Go to the place where terror and
childhood meet with
JOYCE CAROL OATES.

*

Join a woman captive to
an earthbound devil with
REX MILLER.

*

Violate a medieval taboo, and watch stone
turn to flesh, with
GRAHAM MASTERTON.

*

Survive a nightmare cityscape that
takes no prisoners with
NANCY A. COLLINS.

*

Hear the star witness in
an otherworldly trial with
RICK HAUTALA.

*

See a father hurl himself between his daughter
and unseen disaster with
THOMAS F. MONTELEONE.

*

These and 15 other authors leave you
nothing to fear but . . .

Fear Itself

BOOKS BY JEFF GELB

Specters

BOOKS EDITED BY JEFF GELB

Shock Rock
Shock Rock 2

BOOKS EDITED BY JEFF GELB (WITH LONN FRIEND)

Hot Blood

BOOKS EDITED BY JEFF GELB (WITH MICHAEL GARRETT)

Hotter Blood
Hottest Blood
Hot Blood Series: Deadly After Dark

Nancy A. Collins, Rex Miller, Thomas F. Monteleone,
Joyce Carol Oates, Rick Hautala, Graham Masterton...

FEAR ITSELF

EDITED BY JEFF GELB

ASPECT

WARNER BOOKS

A Time Warner Company

WARNER BOOKS EDITION

 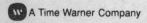
Aspect is a trademark of Warner Books, Inc.

Cover design by Don Puckey
Cover illustration by Steven Crisp

Warner Books, Inc.
1271 Avenue of the Americas
New York, NY 10020

W A Time Warner Company

Printed in the United States of America

First Printing: February, 1995

10 9 8 7 6 5 4 3 2 1

Fear Itself is dedicated to a lifelong best friend, James Crawford, who has always shared and encouraged my interest in various fearsome things.

And for their belief and help in this project, my sincere thanks to Terry Gladstone, Joshua Bilmes, Michael Garrett, John Silbersack, Betsy Mitchell, and Mick Garris.

Contents

Contents

Introduction

What is your ultimate fear?

A salute, but first, an admission.

I've edited horror anthologies for the better part of a decade, since the first *Hot Blood* book took shape. I've worked with hundreds of brilliant writers (contrary to what you may have read elsewhere, there is no dearth of talent or imagination in modern horror fiction). Ask horror writers to come up with a story combining sex and horror, and their creative juices start flowing. Same for rock and horror. Give horror writers just about any topic and watch them go.

But I've often wondered, as I've read those hundreds of stories over the years, what these writers are truly afraid of. They do a convincing job of frightening readers given any topic. But what phobia makes *their* hair stand on end? The one fear that awakens them in the middle of the night, sweating, insecure, less an adult than a child again, feeling lost and alone in an uncaring universe.

I knew that if I could convince horror writers to expose their own personal deepest fears in the guise of a horror story, I'd get a very special, truly frightening collection of terror tales. Not stories of werewolves, witches and vampires. That's grist for a different anthology's mill. When I put out the call for stories that became *Fear Itself*, I asked writers to do something quite different, quite brave: to admit their greatest fears to their greatest fans. Then, to write a story surrounding that fear, the one story they never felt they could write, let alone find a home for.

You think it's easy facing your worst fear? Just try it sometime. Can you even admit it to yourself, let alone an audience of strangers? It's pretty damned hard. I know, because I didn't face my own fear until this book was two weeks away from deadline. Finally, my subconscious fought its way to the surface and showed me a way to shape my greatest fear into a scary yet satisfying story. The experience of writing about it has been the toughest challenge of my professional writing career, but as I suspected, cathartic as well. It hasn't erased the fear—but it has lessened its terrifying hold on my subconscious.

Writing my story for *Fear Itself* has given me an incredible respect for all the writers who agreed to do work for this collection. I know how hard this was for you, and you have my infinite respect and appreciation. After readers devour this book, you'll have theirs as well. And I hope the writing was cathartic for you, too.

So I salute the brave crew of *Fear Itself*, who somehow overcame their own personal nightmares and elected to share them with you. More than professionals, they are pioneers who allowed their skills to take them down life's darkest unexplored roads.

A word of warning: *Fear Itself* ups the usual horror anthology fear quotient exponentially, because its stories were written from a place in a writer's psyche that short-circuits rational thought. They are stories of true, visceral fears you will experience with all your known senses and more. Fears calculated to elicit responses beyond your worst nightmares.

You may never know what truly frightens you—and with whom you share that fear—until you read *Fear Itself*. I dare you to face it. And afterward?

Pleasant screams.

                                                    Jeff Gelb

Victims

Scott H. Urban

Before . . .

I brought my head up off the pillow with a start. Had I heard a clatter in another part of the house? Or was it just an echo from a dream? I knew it wouldn't do any good to ask Maureen—if the Indy 500 were run at night, she could have slept soundly in the pits.

More than likely it was Heather. I still wasn't used to having my daughter, now a freshman in college, home for spring break. She liked to sit up late after Maureen had gone to bed, watching rented movies on the VCR. Although I tried to watch a few of them with her I could never follow the plotlines, and eventually I would retreat to the bedroom, shaking my head, while she cradled a mug of coffee and laughed to herself.

Still, tonight I couldn't detect the telltale murmur of the TV turned low, and it wasn't like Heather to drop something in the kitchen. I got out of bed and, after stepping into a pair of underpants, went to the door. I put my hand on the knob and was turning it when I heard—or thought I heard—a man's voice.

What the hell? I wondered. She wouldn't have invited a boyfriend here this late—would she?

With my daughter growing up and away, I couldn't be certain anymore. Yet something made me withdraw my hand and cross to my closet. I opened the door and reached inside.

Leaning against the corner formed by the edge of the door jamb and the interior wall was a mächete. I had put it there some years ago after a neighbor's house was robbed. Usually I didn't think about the long-bladed weapon being there. It was never in the way. Even when I was selecting my clothes in the morning it was out of sight. Maureen was adamant about not keeping a gun in the house, so this was a compromise that made me happy.

With my fingers wrapped around the mächete's handle, I went back to the door and held my breath for a moment. Was that another voice I heard? Or was the depth of the night itself making me hear things?

Like so many other things that night, what happened next would have been—under drastically different circumstances—amusing. If I could have been outside myself, perhaps watching the drama played out on a movie or television screen, I might have laughed, even knowing it was wrong to do so. It would have seemed like a pratfall, timed by experienced comedians.

I started to turn the doorknob.

Then a shove from the opposite side wrenched it out of my hand. There was no time for me to pull back. The edge of the door caught me just above my right eye, smacking my forehead. I think I grunted in surprise and sudden pain. The mächete fell from my hand. I landed backwards on my ass, thinking Heather had just caught me a good one.

Someone's hand came around the corner and slapped the light switch. I turned my head to shield my eyes from the sudden brilliance. Through my distorting tears, I saw two men—strangers—standing in the doorway to my bedroom. A black man had his hand over Heather's mouth. His right hand held a gun to her head. A narrow-faced white man held his gun in a two-handed grip, poised directly between the abruptly-awakened Maureen and myself.

"All right! No one moves! No one fuckin' breathes unless I say so!"

Now . . .

I'm thirty minutes late getting to Maureen's house. I had been hoping the security guard would just wave me through the gate, but it was some fresh-faced kid I hadn't seen before. We had to go through the whole routine: I parked my car beside the hut while he called Maureen, confirming my license and appearance. I sat there, cursing him in my head, even while I understood the necessity for the procedure.

Look, I wanted to say, I'm not a criminal! I'm a decent guy who wants to see his family—and by the way, I pay your goddamned salary!

But I didn't say any of that.

"Yes ma'am, I'll be right here," said the private cop in soothing, carefully modulated tones to my ex-wife. Obstinately refusing to meet my eyes, he hung up and pressed the button to raise the light metal barrier stretched across the road in front of my car.

This is the fourth time I've visited Maureen and Heather at Redfern Estates. Although I helped them select the development, I'm still not comfortable here. I think about all the time and effort that went into planning this enclosed community. I consider what it must cost to keep such an elaborate security system in place.

Someone, somewhere, is getting rich off the fears of victims.

"Evenin', folks. You can call me Fist." I started to get to my feet, and the white man waved the gun in my direction. "Unh-uh. Don't move. I like you right where you are for the moment." He tossed his head back at his companion, still holding Heather. The black man was huge, at least six-feet-six, and muscular. He looked like a piece of the night, come to life. "This is my friend Corey. We're all gonna spend the night together."

"How did you get in here?" Maureen demanded. She was sitting up in bed, holding the top sheet over her emerald-green silk nightgown. I had bought it for her on our anniversary six years ago.

Fist ignored the question. He pulled two ladder-back chairs away from the far wall and placed them near the foot of the bed. He pointed at Maureen, then to the chair on the left. "You. Here." Then he pointed at me and the remaining chair. "And you here."

"Wait a minute," I protested. "We don't have to do it like this." It was hard for me to find the words. Logic and reasoning weren't working. They shouldn't be here . . . *They shouldn't be here!*

Maureen was easing herself out of bed. I could tell she only had eyes for Heather. My daughter's features were distorted by the black man's stranglehold. Fist turned toward me abruptly. "Did I ask you to talk?"

I held my hands out, offering surrender. "No, look, I just want—"

Maureen was lowering herself into the ladder-back chair with exaggerated slowness and care.

"You got a fuckin' big mouth, asshole!" Fist drew his arm back. But he can't reach me from over there, I thought.

He didn't even try. He slapped Maureen across the face. Her head snapped to the side. When she brought it up there was a flushed scarlet bruise on her cheek and a trickle of blood running from the corner of her mouth. She didn't cry out. I saw her lower lip tremble, but she didn't cry out.

"You son-of-a . . . ." I started up from the floor, determined to choke the life from this intruder.

"I wouldn't!" I heard the black man's voice for the first time. It was so unbelievably low I felt it resonate in my chest. He tightened his grasp, drawing Heather up. Her feet came off the floor. Corey poked the muzzle of his gun into the soft flesh behind her soundlessly-working jaw.

At the same time Fist brought his right hand up and the barrel of his gun rested squarely against Maureen's temple. "You don't learn, do you?" He pointed at the remaining chair with his free hand. "Sit down."

I sat in the chair. My arms and legs were trembling so much I thought they would come loose. Fist put the gun down and pulled thin, coarse twine out of a backpack he wore. He began to secure my wife to the chair. Her arms went behind her back. He tied each wrist separately. Then he tied her waist to the seat and her ankles to the chair.

"Please," Maureen said as Fist drew the twine so tight I could see her flesh pucker on either side, "please let our daughter go . . . She doesn't know where any of our valuables are . . ."

Fist replied without looking up from his chore. "You just keep talkin', you want me to slap the shit outta you again."

Fist finished tying up my wife. Then he began to do the same to me. Come on, think! I screamed at myself. What are you gonna do! You can't let these bastards hurt your family! Can I reach down and grab his gun and shoot them both before Corey shoots Heather? What are you gonna do?

In the end I did nothing.

Fist stood up and took a deep breath. Corey stepped fully into the room for the first time. He took his arm away from Heather's neck. She wheezed, holding her hands to her throat. Corey shoved her back against the wall. "Stay there," he said.

"Now let's get acquainted." Fist's tone was smug, mocking. I wanted to pull out each of his teeth one by one and make him swallow them. "You are?" He pointed at me with his gun.

I knew I had no choice except to answer. "Daniel Brandis." My voice sounded small and insignificant, even to me.

Fist moved the barrel in a circular motion: *Go on, go on.* "And what do you do?"

"I'm . . . an ophthalmologist."

"Oh good!" Fist clapped his hands. "I'm sure we'll see . . . eye-to-eye on everything!" He began to laugh at his own pun. His laughter was too loud and continued too long. "And your lovely wife?"

Maureen shook her head from side to side. "Maureen," I said. What else could I have done? "And that's Heather," I added before he could prompt me.

"And they all lived together in a lovely little house!" Fist chanted in a frenzied, sing-song voice.

Maureen couldn't take it anymore. She had been trying to keep still, keep quiet, but it became too much. "Please. . . . mister . . . Just leave us here in the bedroom . . . You and your friend can have anything you want in the house . . . We won't say anything, we won't tell the police . . . Just take what you want and don't hurt us . . . ."

Fist had been facing me, but when Maureen spoke he whirled on her. "You stupid bitch!" he yelled in her face.

"You goddamn cunt! You think this is about money?" She squinted against the spit flying from his mouth. "I don't give a shit about your fuckin' money!"

Fist took two steps toward me. He brought his gun-hand back—then he drove it toward my chest. The end of the barrel connected with my solar plexus.

It was too fast, too sudden. I couldn't steel myself against it. There was no way for me to back up. Agony exploded from my mid-section. Choking, unable to get any air, I sagged against my bonds. I saw darkness rising in my vision and I almost slipped out of consciousness, but I told myself, No—don't—if you leave, Maureen and Heather will be alone with them . . .

Maureen was screaming, "No! Don't hurt him!" She wasn't trying to hold back the tears anymore. "Why are you doing this?" She leaned forward as far as the twine allowed. "Please . . . we'll take you to our automatic teller . . . we'll take all the money out of our accounts and give it to you . . . just let us go free . . ."

Fist got down on his knees in front of her. "You still don't get it, do you?" His tone was wounded, as if he were trying to reach a pupil who stubbornly fought against the lesson. "I don't want your money. I just want to see you squirm, trying to get away from the pain." He brought his free hand up and ran his fingers through her hair. "If you do something I don't want you to, I won't hurt *you*—I'll hurt someone else in your family." Suddenly he wrapped his fingers around her curls and yanked back savagely, causing her to cry out. "And if you scream for me to stop, it'll just make me want to hurt you worse."

A few minutes later I pull into Maureen's driveway. Her house is impressive. It ought to be—I pay enough for it. Contemporary in design, it features arches where one would expect angles, curves where one would expect corners. The lawn is meticulously maintained by the estate grounds crew. Maureen once told me she planned to put in flower beds, but I don't think she's done anything about it.

She opens the door before I can knock. As I enter, she leans outside. She looks right, left, then pulls back inside as if it is all too dark and threatening. She throws a deadbolt home.

"Evening." I put an arm around her shoulders and squeeze for a moment. "How are you?" Even through her blouse I can sense the stiff tension in her neck, shoulders, and back. Is that constantly there? How can she stand it?

She looks up and smiles, rather unconvincingly. "I'm fine." What did I expect her to say? "Come on in while I get us some coffee."

She goes into the kitchen; I take a right and walk down the hall. At the second door, I knock. A muffled voice invites me in. I step inside as Heather turns away from a drafting table. Maureen and I turned this bedroom into a studio. We bought her everything we thought she could possibly need so that she could keep working on her art, even though she wasn't attending college anymore. I always arrive hoping to see the cluttered disarray of creativity—but the room is immaculate. Even the paper on the drafting table is marred only by a few lines, lines she could have made after hearing me pull up.

"Hi honey." I don't try to approach her or kiss her. "How are you?"

"I'm great." She smiles, but the warmth doesn't go any further than her lips.

"Working on a project?" I ask hopefully.

She shrugs. "Kind of . . ." She half-turns toward the table. "I've got lots of ideas. I just have trouble putting them down on paper."

I nod, trying to think of something else to say. I feel a hand at my shoulder and turn to see Maureen standing behind me. Together, we look at our daughter, her elbows on the sketch pad, her head resting on her palms. The open box of artist's pencils remains undisturbed on the corner of the table.

"Come on into the kitchen," Maureen says quietly.

"Fist." Corey pointed to my right. "Check it out."

Fist looked in the direction the black man was pointing. There lay my mächete, half-hidden by the bedroom door. He went over and picked it up. He turned it over slowly, running his eyes up and down the blade as if it were an *objet d' art*.

"What the fuck is this?" He swung the blade through the air, making it whistle. "You were gonna put your shitty little knife up against my Smith and Wesson?" He tossed the mächete into the air like a baton, twirling and catching it. "You thought you were gonna scare me off with this? 'Oh God, mister, please don't hack us to death with your mächete?' " He smiled at Corey and both of them burst out laughing.

Fist put the mächete's tip against my cheek. It rested there so lightly I could barely feel it. "You thought you heard a couple crackheads. Thought we'd come for your TV and VCR." He drew the blade down my cheek with excruciating slowness. "Thought we needed some shit to pawn off so we could make another dope deal, huh?" The razor-tip came to a halt in the cleft of my chin. Beads of perspiration curled around it. "No fuckin' way. I don't give a damn about your crap."

He whipped the blade away. He did it so quickly I couldn't tell whether he had cut me or not. "Man, you sit there in your little asshole corner of suburbia, and you think you done shut the demons out. You think, yeah, I know there's people on welfare and drive-by shootings and muggings and shit, but it can't touch me here, I'm safe behind my walls." He came in close to me. I inhaled his sour, rancid breath. "I'm here to tell you it's all a crock of shit! There's nothin' that can keep me from comin' in your fuckin' house and doin' anything I want!"

He straightened up and looked at Corey. "What do you think? You think he's got anything I don't have yet?"

Corey shrugged. "Not 'less his dick is bigger than yours."

"This cocksucker? He's gotta strap on a dildo to do his wife." He ran the blade of the mächete up through the leg hole of my underpants, past my waist band, and then sliced. He made the same cut on the other side. A cotton flap fell away, leaving me naked. My shrunken genitals lay between my legs like a deformity, something that didn't belong to me at all.

"I don't think so," said Fist.

"You can't tell with a limp dick," sneered Corey. He dragged Maureen's chair closer to mine. Walking behind my wife, he freed her right hand. "Make 'im hard," he commanded. "I know you do it every night before you suck off his little thing."

Maureen moaned. "I—I can't do that in front of you!"

Corey took a step toward Heather, the flat of his hand raised menacingly. He was so huge I knew he would break Heather's neck if he ever slapped her.

"All right!" she shrieked. "Don't hit her, I'll do it!"

It took a long time. I had never felt less like having a hard-on. While Maureen stroked me, Fist unbuckled his pants. He wore nothing underneath. Using his left hand, he began whipping his own penis. His eyes locked on Maureen's hand, moving steadily up and down my shaft. His cock began to rise.

"Okay, let's check," said Corey. He removed Maureen's hand and tied it once more behind her to the chair. Then he used his hands to gauge how long my erection was. He held up his hands as if demonstrating the size of the fish he had caught that morning. Maintaining the distance between his hands, he moved over to Fist's erection and placed his hands along the penis. My erection was longer than Fist's by at least half an inch.

"Oh man," said Corey. "Fist, you done been out-cocked. Whitebread here's got a longer dick than you."

Rage transformed Fist's features. "No way!" He shook his head from side to side. His erection bobbed erratically in synch with his head. "No way he's gonna have anything better than me!"

He looked around the bedroom. Against one wall stood a low side table. It held some of Maureen's expensive imported porcelain figures. Fist shoved them all to the floor, then he swung the table in front of me. He positioned it between my legs so that my penis rested across the tabletop.

Fist spun the máchete in his hand. "What do you think?" Only at that point did I realize what he intended to do. "Should I take off an inch, or all of it?"

"Take off as much as you can," Corey suggested.

I always feel as if I've gone snow-blind in Maureen's kitchen. Almost everything is white and antiseptically clean.

I sit in a chair at the breakfast table. Maureen has already poured black coffee for both of us. She sits across from me and laces her fingers around the mug. The little finger and ring finger of her left hand stick out; she can't bend them like the others. As she talks she tries to keep her voice steady.

"Dan, I need some more money."

I lick my lips. "Maure, I don't have any more money to give you, or I would—"

She waves her hand, cutting me off. "You do whatever you have to do. Practice longer hours. Skip a meal a day. Move to a smaller apartment. I don't care. But I need more money."

I look around the kitchen. "What do you think you need?"

"Look, I've been pricing motion detectors and I've found a system I want, but it's about ten thousand installed, and I—"

"Motion detectors!" I try, but I can't keep the scorn out of my voice. "Why in God's name do you need motion detectors?"

Maureen looks at me with an expression of disbelief and compassion. "Dan, do you know how I spend my days? Do you? I sit in this house and I try to figure out all the ways someone could get at Heather and me if they wanted to. I know what you're going to say. It's crazy, and I agree, but I can't help it. I try to put myself in their minds, and I think to myself, 'Now: if I wanted to rape and kill Maureen Poulos and her daughter, how would I get in there . . . ' "

"This is ridiculous." I'm trying to keep my voice down so Heather won't hear us. "You live in the safest environment we could find. There's a nine-foot wall around this entire development. Ground glass is embedded in the top. A security patrol with attack dogs walks around the perimeter, once an hour. There's a button upstairs that rings directly in security headquarters . . ."

"But Dan," she interrupts, "what if they broke in downstairs, like they did before, and we didn't hear them, and they came upstairs and overpowered me before I could reach the alarm . . . What then, Dan? Would I be any better off than I was before? At that point would it really matter if there were a thousand security guards around the house?"

"Maureen, no one in their right mind would try to break in this house. There are too many security measures they'd have to get around before they even got to the house."

"We're not exactly talking about people in their right minds, are we? I thought we lived in a safe neighborhood before. I thought burglaries and rapes and murders were things that happened in the inner city—but not where we lived."

"What happened could have happened to anybody, anywhere—"

Maureen slams her mug on the tabletop. Coffee slops out onto the glaringly white surface. "But it happened to *us*, Dan. To you and me and Heather. I do not want that world to touch me or my daughter. I will never put myself in a position to be . . . violated that way again."

Maureen's eyes seemed to have come loose in their sockets. "Please don't do this!" she screamed. "Don't hurt him!" She tried to jerk her chair in front of mine, but she couldn't move at all.

Fist brought both hands over his head. "Ready?" He took several deep breaths. "One . . . two . . ." I could see him tensing his muscles. My penis was shrinking back up into my groin, but I still had enough of an erection that a swipe with the blade would cut it in half. My sphincter began to spasm—I almost shit all over the chair.

Don't beg, I told myself. That's what they want, and it won't do any good. Don't beg . . .

But I wanted to, oh, how I wanted to . . .

"Three!"

The mächete flashed over Fist's head, arcing toward the table. He was going to sever my cock, and I would watch my own penis fly across the room. Blood would spurt from the stump between my legs and I would die tied to a goddamned chair . . .

I don't know how he did it. Fist stopped the swing of the blade just as it touched my flesh. I lost control of my bladder. Hot yellow urine sprayed onto the rug in front of me.

Fist pointed at me. Corey looked up from my closet, where he was rummaging through my belongings. Both of them started laughing. "Oh Jesus fuckin' Christ!" howled Fist. "You shoulda seen your fuckin' face! That was great! You were scared shitless!"

Corey brought my video camera out of the closet. "Shit, I wish we'd been taping it. We coulda shipped that to *America's Funniest Home Videos*. We woulda won!"

"Hell, not too late to start!" Fist held up his dangling cock with his left hand. "I still gotta do something about this!" He turned toward me. "Daddy, you get to decide! Which one is gonna suck me off? Your ravishing wife"—and here he pointed at Maureen with the mächete—"or your about-to-be-ravished daughter?"—and he swung the blade at Heather, curled up embryonically against the wall.

Bastard, bastard! I wanted to yell, but couldn't. They were forcing the responsibility of rape onto me, and it felt worse than the gun barrel to my midriff. The eyes of both women were boring in on me, but I couldn't acknowledge them. I stared at Fist and bit down on my lips until I felt the blood flow.

"Come on, asshole!" Corey demanded. "Make up your mind, or I'll put a bullet in the little bitch's kneecap!"

I opened my mouth—and I honestly don't know what I was going to say—when Maureen shouted, "Take me, dammit! Take me!"

Fist wagged the mächete in front of my eyes, his face lit up with a malicious grin. "Awright, Maureen!" he crowed, but he was looking at me. He pulled her chair away from mine, then straddled her, putting his legs on either side of hers. His groin was at the level of her face.

"You rollin', Core?" He reached down and grabbed himself. "Okay, Maureen! Let's make some movie magic!" He ran the head of his cock across her lips. "Open wide for Papa," he crooned.

Maureen looked at me. I don't know what she saw in my face. Then she closed her eyes and opened her mouth.

"You gettin' all this?" Fist's voice was tense. He pumped his hips against my wife's face.

Corey, video camera on his shoulder, came closer to the chair. "Move back a bit. I wanna get that expression on her face."

* * *

"Actually," I tell her, "I came tonight to ask you something. I would like for you to consider moving back with me."

Maureen swivels in her chair. She puts the back of her hand to her mouth. "How can you ask me that? I only just got to the point where I can sleep through the night again!"

"Maureen . . . I still love you. I want to be with you. And Heather too, of course. We . . . don't need to make love. I'm not looking for that. But I miss your company. Despite all that's happened, we're still a family. But it's like you're living on some sort of island, cut off from the world."

"What world, Dan?" Her crying distorts her words. "Why should we ever leave? We can get everything we need here. I don't want to go out into that world again. Not when it can . . . hurt you like that . . . and there's nothing you can do about it! There's no way you can fight back!"

I force myself to remain calm. "Maureen, you never leave this house. You have your groceries delivered. Heather has a visiting psychiatrist. You've made yourselves prisoners!"

She nods vigorously. "I know! And you know what, I don't mind! I like being a prisoner! And if I never have to hear about the economy or traffic jams or crime statistics again, it'll be fine with me!"

I reach for her hand; she pulls away. "You've put a wall between yourself and the world," I say. "There is so much else other than pain and hurt. Your family misses you. And all your old friends. And there are concerts and museums and walks in the park . . . "

She looks out the kitchen window into the night. I know that for her, it conceals countless threats: fists, knives, guns, and worse . . .

"Can't you see it coming, Dan? It won't be very long. It'll probably happen before we die. The countryside will be filled with bands of maniacs, murderous nomads, and they won't obey any laws or rules. Oh sure, the government will try to crack down on them, but there'll be too many, and not enough prison space, and no chance of rehabilitating them. And anyone who cares about decency . . . who cares about love or morality or their family . . . will live in small, guarded communities like Redfern . . . fortresses to keep us safe.''

For a moment I envision what she says—tiny pockets of humanity surrounded by hundreds, thousands, of Fists and Coreys, shifting uneasily from side to side as they scent prey, hoping to find the smallest ones unprotected, to play with for a while and then kill . . .

''Dan, you talk about my friends and family, museums and art galleries . . . well, if it can't come here, inside my house . . . I don't want it.''

''Aaahh! Aaahh!'' Fist's hips were bucking faster, slapping Maureen's cheeks. ''I . . . ah! . . . I want you to watch me puttin' it to your ol' lady, Danny-boy!'' He whistled between his teeth. ''Makes you wanna hurt me, doesn't it? Makes you wanna gouge my eyes out with your thumbs . . . And . . . ah, Christ! . . . you're sittin' there and can't do a fuckin' thing about it! Just think . . . oh, yeah . . . when I'm done, it's gonna be Heather's turn to give Corey a blow job! An' he can choke a cow with his rod! How's that sound? Oooohh, Maureen, I'm about there, baby . . .''

And I hated him, I loathed him, I wasn't even able to look at him and see a human being. The realization that I could do nothing almost killed me. I wanted to save us, I swear I wanted to. Not right then, but later, I would see my hands slick with my own blood, running from open wounds where I'd abraded my wrists against the twine. But it was no use. Everything I had worked for in my life—my education, my business, my home, my good reputation—counted for nothing. None of it did me the slightest bit of good protecting my family.

''Ah, shit, yeah, it's coming, it's coming . . .'' Fist's buttocks clenched and unclenched.

Choking, gasping, Maureen jerked her head back, spitting his semen out of her mouth.

''No! Fuckin' whore! Don't you pull away from me!'' He slapped her across the face. ''Bitch!'' He backhanded her across the other cheek. ''Don't act like my come ain't good enough for you! I know you swallow every bit of what hubby here shoots, so don't act too high and mighty for me!'' He slapped her a third time, and Corey put his hand on Fist's shoulder.

"I think she needs a lesson," said the imposing black figure.

"Yeah, I think so too." He stooped and retrieved the mächete. He ran the blade under the strap of her nightgown and flicked up, then he sliced the strap on the other side. The shimmery green fabric fell to her lap. With her arms pulled back, her breasts were full and high. Maureen had always been proud of her breasts; they hadn't started to sag yet, and I know her female friends often complimented her on their size and shape.

Fist knelt down in front of her. It almost seemed as if he hadn't seen breasts before. He held the mächete in his left hand. He put the gun down on the floor beside him. Then he reached up and cupped Maureen's right breast with his free hand. She turned her head and closed her eyes. Noticing her response, Fist clenched his fingers suddenly, pinching her flesh. "You watch! Don't you turn your head away from me, you slut!" He moved his fingers to her nipple and began to roll it around between his fingers.

Corey, too, got to his knees on the other side. Together, it almost looked as if they were praying front of my wife. Corey lowered his gun beside his knee and began kneading Maureen's left breast.

"You know," said Fist, "I think her tits'd look better without these nipples. What do you think?"

Corey grinned and nodded.

Maureen heaved against her bonds. "No!" she shrieked. Her voice sounded deafeningly loud in the bedroom. Why doesn't someone hear her? I wondered. Why don't they call the cops?

"Oh yeah," said Fist reassuringly. "This is where it gets fun."

He had the nipple of Maureen's right breast hard in a little erection. "Here." He maneuvered himself slightly to the side. "I want Dan to watch while we do this." Fist lowered the mächete's blade to the top of Maureen's areola. "You hold her tit up and pull her nipple out while I cut."

"Jesus, don't . . ." I hadn't spoken for so long that my

voice sounded strange to my ears. "Don't do that . . . go on and cut me," I offered. "Cut my dick off. I don't care. But please don't hurt her . . ."

They paid no attention to me. Maureen's legs seized and released. I heard a trickle hit the carpet. She, too, had lost control of her bladder. Fist pulled the mächete toward him. The sharp edge drew a thin red line across a tiny section of her breast. A wail came from deep inside Maureen's throat. Fist's and Corey's breathing quickened in the presence of another's pain.

I almost didn't see Heather out of the corner of my eye.

I thought she was still huddled against the wall. I had prayed she would rock herself away to some world where nothing could touch her. But as the two intruders began to mutilate my wife, Heather, without making a sound, crossed the several feet from the wall and plucked their guns from the floor. Fist and Corey didn't notice; they were concentrating on my wife's torture.

I shook my head. I was on the verge of telling her, "No"— I don't know why. I suppose I was afraid that if she failed and one of them got hold of her, her agony would never end.

Heather put the Smith and Wesson's muzzle to the back of Fist's head.

I started to cry out—

—Corey turned and began to raise his hand—

—and Heather pulled the trigger.

Fist's head slammed against Maureen, tipping her chair backwards. Since her arms were bound behind her, she couldn't pull them out of the way. Two of the fingers on her left hand were bent backwards and broken. Thankfully she was unconscious at this point.

The bullet must have caromed inside Fist's skull for at least a second. We later found out it exited the left side of his head and lodged in the bedroom wall. I know the brain itself has no nerve endings—it can't feel pain. But I continue to hope he was aware, in that last second, that his brains were being whipped into grey matter froth. He slumped to the side, his head a ruined orb leaking blood from all its openings.

Heather shoved herself with her feet until her back was

braced against the wall. She held Fist's gun in her two trembling hands. Corey's gun was at her side.

Corey was in a half-crouch. His arms were stretched out toward Heather, but they weren't moving. A drama played itself out in the next few seconds, silently, wordlessly. Corey was looking into Heather's eyes—measuring, gauging. Would she do it again? Could he deflect her arms? Could he make it to his gun? Heather didn't look away, didn't even blink. Corey was waiting for her to glance at me; in that half-second he would have been on her like a falling boulder.

The gun shook in her hand but didn't waver. It seemed as if the moment wore on for hours, glacially slow, but in reality it could only have been several seconds.

He must have made up his mind. He took a step—and was gone. He moved so fast I couldn't see him go down the hall. It was almost as if he had never been there at all.

Heather kept her gun on the door. She must have sat there, immobile, for at least half an hour. I didn't say anything. I waited until her eyes flicked up at me, and then back to the door. She watched the doorway for another ten minutes. Then she looked at me again.

"Dad . . . Daddy?"

I nodded at her. I hurt too much to say anything. I knew my voice would collapse into sobs if I tried to talk.

She went behind me and started to untie the twine. It took a long time. She wouldn't put down the gun.

"Sorry to hear about you and your wife," said the police lieutenant as he set down the ink-smeared Styrofoam coffee cup. He was trying to be sympathetic, but I knew I was only one more face in a long line of misery he would deal with before the end of the day.

I looked down awkwardly, uncertain how to respond. "Thanks." It still hurt to think I wouldn't sleep next to her anymore. "She says . . . she can't look at me without thinking about that night. She says she understands I couldn't have done anything . . . but I think she still blames me for not saving all of us."

"If there's anything I can do . . ." He opened a file in front of him. "I asked you to come down to give you some good news. I've also learned some things I want to share with you.''

He belched into his fist. "First, you knew we caught Corey after he left your house that night. He was apprehended switching stolen cars two counties over from yours. We've had him in custody ever since. Well, last night he hung himself in his cell. You won't have to go through a trial.''

I collapsed against the back of the seat. "Oh thank God. Thank God.'' I could feel the tension draining from my form.

"Now. We've learned quite a bit more about your home-wreckers. Do you want me to tell you?''

I nodded. "Please. I'll go to bed every night wondering if you don't tell me now.''

"All right,'' he said, loosening his belt a notch. "Fist's real name was Lester Donnelly. He wasn't a low life. His father's an industrialist on the east coast. Owns a pharmaceutical company and has his fingers in some other pies. Lester himself had a good education, a college degree, and had worked for three years as a stock broker.

"Corey's real name was Eustis Banks. He ain't no slouch either. His parents are divorced. But his father is a professor of Black studies at some liberal arts college. His mother sculpts and paints—goes from school to school as a visiting artist.''

I shook my head, uncomprehending. "Why would two men . . . with those kinds of backgrounds . . . do . . . what they did?''

The cop shrugged. It must have been only another mystery he would never solve. "I don't know . . .''

"Usually,'' I persisted, "people who do things like that . . . They've been abused in the past, or they have a history of mental illness, or . . . something. I mean, ordinary people don't just go on killing sprees.''

The lieutenant reached over and put a hand on my shoulder. "I don't have the answers, Mr. Brandis. We don't know how these two hooked up or what made them decide torturing people was fun. With your testimony, we've been able to tie them to eight murders in six states. We can thank God they won't hurt any more innocent people.''

"But what they did . . . that's not going to go away . . .

maybe not ever . . . Jesus, they turned my daughter into a killer!"

"I understand how you feel. Mr. Brandis, pardon my saying this, but you're goddamned lucky to be alive. If your daughter hadn't pulled the trigger, your entire family would be dead now—or dying. Those other eight people . . . They didn't die quickly. You don't want me to tell you what Lester and Eustis did to them before they died.

"It had to end the way it did. They weren't looking for money or your belongings. They didn't want drugs. They wanted to kill until they got caught and were killed themselves. That was enough for them. That's all they wanted."

Maureen promises she'll think about what I've said, but I can already tell her mind is made up. I finish the mug of coffee and put it by the sink. I stop in Heather's studio one last time. She's fallen asleep on her drafting table. I lean over and kiss her lightly on the cheek. If she were awake, I wouldn't be able to do that. She murmurs something drowsily but doesn't awaken.

At the door Maureen and I face each other. We never used to say goodbye, so we're not very good at it now. She reaches up tentatively and touches my cheek.

"Please be careful."

"I will."

"Can you wait outside . . . until I lock up?"

I nod. I step through the door and stop. Maureen slowly, cautiously, shuts the door in my face. I won't walk to my car until I hear her secure all the locks.

When the deadbolt slides in place, it sounds like a nail being hammered into a coffin.

Here There Be Spyders

Graham Watkins

"You think you can reach her?" Tony asked, concern evident in the tone of his voice.

Down on my hands and knees, I shined my light down into the blackness of the pit. Far down below, near the effective limit of the powerful halogen beam, a pair of equally worried blue eyes looked back up at me. I sighed and shook my head. "Yeah," I told him. "I can get down there. I'm not sure what I'm going to do once I get there, though. How the hell did this happen, anyway?"

His jaw twitched, his cheek bouncing. "It looked to us like it was big enough," he told me. "We were pretty sure we could see a big room down there at the bottom of the shaft. Carol wanted to go down first, and she found out the shaft narrowed—it was real deceptive from up here. We—"

I gave him a cold look. "So why'd you try to force it?" I snapped, cutting him off.

He bristled. "We didn't! She didn't, I mean! She told me it was too narrow, she was coming back up—then the rope slipped—slipped or something, I don't know—up here. She only dropped a few feet, it shouldn't have been a big deal. But—"

"But now she's stuck." I stood up, gazed blankly for a moment out over the steep rocky slopes of Kentucky's Red River Gorge, listened to the river clatter over the rocks down below the outcropping where we were standing. "From what

22

I can see, she has her hips wedged in the hole. She's in a hell of a fix.''

"Can you get her out?" he asked again. "I dropped a line down to her and we both pulled—well, she tried, she's only got one arm free—but she can't move. She's really jammed in.''

I fingered my ropes and my rappeling gear and wondered why I had to be the first one to come across this potential tragedy. I wasn't a member of an organized rescue team, just an amateur—if experienced—spelunker out for a pleasant Saturday, a Saturday to be spent exploring and mapping some of the myriad caves that honeycombed these mountains. Instead, I'd blundered across a frantic man whose girlfriend was stuck thirty feet down in a hole in the hillside. Naturally, he hadn't wanted to leave her while he went for help; also naturally, when he'd seen me walking along the trail carrying ropes and tackle and wearing a hard-hat with a carbide lamp hanging on it, he'd assumed I too was a spelunker—and, unfortunately for me, he'd been right.

Now, I was responsible—or at least, that's the way I felt. "I gotta figure out how," I muttered. "Getting to her isn't hard—getting her out, that's another matter. It's a goddamn Floyd Collins situation here, we might have to—''

I stopped speaking; the man who'd so far identified himself only as "Tony" had turned utterly white. Obviously, he knew the story of Floyd Collins—the locally famous spelunker who'd tried to map the system of caves now named for him and who'd gotten himself so tightly wedged in a passage that his would-be rescuers could not free him. The Floyd Collins who had, while men worked feverishly to reach him and the national media looked on, died a slow and lingering death in one of these Kentucky caves.

"We'll find a way," I said hurriedly, peering down into the hole again and hoping the trapped girl hadn't heard my ill-advised remarks. "All I was about to say was, I might have to go for help. Get a full rescue team in here.''

"How long would that take?" he asked over my shoulder.

I shrugged; I had only a passing experience with such things. "I dunno. We're a good two hours' hike in here— it's that just back to the road, then a thirty-minute drive to a

phone. Rescue comes out of Campton, that's an hour away.
They get right on it, I'd say four hours. But they never get
right on it—they've got to track their volunteers down—so,
I guess, maybe six is more realistic. But, if they use their
chopper, well, that'll cut it back down to four. So, well—"

"I don't think," he said, his voice low and very close to
my ear, "that we have that long. She says a rock's pushing
into her chest. She says it's hard to breathe."

Moving my head slowly, I looked back around at him; he
hadn't shaved for a day or two, and each of his whiskers
looked like a tiny nail stuck in his increasingly pallid face.
"How long," I asked him, my voice carefully controlled,
"has it been since she fell?"

He bit his lip. "At least, uh, three hours—maybe more—"

Wiping my hand down over my face, I said nothing; I
turned back to the pit. "Carol!" I called. "Carol, can you
hear me?" There was a little clattering of stones that indicated
she'd moved, but no voice answered.

"She, uh, she hasn't been able to speak for about the last
hour—" Tony offered helpfully.

I rolled away from the pit and onto my feet. "Shit," I
mumbled with passion as I stripped off my backpack. "Shit,
shit, shit!" Tony was asking me something else; I ignored him
as I ripped open my pack and jerked out a handful of paper.

"What's that?" Tony demanded as I unfolded one and
began studying it.

"Maps of the caves around here," I told him. "I made a
lot of them myself—I've never tried this particular chimney,
but there's a lot of them around here, and I was hoping that
maybe there was a passage around to the base of—yes!" I
smacked the paper with my fingertip, so hard I almost tore
it. "Yes, I've been in—I've been in—"

Staring at my map, I fell silent. While Tony's eyes followed
my every movement, I stood up and surveyed my surroundings again; my delight at finding a passage that might lead
me up under the trapped girl was tempered by what I'd seen,
in my own almost illegible handwriting, scrawled across my
partial diagram of the room and chimney.

As I looked, my heart felt like it was sinking down, down
toward my groin; at the same time, something uncomfortably

cool popped into existence in my stomach. I shivered, even though the day was warm.

The chimney was—again, unfortunately for me—the one I'd first identified it as on the map. The opening at the top— the opening through which the girl had unwisely tried to descend—was in the center of a large bowl-shaped depression in the surrounding landscape; the steepness of the depression increased with proximity to the hole. It was thus a natural trap; all sorts of small wildlife, ground-living insects especially, would fall into it from time to time. No disaster for most of them, for the most part they could easily climb out.

Except for the fact that the local predators had long since understood the situation and taken full advantage of it. I'd looked into that chamber, the "big room" this pair of cavers had seen from the top, looked in from down below. There were bats in there, as might be expected; there were also rattlesnakes, fat and satisfied rattlesnakes that lay coiled down there waiting for field mice and such to drop in.

The rattlesnakes, dangerous though they might be, didn't bother me. What I'd marked on the map did. Old seafarers used to mark their maps "here there be tygers" to indicate dangerous islands, islands to be avoided; in similar fashion, I marked my maps, "here there be spyders."

You might think it strange that a person like me—an arachnophobe—would enjoy spelunking. But, normally, spiders weren't a big problem; except for the pale and gangly cave spiders, they tended to make their appearance only near a cave's mouth, and to disappear quickly as one moved into the interior darkness. This pit was different; all sorts of bugs fell in here, all the time, just like unwary spelunkers. Like the rattlesnakes, the spiders had taken up residence at the bottom in a big way; worse, the larger ones tended to eat the smaller ones—a natural selection process that favored giants. I felt another cold chill as I remembered my one and only look into that room, several years back; I never intended to go there again, ever.

"Well?" Tony demanded impatiently. "Is there a way?" He stared at the map, pointed toward my warning. "What's this mean?"

"Never mind," I almost moaned. I was about to suggest

that he might go instead of me, that I might just show him the way; but a glance at his feet, which were clad in thin sneakers instead of boots, suggested that this was hardly a good idea. Anyone so unaware of the dangers presented by rattlesnakes and copperheads among these rocks as to wear sneakers wasn't going to be able to deal with the real dangers of that room, the rattlesnakes.

Quickly, I explained about the other passage, the entrance down near the river, and I outlined a plan whereby Tony would stay at the top and try to pull Carol out once I had—hopefully—pushed her free from below. We tossed a rope down to her; thankfully, she still retained enough strength to grab it with her free hand. After warning Tony that she might suffer a broken bone or two as a result of my pushing—and that she'd almost certainly suffer the loss of some skin—I took off down the slope, headed for the riverside entrance.

I was trembling already; for a while, I wasn't at all sure I could even get down the hillside. Trying to tell myself that my fear was wholly psychological, that the only truly dangerous spiders in this part of the country, the black widow and the brown recluse, were not really likely to have taken up residence in that hole, I struggled on down over the rocks.

But when I saw the entrance—it was almost covered by the exposed roots of a huge tree, and as if in warning of what was to come, the roots were festooned with spiderwebs—I wasn't sure for a while that I could even force myself to go in there. For quite a long time I crouched near the entrance, taking much more time than usual to put carbide and water into my lantern and spilling both because my eyes were fixed on a big black and yellow argiope spider that sat like a sentinel in the middle of a near-circular web right above the cave's entrance. Kentucky legend has it that if an argiope—locally, a "writin' spider"—writes your name in its web, it means you are doomed. Naturally, no one living can recall seeing their name written in a web; but I could've sworn I could see the letters of my name in the band of silk down the center of that spider's web that day. Feeling like a soldier about to throw himself onto a live grenade to save his friends, I ducked down to miss the argiope's web and entered the cave.

As usual, the spider population—and virtually all other

populations of wildlife except for the normal cave fauna—
vanished after I'd covered fifty yards of this first passage.
What the acetylene flame of my lantern showed me was
familiar, comforting; the twisting passage way was high
enough that I only had to crouch occasionally, and it was of
a generally squarish shape, looking almost man-made. The
centerline of the floor was grooved by a narrow trickle of
water, a trickle that had, over centuries, carved the whole
passageway; here and there pale humpbacked cave crickets
sprang away from the unfamiliar brightness of my beam.
Moving as quickly as possible—I knew that I wasn't going
to move fast once I reached that dreaded room—I made my
way on down the corridor, slowed twice by rockfalls that had
been noted on my map, places where an ancient collapse of
the ceiling caused the tunnel to go up and over loose slabs
of limestone. All the way, I was looking for, but not seeing,
the innocuous white cave spiders; I couldn't help but think
that this was somehow the calm before the storm, and the
thought caused me to grind my teeth in mental agony.

I suppose that in some way—whatever part of my personality it was that felt obligated to take responsibility for Carol's
plight, whatever had forced me into this cave—I wanted to
get to the room under the chimney as soon as possible. Another part, an older and more archaic part, was secretly hoping
that I'd find the way blocked by a new rockfall, that I wouldn't
be able to get to the room at all—even if that meant that the
girl died in the hole like the unfortunate Floyd Collins.

But there was no fresh rockfall, and soon enough I had
reached a point where I could stand and peer into that awful—
awful to me, anyway—room. It was largest at the end where
the corridor joined it; the floor sloped upward toward the
spot, some hundred yards distant, where the chimney had
been formed by another collapse of rock. Whereas the walls
and ceiling of the tunnel had been relatively smooth, all the
surfaces in this room were literally covered with cracks,
nooks, crannies, crevices, pits; as I turned my head and the
beam from my carbide turned with me, multicolored reflections like millions of tiny mirrors flashed back at me. I knew
what those little star-like images were; I knew all too well
how the eyes of spiders reflected light.

   At that moment, I almost turned tail and ran. Tony and
Carol, I told myself wildly, did not know who I was; I was
just some guy who'd been wandering along the trail, they
didn't know me, they couldn't tell any of my friends or
relatives about how I'd fled, how I'd left Carol to suffer and
die. I could go, I could leave, I didn't have to go back up
on top, I could run down the trail and leap into my car and
go, go, leave, never come back here, ever. You do not have
to put yourself through this, I told myself, you don't. Nobody
can force you to be a hero.
   Nobody but yourself. Or perhaps nobody but your father,
drumming notions about your responsibility to your fellow
man into your head when you were a child, when you were
at your most vulnerable. I could almost hear his voice at that
moment, and, just then, I hated him passionately. He was
forcing me somehow, forcing me from his grave like some
malignant ghost; his voice rang in my head and shoved my
right foot forward into that nightmare of a room.
   I took that step, and I took another; right now the ceiling
was six feet above my head. I was not close to any wall, but
I was already quivering in terror, my head snapping around
to both sides and jerking up and down as well; I felt sick,
my bowels were threatening me, and the crazily dancing light
from my carbide was disorienting me and making me even
more nauseous than ever. There was webbing everywhere I
looked; all around me I could see groups of stars, the little
constellations that marked the faces of the spiders. Now and
then a wolf spider, brown and hairy with a four-inch leg
span, scurried away from my boots. Each time one ran, I
jumped hysterically. Even then I couldn't help but notice that
they never ran far; often they would stop less than a yard
away, sometimes posing with the first pair of their legs lifted
and the body tipped back, the spider defensive posture. As
if they weren't even afraid of me, as if they'd lost their fear
of humans over the generations they'd been living down here
in isolation.
   But they weren't all that was living down there. Focused
as I was on my terror of the spiders, I'd forgotten all about
the rattlesnakes—until one of them chimed out a warning a
few feet from my left leg.

Freezing in place, I turned my head and shined my light down on it; it was a big timber, dark chevrons on a yellow-gold background, six feet or more in length. Its strike range, I figured, would be about a yard, which was just about the distance from its flickering black tongue to my calf. I actually smiled. Snakes held no terrors for me; knowing that timber rattlesnakes are not particularly aggressive, I started drawing my leg away, slowly and carefully. The snake drew its head back a bit more and rattled loudly, but it made no stroke.

"You've got to pay attention," I said aloud. My words seemed to echo hollowly around the cavern. "You have to. You can't afford a snakebite down here, that'd be a total disaster." Trying to ignore the ubiquitous spiders, I scanned my path toward the spot where I presumed the base of the chimney was. Although I couldn't see over the top of the rockpile right under the shaft, the floor along the way looked clear—of both snakes and, far more importantly for me, spiders. Carefully, still twitching uncontrollably, I started making my way over there. My eyes suddenly felt very dry; I realized I had not blinked for quite a while.

I made the rockpile without incident; standing up on my toes, I looked up atop it as far as I could and shuddered anew. There weren't any snakes, but the whole damn thing was covered with spiderwebs, and what looked to me like a whole milky way of stars shined back as my light struck the spaces between the loose rocks.

My knees turned to water and I almost fell. "Naturally," I said aloud, my voice cracking and a sob escaping from somewhere inside my chest. "Naturally, of course they'd congregate there. That's where stuff falls in. Like you, Carol whoever you are, you dumb bitch." Knowing that there was no way I was going to be able to step up on that talus, I started looking around for some sort of tool, some way to chase them out. Luckily for me, insects and rodents and unwary young women were not the only things to fall in the hole; a few feet off to my right I located a sizeable tree branch. After inspecting it to make sure it was free of spiders, I picked it up and poked the top of the rockpile with it. A few stones tumbled free. I grinned, sure that would scare the little devils out of hiding.

My ploy succeeded—almost too well. As those stones fell, all hell broke loose. Spiders, hundreds if not thousands of them—it seemed like millions to me—exploded from the pile, racing off in all directions. Naturally, a lot of them were coming straight for me.

I ground my teeth, but I didn't panic; there may have been a lot of them but they were down on the floor, under control as far as I was concerned. The first to reach me, a big funnelweb, fell victim to my right boot. I did a little dance as the swarm came tumbling onward, the faster ones running over the backs of the slower, and crushed dozens. Not one managed to gain so much as a toehold on my boots.

After they were gone, I poked the pile again, several more times, with my stick. A few more came running out, including the largest and ugliest trapdoor spider I'd ever seen in my life, but there wasn't another mass exodus like there'd been originally. Finally—my teeth chattering as if it was freezing cold in the cave—I forced myself to approach the pile. There were still masses of webbing all over it, but the residents seemed to be gone; only in one place did reflections flicker from my light, and that was deep down among the stones. Relaxing just a little—a fraction—I clambered up on it, using my boots to knock out footholes and touching it with my hands as little as possible. Once on top of it, I shined my carbide up into the shaft.

In one way, things weren't too bad; I could see Carol's feet and legs, the soles of her sneakers barely eight feet above my head. In another way, what I saw there was a new nightmare.

It shouldn't have been a surprise. She'd become wedged just above the chimney's narrowest point, and it was there that the majority of insects and such that fell in would first touch the walls. It was a prime place, perhaps the prime place, for the spiders to spin their webs.

And spin them they had; again, by the hundreds. The whole of the shaft was swathed in webbing, as if spun by a single man-sized giant. Blankly, I stared up into it, at the webbing, at the multitude of bright new stars flickering back. The reflections were not all I could see now, though. In dozens of places, huge spiders of various sorts sat in their webs, turning themselves toward me—toward the light, really—as my carbide beam struck them. I stared at Carol's legs and feet; they weren't covered with spiders but there were several on her pants and shoes. One, a brown and cream araneid with a bloated half-inch abdomen, was currently spinning a web between her dangling legs.

I had a new problem, there was no question of that. The shaft here was only eighteen inches wide or so; climbing up using a standard chimney technique—pressing the arms and feet against the sidewalls—presented no problems.

On the other hand, there was no way I could bring myself to do that, not with spiders all over those walls. They'd be all over me, and I was sure, I was positive, that I couldn't tolerate that.

But I couldn't tell Tony that, I couldn't tell Carol that. Not when the girl was dangling within reasonably easy reach and was probably being slowly asphyxiated by the pressure of the rocks. Gingerly, without thinking much about what I was doing, I poked at the thick mass of webbing up there with my stick.

The results were immediate and for me, hideous; the spiders, evidently already on the alert because of my light, began dropping from their webs instantly, their tracklines glistening in the light. I was right under them; all I could see for an instant was hundreds of hairy wriggling legs, falling toward my face. I could see their eyes, too; it was like a whole heavenful of stars was falling on me.

My control was as tenuous as theirs; I screamed and tried to scramble backwards. Beneath my feet the loosely-piled rocks gave way and I tumbled backwards, hitting the floor hard. The strap on my helmet broke, it rolled off my head; I saw it for an instant before it tipped over onto the face of the carbide lamp and extinguished the flame.

The darkness rushed in. My control evaporated; I howled, gibbered, wept; urine soaked my pants and my ever-threatening bowels turned loose. Thousands of tiny running legs touched my hands, my legs where my pants had pulled out of my boots, my face. I could feel them in my hair, I could feel them forcing their way up the legs of my pants, I could feel them slipping inside my shirt, front and back. I flailed, rolled, squealed like a dying pig; with my hands I tried desperately to find my hard-hat and my carbide, but all I found were more spiders, more, everywhere. They were not innocent, either; they were biting me, biting my fingers, my legs, my arms, biting everywhere. I felt like I was on fire, like I'd been plunged into flame. In a frenzy I vomited all over myself and while my mouth was open some unseen monstrosity tried to stuff hairy legs into it.

I swept that one away with my hand, but my limbs were starting to feel leaden; possibly because of the cumulative effect of their venom but more likely just because of the intensity of my panic, I felt myself becoming paralyzed. I wasn't afraid of dying; I think I wanted to die, I wished I could die, anything to escape this situation. I could feel my heart pounding wildly; it felt heavy in my chest and at the same time felt as if it too was trying to escape, trying to tear itself out of my body and find its own way out of this terrible hole.

I suppose that in a peculiar sort of way, it was one of the spiders that rescued me; at that point I was becoming numb, my movements were slowing, I was sinking into a shock that I might well not have recovered from.

But one of the spiders—some large one, a spider large even by the exaggerated standards of this place—had found its way all the way up my pants leg to my groin. Trapped and pressed beneath my jock strap, it sank its fangs into my penis, down near the tip.

I'm not sure if it was the pain—though that was bad enough—or merely the insult that rejuvenated me. In any case, that bite stood out starkly from all the others; I sat up abruptly and brought my fist down on my own groin with all my strength. I felt the spider crush against my genitals, but a new pain, the waving and flowing nausea of traumatized testicles, almost caused me to lose consciousness. But I did not, I stood up. All I could see, then, was a couple of trickles of light from the chimney, light filtering past the trapped girl's body. Like a zombie I moved toward it; like a mechanical man I started up the chimney, ignoring the spiders now, overcome by my experience, operating on automatic. After a moment

I felt Carol's feet against my shoulders; I didn't stop, I just pushed with all the strength I had.

After a moment, I'd pushed her free; she groaned, made a coughing noise, then cried out in pain. I could hardly hear her; I just kept climbing, pushing her out of the way and on upwards as I went. I wasn't even thinking, then, about the fact that I couldn't get through the narrow passage either; I just pushed on, seeking the daylight like some deranged plant. Distantly, from far above, I could hear Tony's voice; he was apparently pulling Carol up, because her weight seemed to lessen. Not that I cared; I really wasn't very aware of her.

I was aware, though, of a strong sheet of horizontal webbing that I was just then pushing my head through, a sheet Carol had managed to miss both on her way down and on her way back up. With glazed and filmy eyes, I saw that the resident of that particular web had not fled like the others. I also saw that I was wrong in presuming that none of the spiders down here would be black widows—because that's what this one was. She was huge, she was prancing right toward my face, and she was so close already that I could not focus my eyes on her, so close I could see her fangs working back and forth as she came.

I screamed again; with a strength I didn't know I possessed I tore an arm free from the entanglements of the rocks and of Carol's legs. I'd left a good deal of my skin on that rock, too, but I didn't know that then; tearing my fingers so that my blood spurted out I ripped a piece of loose limestone free and pounded the widow back into the rock wall. Pulling the rock away, I saw scattered black legs and oozing green and yellow liquid; it wasn't enough for me, I struck again and again until the stone disintegrated, howling my fury each time I struck that spot.

Pounding the wall was accomplishing something else, as well, something I only then became aware of. I now had my shoulders stuffed into the narrowest part of the chimney, my arms above them; I wasn't able to go farther and was about to be faced with the prospect of going back down and out the way I'd come—which meant I'd have to find the carbide in the darkness down there, by touch. I couldn't face it; but, fortunately for me, my frenzied pounding had shown me a fracture in the sidewall, a fracture I then wedged a stone into. A couple of hard pushes and it gave way, allowing a big chunk of the soft limestone to break up and fall free; it almost took me down with it but I managed to hang on, and its absence left the chimney wide enough—barely—for me to squeeze on through.

Finally, spent, I started to climb again; by that time Tony had managed to pull Carol on out, and he helped me negotiate the last dozen feet of the pit.

"My God, man!" he cried when I was out. "What happened to you down there?"

I couldn't explain, not then; all I could do was mumble and sob, "spiders . . . spiders . . ." over and over. That, of course, he could see; there were still more than a few clinging to me, and he knocked them away, back into their hellish pit.

Eventually, I managed to get to my feet; Tony helped Carol up, she thanked me profusely in a weak voice, and we took a few tentative steps along the trail back to our cars.

I didn't get far, though, not far at all. Less than twenty feet back down that trail, I came upon another of the big black and gold argiopes sitting proudly in its oval web in a grove of mountain laurel. It was identical to the one I'd seen at the cave's mouth, the one I'd imagined had written my doom in its web.

I stopped and stared. "I didn't die, you son of a bitch," I told it softly. "Look at me, I didn't die, I'm alive! God damn you, I'm alive!"

Something, some new emotion, swept over me. While Tony and Carol stood and watched wide-eyed, I snatched the spider from its web with my bare hand. It bit me, sinking glossy black fangs into my fingers, but I ignored the bite.

I brought it up near my face. "I'm alive . . ." I said softly.

Then I stuffed it, still living, into my mouth. It bit my tongue, too, but that availed it nothing; I bit it, too, crushing it between my teeth, luxuriating in the satisfying crunch of chitin-enclosed legs, exhilarated by the squirt of thick oily fluid into the back of my mouth. In near ecstasy, I chewed it carefully and swallowed it, every morsel.

Carol turned away; it was her turn now to vomit. "My God, man!" Tony shrieked again. "What are you doing?"

I smiled at him. "Once, they were my greatest fear," I explained calmly, although my voice sounded unnaturally high and shrill. "A phobia . . ." Pausing, I giggled as I began extracting strands of the argiope's remaining web from the bush. "That's all changed now, all changed." Carefully, working slowly, I tacked a piece of the webbing back in, atop the thick band down the center, and bent it around; left, down, right, down, left, stop. "I have to let them know," I muttered, glancing up at the still-staring couple. "That's fair. I have to let them know."

They kept watching and I kept working; the "S" had been easy but it took me quite a while to get a proper "P" formed in that web. There were four letters to go, plus the final pluralizing "S," but I didn't care how long it took. They had to be warned. It was only fair.

Shatter

Tia Travis

The speedometer clocks one more mile. One more. I stare blind-eyed down the double solid line that divides the interstate. J.P. is dead. She lies on an enamel table under the bright electric lights of a preparation room. The collison occurred at 4:04 A.M. on September 4. It took the state patrol and ambulance attendants two hours and fifteen minutes to remove her body from her totalled car, a Lexus LS 400 with excellent crash test results. The pavement was clear, even, and dry. Visibility was good in all directions. There was no explanation; she hit the concrete barrier dead-on. I identified the body. It had no face.

(At accelerated speeds it takes a fraction of a second for pictures to develop on the retina so you can see them. At 125 mph, you can see only one or two degrees to the right or left of your visual field because objects in the side field move too fast to register on the retina of your eye.)
There are no limits.
(Death is a limit.)
There are no limits.
(Death is the extinction of the personality.)

Splash of rain on the windshield. Impact of a million transparent screams. Something is killed every second, but the screams are too small to hear.

* * *

As I drive I reconstruct J.P.'s death behind a shattered and incomplete picture frame. Her yearbook photo—Class of '81—transforms itself into a death machine: dark hair a spill of motor oil over a steel frame, eyes broken headlights. Her last breath smells of exhaust.

On the floor of J.P.'s car, an ambulance attendant discovered a blood-smeared notebook. The Theory of Axial Collisions, in ink.

There are no accidents.

I slow to 40 and take the off-ramp. My mind reruns a series of films J.P. and I watched when we were fifteen, driver's education films on a portable white screen the traffic patrol set up in the school auditorium. One hour had been set aside to watch the films and to ask questions of the two uniformed state patrol officers.

An expectant silence fell over the class as we waited on the metal fold-out chairs. The lights clicked off and the credits rolled. The State Highway Patrol, a division of the Ohio Department of Highway Safety, presents *Signal 30*, *Mechanized Death*, *Wheels of Tragedy*, *Highways of Agony*. Produced by Safety Enterprises, Inc., Mansfield, Ohio.

"Where's the popcorn!" somebody yelled.

"Shut up," J.P. said under her breath.

Crash

One man critically damaged (camera pan on a black rubber sheeted bundle on the ground).

CLOSE-UP ON DEAD MAN WITH CREW CUT AND BLOOD-SOAKED PLAID SHIRT.

In the car: Oh my leg. Oh no my leg.

(These are the sounds . . .)

My leg. MY LEG! MY LEG!

(of excruciating agony . . .)

"Can you *afford* it? Are you willing to *pay* it?" The patrolmen stood, arms folded, on either side of the screen. Eyes stared straight ahead, mouths grim lines as we observed traffic fatality after traffic fatality, each death clearly the outcome of the driver's *inability to follow elementary safety laws*.

Crash

This car hit a concrete bridge railing.

Crash

That car had a dead baby in it—bottle stuck between the door and frame.

Crash

That car had a body folded in quarters under the car. It is pulled out (slop-slosh).

One kid said it couldn't be real, that the accidents had been reconstructed on a carefully-controlled sound set somewhere in Universal Studios.

But—

Crash

This man lost control of his car and took out an EXIT sign *(Here's your invitation . . . right before your eyes! There's an exhilarating experience in store . . . just look! The driving thrill of your life!)*

Someone threw up. Splash of sick on the seat behind mine.

End credits, lights clicked on. I looked into the faces of my classmates, pale and terrified, blinking in the sudden bright light. I looked at J.P. with a slick sheen of sweat on her upper lip.

Later, we pedalled our bikes with shaky legs down the streets of our town. We rolled to a somber stop at streetcorners, hands sweaty and jumpy on the handbrakes. A car accelerated past us in a blink of chrome and steel . . .

In J.P.'s apartment, September second. I examined the titles of the books piled on the table, the floor: *The Mechanics of Vehicle Collisions, Complete Human Anatomy, Crash Injuries, The Statistical Interpretation of Quantum Mechanics, Emergency & High Speed Driving Techniques, The Encyclopedia of Medical Practice.* She'd ordered the books from out-of-print dealers at exorbitant rates. They were delivered to her apartment by the truckload, and I pictured them in their plain brown wrappers as they crashed into the overloaded mailbox like smashed headlights.

"Look at this," she'd said. She opened the book to the full-color photo of a car crash fatality. The head looked like one of those inflatable rubber balls with a smiley face painted on it. Deflated, now.

I shut the book and locked the picture back between pages

1248 and 1250. I closed my eyes and smelled transmission fluid and engine oil.

"Stop it, J.P.," I said, and opened my eyes. I looked directly at her. "Stop it."

"I can't." Her face had a pale shine to it, as if all she did was sit in the dark and watch newsreel footage over and over. I wanted to check the pads of her thumbs to see if they were permanently indented from the remote control button. Instead, I picked up another book from the stack on her table, automatically turning to the index. A number of entries had been underlined in red marker:

> *Abrasions 102–118 definition of 102; post-mortem appearances of 104; tire marks 115*
>
> *Blood stains, appearance of 491–528; differences between arterial and venous 494; examination at the scene 531; photography of 540;*
>
> *Body, disposal of 112; measurement of temperature of 118; postmortem cooling of 121*
>
> *Burns 719 appearance of corrosive 720; heat ruptures in death from 723*
>
> *Cerebral hemorrhage, traumatic 828*
>
> *Criminal responsibility and insanity 901*
>
> *Cut throat, accidental, by glass 1120*

Each underlined item excited a different picture, and I retained the imprint of each in a mental reference file.

> *Death, molecular 12; moment of 18*
>
> *Features, reconstruction of 712*
>
> *Head injuries 232; mobility of skull at time of blow 233; intracranial hemorrhage 239*
>
> *Lacerations 455*
>
> *Putrefaction 481*

I knew she'd memorized the entries. I'd memorized them myself, or ones like it, when I was a university student with a part-time position in the medical library. I'd sit and read after hours in the dim illumination of a basement bulb, mentally participating in the putrefaction of the human body.

I turned to page 481 of J.P.'s book to check the definition.
The excitement intensified as I speedread the section heads:
*Drowning, Mechanical Asphyxia, Electrical Injuries, Infanti-
cide and Child Destruction, Criminal Abortion.* Uncon-
sciously, I licked my lips. *Stop it.* I'm just looking! Stop it.
Alarms sounded, back of my mind.

There it was. Delirious excitement.

(You're sick.)

The Moments of Death. p. 481.

(Stop it.)

Putrefaction: the bacterial dissolution of the body into gases
and liquids. A green or greenish-red discoloration of the ante-
rior abdominal wall that later extends to the entire abdominal
wall followed by three or four inch blisters filled with a
reddish, watery fluid containing protein and white blood cells.
Tumefaction of the subcutaneous tissues. Pressure increases
in the body cavities and red fluid leaks from the orifices.
Impatient, I turned to page 482, still reading page 481. My
eyes moved like blips on an EKG. There. There, second
paragraph. The climax.

Putrefaction: liquefication of the body organs. The eyes
are the first to dissolve, followed by the brain, stomach and
liver . . .

Putrefaction: the only irrefutable test of death.

"I know what you're looking for," J.P. said. She stood
quietly behind me.

I didn't reply.

"Proof of the inevitability of death, of the limits of the
human condition."

(There are no limits)

"There's no escape, Kelly. Believe me, I've tried. Tried
it all. Quantum mechanics was my last bet, the last roll of
the dice. The universe is unpredictable on a subatomic level;
electrons jump from place to place. But for you and me . . ."
She shook her head. "For you and me there will always be
A and B and the distance between. That's why we have cars.
To get from A to B." There was a finality in her tone that
frightened me. In that moment I think I understood J.P.'s
mind: how it worked, the tracks it tread, the tires it tested.
She had no more control than I did.

I hardly breathed when I said it: "I don't want to die, J.P."

(Death is the extinction of the personality.)

"We all die," she said.

Later: blood-smeared handprint, chrome reflected in a pool of blood. Bodies like bruised grapes, slumped in sacks. Sneakers torn from the driver's feet lay, inexplicably, yards away on the asphalt.

"Turn it off," I told her.

She looked at me blankly, remote control in her hand. Click as the VCR backtracked ten seconds. The body on the screen folded back into quarters. White sheet, rubber gloves. My eyes were drawn to the dark diluted stains on the bottom of the white sack.

"Turn it *off*."

Men in rubber boots, picking at the incinerated steel. The driver had violated the laws of physics. I saw the universe in black and white, cause and effect. Terror in me like a low-grade fever. *No escape* . . .

"At the time this documentary was made there were one hundred million vehicles on America's roads," J.P. said. "If you laid out car crash fatalities end to end on a highway they'd make a line more than fifty miles long. Next year the line will be two miles longer. In the time it took us to watch this film, another fifteen feet were added to that line. Don't you see? It doesn't stop. It will never stop."

"No, J.P." I said carefully. "*You'll* never stop."

"You remember the man who lived down the hall in 4B?"

Friendly man, mid-fifties. Looked like Barney Miller. I said, "I remember him."

"Yeah, well he bought a new car last month, a retirement present for himself. He sure was pleased—an Infiniti Q45. Infinity is right. He was killed last week. Head-on crash on the 101 with a flat black Trans-am. The kid tried to pass a semi on a double solid. The Infiniti retails for $50,400. It has a 4.5-liter DOHC 32 valve V-8, 4-speed automatic transmission, 4-wheel anti-lock disc brakes, power steering, limited-slip differential and a driver's side airbag that failed to perform on this particular occasion. 4B was killed instantly.

Crushed by the steering column. The kid in the Trans-am walked away, Kelly. *Walked away*, with minor cuts and a fractured radius. They took 4B out in a bucket. What was left of him, that is. The day before he became a stat I was at his apartment looking at pictures of 4B, Junior. He'd just landed his first job as an test engineer for the Chrysler Corporation. You want to tell me what's happening here?''

"I don't know, J.P.''

She stared at me, eyes luminous disks in the semi-dark of the apartment. She walked back to the living room and sat on a metal tube framed chair she'd pulled up within two feet of the 48″ TV monitor. She rewound to the start of the video, a dub of a dub with bad lighting and terrible audio. I remember it: *Mechanized Death*.

On her coffee table were full-color laser copies of 1950s medical case studies. Multiple compound fractures, bodies stiff and yellow and rubberlike—

(*THIS is the car . . . THIS is the power team . . . Try the Rocket hydra-Matic "88" at your Oldsmobile dealer soon . . .*)

—little black rectangles over their blind eyes to preserve their identities.

(Death is the extinction of the personality.)

Beside them: J.G. Ballard's *Crash*. Pamphlets offering protective clothing and safety products for morticians. *Your Lucky Numbers!* License plate renewal form. *New Car Price Guide*. A fold-out from the *American Funeral Director's Magazine* for 1994 Cadillac Funeral Coaches caught my eye, and I picked it up. It still smelled like ink and printing presses. The specifications and features of different models of hearses had been underlined. I had a vision of J.P. at the kitchen table, her face an illuminated blue under the artificial track lighting as she read and reread and made her notes:

1. Measurements (wheelbase, overall length, overall height, overall width, rear door opening height, loading height.)

2. Standard Coach Features (full sliding partition glass, rear floor rollers, forma style velour drapes, nameplate holders in side doors.)

Plus a six year, 60,000 mile guarantee. She thinks of the territory 60,000 miles will cover, the cemeteries it will include, the funerals for the car crash fatalities from shattered prom nights. Blood-stained carnations on tire-tracked lapels.

I zoomed in on J.P.'s face, on the tired lines etched below her dark eyes. I see the exhausted motions of pale hands on demi-matte stock as they outline the specifications, once, twice, a thousand times.

If I could choose three features. If I could choose two features. One feature . . . Decisions become harder. She is so tired. Stands up, rubs the back of her neck. Walks stiffly to the window and looks down into the street at the fall of rain, the shimmer-slick pavement. There's a car below her, approaching a four-way stop sign. A Ford Taurus, new model, with speed sensitive powersteering. Steady, reliable. The car stops at the intersection. Brake lights flash red in the dark.

J.P. watches, waits.

The clock ticks.

The Taurus accelerates through the empty intersection and disappears.

The driver could make it home, in theory. Could, that is, if he is careful and has his seatbelt on.

Accidents are the result of inattention to traffic laws.

J.P.'s eyes become windshield screens. She constructs the crash, the Taurus in a collision at the uncontrolled intersection. There is permanent deformation of the car's frame at impact. She examines velocities, momentums, elastic rebounds. Blood pools under the driver in a deep circle. Poker chips of glass crunch on the road.

J.P. rubs her neck, lets the Taurus continue home. Back to work. There are 60,000 miles to cover . . .

There are no limits.
(Death is a limit.)
There are no limits.
(Death is the extinction of the personality.)

Looking at J.P. on the preparation room table, I had been compelled to roll back her death clammy eyelids, to cover the pupils with my thumbs and press them in. *Don't look, J.P. Don't look.*

Instead, I watched them prepare her, listened to the whine of the embalming machine. It didn't seem like J.P. at all, dead on that table, with Celtrol Anti-dehydrant (complete preservation, cosmetic perfection, life-like appearance) being pumped through her arteries. I picked up my car keys and walked out into the dark. Unlocked my car and started to drive. Same drive J.P. took ten hours before. I don't know what I was looking for. A little piece of that 60,000 miles, maybe.

So now I drive, and I think about the parts of a car.

There are no limits

(Death is a limit)

There are no limits.

I accelerate to 90 mph. I lose my peripheral vision, if I had it at all.

100 mph

It occurs to me

110 mph

that J.P. was in error.

120 mph

There are no limits

(Stop me if you've heard it, J.P.)

125 mph

There are no limits (A to B, and everything inbetween.)

130 mph

There are no limits on the interstate. Death is the extinc—

Once Upon A Darkness

Stephen Gresham

The plastic gloves.

Diaphanous, yet milky white, they had arisen from his subconscious as the catalyst image for the novel. A disembodied pair of gloved hands reaching for the throat of a child. The narrative unfolded from there, taking on a life of its own. He had pulled out all the stops. Blown a few mental fuses. He had surrendered wholeheartedly and wholemindedly to the project. He had created a monstrous character. And the experience had been exhilarating.

Even rereading scenes from the manuscript was a joy . . .

For a timeless instant, Jaynie relaxed. She felt as if she were sinking within a whirlpool of warm water. She looked into the nurse's eyes again and saw the day's final light slip away. The nurse's strong hands were around her throat. The plastic gloves squeaked like a frightened animal.

Lifting. And on the road a car shifted gears, its headlights dim against the black matrix of the woods.

Slowly lifting.

Wind soughed high in the pines.

The nurse lowered her face. Her teeth found the girl's throat, gripped and lifted.

Jaynie's penny loafers dangled a few inches off the leaf-strewn floor of the woods.

* * *

John Newland could tell a chilling horror story.

But he never suspected that he would live one.

In the coziness of his study, such a possibility was indeed remote. Things were going too well. He sipped at a fresh cup of coffee and felt the deep down satisfaction that a writer feels when he's produced a piece of work that he wants to live with.

He leaned back. Yes, life's good, his pose suggested.

Movement outside his door drew his attention. There was a soft knock and the door opened halfway. Newland looked up from the manuscript of his soon-to-be-published second novel and chuckled at the timid expression on the face of his son, Clay.

"Dad, say it for me, will ya? Say what our pirate says."

Squinting and snarling, Newland swung around and gestured for the boy to jump into his lap. To the boy's expectant grin, he exclaimed, "I'm Greenbeard the Pirate, I am. I am. There's never a man looked me 'tween the eyes and seen a good day a'terwards."

Clapping his hands in delight, Clay squealed; his shoulders twitched with an involuntary shiver.

"I want some more story about Greenbeard. Is he gonna have to kill somebody like last time?"

"Wouldn't surprise me," said Newland. "He hardly gets the blood cleaned off his sword before he's got to run it through someone else."

He playfully thrust an imaginary sword into his son's stomach. Clay howled a howl of total pleasure.

"Lots and lots of blood," he giggled. "Tell a long story, Daddy. Okay? Make it a long, long story. Okay?"

"Have you eaten your breakfast? You can't hear a Greenbeard story on an empty stomach, you know."

"I did eat breakfast. Mom fixed me Toaster Pops. Strawberry ones. And some milk."

Newland patted Clay's stomach.

"Good enough. So, let's see. There was the time Greenbeard had taken over a cargo ship loaded with treasure, and he said to the captain: 'We want that treasure, and we'll have it, by thunder. Give it to us, or avast thee, you'll be seein' nothin' but musketballs.' ''

Frowning menacingly, Clay said, "I bet Greenbeard was gritting his teeth. Right, Dad?"

"By the devil, he was. Just exactly the way you are."

Pleased, Clay beamed from ear to ear, though it made gritting his teeth difficult. Newland had to fight back a smile. As his mind slid along in search of the next scene, he heard his wife, Trisha, call out his name from downstairs.

In a disappointed tone, Clay said, "Oh, shoot, it's Mom."

"Must be pretty important to interrupt an episode of Greenbeard the Pirate," said Newland.

Clay nodded in agreement.

At the bottom of the stairs, Trisha flashed a smile at Newland and said, "It's Gwen. I thought you'd want to take the call right away—hot news, maybe?"

Newland pulled her close. His wife of twelve years, Trisha had supported him every step of the way in pursuing his dream of becoming a writer, always there as both editor and cheerleader, yet wisely cautioning him not to quit his teaching job—not until the "breakout" book came along. She had the blackest hair and the biggest, brownest eyes he'd ever seen; and she remained, in his view, the most beautiful woman on the planet.

"*You're* hot news," he whispered, kissing her ear and the hollow of her throat.

"That's what all the men say," she whispered back seductively. Then pushed away slightly from him and added, "What's going on upstairs? More pirate stories?"

"Uh-huh. Granny Ruth would be proud of her legacy," said Newland. He kissed his wife full on the mouth and felt the playfulness of her tongue. "Hey," he pulled away, "save *that* for later. I better go see whether my agent is earning her commission."

His grandmother had helped put the demon in him long ago. The demon which demanded that he write. She had been the one who, when he was Clay's age, read to him from the classics of children's literature, her favorite writer—and soon his—being Robert Louis Stevenson. *Kidnapped* and *Treasure*

Island became the catechisms of his imaginative life. Dark adventure and easy violence the stuff which stuck in his mental filter. And maybe they would stick in Clay's mental filter as well.

Thanks, Granny Ruth.

"Hi, Gwen. No, I can't do *Donahue*, but maybe I could squeeze in the time for a spot on *The Today Show*."

His agent's laugh was throaty and sexy, her voice well-traveled on phone lines exercising the glib and oily art of negotiating. He imagined her metallic-blonde hair and large, hoop earrings and frosted lips.

"You jest, buster, but listen to me: if *Sometimes Darkness* takes off the way I think it may, you'll be playing in a different league."

Her words had a pleasurable burn.

"My ego thanks you—this isn't some front for bad news is it?"

He held his breath.

"John, you know I always write when the balloons have to be burst. No, this is a good quickie. *Sometimes Darkness* will be in bookstores in three weeks, and I have you set to do a signing at your local Bookland a month from today— did you get the pre-print cover samples? I put them in the mail three or four days ago."

"No. How's it look?"

"Creepy. Yeah, a dynamite cover. Really, really creepy."

After he and his agent finished their business, he walked down to his mailbox. The Southern winter sun was bright and forceful, diminishing a slight chill. Granite Heights, the quiet subdivision he and Trisha loved, seemed to flow around him like the dream vision of some chamber of commerce. With slightly nervous fingers he tore open the manilla envelope—*hope the hell this is better than what they slapped on* Night Tracks—and unsheathed the cover samples.

Yes, it was better than the cover on his first novel.

Weeks later he would look back and realize when the nightmare started: with his first deep stare into the figure's eyes. The artist's conception was terrifyingly on target. Against a black background a heavyset man wearing a nurse's white uniform cradled a large doll, the forehead evidencing a jagged crack running from the blond curls down to the unblinking, blue eyes. The man wore a reddish wig; his face was powdered and his lips were painted scarlet. And on his hands, plastic gloves.

Newland's heart swelled like a vicious bruise and beat so rapidly that he had to cough and sputter to catch his breath. And his only thought was: *this is my monster*. This was Maris Macready, the cross-dressing, child-killing psychopath who had grown from a dark seed in his imagination and blossomed grotesquely in the pages of *Sometimes Darkness*. But confined to Newland's imagination and caged in Newland's manuscript, the character had not seemed this repulsive—this *real*. It was as if the artist had somehow released the writer's monstrous creation.

To Newland it was such an obvious cliche, and yet . . . and yet as he returned to his house he felt cold, and Granite Heights, the model for the fictional subdivision in which Macready stalked his prey, seemed crouched and hushed as if protecting some secret evil. A secret known only to Newland.

"But it's a *woman*. Of course, it is. The nurse's outfit. The little nurse's cap. Why yes, she's kind of on the heavy side, but not unpleasantly so. Favors my cousin, Julia, just a bit."

"Mother, no, look closer. See, it's a man. The hair's a wig. It's a man dressed up like a nurse. That's what the book's about. This psycho guy who dresses like a nurse so kids won't be scared of him, and he can approach them and kill them. I've read it—it's a man. Trust me."

"Well, I never would have thought . . . oh, goodness."

"It's a horror novel, Mother. The covers are supposed to be like this. Weird and scary so you'll buy the book."

The woman frowned and looked over at Newland.

Newland smiled sheepishly. He was seated at a folding table just outside Bookland in the Village Mall exactly four weeks from the morning he had first glimpsed the cover for *Sometimes Darkness*. And he felt uncomfortable there by the three-foot blowup of that cover and several stacks of his novel. More accurately, he felt rather like an imposter. Horror novelists such as King and Koontz and McCammon could rightfully have book signings—but John Newland? Who's he?

Before the first sprinkling of book buyers and requests for autographs arrived, Newland had a few minutes to reflect upon the weeks leading up to the signing. He had shown the cover to Trisha who had said "Oh, my, it's . . . *vivid*, isn't it?" but he hadn't shown it to Clay. He had admitted to Gwen that the cover "bothered" him, but couldn't explain precisely why. She countered by claiming it was a "gangbusters" cover that had everyone talking about it. His concerns were not allayed, although his brother, Roger, who lived in Wichita, Kansas and was his biggest fan, had called a week ago to tell him that he had seen copies of the book and that he loved the cover. At home, Newland had slowed down on his third novel, had spent more time with Clay, marveling at his enjoyment of the Greenbeard tales.

Newland had committed himself to do an interview with the Columbus, Georgia daily newspaper after the signing, his first interview beyond one he had given to the pissant rag sheet that passed as the Goldsmith, Alabama paper. And that had been just after his first novel was published.

The signing.

To Newland's relief, it went well. A real ego boost. Though he didn't keep count, he guessed that he signed 40 or 50 copies, a decent number if one weren't aware that his publisher had sent over 200. For the most part, people were great, treating him like a legitimate celebrity.

There was, however, one somewhat troubling development. Twice during the two-hour signing Newland noticed a curious fellow in a khaki jumpsuit who paused in front of the blowup of the cover, staring at it as if mesmerized. With muscular arms and thinning, grayish hair greased down, the man possessed a menacing quality which was not difficult to account for. His jaw ticked and his eyes went milky when he approached the cover, but he did not buy a copy of the book; he had not brought a copy for Newland to sign—he did not, in fact, appear even to acknowledge the presence of the author. And when the signing concluded and Newland was making his way to the food court, he noticed the man again; he was seated on the wall of the fountain jotting something in a small, spiral notebook.

Her name was Katie Doyle and she had magnificent red hair and green eyes and a smile filled with questions. They sat in plastic chairs at a plastic table with the aroma of pizza slices and burritos and french fries wafting over them. Newland rubbed at his elbows, not because of the interview, but rather because the sight of the man by the fountain had given him a shiver, an intense frisson, which had spread up his back and down his arms.

But the pre-interview small talk and Doyle's pretty face transported him into a pleasant, ego realm far removed from malicious strangers. Doyle switched on her portable tape recorder, and they talked about Newland's childhood—to Doyle, a disappointingly normal one—and the influence of Granny Ruth and Newland's reading in English and American literature. There was the usual litany of obligatory questions, including "Where do you get your ideas?" to which Newland replied with a practiced, devilish smile, "I write what I know."

Toward the end of the interview, Doyle shifted to *Sometimes Darkness*. "What's behind it?" she asked.

Newland raised his hands and wiggled his fingers, and in a bad imitation of Bela Lugosi, said, "Plastic gloves, my dear. Plastic gloves." He elaborated, and there was a foray into the psychology of psychopaths and serial killers, and then the question.

The question.

It could have been that Doyle asked it because, in effect, the interview had been going too smoothly—it was a question designed, it seemed, to put a little "fierceness" in the evolving dialectic. And it worked.

She had paused after exploring what Newland had to offer about the writing of *Sometimes Darkness*, and in her most serious tone she had said, "Doesn't it worry you that some borderline personality, some guy with a kink in his brain might read your book and be 'inspired' to commit similar atrocities? I mean, what if your book triggers extremely violent behavior? Wouldn't you feel, in a way, responsible?"

The question hit him like a fist of thorns.

He felt the flash of anger viscerally; his stomach tightened, and he laughed softly, nervously. But his smile was forced and did not fit his face; it was like a glove on the wrong hand. He shook his head as if to summon every ounce of denial he had at his disposal.

"I can't be responsible," he began, "for every nut out there who *might* read my book and *might* be pushed over the edge into psychotic behavior. No writer should have to bear that kind of responsibility."

He stared at her, conscious that he had raised his voice. She nodded solicitously. Still intensely irritated—an intensity which surprised him—he found himself shifting his rhetorical strategy to accommodate her.

"Look," he said, "at the core of your question is the issue of censorship. And censorship, no matter what anyone else says, is a mindless force. Its passionate purpose is to make zombies out of us—it's as simple as that. But yes, on the other hand, democracy demands a price, and as I see it, that price means tolerating a lot of horrible stuff I'd rather not see printed or not see showing at our local theaters. And maybe, I just don't know, *maybe* some of what gets printed or shown to the public could provoke acts of violence. But you can't tell the writer or maker of films to curtail his or her freedom of artistic expression—*that* price is much too high. It's a price I won't personally pay."

Newland blanked out the remainder of the interview. Later, he assumed that it had ended amicably enough; Doyle had not been out to get him, and, in fact, having space given to the interview in a paper with the circulation of the one in Columbus promised a salubrious effect upon his career.

But at 3:00 A.M. the next morning Newland was wide awake framing different answers to "the question"—and some demons of doubt had entered the shadow side of his vision of reality. He stared at the seamless darkness of the bedroom ceiling; he was ashamed of himself for even entertaining the possibility that his book—*his book*—could touch off a volatile psyche. And yet. And yet, onto that darkness above him his demons of doubt projected two milky white, plastic gloves closing around the neck of a faceless child.

By mid-morning, the image had dissolved and only a residue of his irritation over "the question" remained. In his study he reviewed his outline of the next chapter of his current novel; well into his second cup of coffee he focused his mental energy on the narrow task of putting words on the screen of his monitor. Trisha's timing—or rather the timing of the event which forced her to have to interrupt him— couldn't have been more unfortunate.

She barged into his study without knocking, and, in an exasperated tone said, "Would you just look at this? *This* . . . this is the work of your Greenbeard the Pirate, aka your son, and he's gotten himself into big trouble. I've already reprimanded him—your son, that is—but maybe I ought to reprimand you, too."

She wasn't serious about the latter. Newland could see that. And his gorgeous wife couldn't know what her mixed expression, one of anger and comic bewilderment and fear, touched within him. Nor could she have understood what effect the object she was holding out for him to see had upon him. The small, gray and white teddy bear had been gutted; whitish blood-stuffing leaked out like oatmeal.

"What happened to Freddy?"

That was all he could think to say.

One hand on her hip, Trisha raised the mutilated bear a little higher and said, "He was murdered. With my best butcher knife. By your son in a fit of Greenbeard mania. And he's been sentenced to no television for a week and told never . . . *never ever* to get into Mom's kitchen utensil drawer again. Looks as if your Greenbeard stories were more stimulating than Clay could handle."

Newland could see that as she talked she lost some of her fear—she even laughed ever so softly at the teddy bear's condition. But when Newland took the bear from her and surveyed where it had been cut—cut viciously—he found suddenly that he couldn't swallow.

In the days afterwards Newland began to imagine things. He began to imagine, for example, that Trisha was far more troubled about the teddy bear incident than she was letting on. Newland had had an obligatory talk with Clay—"You know better than this, son. I'm very disappointed in you. Knives are very, very dangerous objects. You could have hurt yourself. Don't you understand that Greenbeard isn't real? Little boys shouldn't ever try to act like Greenbeard.''— but he didn't want to admit that his storytelling might have provoked Clay's behavior. No, not that. Over Clay's protests, Newland declared a moratorium on Greenbeard stories.

But the wordless dialectic with Trisha continued. He imagined her thinking: What has he done to my son? There's so much violence in our society, how can a small boy develop the proper interpersonal attitudes when his father writes about the horrors of our society for entertainment? This same father who tells stories of a terribly violent pirate—what could it lead to?

Newland never asked his wife whether she was thinking such thoughts. He was afraid to. He noticed his fear, just as he suddenly noticed how difficult it had become for him to write anything. Anything. He also noticed the aversion he had developed to reading about or listening to news reports of murders. He avoided the daily newspaper and the nightly news religiously.

What the hell's going on with me?

He wasn't certain.

He began taking long evening walks through the neighborhood, breathing in the brisk winter air, cursing the elements whenever rain prevented him from his brief sojourns. And what did he do on such walks?

He thought.

And he kept an eye out for . . . for strangers. He studied each house in the four-block area. In a matter of days, he knew much about the habits—the goings and comings—of his Granite Heights neighbors. Then one evening a frightening thought occurred to him.

This is just exactly what Macready did. I'm acting like my child-killer.

So Newland called a halt to his curious routine.

He began spending his evenings watching basketball on ESPN. Trisha and Clay gave him wide berth. His computer gathered dust. He began to feel better. But just when the edge was starting to wear off his anxieties, he received a call from his brother, Roger.

"Is Mom Okay?"

Whenever his brother called, Newland assumed it might concern his mother's health.

"Oh, not too bad," said Roger, "considering she won't take her high blood pressure pills. She claims they make her see things—green footballs and pink and blue rainbows. I don't know. She says she wants to change doctors."

"Don't let her."

Roger coughed and cleared his throat. Newland detected something odd in his brother's manner. He seemed nervous and ill at ease.

"Everything all right on your end?" Newland asked.

"Sure, yeah. Fine. How's, uh . . . how's Trisha and Clay?"

Newland felt an icy trickle of saliva inch down his throat. Roger never, *never* asked about Trisha and Clay. The conversation thrumped and bumped along like an engine running with a couple of blown pistons. Newland waited for his brother to swerve metaphorically into a ditch.

After ten or fifteen minutes, he did.

"We had something weird happen yesterday," he began. As a police dispatcher, it was hardly unusual for Roger to relate bizarre occurrences. But as Newland listened, he could feel his heart quicken.

Roger continued. "Yeah, it was in north Wichita. You remember the 53rd Street area, don't you?"

"Of course. God damn, Roger, we lived there for two years."

"Yeah, I know . . . well, you see . . . they found a body. Found this little girl's body. Well, and she'd . . . been strangled."

"Jesus."

Newland had been standing at the kitchen phone. He sat down. He was suddenly shivering as if it were twenty below zero in the room.

Roger's voice clicked. He gave a sharp, sudden, nervous start of a laugh. "Jesus is right. I mean, this was really horrible, you know . . . and I heard our chief detective talking about it. About what they found."

Roger was stalling.

And Newland didn't know why. Not precisely.

"Roger? What the hell are you . . . what did they . . . there some special reason for telling me this?"

"No, I mean . . . well, in a way, I guess, yeah. Coincidence. Just . . . just the damndest coincidence, you know."

Newland took a deep breath. The terror which had seized him was a razor poised a millimeter from slicing into his rapidly beating heart. He thought maybe he could anticipate his brother's news.

"Roger? Did they, uh, did they find tape across the girl's mouth? If that's it, then I can tell you—from all the research I've done—I can tell you that's sometimes part of the murder profile. So you see, that explains it."

In a feathery soft voice, Roger said, "Yeah. Yeah, there was tape across her mouth, but . . . I mean, you remember in your book how the guy, how Macready wrote stuff on the tape?"

"Sure. God damn, of course. I wrote the fucking book. Macready would take a magic marker and he'd write, 'Children should be seen and not heard.' "

"Yeah, I know," said Roger. "I got out my copy of your book, and I went back through to check . . . and then I double checked with our detective and . . . but I never said anything. I haven't told anybody else—not a soul—what I'm, you know . . . wondering."

For Newland, the room disappeared. A huge, nebulous blackness sucked him into a timeless void. How long he was there he couldn't say. Coming out of that void he could hear his brother, a buried voice, frightened, wanting to but failing to reassure.

"Coincidence. Just the damndest coincidence," it said. Again and again.

Three days passed in which Newland was on fire with fear.

And what he dreaded most, a cosmic dread, was a phone call. A very particular kind of phone call. A phone call from the parent of a strangled child.

For an excruciating run of evenings, Newland cringed whenever the phone rang. He discouraged Trisha from responding, saying that he was expecting an important call. But then he often delayed long enough so that his answering machine would be activated and he would have an opportunity to listen carefully to the messenger. Did the caller sound like a distraught parent?

Reason did not enter the circle of his raging fear.

That such a phone call was improbable mattered little. That it was highly unlikely for a connection to be made between his novel, a work of pure fiction, and an actual murder also mattered virtually not at all.

What his brother had passed along wounded Newland deeply, a wound inflicted by the sharp point of suggestion and implication and coincidence. But was it coincidence?

Children should be seen and not heard.

What were the odds that a psychotic killer would choose those words? Precisely those words? Was it so difficult to imagine that such a killer had read the kind of book which he knew would stimulate him?

A book about his own kind.

Maris Macready would be the hero of such a monster.

And every child became a potential victim.

Even a little boy like . . . Clay.

That thought sent Newland on a more irrational mission than ever. He tracked down as many stores in the east Alabama, west Georgia area that sold paperback novels as time and energy permitted. And he bought every copy of *Sometimes Darkness* he could locate. Several dozen before he completed his fear-crazed mission.

At the Goldsmith mall, he spent part of nearly every afternoon camped out on a bench in front of Bookland to survey the horror section. What was he watching for? The man in the khaki jumpsuit, of course. Not sighting the man in Bookland, Newland would move to the fountain area or to the food court—once he even brought along his camera to snap shots of the would-be psycho.

But the man never appeared.

At home, Trisha grew concerned about him, but he dismissed his fits of anxiety by claiming that he had a virulent case of "writer's block." She reluctantly believed him. Then one evening as Newland sat before the blank screen of his computer, Clay stole into the room and wormed onto Newland's lap.

"I miss Greenbeard," he whispered.

And when Newland looked down at his son's angelic face, all he could see was a sudden projection of an innocent body, strangled, a piece of tape placed over the mouth. With writing on the tape.

Children should be seen and not heard.

Newland began to shadow Clay's every step to school and back. Trisha couldn't help noticing his paranoia and voiced her concern.

"John, what's wrong? Honey, what is it?"

He read her questions as doubts about his emotional stability.

"Nothing's wrong. Nothing," he responded, his manner strained and tense. "You can't be too careful these days. You read about the worst kind of things. Things happening to kids. Better safe than sorry."

The platitude tasted more than bitter.

So he kept to his overly protective routine.

The stream of his writing had dwindled to a trickle.

This is not the legacy of Granny Ruth.

He embraced his own fearful thoughts.

And waited.

Spring was in high gear when something finally occurred.

When the darkness sank its fangs into him.

It was early one Saturday morning. Trisha and Clay were still asleep when Newland decided to call his brother in Wichita. What he learned from his brother was that the child-strangler had not been caught. He had, indeed, killed a second time, same type of killing as before. Four weeks had passed since the second killing. No one had pressed the improbable connection between the killings—*Children should be seen and not heard*—and Newland's novel.

"Thanks, Roger."

"Hey, big brother, this is really bothering you, isn't it?"

"Yeah. Like nothing else in my life ever has."

"But, hey, I mean . . . you don't really believe . . .?"

"Not sure what the hell I believe. All I know is . . . this whole business is eating me alive—can't sleep, can't write. Scared to let my son out of my sight."

"John . . . take it easy, will you?"

"Yeah . . . I'll try."

Newland sat in the empty kitchen at the empty table and then got up and made himself some coffee. While it was brewing, he decided to check the mail. Sometimes it came early on Saturdays. The outside air which greeted him was already humid, promising a hot day. The summer would likely be vintage Alabama—white haze, smotheringly hot.

Walking to the mailbox, Newland perked up. Every writer, he reasoned, has a special relationship with his or her mailbox. For that homely, prosaic object often houses the communications which signal either acceptance or rejection. From another angle, a writer's mailbox is a sacred place, a *temenos*, the repository of one's hopes and dreams, of one's frustrations and nightmares. Of one's fragile ego.

So it was fitting that Newland's mailbox should contain a manifestation of his darkest projections. What he found in his mailbox was this: a cover from a copy of *Sometimes Darkness*; it had been ripped free of the book. That seemed odd in itself. Then Newland noticed the back of the cover. There, in black magic marker letters, was written the following: "Children should be seen and not heard."

He wanted to call the police.

Decided against it because, more than likely, this was a harmless prank. He tried to think of potential jokesters—but came up with none.

The new horror which gripped him was not knowing for certain.

Who's out there?

Who's watching? Waiting?

He floated through the rest of the day in a bubble of terror. He spent much of the time alone in his study. Just thinking. Digging through an attic of memories which might explain something slightly beyond his mental reach. He thought about Granny Ruth reading Stevenson to him. Those wonderful tales. *Kidnapped* and *Treasure Island* and one she had read to him only once: *Dr. Jekyll and Mr. Hyde*, a tale which had never released its hold upon him.

Why didn't I mention that one to Katie Doyle?

Near evening he looked again at the cover he had found in the mailbox, at the writing on the back.

Then Trisha called him to dinner.

Where he heard his son complain, "Why can't I go to *Jurassic Park*?"

"It's too intense for someone your age," said Trisha.

"But Todd got to go and he's the same age I am. So why can't I go?"

"I just explained why."

"But Todd—."

Suddenly Newland had Clay's elbow and was lifting him from his chair, and in a silent fury he sent his son to his room.

Back at the table he said to Trisha, "Children should be seen and not heard."

"I don't know what's gotten into him," she said.

And after they finished dinner, Newland volunteered to help with the dishes. Trisha rewarded him with a kiss. She would wash; he would dry.

Then she slipped on a pair of plastic gloves.

And Newland found, quite suddenly, that he couldn't breathe.

"I have to go," he muttered. "Have to . . . get away from here."

"Honey?"

But he was out the back door and walking across the lawn toward the street, not bothering to explain, not allowing himself to slow down.

He believed he was looking for someone.

When he returned ten minutes later, Trisha had just finished the dishes.

"That was good timing," she teased. "I'm going to get in bed and read. Are you coming up?"

"No, go on without me. I'll be there in a little while," he told her.

He brushed aside her look of concern, and she left him

sitting alone at the kitchen table; he tried not to glance at the dishes standing in the drainpan drying. He was restless. His walk hadn't turned up anyone. From behind a bottle of liquid shortening on the counter he retrieved a pencil and notepad, the notepad they always used to make out the week's grocery list. On a fresh sheet of notepaper he wrote, "Children should be seen and not heard." He studied it a moment, and then he got out the book cover which had been left in his mailbox, turned it over, and compared the two hands.

He sighed heavily.

He thought about a killer somewhere in the Wichita area. He thought about the man at the mall. Dark twins?

There's so many of us.

The thought surprised him. He sighed again.

And surrendered wholeheartedly and wholemindedly to the truth. It was like giving in to the rush of inevitability a writer sometimes encounters in the midst of a narrative.

He took the plastic gloves from atop the drying dishes. He put them on. They squeaked like a frightened animal.

So many of us.

Just waiting for the right trigger.

Then he went upstairs to say goodnight to his son.

And the boy looked into his father's eyes and saw the day's final light slip away.

Home Again

Jeff Gelb

Bruce awakened crying. He turned onto his back, grimacing at the feel of the sweat-soaked sheets. His heart was slamming against his chest.

He stared at the darkness of the ceiling. It was a darker night than usual for L.A.; normally he could make out the wooden beam bisecting the room above his head; tonight there was no sign of it in the stygian darkness.

As his heartbeat struggled to reclaim its normal pace, he realized he had been dreaming. And what a terrifying nightmare it had been:

He was at work selling advertising for "Radio & Records," the music industry trade publication, when his phone rang. It was his son, Franklin, light of his life and the best gift of his marriage to Hope, his wife of thirteen years. Franklin's voice sounded upset, on the verge of tears.

"Dad, I have something to tell you, but don't be mad."

Bruce frowned. "Are you okay?"

"Yeah, but . . ."

Bruce could hear the fear in his son's voice, a foreign element that soured Bruce's stomach. It was 4:40 in the afternoon; Franklin was at a summer day-camp program. Had he scraped his elbow roller-blading? Or was it something worse?

It all poured out in a rush of words: "See, we were playing at the park, and we were making a fort in these bushes off the trail, and my friend found this syringe—"

62

Bruce gasped involuntarily. He'd never heard his son use the word syringe before. The boy was only nine; Bruce and Hope had always considered Franklin too young to have a talk about AIDS and other diseases that could be communicated through things like dirty needles. He felt sweat rolling down his shirt sleeve.

"—and the needle was bent so I couldn't see it, and I accidentally poked my finger."

Bruce gasped. "Did it draw blood?"

"Yes, Dad, a little, but I'm gonna be okay, aren't I? The kids said I'm gonna get AIDS now. Am I gonna die, Dad?"

Bruce felt like the office had gained twenty degrees of heat in the last second. "Jesus Christ. What did you do?"

Franklin started sobbing.

"Honey, it's okay, you're going to be okay. Tell me what you did."

Franklin cried, "I brought the syringe to the counselor and she threw it away."

"Did you wash off your finger?"

"Yeah, Dad, but am I gonna die? Am I?"

Then, as dreams do, his jumped ahead months to the day his pediatrician had gotten back the AIDS test results, and their worst nightmares had been confirmed. Against all odds, the needle had, in fact, just been used by an infected person, and it was still fresh enough to transmit the deadly germs to their son.

Another dream jump and he was at his son's hospital bedside, the boy now just a hollow shell of his former vibrant self, fighting for each breath, unable to speak. Bruce and Hope, devastated by this brutal act of an incomprehensible God, were mopping his forehead with a wash cloth and speaking softly to him, telling him it was okay to drop his body and move into the light. And finally, with a pitiful shudder, he had done so.

At the dream's funeral, Bruce told his parents he felt the entire event was his fault. If he had only warned Franklin of the dangers of syringes. How could Bruce live with the knowledge that his negligence had caused his own son's death?

As if unable to handle the pain of the realization, his brain woke Bruce up. He felt warm tears running down his cheek as he remembered the dream. Thank God it wasn't real. He was embarrassed that his subconscious would even dredge up such a nightmare, and he cursed himself for it. He loved his son; how could he have dreamed such a horrifying thing? What the fuck had brought it on? The chocolate cake he'd had just before bed? He silently promised himself that would be the end of midnight snacks.

Eyes still slick with tears, he struggled to see the lit numerals of the bedside clock. But they were invisible in the darkness. Frustrated, Bruce reached for the switch of the bedlamp, but his hand hit a wall. Where was the lamp? Had the cats knocked it over?

"Hope?" he whispered into the darkness, his voice shaky. But of course, she was doing a fill-in overnight airshift at an L.A. radio station, and wouldn't be home till about six A.M.

Bruce fell back on the wet bedsheets, cursing the dream and the darkness, then remembering his son, who, even at nine, still crept into their bed in the middle of the night. Bruce reached over but felt only rumpled sheets and blankets.

He bolted out of bed, suddenly aching with the need to see his son, hold him, kiss his moist forehead, listen to his soft breathing. Bruce stumbled around the room, knocking his shin against something, hissing at the sharp pain. What the fuck was that? He couldn't recall any hard-edged furniture in this part of the spacious bedroom of the home he and Hope loved so much.

His hands lashed out blindly, searching for a lamp, a light switch, finding picture frames, book shelves. Had he gone blind? No, there was a tiny sliver of light falling across the dresser he'd had as a kid, and . . .

He stopped in his tracks. What was that dresser doing there? It should have been 3000 miles away in upstate New York in his old bedroom, now a guest room in his parents' home. *What the fuck?*

Finally, he felt a light switch and turned it on. He clasped a hand to his mouth to stifle his scream as he realized he was in his parents' home, not his own. He pinched himself to make sure he wasn't dreaming.

When had he come back home? And why?

He looked around. It was his old bedroom alright, with the double bed, the simple dresser, the bookshelves his dad had built for him when he was a teen-ager to hold Bruce's collection of horror comic books. Right now, he felt like he was in the middle of one of those stories, where reality was bent like a funhouse mirror.

"Dad?" he tried cautiously, his voice a tremulous whisper, still not really believing he was back home at all. But when he heard the snoring down the hall, Bruce knew for certain that he was back in his childhood home. "Dad?" Louder now, more forceful, though inside he felt more like a thirteen-year-old kid than his actual forty-two years of age.

He heard an interrupted snore, a grunt, and then the sound of someone getting out of bed. In a moment, the hall light was switched on. Bruce blinked his eyes to adjust to the sudden light and then he could make out his father's familiar frame walking toward him, concern etched in his face.

"Are you okay, Bruce?" Howard wiped sleep from his eyes and regarded his son with genuine concern and love. He set an arm on Bruce's shoulder. "Go back to sleep. It's the middle of the night."

"No, Dad, wait. I mean, I'm glad to see you." He put his arms around his father and for some reason felt himself on the edge of new tears. "I had the worst nightmare of my life. Franklin died and, well . . ." he stopped, caught his breath. "I'm . . . kind of confused, Dad," Bruce said. "I mean, I can't remember why I'm here."

Was that a twitch he'd seen behind his father's expression of concern? "We'll discuss it in the morning, I promise."

"No. I want to talk about it now."

His father sighed. Under the harsh illumination of the hall light, he suddenly looked much older than his sixty-seven years. The impression Bruce got was of a very tired, stressed-out old man. It was a frightening vision, not how he saw his father, and Bruce averted his eyes rather than see him like this.

"You're right," Bruce said. "It can wait. I'm sorry I woke you." He turned to head back to his room and then turned back to his father. He kissed him on the cheek. "I love you, Dad. And Mom." Bruce smiled. "I'm glad I didn't wake her. She always could sleep through anything—even your snoring."

His father's smile seemed forced. Bruce went back to bed, somehow setting aside a million questions, and fell into a thankfully dreamless sleep.

The smell of coffee acted as a natural alarm clock. Bruce opened his eyes to the sunlit view of his bedroom, and smiled. He had so many great memories of this room, from the hours spent reading comics on this very bed to the first time he'd brought a date up here while his parents were out, and made it to second base. Debbie Whitehead—where was she now?

Bruce jumped out of bed, relieved himself in the bathroom, showered, shaved, and brushed his teeth. He felt much better this morning, last night's dream already fading into the quicksand where all dreams quickly retreat during daylight hours.

But what am I doing home?

He bounded downstairs in a bathrobe his Dad must have supplied. "Mom?" Bruce asked, expecting to see Muriel making coffee and eggs for both of "her boys," as she'd always called Bruce and Howard. But he was greeted instead by his father, the morning light making little difference to his haggard appearance. He really had gone downhill since the last time Bruce had been home. But when was that?

"Coffee?"

"You bet." He took the mug gratefully, added cream and sugar, and sat down to a stack of pancakes large enough to choke a horse. In other words, his dad's usual portion.

"Mom up yet?"

Howard hesitated a moment. "She's at her sister's. Betsy had a stroke a few weeks ago and Muriel's been looking after her. Remember?"

"As a matter of fact, no. Maybe I'm having a weird hangover or something, but honest, I really can't remember much of anything, Dad. Is that why I came home? Because of Betsy's stroke? To help you guys out?"

His father joined him at the table. Bruce noticed Howard's stack of pancakes was half the size of the one he'd made for his son.

"Watching your weight, Dad? Forgive me for saying this,

but it looks like you could use a pound or two right now. Are you feeling alright?''

"I'm fine, Bruce," he said, putting a slightly shaking hand over his son's. The body contact was somehow more meaningful than usual to Bruce, who clasped his other hand over his father's for a moment. They both sat silently, enjoying the unspoken father-son bond.

"So Dad, what can you tell me? I mean, I love being here, but I have obligations to work, and my family, and . . ."

"Bruce, I've asked Dr. Broughton to join us this morning—he'll be here in about an hour. Maybe he can help answer your questions."

Bruce's brow furrowed. "Dr. Broughton? Isn't that the shrink who put Mom on Prozac a few years ago? What does he have to do with this?" Suddenly, Bruce brought his hand down hard on the table. The pancakes jumped. "Dammit, Dad, what is going on? Why am I here?"

He saw his father's face register what could only be called fear, and it chilled his spine. Now he too was getting scared. "Is it . . . is it Hope? Or Franklin?" He grabbed at his father's flannel pajama shirt. "Tell me they're okay. Tell me the dream was just a nightmare. Please, Dad, tell me!"

His father was silent.

Bruce's eyes drifted to the wall clock. "It's only 6:15 in California. I swear I'll wake them up and get to the bottom of this if you don't tell me what's going on right now."

His father shook his head. "The doctor asked that we wait for his arrival. We've been waiting for this day, and he said he wanted to be here."

"What do you mean, you've been waiting?" Bruce arose, slamming the chair against the back wall, and picked up the portable phone next to the dish washer. He angrily punched in the number of his home in California. "Well, I'm not waiting for Dr. Broughton, or you, or anyone else." He heard the connection being made and then the phone ringing on the other end of the receiver.

"Hello?" It was a *male* voice. Bruce felt his bowels quiver. "Who is this?" he asked.

"Who the hell is this?" An *angry* male voice, one Bruce couldn't place.

"I'm looking for Hope Goldstone."

"You got the wrong number buddy, and it's six-fifteen in the morning."

"Look, I'm sorry, but I'm calling long distance." He recounted the number he'd just dialed.

"That's me, and there ain't no Hope Goldstone here. Now let me get some sleep, will ya?" He hung up.

"What the hell is going on?" He felt reality slipping away from him. "Dad, *please!*"

His father looked at his son and bit his lip, then nodded. "All right, I'm going to say something you're not going to like and you may not comprehend. It's going to make you angry and upset and hopefully by that time the doctor will be here to help you—to help us."

Bruce sat down opposite his father. Setting aside his hardly-touched pancake stack, Howard took his son's hands in his own. Both of them were shaking, and in other circumstances, they both might have laughed, but now, there were tears in both their eyes as Howard began. "You see, Bruce, you got a wrong number in California because you never lived in California."

"What? Are you fucking nuts? I've lived there for twenty years now . . ."

"Please, don't interrupt. You told me to explain everything. Now give me the chance." He took a deep breath and continued. "The truth is, you've never moved out of our house."

"That's impossible," Bruce yelled, disengaging his hands from his father's. "I work at R & R, my son goes to school in Manhattan Beach, my wife works in Hollywood . . ." he stopped midsentence because his father was shaking his head.

"You never married. There is no Hope, and there is no Franklin. They're just figments of your imagination."

"No!" Bruce stood up again, ran back to the phone, angrily punching in the phone number for R & R. The phone rang 15 times before he hung up. "Fuck. It's still too early. No one's there yet. I'll call back." He turned back to his father. "Why are you doing this to me, Dad? Why are you lying?"

"I'm not. I told you we should have waited."

Bruce shook his head. "Goddammit, I can tell you what

songs we listened to while my wife was in labor, I can tell
you how my son's hair smells after a shower. I can tell you
how much money I made in the last five years. I can tell you
what comic books I bought last week and where I bought
them.

"I have twenty years of California memories inside my
head; they can't all be dreams and . . . wishful thinking.
They can't." He stalked around the kitchen, his mind reeling.

"Bruce, you had a nervous breakdown a month ago. We've
been taking you to Dr. Broughton, and he warned us something like last night would happen. The nightmares, the fanta-
sies . . ."

"No." It was unbelievably terrifying. His own father was
telling him that most of his memories were lies, the tricks of
a diseased mind. It was beyond comprehension. He looked
at his father, eyes seething with hatred. "I want to see Mom.
I want to hear what she has to say. You're lying to me. I
don't know why, but Mom won't lie. I'm calling Betsy's
house." He stood up.

"Don't bother—Mom's on her way home. I called her last
night, after you went back to bed. She'll be here by the time
the doctor arrives."

Bruce felt his world slipping through his fingers like grains
of sand. He couldn't stop the tears, which came in a flood.
Oh my God—no Hope, no Franklin, no *life*. Had he really
spent the last twenty years of his life here, at home, a failure
who finally cracked from the weight of his own unfulfilled
dreams? It was too heavy a burden to live with. He wanted
to die.

His father's hands touched his shoulders and he twitched
them away. "Get away. I want Mom. She'll tell the truth."

He walked away from his father, out of the kitchen, barely
registering that he was in his childhood home again. He went
to the front window of the den, decorated in early American
as it always had been. Through watery eyes, he gazed out
the window, hoping to see a palm tree, or better still, his
son's skateboard in the front yard, or Hope's Mercury Capri
coming into the driveway.

A car was approaching—it was his mother's Ford Escort.
He strained to see her behind the wheel but his vision was

too blurry. Furiously, he wiped at his eyes, but the car was already entering the garage.

Bruce ran to the house's side door and opened it as his mother's familiar shape emerged from her car. Behind him, he heard his father approaching. Crying uncontrollably now, Bruce ran to his mother. "Mom!" he cried as he embraced her, smelling her perfume. It was a familiar fragrance, but not his mother's. It was her sister Betsy's favorite perfume.

Bruce stood back to give his mother a kiss and felt his world shatter as he stared into Betsy's eyes.

"Mom?" He asked. Betsy tried to hug him but he pulled away from her. "You're not my mother," he screamed angrily. "My mother is . . . my mother is . . .

"Dead. My mother is dead. Oh my God, Mom is dead." And he fainted.

And dreamed.

He was standing next to his father at his mother's bedside. Her face was frighteningly thin, her eyes closed, her breath shallow. Howard used a wash cloth to wipe the sweat from her fevered brow. Tears flowed freely from his face as he did his task slowly, lovingly.

Bruce kneeled at his mother's side and whispered, "It's okay, Mom, I'll be fine, and I promise to take care of Dad for you. We'll be okay. It's okay for you to let go, to drop your body." He squeezed her hand but felt no reassuring returned pressure. He wondered whether her spirit had already left her comatose body. In case it had not, he continued to encourage her.

"Head for the light, Mom. I know you can see it. Head for the light, and freedom, and peace. And God."

And almost instantaneously, her hand twitched in his as her body let go of its lifeforce and she died.

Bruce awoke to see Dr. Broughton's face above his own. "How are you?" the doctor asked softly.

Bruce sat up, looked around him. Hope and Franklin came from behind the doctor, rushing forward to hug and kiss Bruce. He grabbed them both and cried into their hair as he remembered:

* * *

His mother had endured open heart surgery following a heart attack two years ago, and the blood she was given during the operation had turned out to be tainted with the AIDS virus. It had taken two painful years for her to succumb. In that time, Bruce had all but moved back to his parents' home to take care of her and her husband, Howard. Bruce reclaimed his old room and did his telephone-oriented sales job from their home. The last thing he remembered was her deathbed scene . . . until last night's dream.

He disengaged slowly from his family's embrace and faced the doctor. Broughton nodded and said, "I understand—you want answers, you deserve them, and thank God, I believe you are ready for them. When your mother died, you were certain her death was somehow your fault. You suffered a nervous breakdown. It happens more often than you'd think, but in your case, it resulted in such a strong mental denial of your mother's death that you lost your grip on reality."

Suddenly dizzy, Bruce needed to sit down. He fell onto a couch, the weight of the doctor's words pressing against him, as well as the reclaimed memory that what Broughton was saying was indeed true.

"Medications and counseling did not help. You turned more and more inward, till you refused to eat or take care of yourself. You renounced your life since leaving home twenty years ago, claiming it never happened, perhaps feeling you could have somehow saved your mother had you never left her. Maybe you felt you could bring your mother back to life by killing the life you had created for yourself.

"You wouldn't see or talk to Hope or Franklin, wouldn't even acknowledge their existence. You built a fantasy that your mom was just away, caring for her sister—who is fine, by the way."

Betsy squeezed Bruce's shoulder in support. The doctor continued, "usually, in cases this severe, patients are sent to a hospital where they can be cared for, and given electroshock therapy to jog their memories. It was seen as a last resort way for you to face your mother's death and get on with your own life. But your father felt it was too risky, and wouldn't allow it."

Bruce turned to his father, who was wiping tears from his eyes. Bruce motioned for him to join him on the couch, where he could hold his hands. Neither person's hands were shaking anymore.

Broughton continued, "He forced me instead to think in non-traditional ways. After much discussion, we decided to try an experiment based on some reading I'd been doing. Basically, we hoped that by making a lie of your real life, your mind would disengage from the false one it had created and shock you back into reality.

"After your nightmare this morning, your father called to tell me about your dream, which I took as a sign that your mind's defenses were cracking. That's when we decided to try the plan. A friend of your wife's has been house-sitting while your family was back here, and he agreed to play-act when you called. I had a similar contingency plan if you had called work. And Betsy agreed to the impersonation of your mother. Beyond that?" He shrugged. "We hoped and prayed it wouldn't go beyond that."

The room was silent for a minute, while the weight of the information slowly sank into Bruce. Finally, his father asked, "Do you forgive me?"

Bruce hugged Howard and they sobbed into each others' shoulders, a long, cleansing cry. Finally, Bruce choked, "I love you Dad. And thank you, thank you all, for your courage, for your love."

He turned to his wife and son. Hope smiled sweetly and said, "welcome home again."

Sewercide

Rex Miller

There was always sound, even in this silent place, echoes
that drifted down into hell from far above, the sewer thrum,
distant machine hum, a vague gaseous hiss; these faraway
sounds only a suggestion of humanity's existence. She
waited, terrorized beyond the edge of sanity, a huddled, naked
form chained to something she could not see.

She could see a few yards around her, looming rock canyon
walls and enormous masses of black shadow that flickered
like ghost images in the dancing flames of the small fire
beside her. What she could see and hear was the world for
her now. Nothing else mattered.

Here in the deep blackness of hell she lived—or died—at
the whims of the king of Hades. Here she was fed and watered, tethered to the great chain, performed her bodily func-
tions without embarrassment now, slept . . . waited to be
used. The waiting was of course the worst, and it was what
brought the madness. Not the deeds themselves—the waiting!

She sensed him and shivered under the rough blanket. Her
sense of smell was now gone—the stench never left her nose
and it was overpowering beyond anything humans ever experience. For the first days and nights she was constantly ill
from the stink, but eventually her olfactory senses became
numb and she was able to keep food down. Now she smelt
nothing. Not even the foulness of her own defecation and the
rotting odors of her prison. Nor could she see him moving

silently, gliding through the deep shadows, and he was stealth itself in spite of his gigantic size so there was no noise. She sensed his presence.

She tried to free her mind from what was coming for her, to block it somehow, to remember her identity, her family, who she was, that others would be searching for her. Her name was Lori. Her husband—God! so unreal now—his name was Tom and he was a million miles away—up there up above her somewhere, beyond the borders of her reality. Two children. Gena and Tommy. Tears welled up and overflowed, streaking the grease and filth of her face. She sniffed and spat into the darkness and he came into the illumination of the fire, materializing out of the inkiness, the king of hell!

How many weeks had she been a prisoner? Time had long since lost any meaning. Months? She couldn't guess. He had spoken to her four times that she could remember and she tried to recall each specific instance. They were points to fasten her shaky mental processes on. Three times he scolded her, then hurt her for infractions, once because she kept begging him to stop. That was the time he had explained who he was and what he wanted.

"Why are you doing this to me? I haven't done anything to you," she'd whined, and he had slapped her viciously, telling her if she spoke again he'd put the awful ball-gag back in and leave it in. She knew he meant it. That was when he'd told her.

"You stupid fucking bitch *I followed you*. Shit ass *pro-life cunt*!" he'd called her. The phrase held all his secrets and she had repeated it to herself over and over, finally coming to agree that these few brutal words redefined her.

He left her food. Water. Kept the fire going so that she would not freeze. She knew he probably wouldn't kill her yet and that was the only thing that kept part of her sanity intact.

The massive hands pinched, tore, pulled, rearranged her as he crudely wet himself and achieved penetration, cursing as he moved her back and forth on him; she tried not to break his rhythms because when she angered him he would pull her hair savagely or cuff her face or nearly rip her breasts off with his angry fingers of steel. It was not intercourse so much as masturbation—him moving her back and forth or up and down on him, controlling her easily with his powerful hands. A minute or two was all that was usually necessary and he would ejaculate, pull out and smack her away.

He finished this time, as always, in a few moments and moved off into the darkness. Did he go away between the times when he used her? Did he live there in the shadows somewhere nearby? Did he watch her? She didn't know.

She felt sticky and even in the beginning stages of madness her intelligence was enough that she knew to fight the itching. Meticulously, carefully, she wet a small corner of the coarse blanket using a tiny amount of water from the jug he left with her and—as best as the situation would permit—gave herself a cold water sponge bath. When that was finished she did as she always did—fell into a long, drugged sleep.

During the terrible sleep she saw his fat, grotesque features, the doughy body—huge but heavily muscled—heard the voice telling her over and over "I followed you . . . pro-life cunt . . ." Then she was awake, or half-awake, or still inside the nasty folds of the dream—what did it matter?

If she did not fight she would slip away into complete madness; she dug her broken nails into her palms and fought to concentrate, to remember.

Once she'd been a socially involved human, a normal woman with a busy schedule of helping others, of political and ethical causes—pro-life? Yes. Proudly so. Her name was Lori, but her last name—Davis?—had become fuzzy and unreal. She had been one of the most active women in her community, a spokesperson and advocate against the pro-choice crowd. That was what had caused the monster to lock onto her, target her, stalk her.

She could recollect a speaking engagement. A loud public argument—she could recall the face of someone screaming about women's rights—she'd called the face a murderer. Her memory struggled to picture the face of the monster in the crowd but could not.

The first time she'd seen him was in the crowded parking lot at Kmart, where she'd gone to buy . . . something. Lori . . . Davis. She had a husband named Tom somewhere up

above. Children. Gena. Tommy, Junior. She made herself
work to see their faces, to hear their voices, to see the draw-
ings that were held to the front of the refrigerator by magnets
made to resemble vegetables and flowers.

She composed a limerick in her mind: the king of hell and
Lori-belle they live beneath the sewer. Something, something, pro-life cunt, that's why he likes to do her! It made
her laugh and cry and spit again. She suspected that insanity
would claim her soon if she didn't break free. She pulled the
chain over the fire and tried to burn it again, even though she
knew it would grow unbearably hot and she'd only succeed in
hurting herself.

Now Lori-belle she had a chain that held her by the waist.
She liked to hold it in the fire and da da-da da-da.

The woman felt around, feeling the sack of burgers and
ice-cold fries there in the shadows of the fire. The jug of
tepid water. He'd put an apple in the sack—how thoughtful!
He probably remembered she'd need some vitamin C.

The monster had done something to her as he yanked her
into a vehicle in the Kmart parking lot. It was the last thing
she could remember until she'd been rudely brought back to
consciousness with smelling salts that made her gag. He'd
made her wash her mouth out and then shoved a disgusting
thing in her mouth that was like a large rubber ball on a cord.
It tied behind her head, and she'd had to wear it all the way
down into the pit.

She had a frightening memory of storefronts, peeling,
cracked walls adjacent to the old boarded-over subway en-
trances and exits, covered in graffiti-painted lumber.

He pulled her through an opening which he resealed with
a length of corrugated tin, and lit a lantern. It was pitch black.
They started down. She almost fainted with fear.

The beast dragged her down around pipes, massive and
dark, vast expanses of poured, reinforced concrete that stunk
of sewage.

It became colder, wetter, and with the worsening smell
came the shivery feel and echoing sound of a river bottom
beneath a canyon stream. She was sure he was going to kill
her.

There were rock steps like a regular stairway, but eventually these gave way to massive slabs that had wider and wider spaces between them. They hypnotized her. Several times she almost stumbled and once she looked down into the black shafts and became very dizzy, pitching forward and almost falling. She would have fallen to her death but the rough grip of steel held her.

One tiny comfort; apparently they were not alone in all this black nothingness. Here and there lights twinkled off in the darkness. Who could live down here? Criminals? Runaways? The thought of where they were chilled her to the core.

The machine sounds above had become a faraway presence. The raw smell of feces was overpowering.

Beyond the glare of the monster's lantern it was pitch black and as they moved with the light, great circles of sickly yellow ricocheted off into the dark. The shafts pulled at her eyes like deep wells of magnetic energy but she concentrated on not falling, and on keeping the rhythm. She had to stay with the rhythm of the slabs.

They moved beneath the looming pipes, the massive chunks of rod-filled concrete that squatted like secret pyramids far beneath Chicago's high-rises. Sometimes she had a sense of slick and slimy things slithering or scuttling away as they continued to descend.

Were they going into the bowels of the earth? The woman's disorientation became intense as they kept moving down the face of a subterranean monolith, dripping stone and rotting friction piles that drove into the substrata like an upside-down forest of redwoods.

At last, mercifully, they stopped descending. The immense monstrosity who had abducted her made sounds she could not identify and she caught quick glimpses of him at the edges of the lantern light. There was no thought of escape. She had no light, no idea where she was, no clue as to the way up and no hoping of finding it. She was also exhausted. Nonetheless that had been her one blind hope. She knew she should have run into the hellish darkness. In a few moments a small fire was going and he had hold of her again. He was chaining her to the rocks.

Lori tried to shake off the grogginess. Was this real or was she imagining it? Was she back in real time or remembering? Had he just torn the blanket from her and raped her or was it the first time, and was she remembering how he savagely stripped off her clothing and forced himself into her?

At first it had been such a puzzle. Why would he go to such trouble to rape a woman? When he finished with her he'd left her the scratchy blanket and the food and water—keeping her alive as if she were a pet. Why?

In time she'd learned the horrible truth. She'd been like a neon sign to him, advertising her reverence for life, and that was what had made him stalk her. That was why she was going to live—at least until the third trimester. He'd brought her here for breeding.

There was only a vague subliminal awareness of being late with her period—then the boredom and drugged lethargy of time without clocks. Slow hours? Fast days? Interminable nights? A timeless space very near the brink.

He had been gone a long time. It was the longest she'd been left alone since the abduction. There was no way for her to count the minutes, to measure the passage of time, but the water was almost gone and when she awakened now she was ravenously hungry. She could feel herself starving. He would not leave her to starve—because he would not kill the child growing inside her.

This was the thought she was fighting to hold on to when she heard the sounds, faraway voices floating down into the depths of her pit! She tried to scream and nothing came. They were coming to rescue her! She quickly put the dirty jug to her mouth and swallowed the last of the hideous water. This time she was able to scream and she screamed until she lost her voice.

The next thing she knew they were there, the police—a woman who tried to examine her briefly by their lights—she saw eyes staring down at her, caught fragments of floating conversation meaningless as coughs.

She was on her feet and the man was asking her something.

"Can you walk? Do you think you can climb part of the way back up? A stretcher is on the way."

"Yes," she said, "I think so." They helped her, men on either side of her, virtually carrying her as they began the slow ascent back. "Where is he?"

"He's gone. Don't worry. You're safe, now," the kindly, older man told her.

"Wh . . . who . . .?"

"My name's Eichord."

She shook her head. "Who was he?"

The detective answered, "He's the monster son of the 'lonely hearts' killer—the serial murderer I killed. Unfortunately, not before he'd fathered a child born with his tainted blood.

"It's going to be all right." He tried to soothe her with his gentle tones but it only made her more upset. Why couldn't he understand? She tried to explain but it took too much effort. They kept moving toward the brighter lights that winked far above.

"I'm carrying his *baby*."

She was exhausted. She felt pain so widespread throughout her body that she couldn't analyze it or pinpoint the sources. She became very nauseated at one point and they had to stop.

They started again and she began making a kind of keening animal noise. By the time they'd reached the midway point she was trying to pull out of the detectives' grasps but was far too weak.

"Just take it easy, Lori," the woman told her. "Your husband's up ahead." She meant it in a helpful way but the words caused her to snap.

"I was for breeding—" she whispered to Eichord, trying to pull away from him. She had to explain what it was all about.

"You're having trouble breathing?"

"No. Breeding. I was for *breeding*—his *breeder bitch*, he called me. I was his *pro-life* cunt who would have his baby because I could not allow myself to get rid of the fetus. Don't you see? It's how he intends to keep their spawn alive? I'm going to have his monster!"

"Take it easy, now. It will all work out. Let's get you out of here and then we'll deal with everything. I promise." They kept climbing. She became more and more unglued.

Inside her head a battle raged: she could not have this baby and she could not abort the fetus. The moral dilemma she faced was as agonizing as the ordeal she had just survived. How would she tell her husband? What would he think of her? How could she reconcile an abortion with her unwavering belief that all life should be revered? What could she do?

Thoughts swirled inside her mind like pieces of food caught in a blender—they came out incomprehensible and mushy. She tried to ask how long she'd been down there but just forming the question presented incalculable problems in logic.

"How long . . .?" The thought went up like smoke.

"We're almost there."

"No—" Why wouldn't they *listen* to her?

"You'll be *fine*. Just a little further."

What would she say to her husband? It's me, the monster's breeder bitch, back from hell? Lori-belle, back from hell, when her belly starts to swell . . . something.

"Lori!" A man's voice boomed out from up above. She saw the detective smile and she pulled both hands loose, tearing away from them, doing the only thing she could do.

She was screaming before her feet left the cold concrete. In her burgeoning madness she'd seen only one way out and she'd taken it—over the high side of a parapet to her and her baby's death far below.

Unfinished Business

Michael Garrett

Mark Hopson's skin tingled with fear. His pulse soared to uncharted heights, his forehead damp with perspiration and eyelids twitching nervously. He fumbled with a mound of paper clips on his desk and stared blankly at his loose-leaf appointment calendar, reminding him of the employee he'd deliberately scheduled last. Efforts to calm himself through a series of deep breaths had proved fruitless.

Violence in the work place.

CNN cable coverage of business-related fatalities flashed through Mark's mind—employees of an Oklahoma post office shot to death by a disgruntled co-worker. A New Jersey executive gutted and hanged by a respected office worker he'd fired a week earlier. A Florida sales manager permanently paralyzed from a knife wound inflicted by a terminated account executive.

Now, for the first time in his career, Mark faced a similar threat, and no one had listened. No one seemed to care. Relax, his own boss, John Russell, had told him. It's an occupational hazard of the nineties. The odds of anything like that happening here are almost nil. But there was no way Mark Hopson could be calm. Not with Brett Hardiman remaining on the list to be fired—the only employee with a violent temper that Mark had ever had to let go.

Although Brett had earned an excellent reputation on the job, he had exhibited episodes of unprovoked aggression in his personal life. He'd roughed up his wife on several occasions, and only a couple of months earlier had severely beaten a man much larger than himself under the pretense of defending a waitress. Mark trembled at the thought of being the target of Brett's potential rage.

Mark Hopson, the trembling, weak-kneed vice president of HammerStock Industries and presumed heir to the presidency, took a deep breath and exhaled. Having never experienced such an overwhelming premonition of impending doom, he straightened his necktie and drummed his fingertips on the polished mahogany surface of his desk. Convinced that his fear was not the least bit unwarranted, he groaned and ran his fingers through his hair. After all, Brett, the winner of the state-wide Tough Guy boxing tournament, had already been summoned, and was on his way to becoming an unemployment statistic. For Mark, the risk could be akin to spitting in Arnold Schwarzenegger's face.

Suddenly the telephone rang, jarring Mark's train of thought. He snatched the receiver from its cradle, cringing at the sound of his boss's gruff voice on the other end of the line. "Hopson?" the chief executive officer boomed. "Is it over yet?"

Mark swallowed hard. "No, sir. Not yet." He paused, attempting to hide the noticeable quiver in his voice. "But won't you reconsider posting a security guard outside my door? I'm really nervous about this one, sir."

Mr. Russell just laughed. "Hell, Hopson, you're paranoid. Hardiman has never laid a hand on anyone at work. Besides, if I could afford to hire security guards, maybe I wouldn't have to get rid of these people in the first place."

Mark cleared his throat and nervously twisted the telephone cord around his index finger. "But Mr. Russell, I'm willing to pay for a guard myself, for my own peace of mind, if you'll just allow me—"

"Forget it, Hopson," Mr. Russell interrupted. "I won't discuss this again. I don't want anyone getting the impression that we have an unsafe work environment here. How the hell do you think the rest of the staff would react to an armed guard walking around for the first time ever?" He broke into a hacking cough, then added, "We've never needed a security force in the thirty-four-year history of this company and we're not about to start now. Just do your goddam job like I told you to.''

The line crackled and the dial tone buzzed into Mark's ear as Mr. Russell resorted to his famous phone-slamming tactic to terminate the call.

Mark's pulse raced higher. More than anything he'd like to quit this job—it was affecting his health—but for the sake of his family's welfare, he had no choice. All he could think about was Lisa and the kids, especially Randy, his second and most dependent child, who was afflicted with Down's syndrome. Mark slowly shook his head. Working for the world's most self-centered CEO had been a nightmare. But better positions were hard to come by in this day and age, and suffering the wrath of Mr. Russell was better than weekly visits to the unemployment office.

Still, Mark couldn't help being saddened by the impact of today's lay-off on the lives of his co-workers. He'd opposed the staff reduction from the beginning, suggesting more humane options for cutting expenses instead, but Mr. Russell— John Vincent Russell—had refused to back down. "Let 'em go," he'd growled. "It's happening everywhere. It won't come as a surprise." And with a cruel smirk he'd added, "They'd better get used to it.''

And at least so far today, Mr. Russell had been right. The five employees Mark had fired already, two men and three women, appeared to have seen it coming. Only one had exhibited any hint of surprise at all. The others had sat in cold silence as if in a daze, their expressions pale, their eyes blank and lifeless.

Unlike those, however, Brett Hardiman's performance had been exemplary. But after eight years of procurement improvements and installing a computerized inventory management system, Brett would fall victim to his own efficiency.

Mark felt his forehead. Did he have a fever? Was he coming down with something? Or was the tension of the moment simply inflaming his skin? He checked his watch. Brett should have arrived by now. Scratching an eyelid, and anxious to get the unpleasant task over with, Mark stood and tugged a line of wrinkles from his vest, then stepped to his office door and stuck his head outside. Brenda Graves, his secretary, was busy tapping away at her keyboard, a long lock of frosted blonde hair dangling over her forehead. "Brenda," Mark called to her, so preoccupied by the unpleasant task at hand that he forgot his usual acknowledgement of the tight sweater she was wearing. "Did you call Brett for me?"

"His line has been busy," she whispered as if sympathizing with the pressure her boss faced. "Mr. Russell just called me to ask if Brett was in your office yet. When I told him I hadn't been able to reach him, Mr. Russell said he would send a messenger for Brett."

Mark shook his head.

"You know how impatient Mr. Russell is," Brenda continued with a sigh. "He told me to call him as soon as Brett leaves."

Mark groaned and returned to his desk, collapsing into his executive leather chair. Since Brett had always received outstanding performance reviews, he wouldn't suspect that his job was in jeopardy.

And those were the ones most likely to explode.

With Brett's violent history, Mark was determined to take no chances. He closed his eyes, massaged his graying temples, and reached for the second drawer on the right side of his desk. With a gentle tug, the drawer glided open to reveal his last resort—a Smith & Wesson .38 Special. As far as Mark knew, the weapon had never even been fired, but with Mr. Russell's refusal to allow a security guard on the premises, Mark felt there was no alternative but to take drastic measures to protect himself.

He ran his fingers again through his thinning hair, past the bald spot at the crown of his head, and scratched the back of his neck. The gun was a blatant infraction of the company's weapons policy, but the termination of so many innocent people was also against all human decency. Somehow, violating the firearms policy seemed minor by comparison.

Mark groaned. The headache he'd nursed all morning was getting worse. And in his mind, he recalled reports of the gut-wrenching impact of Brett's massive fist slamming against his challenger's face. Blood had reportedly squirted from the wound like juice from a grapefruit. Would Brett's temper flare when he heard the news? Would he lash out in an uncontrollable rage? Would Mark Hopson of HammerStock Industries be the next corporate casualty to appear on CNN?

Not as long as a gun separated him from Brett, Mark thought as he clumsily flipped open the snub-nose revolver's cylinder. He decided at the last minute that perhaps the gun should be loaded after all, in case Brett charged and there was no way to stop him other than shooting his legs to slow him down. From his coat pocket Mark retrieved a handful of cartridges and filled the five chambers with shaky fingers.

Suddenly a light knock sounded at the door. Mark returned the weapon to the drawer, took a final deep breath, and adjusted the cuff-links of his heavily starched white shirt sleeves, then closed his eyes for a moment of brief meditation, his heart racing. He exhaled, closed his eyes, and counted to ten. "Come in, Brett," he eventually called out.

Brett Hardiman eased through the door. It was Friday, Casual Day, and Brett was dressed in jeans and a colorful sweater. He looked younger than his 34 years, his face rugged and sporting a full head of dark brown hair without a trace of gray. Brett had maintained an excellent physique through the heavy lifting required of his storeroom position. Normally a stone-faced rock of Gibraltar, a look of bewilderment now marred the big man's face. Mark motioned to one of two chairs facing his desk and asked Brett to be seated.

Brett swallowed hard and glared around the room. "Where's Mr. Russell?" he asked. "I thought the three of us were going to review the latest inventory figures."

Mark reacted by clearing his throat. "I want to make this as painless as possible for both of us, Brett," he recited the prepared statement. "I'm sure you already know that we've been downsizing today, and I'm sorry to say that your position at HammerStock has been eliminated, effective immediately." Mark paused, taking note of the sudden shock on Brett's face. "I'm sorry to see you go, Brett," he added. "You've done an excellent job here, and I've enjoyed working with you."

Brett sat motionless, his cheeks turning red.

"You'll receive one month's severance pay, as well as payment for all untaken vacation," Mark continued as he pushed a manila folder of termination documents across the desk. Brett swallowed hard and exhaled deeply, his temples throbbing like the throat of a frog. "The company will pay your insurance premiums for six months," Mark added. "And with as much as you have to offer, Brett, I'm sure that you won't have a problem finding another job."

Brett hung his head. Mark watched the glow of redness grow deeper and richer across the dejected man's face, and cautiously eased his right hand closer to the partially open desk drawer, his fingers inching toward the protective aura of the gun.

Brett coughed and glanced around the room. "Is that it?" he asked through clenched teeth. "I can't wait to tell my wife." He stood and took a couple of steps toward the door leaving the manila folder behind, his head hanging low in defeat, his breath seething.

Mark exhaled with relief. Brett was obviously angry, but had controlled himself and taken it like a man. Mark scooped up the paperwork and met the despondent employee at the door to shake hands and offer condolences. "I'm truly sorry," Mark said. "This hasn't been easy for me."

Brett took Mark's extended hand and squeezed with all his might, crushing his boss's fingers together. With his other hand, Brett grabbed Mark's collar and practically lifted him from the floor. The termination papers slipped from Mark's grasp and glided across the office. "You son-of-a-bitch," Brett growled. "Don't expect any sympathy out of me for what you've done. I've worked my ass off for this company."

Mark struggled to speak, cursing himself for having let down his guard. "Brett . . . I told you . . . there's nothing wrong with your . . . *work*," Mark gasped for air. "It's just a . . . cost containment measure . . . that's all."

"Shit!" Brett spat. "Is that supposed to make me feel better?" Brett slapped him across the face, splitting Mark's lower lip. "You know, you're not just firing me, you son-of-a-bitch. You're firing my wife and my kid, too. You're firing our house and our cars and everything we own. And you won't get away with it—that's a promise!"

Mark's face stung from the force of the blow. "Brett!"

Mark pleaded. "Don't do anything you'll regret. This is . . . bad enough already."

Brett gritted his teeth and rammed a knee into Mark's groin. As his boss collapsed helplessly to the floor, Brett stepped over the crumpled form and hissed, "There's more hurt to come, Big Boss Man." Brett rattled the door knob as he left the room, then stopped for one last look inside. "We've got ourselves some unfinished business here."

The pain was excruciating. Mark's vision wavered; a loud whistling sound roared in his ears. He held his crotch as if his hands cupped over his genitals would somehow diminish the pain. Mark realized he'd have to carry the gun at all times—Brett could surprise him anytime, anyplace, and the police couldn't protect him twenty-four hours a day. Maybe he should even hire a bodyguard to transport him to and from the office. He'd have to be damned cautious every waking minute—

"*Mark!*" Brenda called as she hurried into the room. She kneeled at his side and wiped a stream of blood from her boss's chin with her fingertips. "Are you all right? Do you need a doctor?"

Mark struggled to catch his breath. "No," he gasped, slowly shaking his head. "I'm okay. Just give me a few minutes to myself."

"But Mark—"

"*Please,*" he rasped as he stood on wobbling legs. "Just go."

After a brief pause Brenda left the room, closing the door softly behind her.

Mark staggered to his desk and stared at the gun in the partially open drawer. All of his precautions had proved worthless, but at least he hadn't been killed. Sweat dribbled down his brow. The throbbing between his legs and his headache merged somewhere in his chest. He felt like he'd been plowed down by a Dallas Cowboys linebacker.

Moments passed. The headache grew more intense. The throbbing in his ears thudded harder and faster. His hand still shaking, Mark reached for the weapon. His arm felt like a phantom limb, the cool steel grip of the revolver alien to his touch and oddly out of place. He tested the gun's weight and couldn't imagine himself carrying a concealed weapon. But just as his hand closed around the pistol to familiarize himself with its feel, the office door jerked open. Mark trembled awkwardly in response, the gun dropping with a dull thud to the bottom of the drawer, blood draining from his face as Mr. Russell stepped inside, flaunting his one thousand five hundred dollars pin-striped suit. "Well, I'll be damned," Mr. Russell said as he noticed Mark's swollen lip. "I guess you were right about Hardiman after all. Do you want to press charges against the bastard?"

Mark exhaled deeply. "I haven't called the police yet, but I will," he moaned, still trying to catch his breath, "as soon as I get my composure back."

Mr. Russell stared back in silence, making no effort to leave. Instead he reached over and swung the office door shut, then casually removed one of the scattered termination papers that had landed on the arm rest and sat in the same chair Brett had occupied moments earlier, his hands folded confidently across his lap. "I'm afraid there's another change in the organization that you haven't been aware of, Mark," he began with an air of superiority. "Since I first came to HammerStock, I've wanted to bring a right-hand-man on board who first worked for me in Memphis. I think that time is now, and unfortunately it will be your position that James will be taking."

Mark sat dumbstruck. Was this a joke? Suddenly the room swirled around his head.

"I know this comes as a shock to you, Mark," Mr. Russell's words echoed as if from a distance, distorted like Linda Blair's voice in *The Exorcist*, "but I have a responsibility to the stockholders." It was a speech Mr. Russell had obviously made many times before.

Mark's heart pounded harder; the whistling in his ears became more shrill and intense. Like Brett, he immediately perceived his own family being fired as well. There would be no Christmas for the kids. And Lisa would be forced to live on an incredibly tight budget. They'd have to give up one of the cars, maybe even lose their home. Unemployment compensation wouldn't begin to provide for their needs.

A rage grew like a spreading cancer inside Mark's chest. He recalled the hundreds of family-time hours he'd sacrificed to be at the office on weekends; how, in every case, he'd executed his boss's orders to the letter without question. He stared into Mr. Russell's cruel, heartless eyes and felt his stomach roll. This moment, this agonizing God-forbidding place in time was what blind corporate loyalty had brought him. Hatred coursed through his veins and screamed to escape. An exasperating ear-splitting shriek spilled from Mark's quivering lips as he wobbled to his feet and reached for the second drawer on the right side of his desk. He heaved to catch his breath.

And as he pointed the revolver in John Vincent *Asshole* Russell's trembling face, Mark Hopson realized that he would be featured on CNN after all.

War And Peace

John Shirley

Butch starts fucking around with the dead girl's body. "Butch," I tell him, real dry, "I'm pretty sure that's not standard police procedure." This, see, was two years ago; the first time I looked at Butch different.

Butch has pulled on the rubber gloves, because when there's blood we watch it real close now. I knew a cop got AIDS from touching a fresh stiff; cop with a cut on his hand turning the dead guy's bloody face for a better look: Boom, an officer's ass shriveling up with HIV. We put on the gloves now.

This stiff is a Chicano girl, big breasted, and she has a little horizontal knife cut about two inches long in the top of her left tit, and there really isn't much blood, I don't know why, most of the bleeding was internal. But somebody has . . .

Butch says it out loud. "Long thin blade ri-i-ight through the titty and ri-i-ight through her itty-bitty heart."

She's propped up in bed in a motel, wearing a black leather skirt, one red pump, no top, one eye stuck open, the other shut, like a baby doll. There's some ripped clothes lying around.

Butch reaches out and runs the rubber-covered tip of his thumb, real slow and tranquil, along the lip of her wound. Then he pinches a nipple. This is making me nervous. I mean, we're a couple of white cops in the Hispanic neighborhood, shit.

"What the hell, Hank," Butch says to me, grinning. "Let's pump a fuck into her. She's got one more in 'er."

You get into gallows humor, this job, so I grin back and says, "She's still warm and soft."

But he isn't kidding. He starts playing with her titties, even the slashed one, and lifting up her skirt. "You can turn your back if you want, or not, I don't care," he says, his hand on his zipper. I get this feeling he's hoping I won't turn away. "Come on," he says. "She was a fuckin' whore anyway."

"We don't know that, Butch. All we know's a motel manager found a stiff." But he goes on playing with her. "Butch—no fuckin' *way*," I say. "They called her family from the ID in her purse, her fuckin' *mom* might show up and come in and see that shit. 'The white police officers were fucking my dead daughter, Mr. DA! I'm suing the department's ass!' I mean, Christ, are you . . ." I didn't finish saying it.

He steps back, the same cool grin, but then he catches the tip of his tongue in his teeth like he was just kidding. "Fuckin' with ya. Gotcha didn't I." He walks out past me. But I see him re-arrange his dick in his pants as he went. He has a hard-on.

Believe it or not, I read about it in the papers. No one called me. I'm just coming off vacation but, shit, somebody should've fucking called me. Della, Butch's wife—the wife of my partner, my best friend—turns up dead in the trunk of her own car, and no one calls me.

Now I'm over at Butch's, just being there with him. Making us some coffee. It feels funny, looking at Della's stuff in the kitchen. My own wife Jilian gave Della those dish towels; *Love Our Planet* machine-embroidered on them. Some kind of soybased dye used in them. My wife goes on these spending sprees in Berkeley.

Della not long ago re-did the kitchen, and put everything in its place, and picked out the curtains and the other new gewgaws about two weeks before; spending too much money, Butch had said. But the kitchen now looks like a picture out of *Ladies' Home Journal*. And then some dirtbag strangled her, and her new kitchen things all seem like placemarkers for her going. *You knew me for years. I babysat your kids. Where am I now?*

I'm just a patrolman, but I see dead people all the time, mostly old people that croak out, and I got to make a report. But this is different: Butch's wife Della, she babysat my kids, made me and my wife dinner. She could be bitchy but Jilian liked her and Ben liked her and Ashley liked her and we were used to her. And some *bug* killed her to make a point, and put her in the trunk of her car. I was glad I wasn't on the detail that found her, after two days . . . the smell of someone dead two days in a trunk; someone that you fucking went *golfing* with.

I look through the door at Butch sitting on the couch quiet as a mannequin in a store window. Butch wears a yellow golf shirt, and tan Dockers pants, and brown loafers with tassels, and no socks. He has that same butch haircut, going a little gray now, that got him his tag, which he says he wears just because you pretty much never had to comb it. Although I think he wears it because his dad had one, his whole life. His dad was a Marine Corps flyer, stationed right here in Alameda, a real big old hard-ass who shriveled up like a used condom with cancer and died whining. I shouldn't talk about him like that, but I always hated the old fucker.

The Gold Tins are searching the house. Just a routine, but it ticks Butch off. "Treating me like a fucking suspect," he says. "God, Della." Starting to cry again. His eyes are still red from crying for two days. He was talking about Della for hours, what a patient woman she was, how she put up with all kinds of shit being a cop's wife, worrying about him, and it ends up they got her and not him, and how it isn't right. The captain was there for an hour or so of that, yesterday, a hand on Butch's shoulder, sometimes starting to cry himself, and later on the captain tells the reporters from the Oakland Trib, "This is genuinely tragic. Officer Behm feels it so deeply. He's got just about the biggest heart of anyone I know." And he talks about Butch's work with the Eagle Scouts and the vocational fair, lots of good stuff he's done.

I tell Butch, "They're looking for stuff that could connect your wife with a killer, like a letter, say—I mean, no offense but they got to consider maybe she had an affair, Butch, and her boyfriend did it. You know?"

He snorts, "Boyfriend. Not Della, not ever." There might be a little contempt in the way he says it. He starts to say something, doesn't say it, then he goes on, "What the fuck is the point of looking for a boyfriend when they got the message painted right on the car?"

Meaning the spraypainted graffiti on the side of her car. They found her car, her body in the trunk, in the Oakland ghetto, right there in gang-banger country, and spraypainted on the side in red was "WAR." And the killers sprayed a little circle around the bumper sticker that said, "OPOBA." Oakland Police Officers Benevolent Association. To let everybody know that *they* knew this was a car belonging to a cop, and the woman was a cop's wife.

For maybe four weeks now, we've been campaigning a "War on Drug Gangs" in Oakland, because of all the drug-related killings, so now, it's figured, their retaliation has begun. Two weeks ago Butch arrested a projects gangster for breaking into a car, and maybe the perp flipped Butch for the target. Who knows, the dirtbag could be related to some big crack gangster. So maybe the gang-bangers start following Butch and decide to hit him where it's easier for them and for a bigger psychological effect on the department. We can get you right in your homes, cops. You can run but you can't hide.

"Thing is, they know the spraypaint could be a fake, Butch," I tell him. "Planted to throw them off. Could be some fucking lunatic who's been watching her for a while, got obsessed with her, maybe somebody she knows."

"I hope so," Butch says, "because then maybe we could nail him. And I could kill him myself." With a catch in his voice.

It's while I'm watching *Jeopardy!*, Jilian's favorite show. All of a sudden, right at the start of Double Jeopardy, I think: *He's a suspect*. After *Jeopardy!*, I'm watching *Wheel of Fortune*. The phrase letters the contestant has, are: __ A__ ____D PE__C__. Something makes me squirm in the La-Z-Boy while I'm watching this. The contestant starts to fill in the letters. My wife, who's the brainy one, figures it out first. "War and Peace," she says.

"Yeah, that's . . ." I don't finish what I started saying, and she looks at me.

"You okay?"

"Yeah." I'm feeling sick, though.

"I feel weird too," Jilian says. "God, Della was just over here taking care of Ashley and Ben. It was hard explaining it to them, Hank." She starts to sniffle, and I go to the couch and put my arm around her.

"I know. But they're a cop's kids. They know the world a little better than their friends."

She shakes her head, her face getting swollen from crying. Her nose going red on the end, the way it does. "That's maybe the worst part of being a cop's kids."

Another time, I might get a little put off. *The worst part*, like it was all bad one way or another. But I'm thinking about War And Peace, and Jilian's attitude is low on the priorities.

I remember Butch, the older kid across the street, helping me with football, soccer, basketball. I was twelve and thirteen, the nerdiest kid with a ball, the Jerry Lewis character, and Butch was like my surrogate big brother. Or my dad. He liked to talk about sex with me, looking at those *Playboys*, and that was some heavy duty intimacy for a thirteen-year-old kid, when it came to hanging with a senior. There was a circle-jerk feeling about it, though he never touched me. Makes me embarrassed now.

He took me to the drive-in with him sometimes too, and he'd leave me in the car to watch one of those 60s movies where hippie girls in paisley miniskirts get involved with Hell's Angels and paint flowers on their chests and do a lot of making out to psychedelic music but never quite screw— while Butch went to drink some beer with his football friends in Andy's van. But he always came back and snuck me a can of beer, and told me some incredibly dirty joke and asked me how I liked the sex scenes in the movie and what did I think about who did what to who. He could turn back to thirteen with me, just like that, though he was about to go into community college.

I know for sure he strangled Della.

* * *

There's no detective work about it. I just know him, and the "War" thing is like some bullshit from a Mel Gibson movie, and Butch loves that stuff: Mel Gibson, Clint Eastwood, Bruce Willis's *Diehard*. He makes fun of it, like all cops do, because it's such fantasy, but he loves it anyway. Like all cops do. And thinking about that "War" spray-painted on the car . . . how Jilian got a skeptical look when I told her about that. And I remember Butch, oh, six months before Della was murdered saying he thought about divorcing her, but he'd still never be rid of her, there would be alimony fights, and fights over the house and she knew all his friends and it'd be awkward going out with people and he finished up by saying, "So I *still* wouldn't get any peace from her."

People talk about divorcing all the time. It's no big deal. They fought a fair amount. That's no big deal either. Me and Jilian fight our share.

War and Peace.

Here's the thing: Butch and I stole some money from the department. Well really, it was from the bugs. It was money confiscated from drug dealers and it was a *lot of fucking money*, see. It was about four hundred eighty grand. We took it from an evidence locker and covered our tracks clean, but they could still find out. So, we were sitting on it. We weren't going to spend it for five years. That was our deal, a blood oath. No calling attention to yourself. Save it for later. No matter how broke we got in the meantime. *Don't touch it.*

But suppose Butch is about to go down for killing Della. *If* he killed her for sure. Suppose he wants to bargain with the department. Suppose he shafts me. *Hey Captain, remember that half a mil that took a hike?*

By about two P.M. the next day I am almost sort of nearly pretty sure I was wrong. He didn't kill her. You can do that; it's like one of those rides at Great America where you go in a loop, completely upside down. That's how I feel while I'm following Butch over the bridge into Oakland. Like the bridge is going into a loopdeloop.

And it's the worst thing in the world, somebody you knew

all your life turns out to be something *else*. I mean—what's real, then? Nothing. Not a fucking thing.·So it can't be right, what I'm thinking about Butch.

I'm officially supposed to be on a Drug Task Force detail, in the unmarked car, which basically means watching the basketball court next door to the high school to see if anyone buys or sells, and then I buzz the detectives who get the glory of the collar. But I coop it off. I am following Butch.

Why is he driving into Oakland?

He's on special leave, and he might be going to see a therapist or something, and then I'll feel like a jerk.

He didn't fucking kill her, you asshole.

And the whole time I am mumbling this I am keeping my car back in traffic so Butch doesn't see me follow him.

He drives to San Pablo Avenue, and he cruises a whore. She makes eye contact and points down the road, not knowing he's a cop, and he picks her up. *What the fuck.*

She's a black girl, or maybe what they call a High Yellow, wearing an elastic tube-top thing, and that shows her stretch-marked middle, and a short fake-leather skirt. Probably no underwear: if they can't do it all giving head, you cough up a little extra money and they hike up their skirt.

They like to do it in the car. It's easier than keeping a room somewhere—those Pakis who run the weekly-rate hotels wring money out of the whores same as pimps. And it's faster just to do it in the car. They're always thinking ahead to the next trick; to the time·they got enough money to go kick it. And the faster they fuck, the faster they get it over with.

They all have their choice spots picked out getting it done in a car: back parking lots of warehouses; certain kinds of dead end streets; dirt tracks along deserted railroad yards; out next to the dumpster behind Safeway; oh, and parking lots under freeways. The butt-end of the city.

That's where Butch has the pavement princess. They're under a freeway, in a county equipment storage lot. Dull yellow road graders, defunct street cleaning trucks, stuff like that. Butch has some county keys, and he's unlocked the gate.

I watch from across the street, with a piece of fence and a parked truck in between; I'm peering around the truck, through the fence, between a couple of road graders. I can make them out in there. Butch is showing her his badge and she looks royally pissed off. I can read her lips. "Oh, man you mother*fucker*." But it's not a bust. I watch as he makes her bend over his car, spreads her legs, her hands flat and far apart on the trunk, while he checks out her pussy, grinning the whole time, slapping her thighs wider apart with a nightstick he's taken out of the car.

Then he starts shoving the nightstick in her, slapping her ass, pinching her titties, and playing with himself. I can make out what he's saying. "You a *ho* aren'tcha, huh? You a *ho*, right?"

He's having a *good* time. The son of a bitch strangled Della.

I can't watch this.

Jilian says, "You shouldn't go, you're not supposed to bug people with too much attention and giving them all kinds of stuff, you're supposed to leave them to feel their grief." She went to a grief workshop when her mom died. She's like that.

"It wasn't my idea!" I tell her. "The fucking fishing trip is his idea! He wants to go!"

So we go, me and Butch. Driving up in his Bronco, he's really pissed off that Stinson made him get permission from the captain to leave town. "Eighteen years on the force and they're treating me like a dirtbag!"

"Hey and you'd be with me the whole time anyway," I say. That was the wrong thing to say somehow. He gave me this *look*.

I don't say anything about how a few days after they found his wife dead he's gleefully rousting prostitutes and playing with their asses. I don't say anything, but I'm thinking about it. How I could tell, watching him play sick games with the whore, he's done this a lot. You hear people talk about how you know somebody for years but you don't really know them. This case, it's like he's almost not even the sex I

thought he was. I mean I don't know *shit* about this guy.
And now I'm driving up to a remote mountain lake with him.
This is great.

We go to Robins Lake. It's one of those reservoir lakes, a
sweetheart arrangement between developers and some senator
who swung the dam. Except for a little bit of gas slick around
the edges from the outboards and the jet-skis, it's pretty clean,
and they stock it with fish. If you go to the north end, the
jet-skis they keep at the south end scare the fish up to you.

It's the kind of sunny day that looks friendly and waits till
its gets you out in the open and then it pulls out the glare.
Have a headache, buddy. We rent an aluminum outboard,
and since it's the middle of the week we're almost the only
guys out on the lake. We both got sailor hats on, folded down
like bowls on our heads, and Ray-bans. Butch's brought a
Styrofoam cooler full of Coors Lite. I'm wishing I brought
sunscreen for the back of my neck, after just a half hour it's
already rasping. I'm asking myself why I'm out on the lake
with a murderer.

Because I have to talk to him. Because he's been my more-
or-less best friend for, what, fifteen years or so. Because it's
inertia, and he asked me.

We fish, either end of the boat, and he doesn't say much.
Until finally, "I guess you could see the idea of a fishing trip
as kind of weird, now. But I had to get away." I can see
sundogs off the lake in his dark glasses.

It's like my lower jaw got real heavy, as I say what I'm
supposed to. "People adjust in their own ways. If this keeps
you sane, hey, go for it."

He doesn't say anything for a minute. "You think there's
anything weird about how they came back last night?"

I feel some hope, then. Maybe it wasn't up to me.

"Buddy, when they don't have a *name*—I mean, okay,
they got the gang-bangers lead. But when they don't have a
name, or even a description . . . they fall back on the family.
Doesn't mean anything."

"You mean, the 24/24 rule."

"Yeah." The 24/24 rule is that the most important time
in a murder investigation are the last twenty-four hours in
the victim's life and the first twenty-four hours after the

body's found. "So it's been longer than the twenty-four, and they feel like it's getting cold. They clutch at straws."

My lower jaw's *really* heavy now. I can barely force myself to say this horseshit. I'm thinking about his small hands, and figuring he didn't do it with his hands, he did it with a cord or a scarf or something. Thinking he's cute for choosing strangulation so she doesn't bleed all over the place. Only, the gang-bangers pretty much never strangle people. They love guns and knives. Just fucking love them.

I decide I can't sit here like this anymore. It's too quiet out here and I just keep seeing him go through the laundry for just the right scarf and then I see him with the ho.

You have to think things through. That's a rule. You're sorry if you don't think things through.

I come at it from left field. "I mean, shit, even if . . . if a cop flipped out and killed his wife, the department'd be stupid to push too hard on it."

He stares at me. My mouth goes dry. I open a beer.

I make myself go on, not sure what I'm trying to accomplish, and thinking it might be good to leave the lake early in the afternoon. "I'm just thinking about ol' Detective Stinson's point of view. Or anyway, the captain's." He opens his mouth to say something like *What are you getting at?* and I put in real quick, "See, they could *talk themselves into* thinking you did it." (He did it.) "And the DA could get wind of it and then they got to go through with it. I mean, we know you didn't do it." (He did it. By now he knows I know he did it.) "But you know, if they haven't got a suspect they'll keep turning to look at you and you know how people can kid themselves into shit." (He killed her. We have a picture of Della feeding Ashley with a baby bottle.)

"So what's the point?"

The smell of gas from the outboard is making me ill. "Well . . . is there anything that could give them the wrong idea? Something they could misunderstand and think it was physical evidence."

He's almost smiling. I'm wishing I could see his eyes behind the Ray-Bans.

"Naw. No I don't think so. I mean, I'm not . . ."

He doesn't actually say it. *I'm not stupid.*

"You know what?" I stretch, and rub my neck. "This sun is, like, too much for me. Maybe we oughta get back a little early."

He shrugs. He's still not quite smiling. "Hey Hank—there's the money we took."

"We're not even supposed to *talk* about that, man."

"We're out in the middle of a fucking lake, Hank. Just keep that money in mind. You wouldn't want to lose that. And who knows what."

I just nod.

My stomach feels like it's got a bag of sand in it. But I just keep thinking, *You got to think things through.* That's the bottom line, right there.

Stinson's happy. Which is fucked up.

Stinson thinks he's going to make his first detective collar. We're sitting in captain's office. Butch and the captain and Stinson and Mann, the heavyset black guy from Internal Affairs, and me for Butch's moral support.

Stinson disarms Butch, first thing, which freaks everyone out, even the captain, who looks like he's going to object, and then doesn't.

Butch tries to be cool. "You want my Beretta, keep it oiled. I don't want a fucking dust speck in it when I get it back."

I'm groaning inside and thinking, shut the fuck up, Butch.

"What'dya think of Omnichrome, Butch?" asks Stinson, putting Butch's gun on the captain's desk, way out of Butch's reach. Like he's going to start busting caps around the office.

"Stinson you watched too many movies-of-the-week," Mann says. "Butch, you know what Omnichrome is?"

Butch shakes his head. He manages not to swallow.

Mann goes on, "It's this new thing, alternate light source device, picks up stuff you can't see with the naked eye. Foreign matter. The Omnichrome shows up stuff under special wavelengths . . ."

Stinson can't contain himself. "Like paint specks."

Mann gives him a tired glare. "Like paint specks, yeah. Same color and chemical composition as the ones on the car. Forensics found them on a pair of your shoes."

"Like you get," Stinson says, actually grinning now, "when there's a real fine cloud of spraypaint, and you think you're being real careful not to get any on you, but the stuff is so fine you can't see it settle."

Butch's voice is almost a monotone, carefully flat, as he says, "Spraypaint's mostly all the same composition. And I helped Hank here spraypaint his kid's bike-frame. I think it was red or orange or something."

Everyone turns their heads to look at me.

Jilian doesn't say anything about it till we're halfway to Yosemite in our RV. About two months later. No charges against Butch. The kids are playing with a Gameboy far enough in the back they can't hear us talk over the noise of the engine and the tires, and there's been a silence for about sixty miles before she said it.

"He never was there, helping spraypaint Ashley's bike."

I'm wondering how come what she said makes me feel like I'm the one who killed Della. I say, "You remember that for sure?"

"I thought about it a lot, Hank. I mean, *a lot*. He came over the next day after the bike was dry and she was showing it off, the new paint you put on so drivers could see it better, and she was telling Butch all about it when he and Della . . ." her voice catches ". . . when they came over."

Is she, I wonder, going to come out and flat out accuse me of perjuring myself, which I sure as hell did, to protect Butch?

If she does, I'll have to tell her about the money. And I haven't figured out how to tell her about the money yet.

Should I lie to her, and pretend I remember him coming over earlier, some time when she wasn't there, standing there with me when I was using the paint? It sounded too forced. Jilian's smart. I elect to go around it.

"He just figured that's where he got the stuff on his shoes, maybe from some dust that got stirred up or something."

"Oh." She decides to believe it.

I don't say, *You don't really think that Butch could have . . .!* or some such shit, because I couldn't do that believably. I just change the subject. Only, it's not really a different subject. I tell her I'm thinking of joining the Sheriff's Department, maybe around Santa Cruz, so we could get the kids away from the Oakland area, all the crime and drugs and stuff. But I'd never do it if she didn't want to.

She says she'll think about it. It's a big step.

It's a step the fuck away from Butch.

I try to see him enough so he doesn't get nervous, but not so much it'll make me nervous. It's not that I think he'd kill me. It's just like spiders. I'm not really scared they're going to hurt me. I just don't like them crawling around me.

At least spiders are what they're supposed to be.

It's easy to be self righteous. But you got to look at the whole picture. The kids and Jilian and the money and covering my ass and the department. No, fuck the department. It's the fucking money. It's me in the joint with a bunch of dirtbags.

Because, you know, Butch thought it through, himself. He collected her life insurance, too. It was *way* premeditated. He'd get the gas chamber like some dirtbag. But his getting away with it is hard to stand. I hear him say, "You a *ho*, right?"

One night I go over to his house, after he's been drinking heavy, and I go up to his bedroom, same room where he slept next to Della for years and years. He's sacked out, fully clothed on the bed, his head deep in those blue satin pillowcases Della picked out. I know him, he won't wake up after all the beer. I'm standing over Butch, who's snoring these long contented snores, and I've got his gun in my gloved hand, and I think maybe I'm going to blow his brains out. And slip away. Because otherwise the guy'll always have something over my head. The money. And I just can't fucking stomach him walking around.

I put the gun muzzle up to the back of his head. But then, at the last moment, I think it through: if I do it, it might look like suicide. Which would imply that yeah, he killed Della and so I must've perjured myself. And making it look like a gang-banger did it would be a big mess to step into.

Sweat's sticking the gunbutt to my palm. So finally, I take his gun and I put it back in its holster, and I go downstairs.

I'll put in my app at the Santa Cruz SD. They got a great benefits package. That's what I'm half thinking about as I walk out to my car.

You got to think things through. That's the bottom line.

Hey. They're not going to say shit about perjury.

I go back upstairs, get the gun and I blow his fucking brains across that satin pillowcase.

The Merry Go-Round Man

Gary Brandner

William Bobbick's eyes bulged and the veins in his neck popped as the demonic face floated toward him. Fright sweat oozed from his pores and a scream caught in his throat.

Run! Run! Get away! cried his brain, but his limbs refused to respond.

The looming face swam in and out of focus like something terrible and deadly seen at the bottom of a murky pool. Only he was looking up, not down at it. The individual features twisted and puffed and slid out of focus. Worst of all, William Bobbick knew that face, knew it well. The message behind those pale eyes was bad. Very bad. But what, exactly, was the message?

William Bobbick's memory was fogged like a badly over-exposed photograph. His senses were dulled. He clamped his jaw and struggled to locate the face in time and space, and decipher its message.

Think back . . . think . . . remember . . . a day long ago . . .

It started out as the very best day in his life. The sun was golden bright, the morning sky so blue it hurt your eyes. Billy Bobbick lay awake in the bunk bed watching the model P-40 rotate lazily above his head on the thread that suspended it from a thumb tack in the ceiling. His little brother Corky was still asleep below him. As the older brother, Billy had first call on the upper bunk.

He breathed in a noseful of the sweet summertime smell of fresh cut grass. Along with the perfume of lilacs, it floated in through the screened window with the morning breeze. The outdoor fragrances blended with the Sunday breakfast smell of pancakes and bacon. A perfect beginning for a very special day. The carnival was in town, and this year the whole family was going—Dad, Mother, Billy, and Corky.

If there was a tiny cloud on the blue horizon that morning, Billy Bobbick did not see it. He had not yet met the merry-go-round man.

Ever since school let out for the summer, more than a month before, Billy had impatiently awaited the coming of Getchel's Greater Shows. Big splashy posters were tacked on telephone poles and propped in store windows to announce the wonders to come. Billy lived in an agony of anticipation until at last the carnival came rumbling and tootling into town with music to make a boy's blood race, and colors to dazzle his eyes.

Sure, the carnival came every year about this time, but always before the fates or something had kept the Bobbick family away. Either Billy had the mumps or Corky was too little or Mother was worried about Dad. She worried a lot about Dad, always reminding him to take his pills, and not to tire himself. It made no sense to Billy. As far as he could tell, Dad was the strongest and most indestructible of men.

This year Mother was, if anything, more worried than usual. Billy often caught her looking at Dad with a strange fear in her eyes. She was not happy about going to the carnival, but Dad said this year they were going, and that was that. He said there might not be any more carnivals until the war ended, and he did not want the boys to miss out.

The war filled much of the talk of grownups. Billy thought it was exciting and fun. In the comic books strong-jawed American heroes blasted slavering Nazis and bucktoothed Japs to bloody shreds. In the movies, even when one of our guys got killed, it was clean and painless, while the enemy died screaming and spurting blood. Billy did not understand why this one-sided struggle should make a difference in the coming of the carnival, but Dad knew about those things.

Billy secretly hoped the war would last long enough for him
to enlist.

On that bright summer day the comic book war was far
away and forgotten amid the clatter and jangle of the carnival.
It looked like everybody in town was there, strolling around
the circular sawdust path, laughing, eating, reading the bright
canvas fronts on the carnival attractions. Billy did not think
much about it, but his was one of the few complete families.
Most of the smaller kids were with their mothers alone. There
were the boys and girls from high school who talked loudly
and laughed a lot and pretended not to be aware of each
other. A few old people walked slowly and watched the young
ones with sad, remembering eyes. And there was a scattering
of young men in uniform. They were not much older than
the high school boys, but they were quieter.

Over Mother's mild protests Dad bought the boys cotton
candy and Popsicles and hot dogs on a stick and root beer.
Billy threw baseballs at a stack of milk bottles but didn't
knock any down. He threw darts at balloons and popped one,
but that wasn't enough to win a prize. Corky was too little
for the games, but he was mesmerized by a man who blew
flames out of his mouth.

Spaced along the inner rim of the sawdust circle were great
clanking machines operated by hard-eyed men in jeans. The
machines took people up in the air or spun them around or
did both at the same time. The ferris wheel seemed to carry
you right to the clouds, and the octopus whirled its jointed
steel tentacles carrying the pods of screaming people up and
down and around in an undulating thrill ride. The noise and
commotion frightened Corky, but Billy pleaded to be allowed
aboard these wondrous machines. Dad might have given in,
but Mother shot him that look of hers and gave a firm little
shake of the head that meant no chance.

They did go through the Fun House—Billy and Corky and
Dad, while Mother waited outside. With Dad right there with
them it was funny and scary all at the same time. Even Corky
laughed when skeletons and witches danced out at them from
dark corners. They jumped at sudden noises and flinched
when a wall of wooden boxes almost toppled down on them,

then righted itself at the last moment. A dark passageway had slithery things along the floor that half-grabbed at your ankles. They were supposed to be snakes, but Billy knew they were only rubber. At the end the three of them sat down on a bench that collapsed under them and sent them down a slick slide to the sawdust path outside where Mother waited, looking relieved that they had made it through.

The carnival was a world of exciting smells and sounds and exotic sights, and Billy Bobbick felt he could live there forever. But all too soon Mother was saying to Dad, "Don't you think we ought to call it a day? You shouldn't overdo it."

"Please, Mother," Billy said. "Can't we stay just a little longer?"

Dad seemed as reluctant as Billy to leave the carnival, but he never openly disagreed with Mother. He said, "I think the boys should go on at least one ride while we're here. It's never the same when you grow older."

Mother put a hand to her chest and looked up at the great wheel towering into the sky. "Phil, you know what the doctor . . ."

"Just you and the boys," Dad said quickly. "And we'll make it the merry-go-round. How rough can the merry-go-round be?"

"Well . . ." Mother was still not sure.

"How about it, troopers?" Dad said. "One ride on the merry-go-round, then home with no complaints. Okay?"

"Please, Mother?" said Billy.

"May-go-round, may-go-round," Corky cried, jumping up and down.

"All right," Mother said finally. "One ride, then home we go."

The merry-go-round. A magical parade of the proudest, most spirited horses and the richest chariots imaginable, moving to a swelling music that pumped right into your bloodstream and made you as powerful as Superman and as brave as Prince Valiant. Corky wriggled and laughed while Billy was transported beyond mere excitement. It was like looking through a window into another, unbelievably thrilling world.

Dad bought the tickets and they waited, forever it seemed, until the whirling, lunging horses slowed and stopped and the other kids all climbed down. Right away Billy saw the mount he wanted. A fiery midnight stallion with tossing mane and a wild rolling eye. The harness was glittery silver against the horse's black lacquer coat. The saddle a deep blood red. The horse held high his proud head, teeth bared in a cry of defiance to the world.

The family stepped up onto the merry-go-round and Mother settled herself and Corky into one of the sedate chariots that was anchored to the floorboards. She made room on the other side of her, and Billy's heart dropped into his stomach.

Dad looked at him, then quickly back at Mother. "I think Billy would rather have a horse of his own."

At that moment Dad stood taller and stronger than the best of the caped heroes in all of the comic books.

"But if you're not riding . . ." Mother said.

"He doesn't need any help," Dad said.

"Well, if you're sure . . ."

"How about it, son, are we sure?"

"Yeah, Dad."

"Here's your tickets. I'll be down there watching."

He gave two of the pink pasteboard tickets to Mom and one to Billy. "Picked out your horse?"

Billy nodded. It was the first time he had carried his very own ticket to anything, and he clutched it as though it were his soul. His throat tightened and he could not speak, only point at the charging black.

"Good choice. He looks full of fire. Don't let him run away with you." Dad laughed and rumpled Billy's hair. He made his way to the edge of the platform and stepped down off the merry-go-round to take a position behind the low metal fence surrounding it.

Billy hurried between the lesser horses and was relieved to see no one had yet claimed his stallion. He put one foot into a dangling stirrup, grasped the brass pole, and swung up into the saddle.

Billy gave a pat to the hard, muscular neck of his horse and took a look at those flanking him. There was a showy white with his neck bowed, and a bay that seemed about to throw the bit. The black would leave them in his dust.

He turned in the saddle to grin at Mother. She smiled back and waved. Corky was too busy trying to pry one of the glass jewels out of the chariot to look at him.

With a gentle lurch the merry-go-round started to move. The music began—low booming notes, piping high squeals, clangoring bells. Gradually they turned faster. Billy gripped the smooth brass pole and held on as the midnight stallion found his gait and they pulled away from the others.

Billy was surprised at how high the horse leaped, and how quickly they gained speed. The wind was in his face—hot from the afternoon sun and sweet with the smell of cotton candy and relish and raw sawdust. Billy opened his mouth to take big bites of the wind. His heart pounded, his blood rushed, he was in love with the world.

The people standing beyond the fence whirled by in a blur of faces. It took several times around before Billy could find Dad. When he did, he saw Dad was grinning and waving at him. Billy wanted to wave back, but he was afraid to take a hand away from the steadying brass pole.

But on the next turn around, he did. He let go the pole and raised his hand in a triumphant salute. And in that instant the wind snatched away his soul.

Not really his soul, but something just as dear—the pink ticket Dad had entrusted to him. His license to ride the black charger. Without the ticket he did not belong here. He would be found out. They would . . . they would . . .

And here *he* came. The merry-go-round man. Tall, gaunt, dressed in jeans and an old plaid shirt, he came, as relentless as death. One by one he took the tickets from the riders. All of them had their tickets ready. Only Billy Bobbick had lost his to the wind.

Gone was the wild joy of the leaping, whirling ride. The calliope music turned discordant, sinister. The crazy-eyed horse bore him steadily, unstoppably toward the oncoming man who would demand his ticket or . . . or . . . Or what? Hurl him off the merry-go-round? Lock him in jail? Kill him?

Every detail of the man's terrible face was acid-etched into

Billy's brain. The cold gray, seen-it-all eyes. The long, lean jaw with its patchy stubble. The pink-white scar that tilted a corner of his mouth. Ever closer he came, taking tickets left and tickets right, his eyes on Billy, seeming to know this boy had no right to ride.

Boys were not supposed to cry. Billy Bobbick knew that, and he hardly ever did. He surely did not want to cry now with Dad and Mother and Corky and the whole world looking at him. But the breath caught in his throat and the tears spilled down his face and he was crying and crying and squeezing the cold brass pole as the wild stallion bucked and lunged.

And the merry-go-round man came closer.

Then Dad was there. Billy never saw him jump aboard the whirling platform and make his way through the galloping horses, but there he was just in time to intercept the terrible man before he got to Billy.

The rest of the day that had begun so bright and blue was a nightmare in gray. Dad tried to make a little joke out of Billy losing the ticket, but when he looked at the boy's face he fell silent. Nobody said anything on the way home. Billy went straight to his room and lay there on the top bunk and stared at the ceiling and tried to erase the memory of the merry-go-round man. He couldn't do it. Not then, not ever.

It was only a few days after the carnival that Dad stumbled and fell out on the front lawn while pushing the lawnmower. An ambulance came and took him to the hospital. Mother tried to explain to the boys that Dad had been sick for a long time. Something was wrong with his heart. Billy could not understand; Dad had never looked sick to him. It had to be some kind of a mistake. He would not believe it until Mother took him and Corky to the hospital.

They walked into the hushed, medicine-smelling room and looked at the man who had always been so strong, so full of health lying gray-faced and weak in the tall white bed with a tube up his nose. Nobody said it aloud, but Billy knew. Dad was going to die.

When it happened, Mother told the boys how Dad went suddenly and without pain, and how it wasn't anybody's fault, just something in his heart that was not quite right. But

Billy knew why his father had really died. He was to blame. It was supposed to be him who was snatched into the darkness, but Dad stepped in the way and the merry-go-round man took him instead.

The days after Billy's father died dragged into weeks that became months and stretched on into years. Billy's mother married a man named Steve who had his own hardware store and was good to the boys. He took them to movies and ball games and fishing, but the family never again went to the carnival.

Billy Bobbick grew up and became Bill. He went to the State University and earned his degree. There was another war and he finally got to fight, but discovered there was nothing romantic about it. Corky went to California and became a computer programmer. Mother and Steve moved to Florida. Bill started his own construction company and built it into a profitable business. He married a local girl named Ruth Ann, fathered a daughter named Terrie, and joined Rotary and the Junior Chamber of Commerce and became William. The world changed. Wars continued. Carnivals died.

Sometimes William would dream about the carnival and the merry-go-round man who was always coming coming coming for him. He would jerk awake sweaty and trembling, and Ruth Ann would lay a hand on his shoulder and remind him that he was in his own bed and safe. She thought his nightmares were about his time in the war, and he never told her different. He never told anyone about the merry-go-round man.

One thing William Bobbick could not hide was his obsession about tickets. Any ticket—theater, airplane, lottery, parking lot—could set him off. He knew it was irrational, but that made it none the less real—the gut-grabbing fear that he would lose it. Whenever he was forced to hold a ticket he was seized by an icy, unreasoning fear. He would shiver and sweat, gripping the ticket like life itself, until he could deliver it to the taker.

When he was kidded about his phobia William forced a little laugh, but he never talked about where the fear came from. Whenever Ruth Ann was with him he gave the tickets over to her to hold. Even then he pestered her continually to check that she still had them. She thought it was kind of cute. She did not know the cold terror that lived inside him.

A week after his forty-third birthday William Bobbick checked into a hospital for the first time in his life. No big deal, just the removal of a small benign growth. It would be done under local anaesthetic and he would be home the next day. Nothing to worry about.

They made him stay in the hospital the night before the operation. It was a rule. Another rule was that he had to let them push him around in a wheelchair, even though he could walk just fine. Most annoying to William was the pink plastic I.D. bracelet they made him wear.

"We want to be sure who we're treating," a nurse explained on the morning of his operation. "You wouldn't want somebody else's enema, would you?" And she laughed and checked the bracelet and stuck him with a needle full of something that produced a cobwebby floating sensation.

Ruth Ann and Terrie were there at his bedside. The way Terrie's eyes kept straying to the window told William that his daughter would a lot rather be somewhere else.

"You guys don't have to hang around," he said, the sedative thickening the words. "This isn't open-heart, you know."

Terrie looked hopefully to her mother, but Ruth Ann said, "That's all right, we'll stay here until you're out of the operating room."

"If you want to," William said. "But believe me, it's a piece of cake."

"If you're so calm," Ruth Ann said, "why do you keep fiddling with that thing on your wrist?"

He looked down at the bracelet as though in surprise. "Was I fiddling? I guess I'm just not used to wearing anything."

They talked idly for a few minutes about small family things—whether to get the sofa recovered or buy a new one, where to go for their vacation, whose turn it was to write to his parents in Boca Raton. Then an orderly came in wheeling a gurney. He was a friendly young man with compassionate brown eyes. He smiled at everybody, helped Bill ease from the bed onto the gurney, and trundled him off.

Ruth Ann and Terrie went down the hall to wait in the room provided for that purpose. There Ruth Ann read a paperback novel about a courageous frontier woman while Terrie clicked through the channels on the television set without finding anything she wanted to watch.

The minutes passed.

An hour passed.

An hour and ten minutes.

"Why is it taking so long?" Terrie asked.

"I don't know," Ruth Ann said. "I want a cigarette."

"Mom, you were going to quit."

"I know, but I want one now. I left them in my bag in your father's room. Will you get it for me?"

"I don't think they allow smoking here."

"Don't nag, Terrie. I won't light it if it will make you feel better."

As soon as her daughter left the waiting room Ruth Ann stepped into the hallway and stopped a passing nurse.

"Excuse me, my husband's been in the operating room now for more than an hour. Is there some way I can find out what's happening?"

"Doctor knows you're here. He'll be out to talk to you. Don't worry." The nurse clicked a professional smile on and off and went away on silent rubber soles.

Ruth Ann looked down and saw she was squeezing her hands together until the knuckles were shiny white. She made an effort to relax.

Terrie came back carrying the bag in one hand and gripping something in her fist. "Mom, look what I—"

She stopped talking as a tall, lean man in a surgical gown came into the waiting room. His expression was grave. Mother and daughter stood frozen, staring at him.

"I'm terribly sorry—" he began.

"The operation," Ruth Ann broke in. "Something went wrong."

"The operation was never begun," said the surgeon. "It was one of those inexplicable things that happen. I only got as far as checking for your husband's I.D. bracelet." He looked down at Terrie's clenched fist and gently pried the fingers open. "Oh, here it is."

Ruth Ann's voice was flat and without life. "He was picking at it in his room. He must have pulled it loose somehow when the boy was helping him off the bed."

The doctor glanced at the name stamped on the bracelet. "Naturally, we wouldn't begin surgery until we were sure we had the right patient. I saw his wrist was bare and started to ask him about it. When I leaned over him he went into cardiac arrest. We did everything we could."

Terrie began to sob. Ruth Ann held the girl close, stroking her short blond hair.

The surgeon looked away. His pale gray eyes reflected the pain of the women. He wiped a hand across his weary face, one finger tracing the pink-white scar that tilted a corner of his mouth.

Food For The Beast

Paul Kupperberg

New York city night, darkly reflected fluorescence and neon
on autumn rain-spattered pavement. Darker slicks, like oil in
the puddled waters, oozing rivers seeking channels through
dirtied cracks between concrete slabs, seeping from the life
source to the gutter, mingling with the rush of waters sweep-
ing clean to the gurgling sewer grate.

Fingers dip in the viscous stream, rub together to savor
the sensual stickiness between thumb and forefinger. Smell.
Bitter and hot, like liquid metal. Like promise cut short by
the slash of reality.

Dip again, into the steaming wound this time, feeling the
organism's ebbing heat rising from the life source. Flowing
from the source, heat to fuel a heart made to beat faster,
stronger for the nourishment it had so long demanded and
been denied.

No more denial.

The beast would be fed. Its hunger pangs had been resisted,
its cries smothered beneath the drowning voices of conscience
and society, forcing it into an uneasy slumber, barely concealed by earlier debaucheries, before it awoke at last,
screaming, the ugliness beneath surface beauty revealed. Demanding.

He listened, recognizing with surprise the futility, the self-
destruction of resistance. Fighting was painful, a ceaseless
gnawing at what he was. At what he would be.

Howling in discordant concert with the beast, he plunges his hands deep inside the life source and, remembering, drinks in everything it has to offer . . .

Three years, seven months, and however many weeks and days later, Dave Collins was used to waking up sober. He no longer thought about what it felt like to lay huddled in bed, head throbbing with the grungy residue of the previous day's alcohol and drugs. Rising only to stagger without conscious thought to bottle or stash for a revitalizing hit of the hair of the dog. The three years plus, the standing up before groups of strangers to simultaneously proclaim and deny his addictions, had succeeded in suppressing the killing habits and needs of a lifetime that had been his daily ritual and desire.

Daylight was no longer a thing to hide from. Collins had thrown away the matched set of crutches that were addiction and a mindless pursuit of empty pleasures. Living now was accompanied by a clear head, without the tight, pained clamp of hangover crushing his thoughts and energies. Clean and sober had washed away fear and uncertainty and, with it, the abuses that bred deeper, more frightening insecurities that lead, in turn, to deeper abuse.

No need to hide. No reason to abuse himself or those inhabiting his particular corner of the world.

He was happy.

"Riley, you're a real son of a bitch, you know that?"

Just ask him.

"Calm down, will you, Dave."

Collins crumpled the papers in his fist and shook them at the man blinking uncomfortably at him from behind the cluttered desk. "What should I be calm about, you shit? The fact you're telling me I've lost it, or the way you want to rip my book to shreds?"

"Come on, Dave, you know I'm not doing either," Carl Riley said, his voice level while his usual pale complexion turned a splotchy red as he tried to maintain his own temper. "This is going to be the fifth book of yours I'll have edited. I gave you a memo just like this one on all of your other manuscripts after my first readings. It's only my first impressions, comments, suggestions . . .''

"No, no, Carl, comments and suggestions are one thing, but this . . ." Collins waved the memo at his editor before smoothing the pages out to read them. "Check this out, man . . . 'disjointed narrative . . . fuzzy characterization . . . whole sections of chapters four through eleven need to be rewritten . . . chapters twelve, sixteen, and nineteen are clumsy and get in the way of the story flow. . . . ' Christ, Carl, what's left? Did you at least like the dedication?"

"Dave, if you'll just take a seat and cool down, we can talk about it."

Collins shook his head and crushed the papers into a ball. "Nothing to talk about," he said, biting off each syllable. "This's bullshit. I'm not going to let you do it to my book."

Riley felt the color deepen in his cheeks, the back of his neck hot. "We've worked together a long time, Dave, going on ten years now. I think you're a hell of a writer, sometimes almost brilliant . . . but you fell down on this one. It's been—what?—almost four years since your last book and I wouldn't be doing you, me, or this company any favors if I let this one go out the way you wrote it. It's just not there yet, but I'm willing to work with you as long and as hard as it takes to fix it."

Collins hurled the wadded memo to the desk. "You got one thing right, Riley. I am a hell of a writer. What you *don't* have is my book. Consider it withdrawn."

"C'mon, Dave . . ."

But Collins was at the door. "Fuck you, Carl."

And he was gone.

The August issue of *The Metropolitan Review* was waiting for him in the mailbox when he returned to his apartment on West 84th Street. Riding up in the elevator, Collins flipped through it looking for the review he had written comparing three novels by first-time writers of what had become known as the "Soho School." His school. The one he'd been credited with giving legitimacy over a decade ago with the publication of his first novel, *Bleecker Still*.

The piece wasn't there. At least not under his byline. Somebody else's analysis of those novels was there instead.

"Look, I'm really sorry, Dave," Katie Ollenshaw told him over the phone. "But I tried calling you all last week to talk about it. It's not my fault you don't return calls."

Collins looked down at his answering machine, the small red light blinking with rhythmic incessance. He didn't remember the last time he'd bothered listening to his messages. "Don't hand me that, Katie. I don't need your 'check is in the mail' editor's shit, okay? You had a problem with my piece, you could've told me."

"I tried, Dave," she said.

"I tried," he repeated, sarcasm dripping. "Look, what's an associate editor doing passing judgment on my piece anyway? I don't even know why I'm wasting my time with you. Just let me talk to Julius, okay?"

Katie's voice was cold, crackling over the wire. "Julius was the one who spiked the review, Dave. He said it was flat and lacked depth. He said it was a 6,000 word justification of the superiority of your work compared to anyone else who dared write about what you've staked out as your turf."

"You've been trying to get your own writers like the moron you reassigned *my* piece to into that rag since you got there, you snotnosed bitch," Collins hissed. "Julius'll be real interested with the way you're looking to poison his people against him. *He's* my editor, honey, not you. Now put him on the line."

"He was your editor. He handed you to me, thought maybe some new blood'd help wake you up and get your act together. But you know what? I don't think you're worth the effort. I think whatever it was you used to have is gone, and what's left isn't worth killing a tree to print, you used up old hack," she said calmly and hung up in his ear.

That was the first time it had reached out to him, its hollow whimper vibrating across staticy silence. Pleading. Begging for release. He knew the sound, half remembered from a time long removed from who he had become. Hadn't it been stronger then? A howl instead of a whimper. Hadn't its voice once filled his head, echoing and rebounding from subconscious to infinity, charging him with inspiration and heat? Its presence had made him throb with righteous anger, delicious pain, caused the reflexive lashing out to draw blood and splash it across paper like a demented surrealistic word painting.

What name did the beast call itself?

How did its bloodied rage and self-destructive hunger lead him to fulfillment, satisfaction?

He could not recall. Answers lived, but buried deep beneath the beast itself, made invisible by the present. He pressed the telephone to his head until it hurt, eyes squeezed shut and hand covering his other ear to block out noise. The whimper was there, just barely, just below the threshold of reality.

"Who?" Collins whispered.

But the static hiss gave no answer.

"And that made you angry?" Dr. Raucher prompted.

Collins stared past his therapist's head, at the floral print hanging across the room from where he sat. Neutral. He had been looking at that print for almost four years and it meant nothing to him. It was just there, a focal point for those times he wanted to avoid Raucher's eyes. He realized with a start that for all the time he had spent looking at it, he wouldn't have been able to describe it if pressed to do so outside this office. Pretty lame for a writer who prided himself on his powers of observation.

"David?"

"Yeah, sure I got angry. Two major kicks in the ass in one day, who wouldn't be? But . . ." Collins paused, searching, afraid of what he might say next, feeling, irrationally, that saying it would be what made it true.

"But what, Dave?"

"But . . . what if they're right, okay? What if the book *does* suck? What if I *can't* do it anymore?"

"Do you believe that?"

Collins shrugged. "I didn't . . . no, I don't . . . I don't know. I mean, maybe I'm just too close to it to see what they're seeing. The thing is," he started to say, then stopped. But the pause only bought him time, not a reprieve from his thoughts. Raucher would just sit there, waiting patiently until

Collins continued. The bastard had no mercy. "The thing is, I spent the last couple of days rereading my earlier books and . . . Christ! They were real good. Really raw, powerful stuff. I don't think there was an ounce of deceit or bullshit in any of them, I don't even think I *knew* what inhibition was back then. I felt it, it got put on paper and fuck the consequences. The first two sold maybe ten, twelve thousand copies between them when they were first published, but they were really good."

"I've read them," Raucher said. "They were excellent. But there was a lot of pain in them."

"Yeah, so?"

"So how happy were you when you wrote them?"

Collins laughed. "I don't know. Not very, I guess. What's it matter? It's the result that counts."

"I don't agree. What matters is how you dealt with your life then versus how you deal with it now," Raucher said. "The financial insecurity, the drug and alcohol abuse, the destructive relationships of then versus the security, the sobriety, and the healthy relationship of today. What you had then didn't signify a healthy or happy mind."

"Maybe not, but it was a mind capable of conceiving some good writing that fifteen or twenty years later, I'm still proud to have my name on and that . . ." He stopped himself dead and shook his head, looking away to the floral print. "Never mind."

"That what?" Raucher insisted.

He heard the metallic buzz in his ear then. It's just my heart's pounding, he thought, my blood shooting through me, like the sound that's always there, even in the presence of silence. The body's a machine, its engine makes noise.

"That I'm," he said softly, barely audible over the rush of blood in his ears, unaware that his fingernails bit into the soft flesh of his palms as he clenched his fists to keep the thought there. *This is important. So simple I didn't even know I knew it.* "I'm envious of what I used to be. Of how I used to be able to live before I was married and how to worry about being a husband and a responsible human being and what I was able to write as a result of it. I mean, I got the feeling reading the older stuff that I get when I read someone else's work that I wish I'd written, you know? Like it was someone else who wrote it. Not me, but some stranger.''

"I think that's the point. The David Collins who wrote those books has grown up, changed. A different person *did* write those books, an immature, unhappy, self-destructive person. Nobody stays the same, Dave. Life is change, and in your case, that change, with your wife's help and support, has been beneficial.''

Collins realized his fists were clenched into tight balls and it took a conscious effort to loosen them. The same effort it took to breathe without gasping as fear ran through him, as though the hungry truths lying beneath the even tones of their conversation were a living creature chasing him through dark alleyways. "But if I can't write," he said, his throat dry, his voice a harsh rasp. "What's the point of being this happy, adjusted grown-up if it robs me of my talent?''

"It doesn't," Raucher said. "It just means you have to readjust your priorities, write from your strengths rather than from your weaknesses. Well," he looked at his wristwatch and then back at Collins and smiled. "We're out of time today. We'll pick this up next time, okay?''

In the throbbing rush of blood, Collins thought he detected a rhythmic pulse. Over and over, a steady pulsating refrain that came, simultaneously from within and without.

He lies, he lies, it throbbed.

"Mis-*tah* Uptown!''

Bill Hardin's voice slashed through the babble of voices and raucous bass jukebox rumblings of the Prince Street bar even before Collins's eyes could adjust to the dim, smoke-hazed interior from the outside sun. He squinted, searching the press of barfly regulars and downtown trendoids for the source of the voice, finally spotting his friend in a booth at the rear of the bar, waving for his attention. Collins waved back as he started threading his way through the lunch hour crowd.

"How the hell you been, man?" Bill demanded, grasping Collins's hand in his insistent handshake.

"Hangin' in there, Billy," Collins said. They slid into the booth whose table was already littered with a trio of empty beer bottles and an ashtray holding half a dozen crushed Marlboro Lights smoked down to their filters. "Been waiting long?"

"Naw, half hour, an hour, like that." Hardin turned in his seat and lifted his arm, signaling to the busy bartender across the room. "Yo, Murph," he bellowed. "Another Bud and a club soda." He turned back to Collins, his canines like a vampire's fangs showing in his smile. "So, it's been a while, man. Like six, eight months since I hopped the rails to Chicago."

"Yeah, I was kind of surprised to hear from you. I thought you were planning on hanging around out there for the long haul."

Bill let loose with his self-deprecating laugh and took a quick, powerful draw on his cigarette. "Best laid plans, right? Went home to patch things up with Karen, make another go at this being married thing . . ."

". . . And she tossed you out on your ass."

The laugh and he stabbed out his cigarette in the ashtray. "A bitch, right? Man, I'm starting to think I'm not cut out for marriage."

"What clued you, besides your three divorces? You can just barely handle one-night stands."

Bill arched an eyebrow and reached to pluck the bottle of beer the bartender was about to put on the table out of his hand. "One of 'em doesn't count, remember. I married Chrissie twice."

"Thereby proving," Collins said, "that both of you are without clues."

"No shit. How's your ball and chain doing?"

"She's got a name, asshole. And Rebecca's doing great."

"Yeah, well, fuck marriage." Bill Hardin lifted his beer in a toast. "To hedonism."

Collins tapped his bottle against Bill's with a shake of his head. "Yeah, 'cause look where it's gotten you, pal."

"Don't be bitter, Davey. Not everybody can be happy with a co-op mortgage and their American Express bill paid in full every month."

Listen!

"Oh, please. You're back eight minutes and you're starting

with me? Besides, I've been where the rent's overdue, the credit cards're maxed out, and I didn't know if or when the next check's coming in. There's something to be said for having a bank account.''

"Don't get defensive, man . . .''

"I'm not. I'm just saying . . .''

". . . In the soft, whining voice of complacency . . .''

"The day I get complacent's the day I hang it up. Stop putting words in my mouth.''

"Your words," Bill said between swallows of beer and a drag on his cigarette. The smoke curled out of his nostrils. "I'm just interpreting tone.''

"No you're not. You're judging me by your standards. C'mon, man, you're probably the best writer I know, but you're so soaked in beer and self-destruction—''

"Don't forget flake and pussy," he reminded him happily, smiling his devil smile.

"—yeah, and cocaine and babes, that your chops are totally fucked. But, okay, you went with debauchery over your writing, that's your business. But I'm not about to excuse it for you either. A guy can work words like you ought to put some of that energy into writing instead of frying your brain and getting your wick waxed.''

Bill's eyes were wide and shiny behind the thick lenses of his glasses, the smile fixed and genuine on his face. It was just past noon, but he was on his fourth beer in less than an hour, and God only knew what had gone up his nose before he got here. "I know what I can do," he said. "I knew I could be a writer or I could live my life the way I wanted. Being a writer takes giving it the whole wad, not just *some*. It's the same with debauchery, man. And I like doping and whoring a whole hell of a lot more than locking myself away in a room to write, so that's what I do. And," another swallow of beer, "I'm pretty fucking good at it.''

"Jesus, I could accuse you of giving blowjobs to German shepherds in Macy's window and you'd cop to it just to prove what a big, fucking pervert you are.''

"At least I'm committed to something, Davey," he said around the mouth of his beer bottle, arching an eyebrow and fixing his friend with a wicked look.

"Give me a break, you asshole. I've been writing and publishing over twenty years, busting my ass to sell books. All of them're still in print . . . you remember the reviews the last two got?"

Bill laughed and waved to the bartender for another round. "So what you're telling me," he said slowly, "is that the great unwashed who make Jackie Collins and Danielle Steel rich and a few pretentious dickweed reviewers who shouldn't be allowed near a typewriter actually like your stuff."

"Let's get more simplistic, why don't we," Collins sneered. "You think everybody but you's an asshole. You figure it's cool to sell your soul to the devil."

"Fuck the devil, man," Bill said. "I got other priorities. And I've got my point of view and the rest of the world's got its own."

Listen!

Collins leaned back in the booth, suddenly exhausted by Hardin's casual disdain, the smoke-clogged air and crushing rumble of human voices, by the rock music pounding from the jukebox. Its bass throb smacked at his ears, sending a vibration *Listen!* through him that was almost a physical presence commanding his attention. "I know I'm going to be sorry I asked," he said, trying to ignore the heavy slap of the presence clawing through to his consciousness. "But you still haven't mentioned the manuscript. I sent it to you over a month ago. You ever get it?"

"Got it." Bill leaned down and reached into the tattered, bulging old leather briefcase he always carried that was dumped on the floor under his chair, stuffed with newspaper and magazine clippings, file folders, books, and scraps of who knew what else. He came back with the photocopied manuscript of Collins's *Tales of Bernstein*, its pages dog-eared and soiled, and tossed it on the table between them.

"I had to read this one twice," he said. "Mainly because I couldn't believe it the first time around."

"See, what'd I tell you? I'm already sorry."

Listen, listen, listen

Hardin paused to light a fresh cigarette while the previous one still smoked in the ashtray. "I hope you are, man," he said darkly, sucking in smoke with a hiss and losing his smile for the first time since Collins's arrival. "'Cause this thing sucks."

"That'll make a swell quote for the book jacket," Collins snapped.

"You telling me you thought there was any blood and guts to it?"

Collins didn't answer, couldn't answer. Hardin was talking, his voice vying for attention with the throbbing bass that had now settled somewhere in his gut. *The answer is here*, it beat over and over again, until the beat of his heart fell into synch with the unspoken but somehow audible words.

"Okay, there was something to the premise, but the plot just wandered all over the fucking map. And the characters were nothing but cardboard idiots dancing to contrivances while you pulled strings that I could see on every page." Hardin stabbed out the cigarette and leaned forward, fixing Collins with a look that scared him, that he couldn't turn away from. "The stuff you used to write, man . . . that was raw. When I finished your first book, I could *taste* the blood in my mouth. But this shit you've been churning out since you got clean and happy . . . best-seller material with no emotion, no heat."

The jukebox changed records, a new song pounded on, but the beat was the same, shouting louder, growing angry. Its anger was becoming his. "So what's that leave," Collins said, his voice low and hard. "Everything's going to be crap to you except what's written by someone like you. Only you're too fucking dissipated to sit down and do it. All you can do is pass judgment on the rest of us. The proverbial eunuch at the orgy, you can watch, you can give pointers . . . but you can't fuckin' do it, can you?"

"I don't have to be an asshole to know shit when it passes by me, Davey. Look, man, by my standards, you were never much more than a dilettante dabbling in hedonism, but at least you used to be willing to get your hands, not to mention your head and your dick, dirty. Now all you've got is some politically correct, oh so angstified urban yuppie riff going that doesn't say squat. You probably think you've grown up, but all you've really done is *give* up, surrender to the big literary homogenizing machine that your wife and shrink's got you convinced is so cool.''

''Just because you're unhappy's no reason for everybody to . . .''

''Oh, fuck that and fuck you if you really believe this's about anybody but *you*. Shrinks are death to a writer. They want to make you healthy and happy, take away all your nasties and make you whole. Well, I got a flash for you, pal . . . art doesn't come from happy. Art comes from disease and despair, from the shit stew of emotional turmoil that's got to be kept simmering with every trauma you've ever experienced.''

The howl was a physical blow that set Collins reeling, slamming back in his seat, gasping for breath. *Yes, yes, yes,* in rising pitch until the metal throb shrieked like pain from a raggedly new and raw wound. The scream was mingled with maniacal laughter, the relief of truth unleashed. ''I don't believe . . .'' Collins gasped, grasping for words that were his own and not those of the beast screaming in his gut.

''Yes, you do,'' Hardin hissed. He spoke, but the words were the beast's, echoing inside him a split second after they left Hardin's lips in hellish reverberation. *You know what feeds art has to eat the soul of the artist. You believe you've been lied to and have lied to yourself because the truth is a frightful thing. You've stood too long at the precipice of that fear until you've become frozen. But the time's come to choose . Back away from the edge, accept the pretense and live with it*

Or jump

Collins's fist shot across the table, smashing into the face with its devil's glare hovering inches from him. It snapped back, blood spurting, fire flashing from glasses that flew from its face. Hot, red wetness splattered on his fingers, burning and pleasurable. Heat, heat was everywhere in him, around him, searing his lungs, pumping through his veins

Jump

over the table, red slicked fingers reaching for its neck while his fist pistoned into Hardin's face, not caring what damage was done to the face or to himself, until he was pulled, dragged still flailing madly from his victim by the grasping hands of startled, yelling patrons.

Collins let himself be held, panting, deafened to their words by the rush pounding through his head, blind to their faces by the haze of anger. Dizzied by the delicious scent of blood.

Someone was helping Hardin to his feet, was he okay? Did he want them to call an ambulance? A cop? Hardin waved them off, shaking his head as blood oozed from his nose and cuts on his face, running down the contours of his lips, seeping over his teeth. No I'm fine no problem just a misunderstanding you can let him go it's cool.

Collins shook off the restraining hands and stared at Hardin who stared back, unblinking, seemingly unaffected by the beating he'd just taken. Collins whirled, smashing his way through the bar patrons who had gathered around to watch the fight, desperately seeking the door and escape as Bill Hardin watched.

And smiled, blood and saliva coating the white of his teeth.

"Jump," he whispered.

Rebecca Collins came home to find her husband sitting in the dark in the middle of the floor of his office, a hollow-eyed island in a sea of scattered and torn papers, a half-empty bottle of vodka clutched in his fist. He blinked at her when she turned on the light, his face a pale, unreadable mask that gave no reaction to the look of horror that greeted the vodka.

"Jesus Christ, Dave," she breathed. "What are you doing?"

He shook his head and looked away. "It wasn't working," he said in a voice reeking of sadness and despair.

She was afraid to take another step into the room. "How the hell could you . . ." she started, but stopped before she said anything that might further the damage. She searched her mind for the right words, the things they drilled into relatives of alcoholics at the Al-Anon meetings. Now wasn't the time for recriminations, not when he was back on the bottle after almost four years of sobriety. No, now was the time for deep breaths, to seek composure and understanding.

"What . . . what's not working, babe?" she asked.

Jump, into the abyss of truth, leave the lies and delusions of happiness behind

The fragile, whispering voice had become strong, piercing the hiss and clutter of his denial and fear. He could hear again, for the first time in years, he could hear everything, clearer now for his attempts at suppression than he had ever heard it in his life.

"Me," he said and lifted the bottle to his lips to drink with enthusiasm, to satisfy the beast's thirst after having withheld what it had craved for so long. "Us. Everything. I've been lying, Rebecca."

She won't understand

Her heart sank some more. "You mean . . . you've been drinking all this time, Dave?"

Collins looked at the bottle as though unaware it was in his hand until she had discovered its existence. "No, not this, I haven't touched a drop the whole time," he laughed, again startled, this time by the sounds emanating from his throat. "About happiness. About contentment. About . . . about everything. This isn't what I'm supposed to be . . . this thing that robs me of what I have to be to be who I am."

She can't understand

He held up his hands, stained reddish brown with dried blood. Rebecca recoiled from the sight and he laughed. "Don't even try, Rebecca. You're one of the ones who tried to make me forget that I need this," he looked with wonder at the bloodstains, then at the vodka bottle, "and this to be who I am. I didn't need to be fixed, Rebecca. I wasn't broken."

"You're an alcoholic, Dave. If you'd kept drinking the way you were, you'd be dead by now."

He was on his feet, roaring the beast's roar, *his* roar, without realizing he had moved. *"I am dead,"* he cried, pain and anger cracking his voice. "You and the shrinks and the twelve-step programs and personal managers killed me. Me!" The fist clutching the bottle thudded against his chest, splashing vodka over his shirtfront. "I let you all fuck with the one thing that gave me any real worth, any true, *true* happiness and fed my talent. My pain!"

She was afraid now, her fear a scent that stained the air and he liked it. How long had he feared her disapproval that she should now be frightened of his? How much deeper, more righteous was his anger than her attempts to create the man she wanted out of the artist he had been? He swept his arm in a wide arc, taking in the paper strewn floor. "Nine fucking drafts of *Tales of Bernstein*, and still not a single paragraph that deserves to live . . . that's what I've been reduced to, Rebecca. A failing hack, a scared, self-pitying used-to-be. I can't do it anymore. I will not commit another fucking lie to paper," he raged. "I will not live another goddamned minute as this shell of what I was!"

Rebecca's heart went cold. "Honey, please, you're scaring me, okay? So you fell off the wagon, it happens. Remember, it's supposed to be about one day at a time, but talking about killing yourself is . . ."

Collins's arm swung wildly, the bottle catching the edge of the desk and shattering in a spray of glass and liquid. *She will never understand*

"Listen to me," he sobbed, and he didn't realize he was waving the broken bottle before him as he stepped toward her, but she did. "I've been starving myself because I thought I'd find my happiness through you, but it doesn't work that way. Now I've got to be fed . . . I need food for it before it's completely dead . . ."

It was singing now, a wild, primal song that screamed in celebration of freedom reborn. Collins added his voice to the beast's. Rebecca's scream was wilder still, rich with fear and pain as the warmth and nourishment of her blood flowed down the neck of the broken bottle and over his hand.

The beast licked its lips and began to feed.

Dr. Raucher didn't try to hide his annoyance when Collins stepped out of a doorway and blocked his way on the street to his Greenwich Village brownstone. The writer was wearing an old, ratty overcoat against the light autumn rain, his shoulders slumped as he dug his hands deep into the pockets. It took the psychologist an instant to recognize his client, and another to realize that there was something terribly wrong. "Dave, what are you doing here?" Raucher demanded.

"I had to see you," Collins said softly.

"This really isn't appropriate, Dave," he said. "We should do this in the office, so why don't you call me tomorrow morning and we can schedule an appointment to . . ."

Collins took a shuffling step forward, into the illuminated pool cast by the streetlight. Raucher was taken aback by the staring black-ringed sunken eyes, the unkempt air.

The rust red streaks like warpaint slashed across his cheeks and forehead.

"I said I had to see you, Raucher."

And his voice. A low rumble from deep in his chest, not sounding anything like the man he had spoken to every week for so many years.

Another step, and Raucher blinked, swallowing hard. Right then and there, his animal logic told him to back away, to run. But intellect decided he knew David Collins and had nothing to fear.

"I have something to show you," Collins said, calmly, drawing his hand from his pocket.

"Tomorrow," Raucher gently, but firmly. "In the office, Dave."

"Tonight. Up your ass, Doc."

Collins's hand swept up, driving the blade of the kitchen knife up into Raucher's stomach, slicing through tweed and cotton, driving into flesh and viscera. Raucher doubled over Collins's fist as the air rushed from him and he felt a warmth ooze across his belly. Collins laughed, his free hand clutching Raucher's collar to keep him from collapsing to the ground.

"You robbed me," Dave Collins said in an easy, steady voice. "You helped steal my soul. I almost lost it altogether, but it was stronger than you. Stronger even than I could have guessed. Since you tried to destroy it, it's only fair you help bring about its renewal."

Raucher grunted. The wound hadn't started to hurt yet, but he knew it would. He had seen the glitter of light on the serrated edge of the knife in its arc towards him, felt it puncture his gut—oh, God, why was he doing this? But the psychologist couldn't speak to ask Collins.

"Come with me, Doctor." Collins half carried, half dragged Raucher up the street, watching with fascination the trail of blood that dribbled along in their wake, abstract dabs on the rain slicked pavement. He kept the knife in the doctor, his hand pressing it in place. He knew if he were to withdraw it, the blood would wash out of Raucher, spill onto the street in a great, steaming torrent. But that wouldn't do; it would be wasteful. He only need wait a few moments longer and he would be able to savor it all.

Collins smelled the cigarette smoke at the mouth of the alleyway and paused. Somebody in there? Dave smiled. More food for the beast. He continued on his way, the cool of the rain dripping down his neck a delicious contrast to the blood warmth oozing over his fist as he gave the knife just a little tug, biting deeper into Raucher's flesh and increasing the flow.

"Got yourself another one, Davey?"

Collins laughed some more and said "Hiya, Bill," to Hardin, who leaned casually against the alley wall, a soggy cigarette dangling from his puffy lips.

"I came looking for you at your place, man. Good thing for you I did, too," Hardin said, shaking his head. "A fucking blind man could've figured it was you offed your wife. But," he smiled, "I did a little clean-up, wiped away a few fingerprints, and *bah-dah-bing*, you can play it all innocent and grief-stricken when the cops start asking questions."

"Thanks, Billy. You're a pal." Collins dropped Raucher's body behind the shelter of some garbage cans and knelt beside him. He looked up at Hardin. "How'd you know I was here, man?"

"The white pages, man. You left it open to the page with his name, with your bloody fuckin' fingerprint under his address. Sloppy shit, man, but I got rid of it for you. You're gonna have to be more careful if you're gonna make a habit of this, start picking people at random."

"Son of a bitch." Collins's eyes were wide. "You know about the beast, don't you?"

Hardin shrugged. "Remember you said I thought it was cool to sell my soul to the devil and I told you I had other priorities?"

"Yeah?" Raucher started to thrash around on the ground.

"Well, maybe I chose hedonism over writing, but that's

just me. You gotta write, but all you're gonna produce is shit if you're pussywhipped into sanity. You didn't want it to happen, but the civilians talked you into it.''

Collins glanced at Raucher as the psychologist yelped, regaining his wind and finding his voice. Collins cursed and slashed the knife once, hard, across Raucher's throat, then turned his attention back to Bill Hardin.

"The beast?"

Hardin started to flick the cigarette butt to the ground, but thought better of it and held it in his cupped hand. "It's no beast, man. Beasts are ugly. What you got here is beautiful.''

Collins nodded and squeezed his eyes shut in ecstasy, near tears. *He knows*, it howled inside him, sharing his joy. "It is, Billy. She's just so fucking beautiful.''

"That's what I figured," Hardin said, his voice a soft, sad whisper. "She's why you wrote the way you did when you were at your best. She's the inspiration that kept you going. You had her . . . and I wanted her, man. I was so fucking jealous, and then so angry when you turned your back on this incredible creature . . . and I *still* couldn't have her. I never will, because she's always wanted you. She kept after you even after you stopped caring.

"Now you're back together with that bloody, beautiful bitch who's gonna make you brilliant again. And you know what's fucked, man? I'll bet you don't even know her name.''

Collins smiled. "I do now, man. She's my muse.''

Bill Hardin nodded and pushed away from the wall. "That's the one, Davey. So, you got shit to do now. Meet me at the bar after?''

"Yeah.'' Collins looked down at Raucher and started to cut open the psychologist's shirt. "I got a lot of catching up to do there.''

"Cool.'' Hardin patted the kneeling Collins on the shoulder as he passed by on his way out of the alley. "Don't forget to clean up and ditch the bloody clothes before you go prancing around in public, man.''

Collins laughed. "I know what I'm doing, Billy.''

"Yeah. *Now*.''

"Now's what counts.''

"Welcome back, Davey." Hardin slipped around the corner and disappeared into the night, and was, for the moment, forgotten as Dave Collins turned to embrace his muse. He had forgotten how good it felt to be folded in her warm, raw embrace.

Mommy

Max Allan Collins

The mother and daughter in the hallway of John F. Kennedy Grade School were each other's picture-perfect reflection.

Mommy wore a tailored pink suit with high heels, her blond hair short and perfectly coifed; pearls caressed the shapely little woman's pale throat, and a big black purse was tucked under her arm. Daughter, in a frilly white blouse with a pink skirt and matching tights, was petite, too, a head smaller than her mother. Their faces were almost identical—heart-shaped, with luminous china-blue eyes, long lashes, cupid's bow mouths, and creamy complexions.

The only difference between them was Mommy's serene, madonna-like countenance; the little girl was frowning. The frown was not one of disobedience—Jessica Ann Sterling was as well-behaved a modern child as you might hope to find—but a frown of frustration.

"Please don't, Mommy," she said. "I don't want you to make Mrs. Withers mad at me . . ."

"It's only a matter of what's fair," Mommy said. "You have better grades than that little foreign student."

"He's not foreign, Mommy. Eduardo is Hispanic, and he's a good student, too . . ."

"Not as good as you." Mommy's smile was a beautiful thing; it could warm up a room. "The award is for 'Outstanding Student of the Year.' You have straight A's, perfect attendance, you're the best student in the 'Talented and Gifted' group."

"Yes, Mommy, but . . ."

"No 'buts,' dear. *You* deserve the 'Outstanding Student' award. Not this little Mexican."

"But Mommy, it's just a stupid plaque. I don't need another. I got one last year . . ."

"And the year before, and the year before that—and you deserve it again this year. Perhaps it's best you go out and wait in the car for Mommy." She looked toward the closed door of the fifth-grade classroom. "Perhaps this should be a private conference . . ."

"Mommy, please don't embarrass me . . ."

"I would never do that. Now. Who's your best friend?"

"You are, Mommy."

"Who loves you more than anything on God's green earth?"

"You do, Mommy."

The little girl, head lowered, shuffled down the hall.

"Jessica Ann . . ."

She turned, hope springing. "Yes, Mommy?"

Mommy shook her finger in the air, gently. "Posture."

"Yes, Mommy . . ."

And the little girl went out to wait in their car.

Thelma Withers knew that trimming her room with Christmas decorations probably wasn't politically correct, but she was doing it, anyway. She had checked with Levi's parents, to see if they objected, and they said as long as there were no Christian symbols displayed, it was okay.

For that reason, she had avoided images of Santa Claus—technically, at least, he was Saint Nicholas, after all—but what harm could a little silver tinsel around the blackboard do?

The portly, fiftyish teacher was on a stepladder stapling the ropes of tinsel above the blackboard when Mrs. Sterling came in.

Looking over her shoulder, Mrs. Withers said, "Good afternoon, Mrs. Sterling. I hope you don't mind if I continue with my decorating . . ."

"We did have an appointment for a conference."

What a pain this woman was. The child, Jessica Ann, was a wonderful little girl, and a perfect student, but the mother—what a monster! In almost thirty years of teaching, Thelma had never had one like her—constantly pestering her about imagined slights to her precious child.

"Mrs. Sterling, we had our conference for the quarter just last week. I really want to have these decorations up for the children, and if you don't mind, we'll just talk while . . ."

"I don't mind," the woman said coldly. She was standing at the desk, staring at the shining gold wall plaque for "Outstanding Student of the Year" that was resting there. Her face was expressionless, yet there was something about the woman's eyes that told Thelma Withers just how covetous of the award she was.

Shaking her head, Mrs. Withers turned back to her work, stapling the tinsel in place.

The click clack of the woman's high heels punctuated the sound of stapling as Mrs. Sterling approached.

"You're presenting that plaque tonight, at the PTA meeting," she said.

"That's right," Mrs. Withers said, her back still to the woman.

"You *know* that my daughter deserves that award."

"Your daughter is a wonderful student, but so is Eduardo Melindez."

"Are his grades as good as Jessica Ann's?"

Mrs. Withers stopped stapling and glanced back at the woman, literally looking down her nose at Jessica Ann's mother.

"Actually, Mrs. Sterling, that's none of your business. How I arrive at who the 'Outstanding Student' is is my affair."

"Really."

"Really. Eduardo faces certain obstacles your daughter does not. When someone like Eduardo excels, it's important to give him recognition."

"Because he's a Mexican, you're taking the award away from my daughter? You're punishing her for being white, and for coming from a nice family?"

"That's not how I look at it. A person of color like Eduardo—"

"You're not going to give the award to Jessica, are you?"

"It's been decided."

"There's no name engraved on the plaque. It's not too late."

With a disgusted sigh, Mrs. Withers turned and glared at the woman. "It is too late. What are you teaching your daughter with this behavior, Mrs. Sterling?"

"What are you teaching her, when you take what's rightfully hers and give it to somebody because he's a 'person of color'?"

"I don't have anything else to say to you, Mrs. Sterling. Good afternoon." And Mrs. Withers turned back to her stapling, wishing she were stapling this awful woman's head to the wall.

It was at that moment that the ladder moved, suddenly, and the teacher felt herself losing balance, and falling, and she tumbled through the air and landed on her side, hard, the wind knocked out of her.

Moaning, Mrs. Withers opened her eyes, trying to push herself up. Her eyes were filled with the sight of Mrs. Sterling leaning over her, to help her up.

She thought.

Jessica Ann watched as one of the JFK front doors opened and Mommy walked from the building to the BMW, her big purse snugged tightly to her. Mommy wore a very serious expression, almost a frown.

Mommy opened the car door and leaned in.

"Is something wrong?" Jessica Ann asked.

"Yes," she said. "There's been a terrible accident . . . when I went to speak to Mrs. Withers, she was lying on the floor."

"On the floor?"

"She'd been up a ladder, decorating the room for you children. She must have been a very thoughtful teacher."

"Mommy—you make it sound like . . ."

"She's dead, dear. I think she may have broken her neck."

"Mommy . . ." Tears began to well up. Jessica Ann thought the world of Mrs. Withers.

"I stopped at the office and had the secretary phone for an ambulance. I think we should stay around until help comes, don't you?"

"Yes, Mommy . . ."

An ambulance came, very soon, its siren screaming, but for no reason: when Mrs. Withers was wheeled out on a stretcher, she was all covered up. Jessica bit her finger and watched and tried not to cry. Mommy stood beside her, patting her shoulder.

"People die, dear," Mommy said. "It's a natural thing."

"What's natural about falling off a ladder, Mommy?"

"Is that a smarty tone?"

"No, Mommy."

"I don't think Mrs. Withers would want you speaking to your mother in a smarty tone."

"No, Mommy."

"Anyway, people fall off ladders all the time. You know, more accidents occur at home than anywhere else."

"Mrs. Withers wasn't at home."

"The workplace is the next most frequent."

"Can we go now?"

"No. I'll need to speak to these gentlemen."

A police car was pulling up; they hadn't bothered with a siren. Maybe somebody called ahead to tell them Mrs. Withers was dead.

Two uniformed policeman questioned Mommy, and then another policeman, in a wrinkled suit and loose tie, talked to Mommy, too. Jessica Ann didn't see him arrive; they were all sitting at tables in the school library, now. Jessica Ann was seated by herself, away from them, but she could hear some of the conversation.

The man in the suit and tie was old—probably forty—and he didn't have much hair on the top of his head, though he did have a mustache. He was kind of pudgy and seemed grouchy.

He said to Mommy, "You didn't speak to Mrs. Withers at all?"

"How could I? She was on the floor with her neck broken."

"You had an appointment . . ."

"Yes. A parent/teacher conference. Anything else, Lieutenant March?"

"No. Not right now, ma'am."

"Thank you," Mommy said. She stood. "You have my address, and my number."

"Yeah," he said. "I got your number."

He was giving Mommy a mean look but she just smiled as she gathered her purse and left.

Soon they were driving home. Mommy was humming a song, but Jessica Ann didn't recognize it. One of the those old songs, from the '80s.

It was funny—her mother didn't seem very upset about Mrs. Withers' accident at all.

But sometimes Mommy was that way about things.

Jessica Ann loved their house on Rockwell Road. It had been built a long time ago—1957, Mommy said—but it was really cool: light brick and dark wood and a lot of neat angles—a split-level ranch style was how she'd heard her Mommy describe it. They had lived here for two years, ever since Mommy married Mr. Sterling.

Mr. Sterling had been really old—fifty-one, it said in the paper when he died—but Mommy loved him a lot. He had an insurance agency, and was kind of rich—or so they had thought.

She had overheard her Mommy talking to Aunt Beth about it. Aunt Beth was a little older than Mommy, and she was pretty too, but she had dark hair. They reminded Jessica Ann of Betty and Veronica in the Archie comic books.

Anyway, one time Jessica Ann heard Mommy in an odd voice, almost a mean voice, complaining that Mr. Sterling hadn't been as rich as he pretended to be. Plus, a lot of his money and property and stuff wound up with his children by (and Mommy didn't usually talk this way, certainly not in front of Jessica Ann) "the first two bitches he was married to."

Still, they had wound up with this cool house.

Jessica Ann missed Mr. Sterling. He was a nice man,

before he had his heart attack and died. The only thing was, she didn't like having to call him "Daddy." Her real daddy—who died in the boating accident when she was six—was the only one who deserved being called that.

She kept Daddy's picture by her bed and talked to him every night. She remembered him very well—he was a big, handsome man with shoulders so wide you couldn't look at them both at the same time. He was old, too—even older than Mr. Sterling—and had left them "well off" (as Mommy put it).

Jessica Ann didn't know what had happened to Daddy's money—a few times Mommy talked about "bad investments"—but fortunately Mr. Sterling had come along about the time Daddy's money ran out.

When Jessica Ann and her mother got home from the school, Aunt Beth—who lived a few blocks from them, alone, because she was divorced from Uncle Bob—was waiting dinner. Mommy had called her from JFK and asked if she'd help.

As Jessica Ann came in, Aunt Beth was all over her, bending down, putting her arm around her. It made Jessica Ann uneasy. She wasn't used to displays of affection like that—Mommy talked about loving her a lot, but mostly kept her distance.

"You poor dear," Aunt Beth said. "Poor dear." She looked up at Mommy, who was hanging up both their coats in the closet. "Did she see . . . ?"

"No," Mommy said, shutting the closet door. "I discovered the body. Jessica Ann was in the car."

"Thank God!" Aunt Beth said. "Do either of you even feel like eating?"

"I don't know," Jessica Ann said.

"Sure," Mommy said. "Smells like spaghetti."

"That's what it is," Aunt Beth said. "I made a big bowl of salad, too . . ."

"I think I'll go to my room," Jessica Ann said.

"No!" Mommy said. "A little unpleasantness isn't going to stand in the way of proper nutrition."

Aunt Beth was frowning, but it was a sad frown. "Please . . . if she doesn't want . . ."

Mommy gave Aunt Beth the "mind your own business" look. Then she turned to Jessica Ann, and pointed to the kitchen. "Now, march in there, young lady . . ."

"Yes, Mommy."

"Your salad, too."

"Yes, Mommy."

After dinner, Jessica Ann went to her room, a pink world of stuffed animals and Barbie dolls; she had a frilly four-poster bed that Mommy got in an antique shop. She flopped onto it and thought about Mrs. Withers. Thought about what a nice lady Mrs. Withers was. . . .

She was crying into her pillow when Aunt Beth came in.

"There, there," Aunt Beth said, sitting on the edge of the bed, patting the girl's back. "Get it out of your system."

"Do . . . do you think Mrs. Withers had any children?"

"Probably. Maybe even grandchildren."

"Do you . . . do you think I should write them a letter, about what a good teacher she was?"

Aunt Beth's eyes filled up with tears and she clutched Jessica Ann to her. This time Jessica Ann didn't mind. She clutched back, crying into her aunt's blouse.

"I think that's a wonderful idea."

"I'll write it tonight, and add their names later, when I find them out."

"Fine. Jessy . . ." Aunt Beth was the only grown-up who ever called her that; Mommy didn't like nicknames. ". . . you know, your mother . . . she's kind of a . . . special person."

"What do you mean?"

"Well . . . it's just that . . . she has some wonderful qualities."

"She's very smart. And pretty."

"Yes."

"She does everything for me."

"She does a lot for you. But . . . she doesn't always *feel* things like she should."

"What do you mean, Aunt Beth?"

"It's hard to explain. She was babied a lot . . . there

were four of us, you know, and she was the youngest. Your grandparents, rest their souls, gave her everything. And why not? She was so pretty, so perfect—''

''She always got her way, didn't she?''

''How did you know that, Jessica Ann?''

''I just do. 'Cause she still does, I guess.''

''Jessy . . . I always kind of looked after your mother . . . protected her.''

''What do you mean?''

''Just . . . as you grow older, try to understand . . . try to forgive her when she seems . . . if she seems . . .''

''Cold?''

Aunt Beth nodded. Smiled sadly. ''Cold,'' she said. ''In her way, she loves you very much.''

''I know.''

''I have dessert downstairs. You too blue for chocolate cake?''

''Is Mark here? I thought I heard his car.''

''He's here,'' Aunt Beth said, smiling. ''And he's asking for you. Mark and chocolate cake—that's quite a combo.''

Jessica Ann grinned, took a tissue from the box on her nightstand, dried her eyes, took her aunt's hand, and allowed herself to be led from her room down the half-stairs.

Mommy's new boyfriend, Mark Jeffries, was in the living room sitting in Mr. Sterling's recliner, sipping an iced tea.

''There's my girl!'' he said, as Jessica Ann came into the room; Aunt Beth was in the kitchen with Mommy.

Mark sat forward in the chair, then stood—he was younger than either Mr. Sterling or Daddy, and really good looking, like a soap opera actor with his sandy hair and gray sideburns and deep tan. He wore a green sweater and new jeans and a big white smile. Also, a Rolex watch.

She went quickly to him, and he bent down and hugged her. He smelled good—like lime.

He pushed her gently away and looked at her with concern in his blue-gray eyes. ''Are you okay, angel?''

''Sure.''

''Your mommy told me about today. Awful rough.'' He

took her by the hand and led her to the couch. He sat down and nodded for her to join him. She did.

"Angel, if you need somebody to talk to . . ."

"I'm fine, Mark. Really."

"You know . . . when I was ten, my Boy Scout leader died. He was killed in an automobile accident. I didn't have a dad around . . . he and Mom were divorced . . . and my Scout leader was kind of a . . . surrogate father to me. You know what that is?"

"Sure. He kind of took the place of a dad."

"Right. Anyway, when he died, I felt . . . empty. Then I started to get afraid."

"Afraid, Mark?"

"I started to think about dying for the first time. I had trouble. I had nightmares. For the first time I realized nobody lives forever . . ."

Jessica Ann had known that for a long time. First Daddy, then Mr. Sterling. . . .

"I hope you don't have trouble like that," he said. "But if you do—I just want you to know . . . I'm here for you."

She didn't say anything—just beamed at him.

She was crazy about Mark. Jessica Ann hoped he and Mommy would get married. She thought she could even feel comfortable calling him Daddy. Maybe.

Mommy had met Mark at a country club dance last month. He had his own business—some kind of mail-order thing that was making a lot of money, she heard Mommy say—and had moved to Ferndale to get away from the urban blight where he used to live.

Jessica Ann found she could talk to Mark better than to any grown-up she'd ever met. Even better than Aunt Beth. And as much as Jessica Ann loved her Mommy, they didn't really *talk*—no shared secrets, or problems.

But Mark put Jessica Ann at ease. She could talk to him about problems at school or even at home.

"Who wants dessert?" Aunt Beth called.

Soon Jessica Ann and Mark were sitting at the kitchen table while Mommy, in her perfect white apron (she never got anything on it, so why did she wear it?) was serving up big pieces of chocolate cake.

"I'll just have the ice cream," Aunt Beth told Mommy.

"What's *wrong* with me?" Mommy said. "You're allergic to chocolate! How thoughtless of me."

"Don't be silly . . ."

"How about some strawberry compote on that ice cream?"

"That does sound good."

"There's a jar in the fridge," Mommy said.

Aunt Beth found the jar, but was having trouble opening it.

"Let me have a crack at that," Mark said, and took it, but he must not have been as strong as he looked; he couldn't budge the lid.

"Here," Mommy said, impatiently, and took the jar, and with a quick thrust, opened the lid with a loud *pop*. Aunt Beth thanked her and spooned on the strawberry compote herself.

Mommy sure was strong, Jessica Ann thought. She'd seen her do the same thing with catsup bottles and pickle jars.

"Pretty powerful for a little girl," Mark said teasingly, patting Mommy's rear end when he thought Jessica Ann couldn't see. "Remind me not to cross you."

"Don't cross me," Mommy said, and smiled her beautiful smile.

At school the next day, Jessica Ann was called to the principal's office.

But the principal wasn't there—waiting for her was the pudgy policeman, the one with the mustache. He had on a different wrinkled suit today. He didn't seem so grouchy now; he was all smiles.

"Jessica Ann?" he said, bending down. "Remember me? I'm Lieutenant March. Could we talk for a while?"

"Okay."

"I have permission for us to use Mr. Davis' office."

Mr. Davis was the principal.

"All right."

Lieutenant March didn't sit at Mr. Davis' desk; he put two chairs facing each other and sat right across from Jessica Ann.

"Jessica Ann, why did your mother want to see Mrs. Withers yesterday?"

"They had a conference."

"Parent/teacher conference."

"Yes, sir."

"You don't have to call me sir, Jessica Ann. I want us to be friends."

She didn't say anything.

He seemed to be trying to think of what to say next; then finally he said, "Do you know how your teacher died?"

"She fell off a ladder."

"She did fall off a ladder. But Jessica Ann—your teacher's neck was broken . . ."

"When she fell off the ladder."

"We have a man called the Medical Examiner who says that it didn't happen that way. He says it's very likely a pair of hands did that."

Suddenly Jessica Ann remembered the jar of strawberry compote, and the other bottles and jars Mommy had twisted caps off, so easily.

"Jessica Ann . . . something was missing from Mrs. Withers' desk."

Jessica Ann's tummy started jumping.

"A plaque, Jessica Ann. A plaque for 'Outstanding Student of the Year.' You won last year, didn't you?"

"Yes, sir."

"Mrs. Withers told several friends that your mother called her, complaining about you not winning this year."

Jessica Ann said nothing.

"Jessica Ann . . . the mother of the boy who won the plaque, Eduardo's mother, Mrs. Melindez, would like to have that plaque. Means a lot to her. If you should happen to find it, would you tell me?"

"Why would *I* find it?"

"You just might. Could your mother have picked it up when she went into the classroom?"

"If she did," Jessica Ann said, "that doesn't prove anything."

"Who said anything about proving anything, Jessica Ann?"

She stood. "I think if you have any more questions for me, Lieutenant March, you should talk to my mother."

"Jessica Ann . . ."

But the little girl hear didn't hear anything else; not any-thing the policeman said, or what any of her friends said the rest of the day, or even the substitute teacher.

All she could hear was the sound of the lid on the strawberry compote jar popping open.

When Jessica Ann got home, she found the house empty. A note from Mommy said she had gone grocery shopping. The girl got herself some milk and cookies but neither drank nor ate. She sat at the kitchen table staring at nothing. Then she got up and began searching her mother's room.

In the middle drawer of a dresser, amid slips and panties, she found the plaque.

Her fingers flew off the object as if it were a burner on a hot stove. Then she saw her own fingerprints glowing on the brass and rubbed them off with a slick pair of panties, and put the shining plaque back, buried it in Mommy's underthings.

She went to her room and found the largest stuffed animal she could and hugged it close; the animal—a bear—had wide button eyes. So did she.

Her thoughts raced; awful possibilities presented them-selves, possibilities that she may have already considered, in some corner of her mind, but had banished.

Why did Mr. Sterling die of that heart attack?

What really happened that afternoon Mommy and Daddy went boating?

She was too frightened to cry. Instead she hugged the bear and shivered as if freezing and put pieces together that fit too well. If she was right, then someone *else* she thought the world of was in danger. . . .

Mark Jeffries knew something was wrong, but he couldn't be sure what.

He and Jessica Ann had hit it off from the very start, but for the last week, whenever he'd come over to see her mother, the little girl had avoided and even snubbed him.

It had been a week since the death of Mrs. Withers—he had accompanied both Jessica Ann and her mother to the funeral—and the child had been uncharacteristically brooding ever since.

Not that Jessica Ann was ever talkative: she was a quiet child, intelligent, contemplative even, but when she opened up (as she did for Mark so often) she was warm and funny and fun.

Maybe it was because he had started to stay over at the house, on occasion . . . maybe she was threatened because he had started to share her mother's bedroom.

He'd been lying awake in the mother's bed, thinking these thoughts as the woman slept soundly beside him, when nature called him, and he arose, slipped on a robe and answered the call. In the hallway, he noticed the little girl's light on in her room. He stopped at the child's room and knocked, gently.

"Yes?" came her voice, softly.

"Are you awake, angel?"

"Yes."

He cracked the door. She was under the covers, wide awake, the ruffly pink shade of her nightstand lamp glowing; a stuffed bear was under there with her, hugged to her.

"What's wrong, angel?" he asked, and shut the door behind him, and sat on the edge of her bed.

"Nothing."

"You've barely spoken to me for days."

She said nothing.

"You know you're number one on my personal chart, don't you?"

She nodded.

"Do you not like my sleeping over?"

She shrugged.

"Don't you . . . don't you think I'd make a good daddy?"

Tears were welling in her eyes.

"Angel."

She burst into tears, clutching him, bawling like the baby she had been, not so long ago.

"I . . . I wanted to chase you away . . ."

"Chase me away! Why on earth?"

"Because . . . because you *would* make a good daddy, and I don't want you to die . . ."

And she poured it all out, her fears that her mother was a murderer, that Mommy had killed her teacher and her daddy and even Mr. Sterling.

He glanced behind him at the closed door. He gently pushed the girl away and, a hand on her shoulder, looked at her hard.

"How grown-up can you be?" he asked.

"Real grown-up, if I have to."

"Good. Because I want to level with you about something. You might be mad at me . . ."

"Why, Mark?"

"Because I haven't been honest with you. In fact . . . I've lied."

"Lied?"

And he told her. Told her about being an investigator for the insurance company that was looking into the latest suspicious death linked to her mother, that of her stepfather, Phillip Sterling (at least, the latest one before Mrs. Withers).

Calmly, quietly, he told the little girl that he had come to believe, like her, that her mother was a murderer.

"But you . . . you slept with her . . ."

"It's not very nice. I know. I had to get close to her, to get the truth. With your help, if you can think back and tell me about things you've seen, we might be . . ."

But that was all he got out.

The door flew open, slapping the wall like a spurned suitor, and there she was, the beautiful little blond in the babydoll nightie, a woman with a sweet body that he hadn't been able to resist even though he knew what she most likely was.

There she was with the .38 in her hand and firing it at him, again and again; he felt the bullets hitting his body, punching him, burning into him like lasers, he thought, then one entered his right eye and put an end to all thought, and to him.

Jessica Ann was screaming, the bloody body of Mark Jeffries sprawled on the bed before her, scorched bleeding holes on the front of his robe, one of his eyes an awful black hole leaking red.

Mommy sat beside her daughter and hugged her little girl to her, slipping a hand over her mouth, stifling Jessica Ann's screams.

"Hush, dear. Hush."

Jessica Ann started to choke, and that stopped the scream-ing, and Mommy took her hand away. The girl looked at her mother and was startled to see tears in Mommy's eyes. She couldn't ever remember Mommy crying, not even at the fu-nerals of Daddy and Mr. Sterling, although she had seemed to cry. Jessica Ann had always thought Mommy was faking . . . that Mommy couldn't cry . . . but now. . . .

"We have to call the police, dear," Mommy said, "and when they come, we have to tell them things that fit together. Like a puzzle fits together. Do you understand?"

"Yes, Mommy." Jessica, trembling, wanted to pull away from her mother, but somehow couldn't.

"Otherwise, Mommy will be in trouble. We don't want that, do we?"

"No, Mommy."

"Mark did bad things to Mommy. *Bedroom* things. Do you understand?"

"Yes, Mommy."

"When I heard him in here, I thought he might be doing the same kind of things to you. Or trying to."

"But he didn't—"

"That doesn't matter. And you don't have to say he did. I don't want you to lie. But those things he told you . . . about being an investigator . . . *forget* them. He never said them."

"Oh . . . okay, Mommy."

"If you tell, Mommy would be in trouble. We don't want that."

"No, Mommy."

"Now. Who's your best friend?"

"You . . . you are, Mommy."

"Who loves you more than anything on God's green earth?"

"You do, Mommy."

"Good girl."

There were a lot of men and women in the house, through-out the night, some of them police, in uniform, some of them in white, some in regular clothes, some using cameras, others carrying out Mark in a big black zippered bag.

Lieutenant March questioned Mommy for a long time; when all the others had left, he was still there, taking notes. Mommy sat on a couch in the living room, wearing a robe, her arms folded tight to her, her expression as blank as a doll's. Just behind her was the Christmas tree, in the front window, which Mommy had so beautifully trimmed.

Aunt Beth had been called and sat with Jessica Ann in the kitchen, but there was no doorway, just an archway separating the rooms, so Jessica could see Mommy as Lieutenant March questioned her. Jessica Ann couldn't hear what they were saying, most of the time.

Then she saw Mommy smile at Lieutenant March, a funny, making-fun sort of smile, and that seemed to make Lieutenant March angry. He stood and almost shouted.

"No, you're not under arrest," he said, "and yes, you should contact your attorney."

He tromped out to the kitchen, to bring the empty coffee cup (Aunt Beth had given him some coffee) and he looked very grouchy.

"Thank you," he said to Aunt Beth, handing her the cup.

"Don't you believe my sister?" Aunt Beth asked.

"Do you?" He glanced at Jessica Ann, but spoke to Aunt Beth. "I'll talk to the girl tomorrow. Maybe she should stay with you tonight."

"That's not my decision," Aunt Beth said.

"Maybe it should be," he said, and excused himself and left.

Aunt Beth looked very tired when she sat at the table with Jessica Ann. She spoke quietly, almost a whisper.

"What you told me . . . is that what really happened, Jessica Ann?"

"Mommy thought Mark was going to do something bad to me."

"You love your mommy, don't you?"

"Yes."

"But you're also afraid of her."

"Yes." She shrugged. "All kids are afraid of their parents."

"Beth," Mommy said, suddenly in the archway, "you better go now."

Aunt Beth rose. She wet her lips. "Maybe I should take Jessica Ann tonight."

Mommy came over and put her hand on Jessica Ann's shoulder. "We appreciate your concern. But we've been through a lot of tragedy together, Jessica Ann and I. We'll make it through tonight, just fine. Won't we, dear?"

"Yes, Mommy."

Both Jessica Ann and her mother were questioned, separately and individually, at police headquarters in downtown Ferndale the next afternoon. Mommy's lawyer, Mr. Ekhardt, a handsome gray-haired older man, was with them; sometimes he told Mommy not to answer certain questions.

Afterward, in the hall, Jessica Ann heard Mommy ask Mr. Ekhardt if they had enough to hold her.

"Not yet," he said. "But I don't think this is going to let up. From the looks of that lieutenant, I'd say this is just starting."

Mommy touched Mr. Ekhardt's hand with both of hers. "Thank you, Neal. With you in our corner, I'm sure we'll be just fine."

"You never give up, do you?" Mr. Ekhardt said with a funny smile. "Gotta give you that much."

Mr. Ekhardt shook his head and walked away.

Jessica Ann watched as her Mommy pulled suitcases from a closet, and then went to another closet and began packing her nicest things into one of the suitcases.

"We're going on a vacation, dear," Mommy said, folding several dresses over her arm, "to a foreign land—you'll love it there. It'll be Christmas every day."

"But I have school . . ."

"Your break starts next week, anyway. And then we'll put you in a wonderful new school."

"What about my friends?"

"You'll make new friends."

Mommy was packing so quickly, and it was all happening so fast, Jessica Ann couldn't even find the words to protest further. What could she do about it? Every kid knew that when your parents decided to move, the kid had no part of

it. A kid's opinion had no weight on such matters. You just
went where your parents went.

"Take this," Mommy said, handing her the smaller suit-
case, "and pack your own things."

"What about my animals?"

"Take your favorite. Aunt Beth will send the others on,
later."

"Okay, Mommy."

"Who's your best friend?"

"You are."

"Who loves you more than—"

"You do."

The girl packed her bag. She put the framed picture of
Daddy in the middle of the clothes, so it wouldn't get broken.

They drove for several hours. Mommy turned the radio on
to a station playing Christmas music—"White Christmas"
and the one about chestnuts roasting. Now and then Mommy
looked over at her, and Jessica Ann noticed Mommy's expression was . . . different. Blank, but Mommy's eyes seemed
. . . was Mommy frightened, too?

When Mommy noticed Jessica Ann had caught her gaze,
Mommy smiled that beautiful smile. But it wasn't real. Jessica Ann wasn't sure Mommy knew how to *really* smile.

The motel wasn't very nice. It wasn't like the Holiday Inns
and Marriotts and Ramada Inns they usually stayed in on
vacation. It was just a white row of doorways on the edge
of some small town and a junkyard was looming in back of
it, like some scary Disneyland.

Jessica Ann put on her jammies and brushed her teeth and
Mommy tucked her in, even gave her a kiss. The girl was
very, very tired and fell asleep quickly.

She wasn't sure how long she'd been asleep, but when she
woke up, Mommy was sitting on the edge of Jessica Ann's
bed. Mommy wasn't dressed for bed; she still had on the
clothes she'd been driving in.

Mommy was sitting there, in the dark, staring, her hands
raised in the air. It was like Mommy was trying to choke a
ghost.

"Sometimes Mommys have to make hard decisions,"

Mommy whispered. "If they take Mommy away, who would look after you?"

But Jessica Ann knew Mommy wasn't saying this to her, at least not to the awake her. Maybe to the sleeping Jessica Ann, only Jessica Ann wasn't sleeping.

The child bolted out of the bed with a squealing scream and Mommy ran after her. Jessica Ann got to the door, which had a nightlatch, but her fingers fumbled with the chain, and then her Mommy was on top of her. Mommy's hands were on her, but the child squeezed through, and bounded over one of the twin beds and ran into the bathroom and slammed and locked the door.

"Mommy! Mommy, don't!"

"Let me in, Jessica Ann. You just had a bad dream. Just a nightmare. We'll go back to sleep now."

"No!"

The child looked around the small bathroom and saw the window; she stood on the toilet seat lid and unlocked the window and slipped out, onto the tall grass. Behind her, she heard the splintering of the door as her mother pushed it open.

Jessica Ann was running, running toward the dark shapes that were the junkyard; she glanced back and saw her mother's face framed in the bathroom window. Her mother's eyes were wild; Jessica Ann had never seen her mother like that.

"Come back here this *instant*!" her mother said.

But Jessica Ann ran, screaming as she went, hoping to attract attention. The moon was full and high and like a spotlight on the child. Maybe someone would see!

"Help! Please, help!"

Her voice seemed to echo through the night. The other windows in the motel were dark and the highway out front was deserted; there was no one else in the world but Jessica Ann and Mommy.

And Mommy was climbing out the bathroom window.

Jessica Ann climbed over the wire fence—there was some barbed wire at the top, and her jammies got caught, and tore a little, but she didn't cut herself. Then she was on the other side, in the junkyard, but her bare feet hurt from the cinders beneath them.

Mommy was coming.

The child ran, hearing the rattle of the fence behind her, knowing Mommy was climbing, climbing over, then dropping to the other side.

"Jessica Ann!"

Piles of crushed cars were on either side of Jessica Ann, as she streaked down a cinder path between them, her feet hurting, bleeding, tears streaming, her crying mixed with gasping for air as she ran, ran hard as she could.

Then she fell and she skinned her knee and her yelp echoed.

She got up, quickly, and ran around the corner, and ran right into her mother.

"What do you think you're doing, young lady?"

Her mother's hands gripped the girl's shoulders.

Jessica Ann backed up quickly, bumping into a rusted-out steel drum. A wall of crushed cars, scrap metal, old tires, broken-down appliances and other things that must have had value once was behind her.

"Mommy . . ."

Mommy's hands were like claws reaching out for the girl's neck. "This is for your own good, dear . . ."

Then Mommy's hands were on Jessica Ann's throat, and the look in Mommy's eyes was so very cold, and the child tried to cry out but she couldn't, though she tried to twist away and moonlight fell on her face.

And Mommy gazed at her child, and her eyes narrowed, and softened, and she loosened her hands.

"Put your hands *up*, Mrs. Sterling!"

Mommy stepped away and looked behind her. Jessica Ann, touching her throat where Mommy had been choking her, could see him standing there, Lieutenant March. He was pointing a gun at Mommy.

Mommy put her head down and her hands up.

Then Aunt Beth was there, and took Jessica Ann into her arms and held her, and said, "You're a brave little girl."

"What . . . what are you *doing* here, Aunt Beth?"

"I came along with the lieutenant. He was keeping your mother under surveillance. I'm glad you have good lungs, or we wouldn't have heard you back here. We were out front, and I'd fallen asleep . . ."

"Aunt Beth . . . can I live with you now? I don't want to go to a new school."

Aunt Beth's laugh was surprised and sort of sad. "You can live with me. You can stay in your school." She stroked Jessica Ann's forehead. "It's over now, Jessy. It's over."

"She couldn't do it, Aunt Beth," Jessica Ann said, crying, but feeling strangely happy, somehow. Not to be rescued: but to know Mommy couldn't bring herself to do it! Mommy couldn't kill Jessica Ann!

"I know, honey," Aunt Beth said, holding the girl.

"Mommy *does* love me! More than anything on God's green earth."

The child didn't hear when Lieutenant March, cuffing her hands behind her, asked the woman, "Why didn't you do it? Why'd you hesitate?"

"For a moment there, in the moonlight," Mommy said, "she looked like *me*. . . ."

And the cop walked the handcuffed woman to his unmarked car, while the aunt took her niece into the motel room to retrieve a stuffed bear and a framed photo of Daddy.

The Gray Madonna

Graham Masterton

He had always known that he would have to return to Bruges.
This time, however, he chose winter, when the air was foggy
and the canals had turned to the color of breathed-on pewter,
and the narrow medieval streets were far less crowded with
shuffling tourists.

He had tried to avoid thinking about Bruges for three years
now. Forgetting Bruges—really forgetting—was out of the
question. But he had devised all kinds of ways of diverting
his attention away from it, of mentally changing the subject,
such as calling his friends or turning on the TV really loud
or going out for a drive and listening to Nirvana with the
volume set on Deaf.

Anything rather than stand on that wooden jetty again,
opposite the overhanging eaves and boathouses of the fourteenth-century plague hospital, waiting for the Belgian police
frogmen to find Karen's body. He had stood there so many
times in so many dreams, a bewildered sun-reddened American tourist with his shoulder-bag and his camcorder, while
diseased-looking starlings perched on the steep, undulating
tiles up above him, and the canal slopped and gurgled beneath
his feet.

Anything rather than watch the medical examiner with
her crisp white uniform and her braided blond hair as she
unzippered the black vinyl body-bag and Karen's face appeared, not just white but almost green. "She would not have

suffered much," in that guttural back-of-the-throat Flemish accent. "Her neck was broken almost at once."

"By what?"

"By a thin ligature, approximately eight millimetres diameter. We have forensic samples, taken from her skin. It was either hemp or braided hair."

Then Inspector Ben De Buy from the Politie, resting a nicotine-stained hand on his arm said, "One of the drivers of the horse-drawn tourist carriages says that he saw your wife talking to a nun. This was approximately ten minutes before the boatman noticed her body floating in the canal."

"Where was this?"

"Hoogstraat, by the bridge. The nun turned the corner around Minderbroederstraat and that was the last the driver saw of her. He did not see your wife."

"Why should he have noticed my wife at all?"

"Because she was attractive, Mr. Wallace. All of these drivers have such an eye for good-looking women."

"Is that all? She talked to a nun? Why should she talk to a nun? She's not a Catholic."

He had paused, and then corrected himself. "She *wasn't* a Catholic."

Inspector De Buy had lit up a pungent Ernte 23 cigarette, and breathed smoke out of his nostrils like a dragon. "Perhaps she was asking for directions. We don't know yet. It shouldn't be too difficult to find the nun. She was wearing a light gray habit, which is quite unusual."

Dean had stayed in Belgium for another week. The police came up with no more forensic evidence; no more witnesses. They published photographs of Karen in the newspapers, and contacted every religious order throughout Belgium, southern Holland and northern France. But nobody came forward. Nobody had seen how Karen had died. And there were no nunneries where the sisters wore gray; especially the whitish-gray that the carriage-driver claimed to have seen.

Inspector De Buy had said, "Why not take your wife back to America, Mr. Wallace? There's nothing more you can do here in Bruges. If there's a break in the case, I can fax you, yes?"

Now Karen was lying in the Episcopal cemetery in New

Milford, Connecticut, under a blanket of crimson maple-leaves, and Dean was back here, in Bruges, on a chilly Flanders morning, tired and jet-lagged, and lonelier than he had ever felt before.

He crossed the wide, empty square called 't Zand, where fountains played and clusters of sculptured cyclists stood in the fog. The real cyclists were far busier jangling their bells and pedalling furiously over the cobbles. He passed cáfes with steamy, glassed-in verandahs, where doughy-faced Belgians sat drinking coffee and smoking and eating huge cream-filled pastries. A pretty girl with long black hair watched him pass, her face as white as an actress in a European art-movie. In an odd way, she reminded him of the way that Karen had looked, the day that he had first met her.

With his coat-collar turned up against the cold and his breath fuming, he walked past the shops selling lace and chocolates and postcards and perfume. In the old Flemish tradition, a flag hung over the entrance of every shop, bearing the coat of arms of whoever had lived there in centuries gone by. Three grotesque fishes, swimming through a silvery sea. A man who looked like Adam, picking an apple from a tree. A white-faced woman with a strange suggestive smile.

Dean reached the wide cobbled market-place. On the far side, like a flock of seagulls, twenty or thirty nuns hurried silently through the fog. Up above him, the tall spire of Bruges Belfry loomed through the fog, six hundred tightly-spiraling steps to the top. Dean knew that because he and Karen had climbed up it, panting and laughing all the way. Outside the Belfry the horse-drawn tourist carriages collected, as well as ice-cream vans and hot-dog stalls. In the summer, there were long lines of visitors waiting to be given guided tours around the town, but not today. Three carriages were drawn up side by side, while their drivers smoked and their blanketed horses dipped their heads in their nose-bags.

Dean approached the drivers and lifted one hand in greeting.

"Tour, sir?" asked a dark-eyed unshaven young man in a tilted straw hat.

"Not today, thanks. I'm looking for somebody . . . one

of your fellow-drivers." He took out the folded newspaper clipping. "His name is Jan De Keyser."

"Who wants him? He's not in trouble, is he?"

"No, no. Nothing like that. Can you tell me where he lives?"

The carriage-drivers looked at each other. "Does anybody know where Jan De Keyser lives?"

Dean took out his wallet and handed them 100 francs each. The drivers looked at each other again, and so Dean gave them another 100.

"Oostmeers, about halfway down, left-hand side," said the unshaven young man. "I don't know the number but there's a small delicatessen and it's next to that, with a brown door and brown glass vases in the window."

He coughed, and then he said, "You want a tour, too?"

Dean shook his head. "No, thanks. I think I've seen everything in Bruges I ever want to see; and more."

He walked back along Oude Burg and under the naked lime-trees of Simon Stevin Plein. The inventor of decimal currency stood mournfully on his plinth, staring at a chocolate shop across the street. The morning was so raw now that Dean wished he had brought a pair of gloves. He crossed and recrossed the canal several times. It was smelly and sullen and it reminded him of death.

They had first come to Bruges for two reasons. The first was to get over Charley. Charley hadn't even talked, or walked, or seen the light of day. But amnio had shown that Charley would be chronically disabled, if he were ever born; a nodding, drooling boy in a wheelchair, for all of his life. Dean and Karen had sat up all evening and wept and drank wine, and finally decided that Charley would be happier if he remained a hope; and a memory; a brief spark that illuminated the darkness, and died. Charley had been aborted and now Dean had nobody to remember Karen by. Her china collection? Her clothes? One evening he had opened her underwear drawer and taken out a pair of her panties and desperately breathed them in, hoping to smell her. But the panties were clean and Karen was gone; as if she had never existed.

They had come to Bruges for the art, too: for the Groeninge

Museum with its fourteenth-century religious paintings and
its modern Belgian masters, for Rubens and Van Eycks and
Magrittes. Dean was a veterinarian, but he had always been
a keen amateur painter; and Karen had designed wallpaper.
They had first met nearly seven years ago, when Karen had
brought her golden retriever into Dean's surgery to have its
ears checked out. She had liked Dean's looks right from the
very beginning. She had always liked tall, gentle, dark-haired
men ("I would have married Clark Kent if Lois Lane hadn't
gotten in first."). But what had really persuaded her was the
patience and affection with which he had handled her dog
Buffy. After they were married, she used to sing *"Love Me,*
Love My Dog" to him, and accompany herself on an old
banjo.

Buffy was dead now, too. Buffy had pined so pitifully for
Karen that Dean had eventually put him down.

Oostmeers was a narrow street of small neat row houses,
each with its shining front window and its freshly painted
front door and its immaculate lace curtains. Dean found the
delicatessen easily because—apart from an antique
dealer's—it was the only shop. The house next door was
much shabbier than most of its neighbors, and the brown
glass vases in the window were covered in a film of dust. He
rang the doorbell, and clapped his hands together to warm
them up.

After a long pause, he heard somebody coming downstairs,
and then coughing, and then the front door was opened about
two inches. A thin, soapy-looking face peered out at him.

"I'm looking for Jan De Keyser."

"That's me. What do you want?"

Dean took out the newspaper cutting and held it up. "You
were the last person to see my wife alive."

The young man frowned at the cutting for nearly half-a-
minute, as if he needed glasses. Then he said, "That was a
long time ago, mister. I've been sick since then."

"All the same, can I talk to you?"

"What for? It's all in the paper, everything I said."

"I'm just trying to understand what happened."

Jan De Keyser gave a high, rattling cough. "I saw your
wife talking to this nun, that's all, and she was gone. I turned

around in my seat, and saw the nun walk into Minderbroeder-straat, into the sunshine, and then she was gone, too, and that was all."

"You ever see a nun dressed in gray like that before?"

Jan De Keyser shook his head.

"You don't know where she might have come from? What order? You know, Dominican or Franciscan or whatever?"

"I don't know about nuns. But maybe she wasn't a nun."

"What do you mean? You told the police that she was a nun."

"What do you think I was going to say? That she was a statue? I have two narcotics offenses already. They would have locked me up, or sent me to that bloody stupid hospital in Kortrijk."

Dean said, "What are you talking about, statue?"

Jan De Keyser coughed again, and started to close the door. "This is Brugge, what do you expect?"

"I still don't understand."

The door hovered on the point of closing. Dean took out his wallet again, and ostentatiously took out three 100 Bf notes, and held them up. "I've come a long way for this, Jan. I need to know everything."

"Wait," said Jan De Keyser; and closed the door. Dean waited. He looked down the foggy length of Oostmeers, and he could see a young girl standing on the corner of Zonnekemeers, her hands in her pockets. He couldn't tell if she were watching him or not.

After two or three minutes, Jan De Keyser opened the door again and stepped out into the street, wearing a brown leather jacket and a checkered scarf. He smelled of cigarettes and liniment. "I've been very sick, ever since that time. My chest. Maybe it was nothing to do with the nun; maybe it was. But you know what they say: once a plague, always a plague."

He led Dean back the way he had come, past the canals, past the Gruuthuuse Museum, along Dijver to the Vismarkt. He walked very quickly, with his narrow shoulders hunched. Horses and carriages rattled through the streets like tumbrils; and bells chimed from the belfry. They had that high, strange musical ring about them that you only hear from European bells. They reminded Dean of Christmasses and wars; and maybe that was what Europe was really all about.

They reached the corner of Hoogstraat and Minderbroederstraat; by the bridge. Jan De Keyser jabbed his finger one way, and then the other. "I am carrying Germans; five- or six-member German family. I am going slow because my horse is tired, yes? I see this woman in tight white shorts, and a blue T-shirt, and I look at her because she is pretty. That was your wife, yes? She has a good figure. Anyway, I turn and watch because she is not only pretty, she is talking to a nun. A nun in gray, quite sure of that. And they are talking as if they are arguing strongly. You know what I mean? Like, arguing, very fierce. Your wife is lifting her arms, like this, again and again, as if to say, 'what have I done? what have I done?' And the nun is shaking her head."

Dean looked around, frustrated and confused. "You said something about statues; and the plague."

"Look up," said Jan De Keyser. "You see on the corner of almost every building, a stone madonna. Here is one of the largest, life-size."

Dean raised his eyes, and for the first time he saw the arched niche that had been let into the corner of the building above him. In this niche stood a Virgin Mary, with the baby Jesus in her arms, looking sadly down at the street below.

"You see?" said Jan De Keyser. "There is so much to see in Brugge, if you lift your head. There is another world on the second story. Statues and gargoyles and flags. Look at that building there. It has the faces of thirteen devils on it. They were put there to keep Satan away; and to protect the people who lived in this building from the Black Death."

Dean leaned over the railings, and stared down into the water. It was so foggy and gelid that he couldn't even see his own face; only a blur, as if somebody had taken a black-and-white photograph of him, and jogged the camera.

Jan De Keyser said, "In the fourteenth century, when the plague came, it was thought that the people of Brugge were full of sin, yes? and that they were being given a punishment from God. So they made statues of the Holy Mary at every corner, to keep away the evil; and they promised the Holy Mary that they would always obey her, and worship her, if she protected them from plague. You understand this, yes? They made a binding agreement."

"And what would happen if they didn't stick to this binding agreement?"

"The Holy Virgin would forgive; because the Holy Virgin always forgives. But the statue of the Holy Virgin would give punish."

"The statue? How could the statue punish anybody?"

Jan De Keyser shrugged. "They made it, in the false belief. They made it with false hopes. Statues that are made with false hopes will always be dangerous; because they will turn on the people who made them; and they will expect the payment for their making."

Dean couldn't grasp this at all. He was beginning to suspect that Jan De Keyser was not only physically sick but mentally unbalanced, too; and he was beginning to wish that he hadn't brought him here.

But Jan De Keyser pointed up to the statue of the Virgin Mary; and then at the bridge; and then at the river, and said, "They are not just stone; not just carving. They have all of people's hopes inside them, whether these hopes are good hopes; or whether these hopes are wicked. They are not just stone."

"What are you trying to tell me? That what you saw—?"

"The gray madonna," said Jan De Keyser. "If you offend her, you must surely pay the price."

Dean took out three more hundred Bf bills, folded them, and stuffed them into Jan De Keyser's jacket pocket. "Thanks, pal," he told him. "I love you, too. I flew all the way from New Milford, Connecticut, to hear that my wife was killed by a statue. Thank you. Drink hearty."

But Jan De Keyser clutched hold of his sleeve. "You don't understand, do you? Everybody else has told you lies. I am trying to tell you the truth."

"What does the truth matter to you?"

"You don't have to insult me, sir. The truth has always mattered to me; just like it matters to all Belgians. What would I gain, from lying to you? A few hundred francs, so what?"

Dean looked up at the gray madonna in her niche in the

wall. Then he looked back at Jan De Keyser. "I don't know," he said, flatly.

"Well, just give me the money, and maybe we can talk about morals and philosophy later."

Dean couldn't help smiling. He handed Jan De Keyser his money; and then stood and watched him as he hurried away, his hands in his pockets, his shoulders swinging from side to side. Jesus, he thought, I'm getting old. Either that, or Jan De Keyser has deliberately been playing me along.

All the same, he stood across the street, cater-corner from the gray madonna, and watched her for a long, long time, until the chill began to get to his sinuses, and his nose started to drip. The gray madonna stared back at him with her blind stone eyes, calm and beautiful, with all the sadness of a mother who knows that her child must grow up, and that her child will be betrayed, and that for centuries to come men and women will take His name in vain.

Dean walked back along Hoogstraat to the market-place, and he went into one of the cafes beside the entrance to the Belfry. He sat in the corner, underneath a carved wooden statue of a louche-looking medieval musician. He ordered a small espresso and an Asbach brandy to warm him up. A dark-looking girl on the other side of the cafe smiled at him briefly, and then looked away. The jukebox was playing "Guantanamera."

He was almost ready to leave when he thought he saw a gray nun-like figure passing the steamed-up window.

He hesitated, then he got up from his table and went to the door, and opened it. He was sure that he had seen a nun. Even if it wasn't the same nun that Karen had been talking to on the day when she was strangled and thrown into the canal, this nun had worn a light gray habit, too. Maybe she came from the same order, and could help him locate the original nun, and find out what Karen had said to her.

A party of schoolchildren were crossing the gray fan-patterned cobbles of the Markt, followed by six or seven teachers. Beyond the teachers, Dean was sure that he could glimpse a gray-robed figure, making its way swiftly toward the arched entrance to the Belfry. He started to walk quickly across the market-place, just as the carillon of bells began to ring, and starlings rose from the rooftops all around the square. He saw the figure disappear into the foggy, shadowy archway, and he broke into a jog.

He had almost reached the archway when a hand snatched at his sleeve, and almost pulled him off-balance. He swung around. It was the waiter from the cafe, pale-faced and panting.

"You have to pay, sir," he said.

Dean said, "Sure, sorry, I forgot," and hurriedly took out his wallet. "There—keep the change. I'm in a hurry, okay?"

He left the bewildered waiter standing in the middle of the square and ran into the archway. Inside, there was a large deserted courtyard. On the right-hand side, a flight of stone steps led to the interior of the Belfry tower itself. There was nowhere else that the nun could have gone.

He vaulted up the steps, pushed open the huge oak door, and went inside. A young woman with upswept glasses and a tight braid on top of her head was sitting behind a ticket-window, painting her nails.

"Did you see a nun come through here?"

"A nun? I don't know."

"Give me a ticket anyway."

He waited impatiently while she handed him a ticket and a leaflet describing the history of the Belfry. Then he pulled open the narrow door which led to the spiral stairs, and began to climb up them in leaps and bounds.

The steps were extravagantly steep, and it wasn't long before he had to slow down. He trudged around and around until he reached a small gallery, about a third of the way up the tower, where he stopped and listened. If there *were* a nun climbing the steps up ahead of him, he would easily be able to hear her.

And—yes—he could distinctly make out the *chip—chip—chip* sound of somebody's feet on worn stone steps. The sound echoed down the staircase like fragments of granite dropping down a well. Dean seized the thick, slippery rope handrail, and renewed his climbing with even more determination, even though he was soaked in chilly sweat, and he was badly out of breath.

As it rose higher and higher within the Belfry tower, the spiral staircase grew progressively tighter and narrower, and the stone steps were replaced with wood. All that Dean could see up ahead of him was the triangular treads of the steps above; and all he could see when he looked down was the triangular treads of the steps below. For more than a dozen turns of the spiral, there were no windows, only dressed stone walls, and even though he was so high above the street, he began to feel trapped and claustrophobic. There were still hundreds of steps to climb to reach the top of the Belfry, and hundreds of steps to negotiate if he wanted to go back down again.

He paused for a rest. He was tempted to give it up. But then he made the effort to climb up six more steps and found that he had reached the high-ceilinged gallery which housed the clock's carillon and chiming mechanism—a gigantic medieval musical-box. A huge drum was turned by clockwork, and a complicated pattern of metal spigots activated the bells.

The gallery was silent, except for the soft, weary ticking of a mechanism that had been counting out the hours without interruption for nearly five hundred years. Columbus's father could have climbed these same steps, and looked at this same machinery.

Dean was going to rest a moment or two longer, but he heard a quick, furtive rustling sound on the other side of the gallery, and caught sight of a light gray triangle of skirt just before it disappeared up the next flight of stairs.

"Wait!" he shouted. He hurried across the gallery and started to climb. This time he could not only hear the sound of footsteps, he could hear the swishing of well-starched cotton, and once or twice he actually saw it.

"Wait!" he called. "I don't mean to frighten you—I just want to talk to you!"

But the footsteps continued upward at the same brisk pace, and with each turn in the spiral the figure in the light gray habit stayed tantalizingly out of sight.

At last the air began to grow colder and fresher, and Dean realized that they were almost at the top. There was nowhere the nun could go, and she would *have* to talk to him now.

He came out onto the Belfry's viewing gallery, and looked around. Barely visible through the fog he could distinguish the orange rooftops of Bruges, and the dull gleam of its canals. On a clear day the view stretched for miles across the flat Flanders countryside, toward Ghent and Kortrijk and Ypres. But today Bruges was secretive and closed-in; and looked more like a painting by Brueghel than a real town. The air smelled of fog and sewers.

To begin with, he couldn't see the nun. She must be here, though: unless she had jumped off the parapet. Then he stepped around a pillar, and there she was, standing with her back to him, staring out toward the Basilica of the Holy Blood.

Dean approached her. She didn't turn around, or give any indication that she knew that he was here. He stood a few paces behind her and waited, watching the faint breeze stirring the light gray cloth of her habit.

"Listen, I'm sorry if I alarmed you," he said. "I didn't mean to give you the impression that I was chasing you or anything like that. But three years ago my wife died here in Bruges, and just before she died she was seen talking to a nun. A nun in a light-gray habit, like yours."

He stopped and waited. The nun remained where she was, not moving, not speaking.

"Do you speak English?" Dean asked her, cautiously. "If you don't speak English, I can find somebody to translate for us."

Still the nun remained where she was. Dean began to feel unnerved. He didn't like to touch her, or to make any physical attempt to turn her around. All the same, he wished she would speak, or look at him, so that he could see her face. Maybe she belonged to a silent order. Maybe she was deaf. Maybe she just didn't want to talk to him, and that was that.

He thought of the gray madonna, and of what Jan De Keyser had told him: "They are not just stone; not just carving. They have all of people's hopes inside them; whether these hopes are good hopes, or whether these hopes are wicked."

For some reason that he couldn't quite understand, he shivered, and it wasn't only the cold that made him shiver. It was the feeling that he was standing in the presence of something really terrible.

"I, er—I wish you'd say something," he said, loudly, although his voice sounded off-balance.

There was a very long silence. Then suddenly the carillon of bells started to ring, so loudly that Dean was deafened, and could literally feel his eyeballs vibrating in their sockets. The nun swiveled around—didn't turn, but smoothly swiveled, as if she were standing on a turntable. She stared at him, and Dean stared back, and the fear rose up inside him like ice-cold sick.

Her face was a face of stone. Her eyes were carved out of granite, and she couldn't speak because her lips were stone, too. She stared at him blind and sad and accusing, and he couldn't even find the breath to scream.

He took one step backward, then another. The gray madonna came gliding after him, blocking his way to the staircase. She reached beneath her habit and lifted out a thin braided ligature, made of human hair, the kind of ligature that depressed and hysterical nuns used to plait out of their own hair, and then use to hang themselves. Better to meet your Christ in Heaven than to live in fear and self-loathing.

Dean said, "Keep away from me. I don't know what you are, or *how* you are, but keep away from me."

He was sure that she smiled, very faintly. He was sure that she whispered something.

"What?" he said. *"What?"*

She came closer and closer. She was stone, and yet she breathed, and she smiled, and she whispered, *"Charley, this is for Charley."*

Again, he screamed at her, *"What?"*

But she caught hold of his left arm in a devastatingly strong grip, and she stepped up onto the platform that ran around the parapet, and with one irresistible turn of her back she rolled herself over the parapet and slid down the orange-tiled roof.

Dean shouted, *"No!"* and tried to tug himself free from her; but she wasn't an ordinary woman. She gripped him so tight and she weighed so much that he was dragged over the parapet after her. He found himself sliding and bumping over the fog-moist tiles, and at the end of the tiles was a lead gutter and then a sheer drop down to the cobbles of the Markt, one hundred and seventy feet below.

With his right hand, he scrabbled to get a grip on the tiles. But the gray madonna was far too heavy for him. She was solid granite. Her hand was solid granite; no longer pliable, but still holding him fast.

She tumbled over the edge of the roof. Dean caught hold of the guttering, and for one moment of supreme effort he swung from it, with the gray madonna revolving around him, her face as calm as only the face of the Virgin Mary could be. But the guttering was medieval lead, soft and rotten, and slowly it bent forward under the weight, and then gave way.

Dean looked down and saw the market-square. He saw horse-drawn carriages and cars and people walking in every direction. He heard the air whistling in his ears.

He clung to the gray madonna because that was the only solid thing he had to cling to. He embraced her as he fell. Hardly anybody saw him falling, but those who did lifted up their hands in horror in the same way that serious burn victims lift up their hands.

He dropped and dropped the whole height of Bruges Belfry, two dark figures falling through the fog, holding each other tight, like lovers. Dean thought for one illogical instant that everything was going to be all right, that he was going to fall forever and never hit the ground. But then suddenly he saw the rooftops much closer and the cobbles expanded faster and faster. He hit the courtyard with the gray madonna on top of him. She weighed over half a ton, and she exploded on impact, and so did he. Together, they were like a bomb bursting. Their heads flew apart. Stone arms and flesh arms jumped up into the air.

Then there was nothing but the muffled sound of traffic, and the echoing flap of starlings' wings as they resettled on the rooftops, and the jangling of bicycle-bells.

Inspector Ben De Buy stood amongst the wreckage of man and madonna and looked up at the Belfry, cigarette-smoke and fog-vapor fuming from his nose.

"He fell from the very top," he told his assistant, Sergeant Van Peper.

"Yes, sir. The girl who collects the tickets can identify him."

"And was he carrying the statue with him, when he bought his ticket?"

"No, sir, of course not. He couldn't even have lifted it. It was far too heavy."

"But it was up there with him, wasn't it? How did he manage to take a life-size granite statue of the Virgin Mary all the way up those stairs? It's impossible. And even if it *was* possible, why would he do it? You might need to weight yourself down to drown yourself, but to jump from the top of a belfry?"

"I don't know, sir."

"No, well, neither do I, and I don't think I really *want* to know."

He was still standing amongst the blood and the broken stone when one of his youngest detectives appeared, carrying something grayish-white in his arms. As he came closer, Inspector De Buy realized that it was a baby, made of stone.

"What's this?" he demanded.

"The infant Jesus," said the officer, blushing. "We found it on the corner of Hoogstraat, up in the niche where the stone madonna used to stand."

Inspector De Buy stared at the granite baby for a while, then held out his arms. "Here," he said, and the officer handed it over to him. He lifted it over his head, and then he smashed it onto the cobbles as hard as he could. It shattered into half-a-dozen lumps.

"Sir?" asked his sergeant, in puzzlement.

Inspector De Buy patted him on the shoulder. "Thou shalt worship no graven image, Sergeant Van Peper. And now you know why."

He walked out of the Belfry courtyard. Out in the market square, an ambulance was waiting, its sapphire lights flashing in the fog. He walked back to Simon Stevin Plein, where he had left his car. The bronze statue of Simon Stevin loomed over him, black and menacing in his doublet and hat. Inspector De Buy took out his car keys and hesitated for a moment. He was sure that he had seen Simon Stevin move slightly.

He stood quite still, right next to his Citroën, his key lifted, not breathing, listening, waiting. Anybody who saw him then would have believed that he was a statue.

The Highway

Edo van Belkom

Darryl Bedard struggled in the dark to find the windshield-wiper control switch. As he leaned forward, his left hand fumbled with a half-dozen different knobs, none of which controlled the wipers. The car's interior light came on, then the headlights went out. The horn blew, then he signaled for a right-hand turn.

Splat!

The semi-trailer ahead and to the left of him had driven through a deep trough in the highway, throwing gallons of dirty water and slush across his windshield.

Momentarily blinded, Darryl panicked. He grabbed at the steering wheel with both hands, sending the car swerving into the empty lane to his left.

When he regained control of the Japanese rental car, he again searched for the wiper control. At last he found it and the wiper blades immediately began clearing off the windshield.

Darryl leaned back in the driver's seat and breathed a deep, long sigh. Even though his job as a salesman required him to travel tens of thousands of miles each year, he hated driving, especially in bad weather.

He turned on the radio in the hopes that some music would help settle his nerves. Instead of music however, there were endless reports of canceled events and services, and repeated pleas by announcers to stay indoors. He tried another station, same story. He turned the radio off and listened to the rhythm of the wipers as they hummed and squeaked across his windshield.

Normally he would have flown to Detroit, but flights over half the continent had been canceled and many planes caught in the air by the sudden storm were still struggling to find places to land.

Even so, Darryl wished he were in the air. Flying, after all, was infinitely safer than driving, even in the middle of what the radio called the worst snow storm since the second World War. Better still, Darryl would have liked to have put the trip off until the weather had cleared and a flight had become available. Unfortunately, this was a business trip unlike any other; this one could not be postponed. Darryl was on his way to the annual general meeting of company executives and salesmen from both sides of the border. If he ever wanted to move up within the company, to get a position that didn't require a lot of traveling, this was the place to shmooze and press some flesh.

But knowing that didn't make driving any easier. In fact, it made it more stressful. If he wanted to be in Detroit in time for the company chairman's dinner, he'd have to keep his speed up around fifty-five; no mean feat considering he couldn't see more than twenty feet of highway in front of him, but not impossible since the highway had recently been plowed.

He glanced at the speedometer, noticed it slipping below fifty and gently pressed his foot down on the gas.

As the car's numbered LCD readout slowly climbed back up to fifty-five, Darryl noticed flashing red and white lights in his rearview mirror. He turned around to look behind him and, through the falling snow, could just make out a fire truck pulling across the three-lane highway, blocking it off. He eased up on the gas and prepared to pull over, then turned around for another look. He saw what looked to be the flashing strobe lights of an ambulance or some other emergency vehicle coming to a stop next to the fire truck. He pulled into the right-hand lane and glanced back one more time. The lights were now little more than soft pulses in the snow-shrouded darkness. Obviously, the emergency vehicles were stationary. Whatever the problem was it had to be behind him since he hadn't even been able to see it through the storm.

"Well, that's a lucky break," Darryl said under his breath.

If he'd been caught behind a pile-up on the highway—or even worse, involved in one himself—who knew what time he'd end up making Detroit. It was just one more little data point that reinforced his belief that flying was always safer than driving, no matter what the conditions.

He pressed down on the gas and carefully piloted the car back up to speed.

Just then, the car's front end received a terrific jolt—

"What the . . ."

—and the entire car began to shudder.

Darryl held tightly onto the vibrating steering wheel as he eased up on the gas and tried to guide the car onto the shoulder. He was able to control the car well enough to bring it to a stop a few hundred feet down the road. As he sat in the car, breathing hard and fast, his heart pounding against his chest like an angry fist, he realized the car was listing forward and to the left.

"I don't believe it," he said in a voice that bordered on a scream. "Who the hell gets flat tires, anymore?"

He rolled down his window and stuck his head out into the storm to inspect the damage. As he'd feared, the front left tire was little more than a shredded black rubber husk.

He quickly fell back into his seat, his head already cold and wet from the storm, and rolled up the window. After a moment's reflection upon his situation . . . he began pounding on the steering wheel with both hands.

"Why did I agree to a Japanese car?" he cried. "Why didn't I hold out for made in the U.S.A.?"

He slammed his fists against the wheel for several more seconds. When they began to ache, he tucked his battered hands under his armpits and rocked back and forth in his seat.

He wasn't so much upset about the car as he was about having to change the flat. While he detested driving in bad weather, he was absolutely terrified by the prospect of having to step out onto the highway. After all, the side of a major highway was a dangerous enough place at the best of times. In the dark, and in the middle of a snow storm, stepping out of the car would be like thumbing your nose at the Grim Reaper.

Again, Darryl thought about how much safer it was to fly.

He glanced at his watch. If he changed the tire in less than thirty minutes, he might still make the dinner in time for dessert. It would make a great entrance, he thought. I'd have a great story to tell, too. Wouldn't hurt to show them all how dedicated to the company I am, either . . . provided I don't get killed out on the highway.

The last thought made him shudder.

He did his best to clear it from his mind, then buttoned his trenchcoat and wrapped his silk scarf tightly around his neck. He picked his gloves off the seat next to him and slipped them on, then flipped up the collar of his coat to protect the back of his neck from the wind and snow.

He had no hat. And his black loafers would be little more than house slippers in the heavy wet snow that had piled up on the highway's shoulder, but they'd have to do.

After taking a deep breath to strengthen his resolve, he shut off the engine. He searched a moment for the control for the car's hazard lights, then switched them on. He listened to the lights *tink* on and off for several seconds, then pulled his gloves tight on his hands, and got out of the car.

He was immediately hit by a sharp blast of cold. It pierced his coat and clothes as if they weren't even there, and the snow collected on his head and shoulders like a bad case of dandruff.

Doing his best to ignore the cold's bite, and the fear that was rising up within his chest, Darryl started toward the back of the car.

He was halfway there when the ear-splitting blast of a gas horn suddenly ripped through the air like a dull knife blade. Darryl looked up . . . and saw the lights.

It took him a moment to realize there was a semi-trailer heading straight for him. He tried to move out of the way, but his shoes slipped on the snow and he fell to the ground. By the time he was back on his feet, the truck was on him. He dove toward the car, landing on the trunk lid.

The truck roared past as quickly as it had come and before Darryl could get off the car and back onto his feet, it was gone.

For a few moments, Darryl's whole body trembled, so numbed with shock that he no longer felt the cold. Then, with each snowflake that fell on his body, the trembling eased and the cold crept back in, masking his fear like an icy blanket and prodding him to carry on.

With his heartbeat settling down into a heavy thud, he lifted the trunk lid. Although it was dark inside the trunk, and he was unfamiliar with the placing of the spare and its jack, he was able to find them both fairly quickly.

He set the spare up against the car's rear bumper, then looked back down the highway for the longest time. Confident it was safe, he carried the jack around front. Then being careful not to kneel on the snow-covered highway, he placed a gloved hand on the ground to support himself and tried to slide the jack into place behind the ruined left front tire. After several tries, Darryl realized there was no delicate way to change the tire. His coat was already wet and it was obvious that everything else he was wearing would be drenched by the time he was done. "To hell with it," he said, and lowered both knees down onto the dirty brown snow.

He elevated the jack until it was tight between the car and the ground, then set about removing the tire's four lug nuts.

As he worked on the first nut, he felt wetness creeping up his pant leg, spreading the cold and damp evenly to every part of his body. Snowflakes fell onto the back of his neck, melting instantly upon contact with his warm skin and sending ice-water trickling down his back.

A shiver ran the length of Darryl's spine. When the shiver reached the base of his skull, he began thinking about all of the things that could happen to him while he changed the tire by the side of the highway.

He remembered hearing about a guy who got killed by a spare tire that had fallen off a semi-trailer. The guy was changing a flat by the side of the road when he got creamed by this huge spare tire rolling down the highway at fifty miles an hour. The guy didn't see it coming and never knew what hit him.

Darryl suddenly felt incredibly vulnerable, almost naked against the fierce, chill wind. He shook off a shiver and got back to work on the tire, unscrewing the first nut, putting it in his pocket, and setting to work on the second.

Then he remembered another story about a guy who got killed by a hubcap that had come off a 1985 Buick doing seventy-five on the interstate. The guy had heard the hubcap rattling down the highway at him and turned to take a look. Then, while the guy's wife and two kids sat in the car watching, the thing hit a bump in the road, became airborne and just about sliced the guy's head in two.

He adjusted his scarf and the collar of his coat, nervously pulling them tight around his cold, wet neck.

He unscrewed the second nut, put it in his pocket along with the first and began working on the third. For a few moments it wouldn't move, then ever-so-slowly it began to turn.

As he loosened the nut, he remembered hearing about people stopped by the side of the road who'd been mowed down by truck drivers asleep at the wheel. One woman in Quebec, he recalled, had been dragged along for half a mile before the driver even heard her screaming.

Despite the cold, Darryl felt himself sweating beneath his clothes. He took a quick glance over his shoulder at the highway behind him. He couldn't see a thing. The falling snow was like an impenetrable white veil drawn across the road. But he did hear a jet flying high above the storm and guessed he was closer to Detroit than he realized, at least close enough to be along the airport's flight path. Again, he wished he were up there, sitting in a warm and comfortable first-class seat where his most difficult task would be deciding which wine he preferred with his meal—the red or the white.

"Fuck it!" he said.

He unscrewed the third nut, dropped it into his pocket, and began working on the fourth and final nut.

After several seconds it became apparent that the nut refused to budge.

"There's always got to be one!" he shouted, swinging the tire iron against the wheel in frustration. "And it always has to be the last one! Doesn't it?"

The question went unanswered. His words were torn from his lips and immediately carried away by the wind.

"Doesn't it?"

He pounded the tire iron against the wheel a few more times before standing up to take a break. He looked up and down the highway, and saw nothing but darkness and falling snow. He heard another jet overhead, this one closer. Maybe the storm's easing up, he thought, shaking his head in misery.

He knelt down and attacked the last nut with renewed vigor. He grabbed the tire iron with both hands, and lifted with as much leverage and force as he could muster.

Crack!

The nut moved slightly, then again and again until it was loose and spinning freely.

"Thank you!" he sighed under his breath.

Before he removed the nut, Darryl jacked up the car until the flat tire was several inches off the ground. Then he un- screwed the final nut, placed it in his pocket and removed the tire.

He glanced at his watch. He was making excellent time. He just might make the dinner in time for the main course.

For the first time since he stepped onto the highway, he was able to relax.

He carried the flat tire to the trunk and threw it inside. He began rolling the spare towards the front of the car, but after a couple of revolutions the wheel wobbled wildly to the left and rolled out into the middle of the highway.

As the tire fell onto its side and fluttered like a quarter at the end of its roll across a table top, Darryl's eyes opened wide and his jaw fell slack. "I don't fucking believe it!" he screamed, pressing his open hands against the side of his head. "What else can go wrong?"

He stood silent for a few seconds, seriously thinking about getting back into the car, turning on the heater and waiting out the storm.

But he knew he couldn't.

If someone ran over the spare tire lying in the middle of the highway, he'd be up on all sorts of charges of criminal negligence causing bodily harm, maybe even death. And even if he could wait out the storm inside the car, how long would it be until help arrived? Or until a snow plow came along and pushed the car over the shoulder and into the ditch?

The thought of it made Darryl's knees weak. He became aware of how wet and heavy his clothes had become and began to feel faint. He wrapped his arms tightly around his body, then let them fall to his sides in defeat.

There was no way around it. He'd have to venture out into the middle of the highway to retrieve the tire.

Reluctantly, he looked down the highway, squinting his eyes in an attempt to penetrate the snow-shrouded night.

He couldn't see anything but snowflakes and darkness.

He stood motionless to see if he could hear any oncoming traffic. Other than the faint *tink* of his car's hazard lights, all he could hear was the blowing of the wind and the faint drone of jet engines off in the distance.

He decided that now was as good a time as any.

He ran out onto the highway, knelt down on one knee, placed a hand on the spare, and turned around . . .

Just in time to see the airliner emerge from the falling snow. Flaps down, landing gear locked.

He wanted to get out of the way, but couldn't.

Seconds suddenly stretched into minutes as he stood frozen in absolute terror watching the airplane's front wheels touch down on the highway and start skidding toward him.

And when he felt something hot and wet trickle down the inside of his thigh, he couldn't help but think how much safer it would have been to fly.

Avenue X

Nancy A. Collins

June 6th, 199–

I can't wait until I leave town! It's nothing but a swamp of dead-end jobs, burn-outs, and half-assed wannabes. The economy sucks so bad you might as well be living in the Caribbean! Everything's aimed at tourists—no jobs available for anyone over the age of twenty-five, unless you want to go to your grave doing nothing but flipping burgers and changing hotel bed linen. None for me, thanks.

I picked up my bus pass to New York City today. All my friends keep asking me if I'm doing the right thing, chucking it all down here in favor of moving to the Big Apple without a job prospect or an apartment. Maybe I'm being foolish, but I know that if I stay around here another year my brain's going to turn into guacamole paste. Still, my old college roomie, Cynthia Brinkes, lives up there. She says I can crash on her sofa until I can find my own space. What's life about, if not taking chances?

June 13th, 199–

Tomorrow's the big day! I'm so excited I can't sleep! At 7:05 A.M. I'll get on the bus for New York and my new life! A couple of friends threw me a going-away party the other night, and one of them even tried to talk me out of it. Even if I *was* having second doubts, there's no way I'd turn back now. I'm already committed. I've turned in my keys to my landlord and put my furniture and books in storage until I can send for them. New York, here I come!

June 18th, 199–

Sneaking a few paragraphs while I can. Boy, the bus sure is crowded! And smelly! And there are some real weirdos riding it, too! I had to change my seat because of some weird Pakistani guy trying to proposition me. He sat down and started talking to me after the bus left Nashville. He looked kind of harmless, at first, but after a few minutes he pointed at his lap and said "My balls are so full! Please help me!" That's when I moved. Looking forward to seeing Cynthia again, after all this time. She told me she'd be waiting for me at the bus station when I get there.

June 20th, 199–

I'm finally in New York. It took me three days to get here on the bus. When I got off the bus at Port Authority I was so tired it took me a couple of minutes to realize just how scummy it really was. It was three in the morning when my bus pulled into the station and the only thing open was this cheesy fast-food joint in the lower level that sold over-priced hot dogs that looked like they'd spent a few weeks riding the weenie carousel. I looked around, hoping to spot Cynthia, but all I saw were either other people waiting to get on the buses or street people types who'd snuck past the cops guarding the doors to the main entrance by entering the lower level through the bus ports.

I thought maybe Cynthia was on her way, so I sat down at the fast-food place with my bags to wait for her. After a half hour I got tired of waiting and went to find a pay phone. The phone rang several times before Cynthia picked up. She sounded like I'd woken her up. I told her I was at the bus station, waiting for her. She mumbled she was sorry and that she was on her way to pick me up. When I got back to where I'd left my bags, they were gone! All my clean clothes and extra shoes and things like my make-up and toothbrush and spare tampons—gone! All I had was the clothes on my back and my purse. Luckily, I still had all my money on me.

I asked the black girl behind the counter if she'd seen

someone take my suitcases. She looked at me like I was stupid and said; "Don't you know better than to walk off and leave your stuff by itself?"

Welcome to the Big Apple.

Cynthia finally showed up around six o'clock. I didn't recognize her at first. She was wearing too much makeup that she looked like she'd been sleeping in. She was also wearing a really *tight* mini-skirt and a blouse you could see right through. Her hair was frizzed out from a perm that didn't take and looked like it'd been dyed badly two or three times. She didn't look a thing like the young co-ed who'd planned on being a poet and an artist.

When I told her what had happened to my bags she shook her head and looked at me the same way the black girl had. "Jeannie, don't you know any better than to walk off and leave your stuff by itself? You're in New York now!"

I started to get mad, but made myself swallow it. Things were already bad, and I didn't want to make things worse by getting on the wrong side of Cynthia. After all, she *was* letting me crash at her place and had offered to help find me a job.

We left Port Authority and Cynthia waved down a cab. After a seven-dollar cab ride—which I paid for—we reached her place on the Lower East Side. When she first told me she lived in "the Village," I thought she meant Greenwich Village. You know, where the beatniks and hippies used to hang. But this is someplace called the East Village. Whatever that means.

Cynthia's apartment is in a big brick building on East Third Street, between Avenue A and Avenue B. Her place is on the ground floor. She calls it a "studio," but it's really an efficiency. The kitchen, bedroom, and living room are all the same room. There's a tiny bathroom with just enough space for a sink, a shower stall, and toilet. Cynthia sleeps on a loft platform that's four feet off the ground.

The apartment is dark and smells of old grease and dirty clothes. There are roaches everywhere, because of the pile of dishes in the sink and stacked on the kitchen table. I'm writing this while sitting on Cynthia's couch. At least there's that much. Cynthia took off her clothes and crawled back into bed the moment we came in the door. This was hardly what I was expecting.

Still, Cynthia assures me I shouldn't have any trouble landing a job. She's even promised to set me up with an interview. Better get some rest. It's been a long day (*and* night) and I need to look my best if I'm going to go job hunting.

June 22nd, 199–

Wow! Talk about easy! I'm not in New York forty-eight hours and I've already got a job! And one that pays! Cynthia took me to this place over on Lexington Avenue. They're hiring women to answer the phones for twelve dollars an hour! Turns out it's an escort agency. Cynthia introduced me to the woman who runs the business—Maddy—and she hired me right on the spot! All I have to do is answer the phone six to ten hours a day, check credit card numbers on the computer terminal, and relay messages for the girls who work out of the agency. At this rate I'll have enough money saved up to move into my own place within a month! I can hardly wait! Even though Cynthia's hardly ever home—and when she *does* come in, she's so wasted all she does is go right to sleep—this apartment is so damn depressing! You can't even look out the windows! Not that the neighborhood's anything to look at, mind you.

Building next door to this one is abandoned, the windows covered with sheets of plywood. Coke dealers sit on the steps leading to the sealed front door and sell little plastic zip-lock pouches to people in broad daylight. Most of the ones buying are middle-aged Hispanic guys, although I've seen a few young white guys and a couple of black women go up to the steps, too. Some of them are walking dogs or pushing baby strollers.

I still can't get over how blatant the drug dealing is around here. I mean, I'm not stupid or naive. I've used drugs before—but stuff like pot, acid, occasionally speed. Everyone here seems to be into the hard stuff—coke, crack, smack. There's no room for simple buzzes. These people would mainline rocket fuel, if it was at all possible.

July 6th, 199–

There sure are a lot of dogs in this area. Most of them big, brutish attack animals like Rottweilers, pit bulls, and Dobermans. There's also a lot of dog shit on the streets. At least I *assume* it's dog shit. Saw a homeless woman taking a crap between a couple of parked cars late last night. Apparently there's a law about curbing dogs, but when it comes to humans . . . Needless to say, what with all the dogs, homeless, and discarded syringes, I always look where I'm walking. Definitely not a place to walk around barefoot in.

August 1st, 199–

I'm finally out of Cynthia's reeking hell-hole of an apartment. Not that where I am is any better, really. But at least it's my own place. After working overtime answering the phone at the escort service for nearly six solid weeks, I finally had enough money to look for my own apartment.

The rents in the town—even the shittiest part of it—are unbelievable! I looked at places for rent in five different neighborhoods, all of them progressively scarier, until I found this place. It's on Avenue D between Sixth and Seventh. There are stripped and gutted cars decorating the curbs and the fire hydrant seems to always be open to full flood, and there are never less than three dozen half-naked Latino kids running around screaming at any given time of the day.

At night the streets are loud, since the drug-dealers cruise by extra-slow in their cars so they can serenade the neighborhood with the rap and Latino music pumping out of the suitcase-sized speakers in the trunks. Instead of crickets, if I listen late at night I can hear automatic gunfire and the sounds of people screaming and arguing in the near distance.

My building is very old. It was probably originally built in the 1890s. The apartments have been divided and redivided over the years, according to what the building inspectors would allow. My whole apartment is little over three hundred square feet. There is a tiny two-burner gas stove wedged in between a sink and a midget refrigerator in one corner that's supposed to be my kitchen. There is a rickety loft-bed with a mildewing double mattress atop it left over from the previous tenant. What I first thought was the first of two closets turned out to be the toilet. The bath-tub is a huge antique metal creature with lion's feet and a curved back lip. It's in plain sight in the kitchen area. Which is also the living area and the dining area and the sleeping area.

Since I don't have any furniture yet, the place looks kind of empty, although all I have to do is buy a Salvation Army couch and a table and a chair to make things crowded around here. Despite everything wrong with the building—the elevator's perpetually out of order, the mail-boxes get broken into every other night, and the halls reek of piss—it's rent-controlled at $450 a month. The horrible thing is, most people living in the city would *envy* me my rent! Funny how your priorities and standards change once you're in New York.

The big bummer, though, is the fact that while I've been living in the city for nearly two months, I still haven't found the time to check out the museums or even take in a film down at the Angelika. And, outside of Cynthia and Maddy, I don't really even know anybody. I've spent all my time working trying to get the money to set myself up to take the time to go hang out at a bar and check out the scene. Hopefully that'll change pretty soon. After all, what's the point of living in Manhattan if you don't avail yourself of the culture?

August 16th, 199–

Things went really bad today. So bad my brain's still not able to handle everything that went down.

I went into work today just like usual. During my lunch break, Maddy—the woman who runs the escort agency I answer the phone for—Lady Day & Night—came up to me and asked me if I liked my job. I said sure. Then Maddy asks me if I'd like to make more money. I said of course. Then she tells me that if I want to keep my job, I've got to start going on out-calls at least twice a week. I told her I had to think about it. She said I could think until tomorrow.

Man, what am I gonna do? They're telling me if I want to keep my job, I've got to be a hooker. I know *they* call it being an "escort," but it's *still* prostitution. Besides, most of the johns are Shriners and opticians from out of town, in the city for conventions. Men like my dad. Ick. I can't do that kind of stuff. Not for money. Not with strangers—certainly not the kind of strangers who'd use an escort service. Just thinking about it is enough to make me puke.

But what about my rent? And utilities? And the phone bill? Not to mention little things like eating and keeping shoes on my feet. Where's the money going to come from? I'm going to have a hard time finding a job that paid as good as that one. Still, I've got to stand strong. I can't buckle just because I got thrown a curve ball on this.

If I give in, I'll end up like Cynthia, turning tricks and blowing everything she makes on smack so she can live with what's she's become. It's really sad talking to her. It's like communing with a ghost. Every now and then I catch a glimmer of the girl who was going to take Manhattan's art circle by storm with her painting and her poetry, but most of the time she's either strung out or needing a fix. Maddy fired her from the escort service a month ago because of the tracks on her arms.

Cynthia wears long sleeves buttoned down to her wrists all the time now, no matter how hot it is. Last I heard, she was trolling for johns over on Allen Street, where the skankiest of the crack-whores hang out. I refuse to let the city get to me like that. I absolutely *refuse*.

August 23rd 199–
Another day of job-hunting. I feel like I'm taking huge chunks of time and tossing them down the toilet. Most of these jobs don't pay shit, and the ones that *do* pay shit have fifty other applicants waiting in line by the time I get there— and *I'm* there before dawn! Maybe I ought to just sit on my butt and collect unemployment and food stamps and spend the day hanging out on the front steps and watching broadcast TV like everyone else in this fucking neighborhood does.

This place is really scary. I mean, it's *always* been scary, but back when I was making money and thought it was only a matter of time before I could move into a better neighborhood, I ignored a lot of what goes down around here. But now that it looks like I'm stuck here—I've taken to sleeping with a butcher knife under my pillow. I also keep the cheap little black & white portable I bought off one of the street peddlers over on Second Avenue for ten bucks on all night so I can't hear the people next door fighting and fucking and abusing their children. Don't those people ever get tired? It's like living next door to a damn zoo!

August 25th, 199–

I remember how upset I used to get about the people who'd come up and buy drugs from the dealer next door to Cynthia's crib. At least they went somewhere else to do their shit up. In this neighborhood there's no such self-restraint. The junkies and crack-heads buy their poison down on the corner, then wander to the middle of the block to shoot up. Hell, they don't even have the decency to crouch in a doorway or something! It certainly takes the guesswork out of knowing who is or isn't doing crack. When you see a guy standing on the curb, lighting a Coca-Cola can, there's only one thing he could possibly be doing.

August 27th, 199–

Cynthia showed up yesterday looking for a place to stay the night. Seems like she's finally been evicted from her crib. Not surprising, considering she hadn't paid rent in five months. What could I say? She was my best friend in college. She let me crash at her place until I had my own apartment lined up. I couldn't just let her sleep on the sidewalk. Turned out to be a *big* mistake. When I got back from job-hunting today Cynthia was gone—and so was the last of the money I had stashed in the sugar bowl. Three hundred and fifty bucks. Gone. She's probably already nodding out on some corner over on Allen Street, trying to wave down some horny asshole from Jersey. Hope she gets a Rifkin, the skanky bitch.

August 29th, 199–

I hate this fucking neighborhood and all the stinking spic assholes in it! I hate their fucking stupid music and their fucking lousy food and the lousy *bodegas* that smell like someone's peed in them. They're sleazy, lazy, dirty, stupid, violent people. I was walking back from the subway after registering for food stamps. I left the house at seven in the morning and it was already getting dark by the time I got back to the neighborhood. It took all damn day just to do that! But at least I got a packet of food stamps to tide me over for the next week or two.

I was walking down Avenue D, near Third Street, when I saw this group of PR girls hanging at the corner, sitting on the hood of a parked car. There were four of them, wearing leather jackets and too much make-up and I could tell some of them had tattoos on the wrists. Gang girls.

As I got closer to them, one of them stepped out in front of me.

"Where choo goin', blondie?"

"I'm going home. That's all."

"Then how come we never seen you before?"

"I—I live down around Sixth—"

"This is *our* neighborhood, blondie. Choo don't belong here."

Before I could say anything else, the one in front of me grabbed me by the hair and punched me in the face while one of them circled behind me and made a grab for my purse. I guess it's a testimony to how much living in New York City has changed me that I not only didn't let go of my purse, that I also got away from them by ramming the leader in the gut with my head. But I'd be damned if a bunch of sleazy spic whores-in-training were going to take anything of mine.

They chased me for at least a block and a half, screaming "I'm gonna cut choo, blondie! Cut choo good!", but I was too fast for them. God damn spic bitches. The anger is finally starting to ebb away, and with it the adrenalin. My God, I could have been killed! And for what? A five-and-dime eel-skin shoulderbag and seventy-five dollars in food stamps. Shit. I guess this means I can't walk down Third Street ever again.

September 6th, 199–

Finally landed a job waiting tables at this trendy retro Seventies bistro in the West Village. I have to wear bell-bottom flares, stack heels, a Farrah Fawcett wig-hat, and a macramé midi-blouse, but at least I get off easier than the male wait-staff—they have to wear lime green polyester leisure-suits with fashionable clown-width ties. It's not enough to support me entirely, and I'll be damned if I'll take myself off the food stamp rolls. Is this what I spent four years in college to become? A waitress and welfare cheat?

September 10th, 199–

Took the bus home from work tonight. Saw a homeless crack-addict teetering around the bus shelter. I'd heard that crack makes their skin crawl and itch in such a way when they're fucked-up that all they can do is obsessively scratch and claw at their face and arms. What's it called? Tweaking. So I guess this homeless guy was tweaking. He was staring into the rear-view mirror of one of the parked cars, scraping away at his face with what looked like a pen knife. He'd spend several minutes like he was cleaning barnacles off the hull of a ship or something, then take a hit from this bent-up Coke can, rock back-and-forth on his heels for a few seconds, then go back to scraping away what was left of his face. Do-it-yourself leprosy.

September 12th, 199–

The homeless. God I'm so sick of them. I knew New York had a homeless problem, but I never realized just how bad it really was. Jesus, I can't go out on the streets without feeling like I'm walking through downtown Calcutta. They're everywhere! It's making me nuts. Every day I get hit up for spare change at least twelve times. Do I have a sign taped to my back that says "Hi my name's Jeannie! I have spare change!" or something?

I used to think they were people like me, only just down on their luck—and maybe some of them are. But most of the ones I see are either crazy or on drugs or just no-good bums. They stand there, shaking their fucking paper coffee cups like they're some kind of year-round Salvation Army Santa. Giving you dirty looks and calling you fat or ugly or a bitch if you don't give them a quarter. Like I could afford to even part with a lousy dime!

While I was coming home from work last night some homeless geek literally accosted me. I was on the corner of St. Mark's and Second Avenue, waiting for the light to change, when this piece of walking rubbish comes lurching up to me, waving one of those ubiquitous Greek coffee cups.

The geek was so filthy I couldn't tell what sex or race it was. I assume it was male. Maybe I'm wrong. The only thing I noticed was that his skin was gray and gritty—the color of pavement. He shook his cup at me and made some kind of plea for spare change—at least, that's what I *think* he was doing. Maybe he was reciting the Gettysburg Address. I really can't remember, since I was doing my best to ignore him.

When he realizes I'm not going to give him money to go away, he gets *really* belligerent and grabs my arm. I instinctively jerk away from his touch, losing my balance and falling off the curb and into the street, where I come close to getting smeared by a passing taxi. When I turn around, the homeless geek is gone. I managed to escape unscathed, except for where he grabbed me. My upper forearm, just above the elbow, is badly abraded—as if I'd somehow fallen down and scraped myself on the sidewalk. Hope I don't catch anything. A lot of these street people have TB.

September 28, 199–
Landed a second job, this one part-time. I work from two to seven in the morning three to five days a week as an assistant shipping clerk for a novelty company in Midtown. They repackage and distribute all kinds of cheap crap they buy from factories in Taiwan and Korea, most of it knock-off bootlegs of popular, copyrighted characters like the Simpsons, Teenage Mutant Ninja Turtles, and Batman. Lately I've been packing and shipping out lots of cheap purple plush dinosaurs stuffed with Styrofoam pellets. On top of my waitressing gig, I'm averaging sixty-seventy hour workweeks. I still don't have the time to go check out the museums, much less find a boyfriend. I'm still on food-stamps, too.

October 15th, 199–
Had a bad time on the subway. Not from getting mugged or having some perv try and rub up against me, though. This was weirder. I was coming back from my Midtown job, and I fell asleep on the F train. I was sitting down, staring at this homeless guy sprawled out on the seats opposite me, and the next thing I know, I'm nodding off. It was a really strange

feeling, because I *knew* I was no longer awake, but at the same time I could see everything in perfect clarity.

There were other people in the subway car. After all, it was after seven in the morning, the earliest tip of rush hour, and the train—while hardly crowded—was far from being deserted. There were spics, slopes, pakis, hebes, along with the ever-present homeboys. And the minute my head dropped to my chest, they put aside their newspapers and paperback novels and crossword puzzles and rose as one, shambling toward my sleeping figure like extras from a zombie movie.

I was terrified by the sight of their slack, alien features, revulsed by their oppressive stink, as they stood ringed about me, straining forward like beasts eager to be fed. I could feel their hungry stares carving me up, dividing my flesh into rump roast, head cheese, ham hocks . . .

Suddenly the crowd parts, shouldered aside by a homeless person with gray, scabby skin that resembles pavement. His eyes appear vacant, then I realize what I'm looking at are unwashed, empty windowpanes. The homeless person grins down at me, revealing a mouth full of bent and rusty syringes, and reaches out to touch me.

I awoke with a strangled gasp, only to find an elderly Ukrainian woman staring at me disapprovingly. I had missed my station and was halfway to Coney Island.

October 26th, 199–

Really tired. Didn't get much sleep last night. The city kept me awake until six in the morning, screaming and yowling and threatening itself. At one point the distant police and fire sirens, the car alarms, crying babies, screaming women, angry pimps, automatic weapon fire seems to meld together into a single voice. The voice of the city. And I could swear it was calling my name.

Jesus. I need some rest.

November 1st, 199–

Police showed up at my crib today. Cynthia's dead. They found her early this morning under the Williamsburg Bridge, where the coke-and-drug burn-outs blow Hasids for five bucks. I hadn't seen Cynthia in almost three months. Not since she stole the last of my savings. I guess she'd slid even farther, and faster, than even I suspected. I keep thinking I'm going to feel sad or something, but the best I can muster is a sigh of relief. I guess it's up to me to break the news to her parents. What should I say? What *can* I say?

> Dear Mr. & Mrs. Brinkes,
>   Your daughter, Cynthia, came to New York City to become a poet and artist but ended up a prostitute and a drug addict. By the time her body finally died she had turned into someone none of her friends recognized or liked. The city ate her hair, guts, and all. Hope you are both doing well.
>
>   Best Wishes,
>   Jeannie Singleton
> P.S. You owe me three hundred and fifty smackers that your skanky junkie whore bitch of a daughter ripped off from me.

November 12th, 199–

It's getting colder and the drug-dealing, brawling, and pimping has moved from the street into the surrounding buildings. I can't walk up to my crib without having to step over passed-out drunks, junkies shooting up, or whores blowing johns. The steam radiator is always on, turning my shoebox of a room into a sweltering hothouse. I have to keep the windows open to keep from suffocating. As it is, the radiator leaks, steaming the wallpaper off the surrounding walls and loosing the plaster on the ceiling. I expect to wake up one day and find the whole roof collapsed on top of me. Assuming that I wake up.

November 23rd, 199–

I have to write this down. Right now. While it's still fresh. The police are going to want to know. I keep telling myself that I have to remember everything. Just as it was. So they'll believe me. They *have* to believe me.

I was coming home from my waitress job. I didn't have to go to my second job tonight. That's not until the weekend. I was coming down Fourth Street, in between B and C. There wasn't hardly anyone on the street, because it was cold. Not so cold that you would freeze—but cold enough you didn't want to be hanging out if you had somewhere warmer and dryer. I hear what sounds like a bottle breaking behind me, and I turn and look . . .

There were at least four or five of them, clumped together. At first I thought they were a collection of trash bags left out on the curb. Then one of them begins to move. He lifts his head and turns his face towards me and motions with an arm, as if he wants me to help him get to his feet. It's late at night and the light isn't very good, but I can tell his face is gray. The homeless geek opens his mouth and this sound like a car alarm comes out. He grins then, displaying teeth that aren't teeth but broken, rusty syringes.

I take a step backward, too scared to scream or cry or even run. All I can do is stare at this thing's face as it and its friends get to their feet. One of them keeps swinging its head back and forth, the way disturbed children do, and I catch a glimpse of gray skin and dirty, cracked windowpanes where its eyes should be. It produces a forty-ounce malt liquor bottle from its rags and hiccups like an ambulance's siren when it's trying to clear a jammed intersection.

One of them has its pants open. It strokes its exposed penis, which is gray and gleams like wet pavement. The sound it makes as it masturbates is like sandpaper on concrete. It leers at me, drool spilling over its blackened, festering gums.

That's when I ran. I could hear them as they came after me, their voices raised in a cacophony of whooping sirens, booming hip-hop, screaming babies, automatic gunfire, and shrill car alarms. I was so frightened my ribcage felt as if it was going to burst and my heart and lungs spill out onto the street.

I probably would have made it home free if I hadn't slipped in some shit in between parked cars and fallen. I landed hard enough to chip one of my teeth and bite my lower lip hard enough for it to bleed. I was dazed for a second—then one of them grabbed my ankle and began pulling me towards him. It felt like he was wearing a sandpaper glove.

I began to kick and struggle. I glimpsed someone walking on the other side of the avenue and I screamed for him to help me. He paused for a second then turned and hurried away. I screamed even louder, trying to buck my way free of the things surrounding me.

My attackers closed in around me, their gray, stony faces blocking out what little light came from the nearby streetlight. I could feel something like a poured concrete rod pushing itself between my thighs. I shrieked as it penetrated, tearing and shredding delicate tissue into bloody mulch. It felt as if someone had impaled me on a blunt stake, leaving me to bleed to death from my cunt. I screamed one final time before blacking out, joining a thousand other distress calls I'd heard every night and ignored.

I woke up I don't know when—maybe an hour later. I was sprawled across the steps of my building. To my amazement, I discovered that I was still wearing my clothes and the contents of my purse remained untouched. Nor was I bleeding from my vagina. The avenue was empty and I was alone.

I'm going to call the cops in the morning and report a rape. Even though there's no physical or medical evidence anything happened to me. Even though they'll end up thinking I'm some kind of lunatic or drug addict.

It happened. I know it did. What happened may have been a nightmare, but it wasn't a dream.

Write it all down. I have to write it all down before I fall asleep. Or else I'll forget things. Forget details. I can't risk anyone thinking this is a hoax. I have to convince the police that this *really* happened. That it wasn't some kind of hallucination.

I'm so tired. Sleep. I need sleep. The city's been calling my name every time I try to sleep. And I'm so tired. So very tired. I have to get out of this place. Out of this hell. I need to go home. I have to escape before I'm devoured, soul and all, just like Cynthia. I have to get away. The city knows my name.

And it knows where I live.

December 1st, 199–

I woke up today after sleeping over a week. I feel wonderfully refreshed and not in the least weakened. I'm not too sure what my dreams were about, except I'm certain I dreamt of the city.

As I thumb through this diary it is all I can do not to toss it down the incinerator. To think I even contemplated leaving the city! When I stand at my window and look out upon the city, I am awash with the joy and security that comes with knowing that I have a place in the scheme of things. That I have taken the worst and survived—the city has scourged me and, finding me worthy of its cruel affection, made me its bride.

In the dim light of the coming dawn I stroke my new skin, the one that grew while I lay sleeping. It is rough and dry and the color of pavement. I stand before my mirror and smile, my mouth full of broken needles. I think back on my previous fear of my environment and I laugh at my foolishness, and my laugh is the bark of a 9mm handgun. I shake out my hair, which shines and rustles like strips of plastic garbage bags.

Cynthia did it all wrong. She succumbed to the city's mad passions without allowing it to transform her. And for the city there can be only lovers or meat. Cynthia failed the courtship dance and found herself on the low end of the food chain.

Soon I will leave this place to go and join my lover, to wander his graffiti-smeared heart day and night. Jeannie Singleton is dead, tossed aside with the husk of dead skin that served as my chrysalis. From now on I shall go by another name. My *true* name.

Call me Avenue X.

Perfect Witness

Rick Hautala

> . . . see, see! dead Henry's wounds
> Open their congealed mouths and bleed afresh.
> *Richard III*, I. ii. 55–56.

I'm confused, really confused.

I can see bright lights all around me.

Too bright.

I know there are people nearby, too. Sometimes it sounds as though there's a whole crowd, milling around somewhere in the outer darkness behind the blinding lights. A faceless, nameless mass of people, like an audience, unseen, but their presence is sensed behind the glare of stage lights.

At other times, or maybe at the same time, I can tell there are a few of them—maybe three or four—right up close to me.

I think they're doing things to me.

I don't know where I am or what's happening to me.

Can anyone tell me?

I try to move my arms and head, but my whole body feels like it's a wet lump of senseless clay. There's no sensation in my legs. Absolutely none at all. Not even the sensation of pain.

Nothing.

It's almost like my body doesn't even exist.

What the hell's happening to me?
I don't remember a thing, not since . . .
When was it?
Earlier tonight?

Yes, I remember . . . I was walking back from the Mad
Horse Theater to my apartment on Irving Street, in Cam-
bridge, when a man—hell, no! He wasn't a man; he was a
young boy—a kid, for Christ's sake, stopped me and demanded that I give him my wallet. At first I started to reach
for it, but then in an instant I decided not to. I think I might
have tried to fight with him, to wrestle the gun out of his
hand.
Was that what happened?

*"We have to administer the rest of the drug very slowly.
I have no idea if he will experience any pain, but I don't
want to risk losing him again."*

Hey, who said that? Who's there?
It sounds like a woman's voice, but no one answers me.
Did I speak out loud?
Probably not.
I strain to open my eyes but have the dull sensation that
they're already wide open. I keep trying to see better, but
the light gets steadily brighter, almost stinging. My eyes don't
seem to be able to adjust to it, but at least there's a slight
tingle of pain.
Thank God!
If there wasn't any pain, then I might think I was paralyzed
or . . . or dead.
At least I know that I'm *alive*.

Just barely.

I think it's almost funny how those gray shapes keep drift-
ing around in front of me like . . . like there's a group of
people, milling around me.
I wish I knew where I am.

I wish I knew what's happening, but my body still feels totally numb.

"Mr. Thurmond, I hope you keep that video cam running. If this works at all, I don't want to miss a single second of it."

Miss any of *what*?
Who said that?
Where the hell are you?

In the distance, I can hear other voices, buzzing around me like the droning hum of a bee hive. I can't make out anything anyone is saying. It still reminds me of the indistinct chatter of a crowd, talking softly in the dark in expectation of a show which is about to begin.

Come on!
Somebody!
Please!
Talk to me!
Why won't anyone tell me what the hell's going on?
Why can't I see you?

I can't feel anything, but I am positive, now, that they are doing something to me.
What the fuck are you doing to me?
Oh, shit!
Wait a second.
I think I know what's happening. I remember, now. I *did* try to fight with that kid, and I think he might have—Shit, yes, that's it!
I've been shot!
I'm dying!
Oh, God, I'm afraid that might be what's happening!
I remember, now, he was holding a gun, pointing it straight at me. He was standing too close, and I made a grab for his wrist, hoping to push the gun away, but then there was an explosion of light.
Funny, but I don't remember hearing anything. There was

no loud blast. Just a burst of intense white light, and then
. . . then . . .

Nothing.

So that's it.
I've been shot!
I must still be lying on the sidewalk where I fell. Am I
bleeding to death? Why can't I feel anything? Even that
whisper of pain is gone now. These people must be paramed-
ics from the rescue unit or something; and the others must
be the crowd that's gathered to watch.
To watch me die!
Shit, that's it!
I'm dying, and they're trying to save my life.
Oh, *Jesus*! Oh, *shit*!
I'm scared!

*"You have to remember, your honor, that this is the first
time we've attempted to do something like this. We have to
proceed with caution."*

A woman's voice.
Why did she say, "your honor?"
What the hell is she talking about? Is she a doctor or
something? And who's she calling "your honor?"

Hey, wait a second.
I think she—or someone—is maybe doing something to
me. For a moment, there, I could almost feel my body again
. . . at least a little bit. There's something hard underneath
me. Is it concrete? Am I still lying on the sidewalk? It sort
of feels that way, but it feels as though my knees are bent.
Is this the way I hit the ground after I got shot?

*"Given these rather unusual circumstances, do you gentle-
men agree that we can dispense with the usual formality of
swearing in."*

* * *

Swearing in?

What the fuck are they talking about?

Jesus Christ, stop talking nonsense and do something to save my fucking life!

Even as I think this, I can feel a warm current of sensation returning to my body. The heavy, lumpish feeling in my chest is starting to loosen up, and I think—yes! I can even feel the dull throb of pins-'n'-needles spreading slowly into my arms and legs. The center of my chest feels like it's on fire.

I can't tell if I'm turning my head or shifting my eyes, but when I look around, the light is more diffused. The figures leaning over me—I think I can count three of them—are still indistinct. They're surrounded by these weird halos of light that ripple with deep blues and purples like I've never seen before!

It's beautiful, but I'm still scared.

Really *scared*!

"I object, your honor. I think this entire experiment is nothing more than a . . . a charade . . . a mockery of justice. I respectfully ask that we sequester the jury so they won't have to observe this . . . this macabre spectacle."

I wish I knew what this person is talking about, but I'm so swept up by the gushing, almost burning sensation of feeling as it rushes through my body that I can't concentrate on what anyone is saying. I imagine my body is an ice-bound river, and warm spring winds and the steady tug of strong, flowing water underneath the ice are—finally—breaking apart the hammer-lock grip of the frozen surface. I'm dizzy with a heady rush of euphoria as my vision clears even more. I can see that I am not lying in the street, bleeding to death.

I'm in a room.

I'm sitting up in a chair.

My hands are clamped to the chair arms in a vise-like grip. I know, even if I wanted to, I wouldn't be able to move them. Across my chest, I can feel the tight pull of a restraint. I know that it, not my own strength, is what's keeping me sitting erect in the chair. When I try to open my mouth and run my tongue over my lips, there is almost no feeling, as though my whole face has been injected with Novacaine.

"Objection overruled, Mr. Applegate. While I grant you that this is a . . . a most unique situation, I'll reserve judgment as to whether or not the evidence we receive is or is not admissible."

As my vision continues to resolve more clearly, I try to look around. Off to one side, I see the source of light—a high bank of windows, through which bars of iridescent blue light are streaming. The light shimmers in slow, sinuous waves that maddeningly flicker through the colors of the spectrum. Everything appears to be watery and insubstantial. Halos of light surround everything.

Arrayed against this wall, below the windows, are numerous dark shapes . . . People, I realize. They seem frozen in place, as immobile as mannequins.

I try to blink, and it seems to take forever for the rough, sandpaper feeling to scrape across my eyeballs. I jump with a start when I rotate my head slowly to my left and see the dim silhouette of someone standing close to me. The nimbus of light surrounding him—at least now I can see that this is a man—masks his features as he leans close to me. I get a faint whiff of something stale, almost rotten, and that makes my stomach growl.

"Can you hear me, Mr. Sinclair?"

I want to answer him, but when I try to clear my throat and take a deep breath, I have no sensation whatsoever of breathing. My chest feels like it's encased in iron bands. I lean forward, and the restraint presses into my chest, but, surprisingly, there is no pain. The indistinct features of the man's face loom closer to me. I see a terrifying, cartoon face—a wide, smiling mouth frozen in the center of a round, white balloon, and two dark, dimensionless balls that must be his eyes. When he speaks to me again, repeating his question, his lips move in flabby, rubbery twitches that seem to be not at all in synch with his words.

"Do you understand what I'm saying to you, Mr. Sinclair?"

Again, I try to speak, but the best I can manage is a slight nod of my head. I'm not really sure if I've moved at all. There is no pain, but I have the sense that the bones in my neck are dry and splintering. If I move even the least little bit too fast, I fear my spine will snap in two like a piece of rotten wood. I try to focus on this man's face and am surprised to notice that I no longer feel the need to blink my eyes. It doesn't matter, because I can't even move them. The lids are frozen wide open. I stare blankly forward, hoping my vision will resolve so I can turn my head and see who this is talking to me.

"Can you see my hand?"

Something that looks like a huge, black crow flying across a stormy sky flashes in front of my face. It goes by so fast I can't possibly turn my head fast enough to track it.

"I would ask, Mr. Charles, that you not push him quite so hard."

This is the woman's voice again, speaking from somewhere off to my right. She's trying to sound like she's in control, but I detect a near frantic edge of worry in her voice. When I try to turn my head to look at her, the total lack of sensation makes it feel as though my eyeballs are detached and rolling around inside my head, completely out of control.

"I understand, Dr. Murphy, but you indicated that we might not have very much time when he is even semi-conscious. I repeat, Mr. Sinclair, can you see how many fingers I'm holding up in front of you?"

* * *

Again, the black crow flaps across my vision.

This time I see two blurry lines, like fence posts, pointing straight up.

Two, I think, but there is no way I can even begin to say the word. As much as I strain to speak, I can't feel the vocal cords in my throat. They might as well be cut. I feel like I'm a disembodied entity, floating in a hazy, gray soup of vague lights, shadows, and sounds.

"I could administer a small amount more, your honor, but in my opinion, we've already pushed this to a dangerous level."

"I respectfully submit that this is an complete waste of the court's valuable time, your honor. My client and I request that you strike all references to this shameful . . . incident from the record, and that we proceed in a customary manner."

"Again, Mr. Applegate, your objection is noted and over-ruled. Please proceed with your line of questioning, Mr. Charles."

While this exchange is going on, I am only half listening to it because I am trying so hard to make my throat work, but it's like trying to flex the muscles of an arm that has been amputated.

There's nothing there—not even the lack of sensation.

After a few moments of struggle, I feel another, stronger gush of warmth that's centered in my chest. The heat radiates outward, like a faintly glowing coal being fanned by a gentle breath. My throat tenses. The tendons and muscles are as stiff as bars of iron. I can feel a faint thrumming that brings with it an agonizing jolt of pain.

". . . two . . ."

In an almost dizzying rush, my vision resolves more clearly, and I see where I am.

To my right is a tall, oak-paneled desk, behind which, high above me, sits a man dressed in a dark robe. The few wisps of gray hair he has are combed straight back on his wide forehead. His face looks pale and is criss-crossed by thin, red lines of exploded capillaries, particularly on his nose.

Beside me, to my left, is a man wearing a fancy three-piece suit of dark blue. His necktie is a design of squares with dark circles in the center that looks amazingly three-dimensional. He is leaning forward with both hands on the arm of the chair in which I sit.

In front of me, a little to my right, stands a rather attractive, dark-haired woman. She is dressed in what looks like a white laboratory smock that swells out due to her ample breasts. She has a syringe in one hand, and I can see that a needle and the plastic tube of an IV feed have been taped to my exposed forearm, which is strapped to the arm of the chair.

Perhaps the most shocking thing I notice is the color of my own skin. It is a pasty white, almost gray. It looks exactly like the immobile clay I imagine it is.

"Very good, Mr. Sinclair. That is correct," the man in the three-piece suit says, smiling broadly as he leans closer to me. "I'm holding up two fingers."

His features don't look quite so cartoonish, but they are still horrifyingly animated as the smile spreads across his wide face. His teeth looked as big and flat as dinner plates, and for an instant I am consumed by the fear that he is about to bite me.

"I know it must be difficult for you to speak, Mr. Sinclair," he says, "but if you please, can you indicate with either a sound or a motion of your hand that you understand what I'm saying?" He glances over his shoulder. "Is this acceptable to you, your honor?"

As I stare at him, the halo of light that surrounds his head gradually blends from vibrant blues and purples to deep, fiery reds and oranges that shift across his features like flickering flames. Unaccountably, I feel the cold, hollow stirrings of hunger.

Yes, hunger!

* * *

"My name is Raymond Charles, Mr. Sinclair. I'm the lawyer, representing you in this case."

I want to ask him exactly what case that is, but I'm fairly certain it has something to do with the night I was mugged and tried to fight back. I realize that I must have been wounded, and I wonder if I have been in a coma all this time and am just now coming out of it.

"You may remember that, on the seventeenth of December, you were accosted on your way home from work by a young man. Do you recall that incident?"

". . . yes . . ."

It takes every bit of effort I can muster to say that single word, which reverberates like the heavy clang of metal in my ears.

"Mr. Sinclair, I am informed that we don't have much time, so I must get directly to the point. I have to ask you, do you think you would recognize your assailant if he were to be presented to you?"

I turn away from Mr. Charles, sensing that the painful stirrings of hunger inside me are only intensified whenever I look at the glowing curtains of red light that surround his face. The fleshy folds of his skin fairly vibrate with energy and life. I try to concentrate on remembering exactly what happened that night—when?

How long ago?

I have no way of knowing.

It could have been days or weeks ago, or it could have been months.

The image of the young man's features swirls into my memory like a face seen, looking up at me from underwater.

Dark hair, shifting in heavy, oily curls swirls around his face. Eyes, dark and liquid, slide nervously back and forth. Thin, tight, almost bloodless lips are pursed, and the pale skin is marked by the faint wisp of a mustache. His skin is greasy-looking and pimply, but it is what I see *inside* those eyes that I remember most clearly.

Fear . . .

Fear and silent desperation.

". . . yes . . ."

Even as I say the word, I see this boy's face materialize like a mirage in front of me. It, too, is surrounded by a sparkling sheet of red light, and the gnawing hunger that is churning inside me intensifies until it becomes excruciatingly painful.

This hunger is the only pain I know now.

The woman, apparently a doctor or nurse, says something to the man who has identified himself as my lawyer, but her words are lost to me as I stare again into that boy's dark, desperate eyes.

"Is this the man who attacked you, Mr. Sinclair?"

I hear the words, but they mean almost nothing to me. The hunger that is growling like a beast inside me is getting more demanding. I am distantly aware that my mouth has dropped open, and my teeth are grinding back and forth as I strain forward, but the strap across my chest holds me back. I try to raise my arms, but they, too, are firmly held in place by my restraints.

". . . yes . . ."

"I object!" a voice suddenly yells, sounding in my ears like a rolling peal of thunder.

"Overruled."

"I ask you again, Mr. Sinclair, and if you can, I would like you to speak a bit louder for the sake of the jury. Mr. Sinclair, is this man standing in front of you the man who accosted you on the night of December seventeenth and, at gun point, demanded that you give him your wallet?"

". . . yes . . ."

* * *

"If it please the court, I would like it noted for the record that Mr. Sinclair has identified the defendant, Mr. Roy Peterson."

"So noted."

"Objection, we haven't established the credibility of this witness."

"Overruled. Who better to identify his assailant, Mr. Applegate, than the victim himself?"

"Your honor, I'm afraid we're losing him."

When the woman speaks this time, even through the boiling pain of my overwhelming hunger, I recognize the near-panic in her voice. All around me, there are explosions of shadow and light, blending and swirling in an insane riot of color and sound. I am dazzled, confused, and the only clear thought I carry through this confusion is that I am hungry . . .

Hungry!

"Your honor, I realize that this is a rather unusual request, but I would beg the court's indulgence to allow me to ask if Mr. Peterson will please step forward and touch Mr. Sinclair on the hand."

"I object! This has gone on long enough. It's well past the point of morbid curiosity."

"May the court ask, Mr. Charles, exactly why you are making such an unusual request?"

"I beg your indulgence, your honor, but it is an ancient tradition that, if a corpse is touched by the murderer, the wounds which were inflicted by that individual will begin to bleed again, thereby identifying the murderer."

A corpse!
What the hell is he talking about?
I'm not a corpse!

Voices explode around me, but I am so consumed by hunger and the numbing fear that embraces me that I don't understand a single word. Stark terror squeezes me with a mounting pressure that soon becomes intolerable.

* * *

"I object! This is patently absurd! Why, this is a . . . this is medieval superstition we're talking about, not modern jurisprudence. Your honor, I would like to request that these entire proceedings be declared a mistrial, and that the—"

"Please calm yourself, Mr. Applegate. In light of this rather unusual situation, which is certainly something *I've* never experienced before, please instruct your client to do as Mr. Charles has requested."

"I will not!"

"You will, or I'll find you in contempt of court."

Every fiber of my being is charged with tingling jolts of electricity. The raging urge to eat . . . to kill . . . to rip into the throbbing, living flesh so close to me is absolutely overpowering, filling me with a spiralling insanity. I feel myself thrashing wildly against the restraints. My head begins to reverberate with a loud, crashing sound that I soon realize is my teeth, gnashing together. Hot, sour saliva floods my mouth and the back of my throat, and then—through it all— I feel something else.

A touch . . . like a pin prick . . .

On the back of my hand.

It sizzles and crackles, but for only an instant; then dark, rolling clouds churning with thick clots of ropey gray and black descend across my vision. All colors fade, and once again I am clutched by the sensation of being frozen into immobility. My muscles go rigid. My bones feel like iron spikes.

I can *feel* the touch on the back of my hand for less than a second, and then the dull leadenness seeps like poison throughout my body.

"Oh, my God! Look!" a voice suddenly cries out. "He . . . he's bleeding!"

I am so lost in my own internal agony that I can't distinguish whose voice it is.

I no longer care.

It sounds so impossibly far away I would cry . . . if I could.

"It's true! The chest wound is bleeding again!"
"But that's impossible," I hear someone say. It might be the judge or it might be the man who claims to be my lawyer.
"A corpse can't bleed!"

I am past caring as darkening waves engulf me, pulling me under with powerful surges. All of my senses are dimming. The last thing I hear before everything resolves into pitch black again is a faint, echoing voice.

"That will be all for now. Thank you, Dr. Murphy. You may return Mr. Sinclair's body to the morgue now."

Pyre

Th. Metzger

Quinn sat up in bed, gasping. 3:30, by the throbbing orange numbers. Dark and silent. The whole world was asleep and Quinn had never felt more awake.

"It's happening again. I can feel it."

Melanie stirred beside him. "Go back to sleep. It's nothing."

"No! I can feel it. I'm on fire."

He touched Melanie's shoulder—cold, so cold. "Go back to sleep," she groaned, rolling away from him. "It's just the flu. Take some aspirin."

"This time it's real. I can feel it." He sat helplessly on the side of the bed, sure that at any moment he'd burst into flame. No thermometer was needed; the mercury would shoot out the top like a liquid bullet.

"Go back to sleep." She sounded so far away. "Don't think about it." Which was like telling him not to breathe.

He felt his way to the bathroom, closed the door, and turned on the light. Melanie was probably back asleep already. She didn't believe him, just as she hadn't believed him the last time and the time before.

He splashed water on his face, expecting to see steam shroud the mirror. Nothing. Just his bleary face staring back. He studied the eyes, the mouth, the flushed skin, as though trying to see through a mask.

He got in the shower and let the cool water run over him.

Eventually the feeling grew weak. Once more, he'd sent it back wherever it came from. But he didn't know how many more times he had until nothing would work.

He toweled himself off and slid back into the bed naked. Melanie was still on her side, facing away from him. He stared at the curve under the sheet, the blond halo of her hair, until the first sign of dawn shone in the window.

When he woke, the house was empty. As usual, Melanie had slipped out of bed, dressed and escaped from the house without waking him.

He took his time getting to work. He was late, very late, but no one seemed to notice.

He stared at his screen and saw only a chaos of tiny stars, no pattern, no meaning. He tried to concentrate but could barely make his fingers move.

It wasn't just the fever. The new woman—Jeanette—was there. He sensed her presence in the next cubicle. He heard her fingers tapping her keys, the occasional soft groan when she made a mistake.

Quinn logged into the immediate mode of the company's E-mail system and sent Jeanette a message. "How's it going? Are you sorry you transferred yet?"

Her answer came back quickly. "No. But maybe Waterson will regret it." He pictured her smiling.

It seemed ridiculous to be communicating through their machines when he could just as easily walk around the divider and speak. But it was safer to keep it on this level. Let her stay hidden, one more disembodied presence in the system. He found it difficult to reconcile the two forms she took: the string of syllables, commands, architectural data that appeared occasionally on his screen and the woman of real flesh.

He inhaled deeply, trying to calm himself. He went through one of the breathing excercises he'd gotten from his doctor. But with each repetition, he got another whiff of Jeanette. Not perfume. Something more basic, some nameless scent exuded by her flesh. She'd only been in the department a few days and already the climate there had been completely transformed.

"How about lunch?" Quinn keyed in.

"Maybe tomorrow. Got to get these variances cleared."

"Okay. Tomorrow."

His screen buzzed and hissed at him. None of the colors had names, as though the fever had given him the power to see above and below the visible spectrum. He wondered if this was what he looked like inside—a seething stew of heat and light.

He went patiently through the magazines. 1967, 1966, 1965. Old *Life*s and *Look*s. They reeked of mildew. A patina of blackish grime coated his fingers. He might have been eight years old again, squatting in his parents' basement.

Finally he found the picture he was looking for. Three Buddhist monks sitting cross-legged on a sidewalk, engulfed in fire. Their faces grinned through the billowing flame, like skulls seen through diaphanous veils. The men looked so happy, utterly consumed, set free. The flames and their robes were indistinguishable. Their pain and their ecstasy too.

Melanie came home well after seven and found Quinn poring over the magazines.

"You see what I mean?" he said, as his wife kicked off her shoes and began rummaging in the cupboards. "It's happened before."

She ignored him.

"I'm talking to you, Melanie."

She gave a quick glance at the photo. "Come on, Quinn, you know they did that to themselves. They poured gas on themselves and lit it. It was a protest or something."

"I could blow up right here in front of you and you still wouldn't believe it."

"It's not a matter of believing. Look, it says right here." She pointed to the caption. " 'Self-immolation.' It was a protest. A religious thing."

"I know. But every night, when I get in bed, I feel it getting closer. I'm going to go up, Melanie. Just like these guys. Up in flames." He tapped the picture. "Last night was close. I could smell the smoke. My hands were shimmering, you know, like pavement on a really hot day. My blood was starting to boil. I mean really boil. It was turning to vapor in my veins."

"You had night sweats, Quinn. It's the flu. Everybody's got it these days. Half the people in my office were out today, or dragging around like zombies." She paused. "Didn't you get my message?"

The light on the answering machine winked at him.

"I had to put in a couple of extra hours to cover for Ralph," Melanie said. "If you're sick, why don't you go to bed early? You need some sleep. I'll be in later. I've got a ton of work to catch up on."

"I'm not a baby. I know when I need sleep."

"All right, fine. Sit here and stare at these stupid magazines. But you're not going to catch on fire. It just doesn't happen. It's impossible."

"What about those Vietnamese monks?"

"Jesus Christ! You're not listening to me. They poured gas on themselves and lit a match. That's the only way you're going to catch fire."

"Feel my forehead."

"You may say you're no baby, but you certainly are acting like one." She grabbed a carton of ice cream and fled down the hall to her office.

Quinn went to the kitchen sink and wet the dish rag. He held it to his face, picturing the image of his features—eyes, nose, mouth—seared into the cloth.

He dropped it and looked out the window. It was dark outside. He saw himself running down the empty street, like a ghost of flame. Orange, red, yellow, and all the nameless shades in between. Racing through the night air.

He went to Melanie's office and tapped on the door.

"What?"

"We've got to talk."

"Look, I've got a mountain of work here and I—"

"I've got something I need to tell you." He looked at his wife and his vision blurred. He was close, getting closer. His joints ached. His mouth tasted of ash and sulfur.

"This has been a bitch of a day, Quinn. I have a splitting headache, Olsten wants the whole casebook on his desk tomorrow and I've had about all I can take of your idiotic spontaneous human combustion bullshit."

He put his hand on her shoulder. She shrugged it off as if

it were toxic. Her look was unbearable. The contempt was familiar, but there was something else. Guilt? Pity? She couldn't even look him in the eye. He put his hand on the side of her neck. He brought his lips close to kiss her forehead. She'd always liked that.

"Please, Quinn, I need some time by myself." She squirmed out of his grasp.

He turned and fled. Down the hall, to the bedroom, to the corner where his machine was set up on a card table. He made sure the phone was hooked in properly, logged on, then paused, muttering, "It's okay, it's okay." He breathed evenly to calm himself, in and out, in and out, and he was back twenty years, squatting before a campfire, blowing a bed of coals to life.

He looked at the screen to see what he'd written. "I need to talk to you. You name the place, the time. Whatever you want. It's important." With the touch of one key the message would be gone. With another it would be instantly in Jeanette's E-mail box waiting for her. He stared at the message a long time, knowing there'd be no turning back once it was sent.

He thought of the monks sitting in the pools of gasoline, waiting for the match to ignite.

He hit the send key. With one simple motion, one finger moving half an inch, the flame and the pain were transformed. He was one of the monks now. He'd decided.

Quinn met Nick Platt on his way to the men's room. The two men had worked together until a recent company reorganization. Quinn had even invited Nick over a few times for supper, but that ended when Melanie said she felt uncomfortable with him in the house.

As usual, the first thing out of Nick's mouth was about women. "What's her name?"

"Who?"

"You can't keep her all to yourself, Quinn. I saw her the other day. Short black hair, nice ass. Sound familiar?"

"Come on, Nick, I don't—"

"What's her name?"

Quinn sighed. "Jeanette."

"She's new here?"

"No, just transferred from legal. We needed somebody to cover the variances. You know, the codes get harder to understand every year. Waterson thought we should have her in the department."

"So what's she like?"

"I hardly know her. I haven't said five words to her since she came on."

"Introduce me."

"I said I hardly know her."

"You just want to keep her for yourself." Nick gave Quinn one of his ridiculous smirks.

"What's the matter?" Quinn said. "You've already gone through every woman in your own department? Why don't you start over at the beginning again? Just leave Jeanette alone, all right?"

"Geez, Quinn, you sound mighty protective. Did you stake your claim already?"

Quinn turned. "I gotta get going. I've got a lunch thing in—"

"With her, right?" Before Quinn could deny it, Nick was grinning like a jack-o-lantern. "With her! Invite me, let me come along."

"No. It's just a—"

"It is, it is her! Jesus, you're blushing like a house on fire."

At one point, Nick had kept a chart in his desk: all the women at the office that he'd gone after, all that were still possibilities, all that were, as he called them, "direct hits." Quinn didn't want Jeanette's name on that chart. "I really gotta go. See you around." Quinn hurried down the hall. Luckily, thankfully, Nick didn't pursue him.

Quinn paused at the door to his department, trying to calm his breathing.

He went in and Jeanette smiled, seeing him. "I'd just about given up on you. I thought you'd stood me up."

Her face was open; there was nothing veiled or secret in her eyes. He'd spoken with her a few times at meetings. He'd watched her come and go. But until that moment, she'd been pure fantasy, an alternative to the pain he felt whenever he was in Melanie's presence. He helped Jeanette on with her jacket. He caught a whiff of her scent, he felt a trace of her body warmth. She was real now.

They went down to his car.

The first half an hour or so was a haze of small talk: where they'd worked before, gripes about the management. But this soon petered out. They hinted and feinted, trying to figure out what was really going on between them. Quinn made no mention of his wife, and Jeanette let drop that she was divorced. No kids. Apparently no current boyfriend.

Quinn felt the spark, and he thought she felt it too. Perhaps it was mere biology, lunar cycles, pheromones. Or perhaps it was just dumb luck. She fit the woman-shaped void he felt and it seemed he served a similar purpose for her. It had been a long time since he'd felt this way. The old momentum built, the sensation that he was on a sloping plane, the angle growing steeper with each moment he lingered near her. First the small talk, then eye contact and a casual brushing of his leg against hers. Getting no sign of resistance, he upped the stakes. He took her hand in his, to supposedly admire the garnet ring she had on.

Even this he took as encouragement. She wore the fire-red stone just for him, a sign that she'd understand anything he told her.

It was all moving too quickly for him. He was falling so fast he could hardly breathe.

"I want to show you something," he said, pulling the quarter-folded picture from his pocket. This was the real test. If she shrunk back, stared at him blankly, then he'd know there was no point in pursuing this any further.

He brushed crumbs off the table and flattened the picture out. Three monks wrapped in robes of gorgeous flame. "It's called spontaneous human combustion."

He waited. He tried to see through her eyes. She didn't shrink away. There was no sign of repulsion.

"When I was a kid, I saw this picture. It made a big impression on me. I couldn't get it out of my head for months. And just a few days ago, I stumbled on it again. I was cleaning out my parents' basement—they're moving to a smaller place—and I found it." There, it was all out. He'd opened himself up, shown her the truth. Now it was her turn. She could squirm and make excuses about getting back to the office. She could laugh and tell him he was a fool. Or she could—as she did—sit quietly, staring at the picture, winding her napkin in a knot, as though the image had as much power over her as it did over him.

She said nothing. She didn't argue with him. She didn't tell him that this was all kid stuff, no different than Big Foot or fish falling from the sky. No, she sat and listened as he explained it to her. All the way back to the office, she was silent, consumed by the beautiful, awful picture.

And her face wouldn't leave him. It hung like a beckoning spirit the entire day. He saw it behind the schematics on his screen, in the fiery billows that surrounded the monks, in the throbbing crimson of sunset.

Quinn went to bed alone and lay there waiting for the fire. Fever was supposed to cleanse the body of impurity. But Quinn's fever had the opposite effect, opening the conduit wider for new poisons, new shades of darkness.

Melanie came home late and slipped into bed without a sound. Quinn pretended to be asleep at first, and she pretended to believe it, though she must have felt the heat radiating off his flesh. The shadowy bedroom shapes swelled and swayed. Quinn and Melanie lay there, listening to each other breathe.

Finally, Quinn inched his hand across the sheets and touched her shoulder. She drew back, but he didn't care anymore. He rolled onto his side, snaking his arm around her waist. She squirmed, and he brought his lips to the side of her neck. There was a foreign scent in her hair. He grabbed her ear between his teeth and tugged.

"Not tonight, I'm not—"

His hand slipped upward and covered her mouth. "I don't want to hear it," he growled, and yanked on her nightgown.

She fought at first, as he kissed and pawed her. Indifference might have killed his lust. But her resistance only inflamed him further. He threw back the covers, pulled her nightgown over her head, and stared, as if expecting some secret to be revealed. Her skin shone dead white. She could have been a corpse, he thought. I've been sleeping with a corpse.

Then suddenly she held her arms up, as if to welcome him, or surrendering. It was an act, a sham, but it was good enough for Quinn. He descended on her, quenching the awful heat with her cold flesh. She pretended to want him, to like what he did to her. And he pretended not to notice the complete falseness of her every move and sound.

Now Melanie was the fantasy figure, taking the place of Jeanette. He rode her downward, through the fire, the smoke, the moans and cries and gnashing of teeth.

Jeanette didn't come in the next day. And at first, Quinn was relieved. He actually got some work done that morning. But by lunch time, his mind had slipped its moorings again. He went past her cubicle twice, then ducked inside. He closed his eyes and took a deep breath. In and out, in and out. Deep and deeper, expanding his diaphragm, just as his relaxation tapes said.

"She's sick." Nick Platt's voice pulled Quinn out of his dream state.

"Who?"

"Jesus, Quinn, what's wrong with you? Who do you think? Jeanette called in sick this morning. She's got the fever that's been going around."

"How do you know?"

"I asked Lorraine, in personnel."

"Why?"

Nick smirked, like a bad boy caught looking where he shouldn't.

"Leave her alone."

"It's a free country, right? Nobody owns her."

"Isn't there any woman you can keep your hands off?" He fought to keep from shouting.

"She's not married. She's not attached," Nick said. "I'm not cutting in on anybody's turf, am I?"

Quinn felt twinges of heat radiating up from his belly. "No, I guess not." He fought the fire, bit back the foul taste. "Look, Nick, I've been feeling pretty shitty these days. I have the same thing that everybody has. I haven't been sleeping very well."

"I understand."

"Things have been pretty bad between me and Melanie. I don't know what's going on with her. I mean, we haven't . . ."

His voice trailed off. "You think we could get together some time, you and me? Just talk, have a couple of beers, shoot the breeze?"

"Yeah, sure."

"How about tonight?"

"No. Sorry. Tonight's not going to work."

"I've got a lot on my mind. Things have been bad, really bad. I need to . . ."

"Maybe this weekend. Come over on Sunday and we can watch the game." Nick backed away. "Give me a call. Maybe we can do it this Sunday."

He disappeared down the long line of cubicles.

Quinn spent the next few hours in a daze. He tried to work, and got nowhere. His screen hissed at him. His face—reflected in the glass—was a mess. Green, bent, pocked by scars of light.

Near quitting time, he went to the personnel office and asked Lorraine for Jeanette's address. "She took some contract riders home with her yesterday. I thought I'd pick them up on my way home. We'll be needing them tomorrow."

He could just as well have said, "I want the address. I'm going over there right now and burn her house down." Lorraine wouldn't have noticed or cared. She scribbled the address on a scrap of paper and went back to her screen without making eye contact with Quinn.

After the office had emptied, Quinn emerged from his cube. Clutching the address like the relic of a saint, he went down to the car and headed for Jeanette's place. He'd expected a house, an ordinary suburban street. However, Jeanette lived in a three-story building in a huge apartment complex. Countless identical brick buildings. Neatly trimmed grass, parking lots full of cars.

He went to her door and pressed the buzzer. A long wait. He tried again and a faint voice answered. "Who is it?"

Quinn hesitated. He could still turn around. He could go home and she'd never know.

"Who is it?"

"Quinn. I need to talk to you."

Another long pause.

He pressed the button again.

Finally the door buzzed open and Quinn went down the long cinderblock corridor. Jeanette was waiting for him at her door. She had on a ratty pink bathrobe. Her hair was pulled back in a short pony tail. No makeup, her nose red and runny. Her eyes looked swollen, bloodshot. Quinn liked her even better this way. No pretense whatsoever. No acting. The real thing.

"Can I come in?"

"I guess so." She didn't sound very eager.

Her couch was heaped with pillows and blankets. A vaporizer squatted in the corner, sending out weak jets of steam. The room smelled of coughdrops and stale flesh. A man on the TV was rattling on about "instantaneous relief."

"What did you want to see me about?" Jeanette said.

"We need to talk."

"About what?"

"You and me." He closed the door. He went to the TV and shut it off. Silence flooded the room. And with it, the fever returned. No flames licking and crackling this time however. No hiss of smoke. It was as though he'd been suddenly submerged in lava. Every movement was a huge effort, every word was a struggle to get out of his mouth.

"Maybe we'd better talk about this at the office," Jeannette said. "Or we could have lunch again sometime. I'm not feeling very well right now. Maybe this weekend we could—"

"No. We need to talk. Now. It's happening right now. Here. Tonight. I can feel it." His blood was getting thinner, turning to vapor. He saw an orange-red glow around his hands. "It's starting." He reached for her and she backed away. The glow was spreading quickly, fire eating his flesh, the ember of the fuse crawling toward the explosive.

"I need somebody," he said. "I have to have—"

"We've got to take this slower, Quinn. I mean, we hardly even know each other."

He grabbed her hand. The skin was damp and far too hot. Beads of sweat clung to her lip. She had the fire too; he was sure of it now. He pulled her close and kissed her, tasting salt on her lips.

She struggled out of his arms and backed away, staring.

"What's happening to you?" She was trying to hold her panic in, but the wildness in her eyes gave it away.

He grabbed at her again. She pushed him away. "I've been thinking about you non-stop for weeks. I can't think of anything else."

"Get out. Please." She held her robe tight to her throat. Her hands were pale as egg white.

"Feel this," Quinn said, and touched her face. She drew back, scorched by his fingers.

"Get out! Just get away from me!"

He put both hands on her face and she screamed. The sound was like a siren: police, fire truck, ambulance. Quinn raked his hand down Jeanette's face, caught in the collar of her robe and pulled it open. Her screams were unbearable now, rising and falling, an air raid siren as the incendiaries fell to earth. "Please!"

He could take her with him; wrap her in his arms and let the fire loose. They could go up together, bodies and souls united in the pyre.

"Please!"

He grabbed her nightgown and ripped it from her shoulders. Then he paused, stricken by the sight of her that way. Head down, sobbing, fingers clenched in ice-white fists. Her tears were real, the shakes that wracked her body were real. He thought of Melanie and the night before.

Jeanette had the fire too—he was sure of that. But she couldn't or wouldn't admit to it yet. She wasn't ready.

Quinn turned and bolted from the apartment. He headed in the opposite direction he'd come. And though he knew it would just give more oxygen to the fire, he ran down the deserted hallway. By now, there was no point in fighting it. He wanted it to come. He welcomed it. If he was going to die, let it be this way, rather than bit by bit in bed.

He sucked in air, stoking the blaze. He looked down at his arm; it was already swathed in red light. He found a stairway, slammed through the emergency door and took the steps three at a time. As he came to the top, the flame reached his shoulder.

He stopped, closed his eyes, and went up.

The explosion was too loud to hear, an overpowering blast

of sound. Quinn stood there and let the fire consume him. He was lighter than air now, pure flame, free of his body, brighter than any angel.

A new sound penetrated: the fire alarms. He wailed back, as if a rut-crazed animal returning a mating call. This wasn't to express his agony though; his nerves were too overloaded to feel any pain. It was a cry of release, surrender.

The asphalt tile curled and blackened at his feet. The paint on the walls bubbled up. Whorls of soot obscured the ceiling. His flesh remained intact though. The fire erupted from him, out of him, leaving his body unscathed.

Quickly, the fuel—his panic and desire—was used up. He watched the last flickers die back. His breath came in sulfurous blasts.

He knew he had to get away quickly. They'd see the blackened trail on the ceiling, the burnt footprints on the floor.

He went out the back exit and skirted the building to get to his car. Red lights were throbbing in the parking lot. People milled about, dazed, angry to be rousted out of their apartments.

Quinn started his engine and pulled out. Cleansed now, there were no questions anymore in his mind. He traveled like a pure arrow of light—calmly, swiftly, with absolute assurance. He drove out of town, a half hour on the expressway, and easily found the country road where Nick Platt lived. There were two cars in the long gravel driveway. One was Nick's. The other was Melanie's.

He told himself: I feel nothing, nothing can touch me. He sat a while, staring with no thought or emotion at the cars. Then he backed out and parked down the road a short distance. He walked around the side of Nick's house. Most of the windows were dark. He peeked in one, another, then went around the corner to the back. One window was lit, though faintly. He crept up to it and looked inside. By the glow of the TV set, he saw two figures in bed. The shifting blue-green light painted them cold ghosts. A voice from the TV muttered about "amazing deals" and "limited offers."

Quinn watched. This was the thing he'd tried for months to keep out of his conscious mind, yet here it was so banal, so vapid. There was no passion in the figures on the bed. They moved against each other like two snakes trying half-heartedly to crawl out of their skins.

Eventually the listless movement ceased, and the TV, as if in response, lost its channel. The room was bathed now in flickers of static, a sullen hum.

Quinn went back the way he'd come. But instead of getting into his own car, he used his key to unlock Melanie's. He got in the back and hunched down behind the seat.

The wait was long, though Quinn hardly noticed. His knees ached, his thighs cramped, his back stung. This wasn't pain anymore, however, but raw fuel.

He crouched in a fetal ball, waiting for Melanie, waiting to be reborn again in fire.

She came. She unlocked the door and slid in. But before she could put her key in the ignition, Quinn rose up behind her and put his hands over her eyes. "Guess who?" he whispered. She knew better than to scream.

He saw a fragment of his face in the rearview mirror. It was happening already. He had the glow, a halo of red-orange light flickering from his scalp.

He jerked her backward against the seat. "Guess who?" he growled.

"Quinn, listen, I can explain. Really, it's not what—"

"I don't want to hear it. No more lies. I'm sick of lies."

Her hands came up and tried to peel his away from her face. Quinn was stronger now. There was nothing she could use against him anymore—body, voice, the past—that could really touch him. Though hand in hand, though his mouth was almost touching her ear, Quinn was invulnerable now.

"You didn't believe me. But now you're going to see. I was telling the truth all along." The light shone around his hands. His arms flickered on and off like a fluorescent bulb that can't quite get started. He smelled the sweet tang of a snuffed match. "I believed you, but you didn't believe me." Still he held his hands tight over her eyes. He wanted her to have it all at once. He wanted her to wake there, move in an instant from absolute blackness to unbearable light.

"Quinn, please, listen to me. It wasn't anything. It didn't mean a thing. I just—"

"You just have to sit here a little while longer. That's all."

He breathed deeply, sucking in her scent, sucking in oxygen to stoke the coals in the furnace. Inhale, exhale. Melanie squirmed like a little girl. She was afraid; she felt the heat at last. He'd finally made a believer out of her. "It's happening. I'm going up." It was the last second before orgasm, the last inch before going over the precipice. "You believe me now, don't you?"

"Yes."

It happened. The fire came roaring out of its hiding place. He exploded into a cloud of flame and immediately the stench of melted vinyl, scorched flesh, bubbling plastic filled the air. He was the god, the priest, and the burnt offering. He was the altar and the knife. Melanie was the virgin. Her screams could barely be heard above the fiery roaring.

He let go of her. She twisted in the seat, trying to reach him. There were two black handprints on her face, like a child's Halloween mask. Quinn smiled and new flame erupted from below.

The car thrashed like a frenzied animal. Rubber melted, paint writhed, glass buckled and sagged. The smell of burnt hair blended with the gasoline smoke.

Quinn threw the car door open and rolled onto the driveway. Already his fire was dying. He staggered to his feet, and ran across the dewy lawn, leaving a trail of smoking footprints.

He flickered and flared. In the few moments it took to reach his car, darkness had returned to his flesh. He didn't mind though, because he knew it wasn't permanent. As long as there was fuel to burn inside him, as long as there was the fuse and the match to light the fuse, the fire would return.

He passed a police car on the way to Jeanette's, then an ambulance. Their sirens seemed to call to each other, lonely as ghosts.

Quinn parked in Jeanette's lot and sat quietly staring as the dawn light painted her windows. Eventually she'd see

the truth too—she had the fire. He'd wait for her. He had all
the time in the world.

He sat enjoying the colors of sunrise. His hands were
folded, his head was bowed slightly, like a monk at morning
prayer.

Home For The Holidays

Elsa Rutherford

It is not a very long walk from my little house in the village
to the graveyard out here in the countryside. And as I draw
closer to the graveyard I can see Grandmother's house just
down the road, the windows aglow with flickering lamplight.
Rather convenient, her living so near the graveyard. Only a
little farther for me to walk in the dark.

By now her dining room table is piled high with turkey
and all the trimmings, and most of the family is already there.
I catch glimpses of their silhouettes as they drift past the
windows, milling about, a mite anxious, I expect. Aunts,
uncles, cousins. All waiting for me to get on with it and fetch
Grandfather home for the holiday. It is my duty, as I am the
eldest grandson. But it is a duty that is almost more than I
can bear.

This is only the eve of the holiday. Thanksgiving will not
arrive until tomorrow. But our family observes the holiday
on the night before, after the sun has set and darkness has
fallen and there are many long hours before the light of dawn
ushers in the coming day. This is how we keep all the major
holidays now: Easter, Thanksgiving and Christmas. We begin
the festivities, if they may be called that, on the preceding
night and by the time the actual day arrives it seems a letdown,
the way the day *after* a holiday used to seem. But it is a
relief, too, when what must be done is done. At least until
the next time.

This was not always our way. Not so long ago, we celebrated holidays on the prescribed day, like any other family. But that was before everything changed. Before Grandmother had her dream. Before we began to bring the dead home for the holidays.

I'm coming up to the graveyard gate now, shovel in one hand and lantern in the other, and the unnerving silence of this place washes over me like a cold mist, colder than the November wind that ripples past me. And it's dark. Too dark. Even the lantern's soft glow is swallowed up by the darkness, providing only the most meager, limited pool of hazy light to guide my steps. Certainly the pale swatches of lamplight emanating from Grandmother's windows are too distant to cast any illumination here. It is no exaggeration to say I am in a state of mortal terror. Though my trade as a blacksmith has strengthened my naturally well-set form, tonight my flesh feels as weak as water. My body is soaked in an icy sweat, my legs shake so badly I can hardly walk and my heart is pounding loudly enough to wake the dead. Yes, tomorrow is Thanksgiving and, therefore, the horror has begun.

My own slumber was fitful last night as I knew it would be. I awoke hours before dawn, the sickening terror that had hounded me during sleep leaping into my throat as I opened my eyes. So ill was I that I wanted to hang my head from the bed and retch, but I knew it would not lessen the awful strain afflicting me.

I've tried to tell myself that I must conquer this ghastly repulsion I feel, and steel myself for what I have to do. Get hold of yourself, man. Buck up. Just do it. That's what I say to myself. After all, I've done it before and am unalterably obliged to do it again. But the very thought of the task before me fills me with unholy dread.

I can't help wishing that we could have gone on celebrating our holidays just as we used to, in a perfectly regular fashion. It's long been our custom for everyone to gather at Grandmother's house for the holidays, and perhaps we make a bit more fuss about such things than some others might do, but that's because Grandmother has instilled in us the importance of family unity, and she sets such store on renewing family ties during the holidays. One might say that is what she lives for—bringing all the family together on these special occasions. It is a deep-rooted tradition with us; it is how we hold on to who and what we are. From near and far the kinsfolk come. They still do. In spite of what has come to pass. On foot and on horseback. By buggy and by cart. But of course it isn't the same anymore.

I remember what splendid times we used to have, laughing and joking and feasting on good food and drink. A most gregarious assemblage we were, all of us bound together by lineage and proud of it. But that was before Grandmother had her dream.

When she first told us of the dream we were sympathetic, quite naturally attributing it to her continuing sorrow over Grandfather's death which had occurred six months earlier. (We all love her so dearly, and cannot bear it when she is down-hearted; it wounded us deeply to see how she'd lost her zest for life, how she languished beside the window day after day, gazing out toward the graveyard with such a melancholy countenance and who knew what thoughts preying upon her mind.) At the time of the dream, Thanksgiving was fast approaching, and we knew how keenly she would feel Grandfather's absence on that day—it would be the first time in more than fifty years that she'd spent a holiday without him. So we surmised the coming holiday had a great deal to do with the dream. But the dream was only that, a sad, sad dream, we said. Nothing more. Grandmother, however, insisted we were quite wrong.

Her veined hands trembling, her aged, china blue eyes brimming with tears not of sorrow but of resurrected hope, she insisted that Grandfather had called out to her from his grave, communicating a strange but wondrous message. He had told her, she said in a voice quaking with amazement, that it was possible for him to be with us again at certain times. On holidays, to be exact. Yes, that was definitely what he'd said, she insisted. Holidays. Wasn't it wonderful? He could come home for the holidays.

Needless to say, upon realizing that Grandmother was taking the dream as valid fact, we made every attempt to dissuade her from what was obviously a most pathetic misinterpretation. We agreed, of course, that Grandfather's *spirit* would always be with us, especially during the holiday gatherings, but certainly his physical body would and must remain in the grave.

No! no! she cried. He could come home! He *would* come home! It was simply a matter of someone going to fetch him. *Of opening the grave and bringing him out.*

Her eyes fell on me. "You are the eldest grandson, twenty-one years of age, strong and able. So, it is only fitting that you be the one to do it. You must go and fetch him home." As I stood there, my mouth agape, she proceeded to explain that the disinterment should be undertaken on the night before the holiday and that Grandfather would have to be returned to his coffin before the sun rose the following morning. For according to Grandfather's dream-sent message, she said, "the dead do not abide the sun."

So, on that Thanksgiving eve, a year ago tonight it was, I set out on the short walk from my house to the graveyard. But it was only to appease Grandmother, you understand. To prove, once and for all, that her dream had no basis in reality, that Grandfather was as dead to the world on Thanksgiving eve as he'd been when we'd lowered him into the ground six months before.

I must confess that for a brief moment I had allowed myself to consider what it would mean if Grandfather *could* come back to us. For if he could come back to life, Grandmother's own vitality would surely be restored as well. Yes, such thoughts were an offense to reason, I know, and only a fleeting speculation, but something deep inside me yearned for reassurance that the dead are not cut off from us forever, that some part, some essence, still lingers here on this earthly plane, surviving even the cold clutches of the grave. What mortal man has not, at one time or another, yearned for such reassurance? For proof of life beyond death? Surely this is the basic longing at the heart of every ghost story ever told. A desperate desire to believe that some part of the life force remains indestructible, that the dead can and do reach out to us, commune with us. That is our greatest hope and yet, paradoxically, it is also our deepest fear. Even to imagine the dead rising from their tombs sends a cold shiver down the spine.

Of course I knew such conjecture was futile; the Good Book teaches that we shall not know the answers on this side of the veil, and I felt rather like a fool, a common grave-robber, as I readied myself for the distasteful act of plundering the earth where Grandfather lay. But I had promised Grandmother—indeed she had made me swear—that I would open the coffin and see with my own eyes if Grandfather truly was waiting to be released, waiting to come home for the holiday. And I was willing to go to any length to mollify Grandmother.

I set the lantern on the ground, and with only its scant nimbus to see by, I proceeded to penetrate the grave, shovelful after shovelful, heaving the excavated dirt into piles at the edges of the growing aperture until, at last, the chasm yawned open before me and the coffin was revealed. It struck me at that moment that what I was about to do was an accursed thing, an abomination, but I had given my word, I had sworn to do it. I had no choice but to break open the coffin and look on my Grandfather's moldering remains. Thus, I climbed down into the grave and, with a mighty swing of the shovel, smashed the coffin's hasp and lifted the heavy, creaking lid. I thought I heard a sigh as the lid came open, but I reasoned it was only a pocket of stale air escaping its pent-up confines.

I reached for the lantern, held it aloft, and peered down at my grandfather. At first, what I saw was exactly what I'd expected to see—an insensate corpse sleeping the final sleep. To be sure it was a grim sight: the flesh had darkened and begun to wither and fall away, and there was an overpowering stench that gushed upward and took the breath from me. But all in all, it was what I'd expected. Then, just as I was about to lower the lid again, some strange, unexplainable feeling seized me and I knew—*against all constraints of rationality I knew!*—that everything was not as it seemed.

"Grandfather?" I whispered, my voice as scratchy as a rasp upon the chill night air.

Though he did not answer aloud, his dark, dry-looking lips as unmoving as they'd been only seconds before, I *sensed* he was speaking to me. I felt rather than heard the words, felt them in the very marrow of my bones. *I am alive. Though I am dead, I am alive.* That was what he was saying to me.

Calling out to me as he'd called out to Grandmother through the dream.

I was utterly stunned. Who could believe such a thing was possible! But I was sure it was! Somehow some core of life still existed inside Grandfather's dead body, some vital spark that had reached out to Grandmother and was now reaching out to me. Without question, there was nothing for me but to bring him out of the grave and take him home.

He was heavier than you might think, considering that we tend to think of the dead as mere skeletons, nothing but heaps of dried-out bones, but Grandfather had been a large, robust man in life and, dead only six months, much of the flesh still remained, spongy now to my touch, and oozing a putrid fluid. His grave-clothes, too, were moist and slick, so slippery it was hard to get a firm hold, but by draping him over my shoulder, half-carrying, half-tugging, I was able to convey him, albeit clumsily, from the graveyard to Grandmother's house in a matter of minutes.

As I went lurching along, bearing Grandfather's weight, I was caught up in a wild delirium of emotions, aghast and excited at the same time. In spite of the fact that Grandfather's body had deteriorated and putrefication had set in, I was almost certain I could feel the lifeforce pulsing deep inside him, though I grant it was difficult to detect, given that my own blood was churning through my veins and thundering in my ears in such a tumult that it overrode all else.

A few of the aunts and cousins screamed when I came into the house with Grandfather slung over my shoulder. Others were so stricken at the sight that they could not utter a sound, and some of the smaller children ran from the room and hid. To say the least, everyone was astounded. They'd all known that I'd gone to the graveyard and why, but no one had dared believe that I'd actually bring Grandfather home. No one except Grandmother who was beside herself with jubilation, as I knew she would be.

I seated Grandfather at the head of the long table, where he'd always sat, and where he seemed very content to be once again. With an enthusiastic clap of her hands, Grandmother bid us all to take our places round the table and, as usual, we bowed our heads and offered thanks. *O Lord, thank*

you for our many blessings. For surely on this Thanksgiving
eve we did indeed have an extraordinary blessing to be thankful for. However, I couldn't help noticing that some of the
family didn't look particularly thankful, especially when, as
the meal progressed, a few tiny clumps of rotten flesh fell
from Grandfather's face and landed between the mashed pota-
toes and the cranberry sauce. What I saw on a number of
faces appeared to reflect repugnance instead of gratitude, and
I noticed that no one seemed to have much appetite.

After the meal ended and I'd removed Grandfather from the
table to his favorite armchair in the living room, Grandmother
drew up a seat and sat beside him. Holding his decomposing
hand in her own, patting it from to time, she spoke to him
with almost child-like excitement, so effusively warm and
affectionate she was. And how attentive to her he seemed to
be, how absorbed in her words. So satisfied to sit perfectly
still and listen as she talked on and on.

In contrast, the others were standoffish and visibly reluctant
to engage him in conversation, but they did file by and speak
before moving off to talk among themselves. Mostly "Hello,
Grandfather" and "How are you, Grandfather" and "Good
to see you, Grandfather." Correct but restrained to the point
of awkwardness. It made me feel sorry for the poor old fellow.
Surely this was not the sort of response one would expect to
receive upon rising from the grave and coming home for the
holidays. But I thought they were, understandably, simply
too shocked to say more; it was, I admit, an unusual situation.
Grandfather himself gave no indication that he felt slighted
by the lukewarm reception. It was evident to me that Grandmother's heart-felt welcome was all that truly mattered to
him.

As time went on, I became aware of dismaying snatches
of conversations here and there around the room. The gist of
it was that much of the family simply could not believe that
Grandfather was alive again. In fact, some of them were
denying it emphatically, insisting that what was sitting in that
armchair, the focus of Grandmother's loving attention, was
nothing but a dead body. Stone-cold dead, they said. Totally,
completely and without question, dead. Disgusting, they said.
It was clear, too, that they were quite angry with me. One

cousin pulled me aside and demanded to know if I'd taken leave of my senses. "Why, it's the vilest thing I've ever seen, digging up the old man's corpse and parading it about this way," he said. Another quickly declared I ought to be buggy-whipped and that I'd be lucky if the sheriff didn't find out and lock me up for good.

It was then, feeling unjustly put-upon and forced to defend my actions, that I turned and saw what I had not seen before. On the verge of indignant rebuttal, the scales suddenly fell from my eyes and I beheld a sight that filled me with cold horror.

The truth, the reality, of what I was seeing staggered me like a breath-taking blow. God in heaven, my cousins were right! The thing sitting in that armchair *was* nothing but a corpse! Yes! Yes! I saw it clearly now! Why, anyone with eyes could see there was no core of life, no vital spark, left in that awful, cadaverous thing, none whatsoever. Can you imagine the horror of waking suddenly to that realization!

There was only one explanation for it: a mind-twisting hallucination had befallen me, entrancing me as I'd opened Grandfather's coffin, and it had deluded my mind and impaired my reasoning up until that very instant. And—Lord have mercy!—look what it had wrought: Grandmother was talking to a corpse and smiling into its stinking face! Gently stroking its rotted hand! Believing with all her heart that Grandfather had come back to her and that he was responding to her ministrations. This was beyond nightmare, this was depravity, and I alone bore the blame.

For a moment I felt utterly helpless, addled with indecision. But suddenly a rush of adrenalin surged through me, and I hurried to Grandmother's side and fell on my knees before her and began to explain, in what must have been an incoherent babble, that I had to return Grandfather to the graveyard at once. While I attempted to pull her hand from his, attempted to lift her to her feet in order to place her into the care of some of the aunts who'd come forward, she stared at me as if she didn't know who I was or what I was raving about. She refused to be taken away, and when I tried to remove Grandfather from her grasp, she would not surrender him to me. Eyes burning with a frightening intensity, she him tenaciously, surprising me that such a small, frail person could summon such strength.

"Leave us be, you son of a bitch," she said, flinging the startling words into my face with such vehemence that it drove me backwards as surely as if she had struck me. Then she turned to Grandfather, her hands sliding up his dark, withered neck, and she began to whisper in his ear, imparting secrets that were for him alone. I knew she was reaching deep into her dreams, trusting in something that none of us could begin to fathom. And I also knew, it was plain to see, that she was quite mad. But in that madness there was something else that was plain to see: there was a bliss, a new-found bliss that had totally obliterated her grief, wiped it away as if it had never been, and transported her beyond her dreams and her hopes to the conviction that the bond of family truly does transcend even the grave itself.

I understood at that moment that I could not take that bliss from her. I would sooner have been damned to perdition than to do so. Even if it was based on a lie, a terrible lie, I could not take it from her. And so I did leave them be, both she and Grandfather, the living and the dead, to commune in whatever incomprehensible way she believed them to be communing.

My family, though relieved that I had finally come to my senses, was appalled that I insisted on Grandfather remaining where he was for the rest of the night. "You must take him back immediately," they urged. A few even offered to help. The aunts said, "We'll put Grandmother to bed straight-away, give her a strong draught of sleeping potion and come morning she will think it was all a dream." But I remained firm in my resolve, and eventually, grudgingly, they resigned themselves to it and waited for the night to pass.

In the hour before dawn, I took Grandfather in my arms and heaved him over my shoulder, just as I had done before. This time Grandmother relinquished him willingly if regret-fully. "Yes, yes, it's time, I know," she sighed. "He must go back before the sun comes up."

In the fading darkness, the gray shadows swirling about my feet as I made my way to the graveyard, I tried to numb my mind and shut off my senses so I wouldn't feel that smeary, pulpy flesh against my own, wouldn't smell the rank stench, wouldn't acknowledge what it was I held in my arms. When, at last, I'd returned Grandfather to his grave, lowered him into his coffin and shoveled the last shovel of dirt over him, I was immensely relieved to be rid of my loathsome burden.

But of course I was not rid of it. The guilt, the obscenity of what I'd done, would continue to haunt me. How could there be a greater sacrilege, a greater wickedness than to deliberately defile the dead? Yet, God forgive me, I knew I would do it again. The bliss I had seen on my Grandmother's face, the deliverance from dark despair to ecstatic joy, would compel me to do it again. No matter the burden it placed upon my conscience, no matter the revulsion and fear I would feel, for her sake I would do it again. And I did, just over a month hence, when Christmas eve came round.

And again when Easter came. By that time, Grandfather had deteriorated to an even greater degree, his bones showing beneath the stringy, rotted flesh, and his head shrunken to a wizened skull. The family turned their own heads in disgust as I brought him in, but they, too, understood by then that it was this gruesome holiday recurrence that gave Grandmother courage for all the other days of the year. Some part of her mind was gone, that is true, but because she believed Grandfather would return to her periodically, she continued to function, to live and breathe and laugh and love, in a relatively normal fashion. And none among us had the heart to deprive her of that. Nor to deprive ourselves of the grandmother who'd been restored to us. For, by then, there was something else we all understood: *if she stopped believing, then something inside all of us would wither and die . . .*

Now Thanksgiving eve is upon us again and seven months have passed since Easter, since last I dug up Grandfather. Most likely I will find him beyond recognition this time, the seeping rain, the moldy damp, and the grave-worms having taken their toll. It will be a revolting, skeletal thing I shall carry to Grandmother's house this night. Still, I plunge on, my heart racing, my hands clammy as the lantern swings at my side.

Ah, yes, there it is, just ahead there, Grandfather's grave.

Of course I am fully aware that what I do here is an offense against every law of heaven and earth, and I do not know if God will have mercy on my soul, or if I shall be condemned to the everlasting fires of hell. All I know is that, in the meantime, Grandfather will come home for the holidays. Now, I must dig.

Time Enough To Sleep

Thomas F. Monteleone

> *Your children are not your children.*
> *For their souls dwell in the house of tomorrow,*
> *which you cannot visit,*
> *not even in your dreams*
>
> Kahlil Gibran

I'm not sure how much longer I can hold the son-of-a-bitch off.

For the past few days, I've seen more signs of his arrival. Each time I enter Becky's room, I think I smell the faintest of scents—a grim, olfactory wake of his passage.

He's so bold, coming here flirting with my daughter, thinking I have no sense of it. And yet, it is the driving force in my life. There is nothing that will give me more strength than to have the chance to beat him. He knows now that I keep an old Little League aluminum baseball bat in the pantry, but he also knows I am not afraid to use it.

It began the day Rhonda and I brought her home from the hospital. There is nothing more fragile than a newborn child—something I had never realized till that moment. I admit, being a cost accountant for Proctor & Gamble all my adult life, had perhaps kept me somewhat removed from the mainstream of life. When I brought a new life into the world, it was like getting slapped in the face.

The very first night, Rhonda kept her in a bassinet in our bedroom. I questioned the need for it until darkness fell over everything and the house shut down to the point of the occasional creak of an old foundation. I could hear my wife's breathing at my ear, a signature of her exhaustion and a final release of tension, anxiety, and fear.

Little did I realize that mine had just begun.

I never slept that first night. An endless stretch of black time wherein I lay listening to what seemed like breathing of the most labored sort. I had no idea a tiny, living human could make such scary noises and survive till morning. Wheezing, coughing, rattling, mucous throttled sucking were only a few of the horrible sounds through which I suffered that night. It was so intensely awful, I became quite certain we would lose Becky before dawn.

But we didn't.

The bassinet remained in our bedroom another three or four weeks before I allowed my wife to have the baby sleeping in a crib so far away from us—her own bedroom down the hall. I had grown accustomed to the travail of her breathing, and it measured out the nights as a metronome of life itself.

It was just about that time when I was watching the Game of the Week (the Orioles against the Blue Jays, I think), and I saw the commercial. Actually, it was probably one of those Public Service Announcements, and what it was doing shoehorned among the endless array of beer and razor commercials I could not imagine.

(Of course, I now know the message was placed there by Divine Intercedence. It was important that I receive the message when I did.)

The message? Oh yes, it was important all right. Have you ever heard of SIDS?

Neither had I! Imagine my shock as I sat there in my La-Z-Boy to see that there is this hideous phenomenon know as Crib Death or Sudden Infant Death Syndrome. Newborns, up to the age of six months, are suddenly found dead in their cribs, and no one has the foggiest notion as to how or why.

How come I've never heard of this? I ask myself. How come I've *never* seen anything about this terrible syndrome until *now*, until the *very moment* I have my *own* little baby who may be victim to this horrible thing?

This was positively *incredible* to me. But stunned though I may have been, I remained lucid enough to realize I had been given a Sign, a celestial memorandum so to speak, to be ever vigilant.

As the months ticked past, I took it upon myself to nightly approach the crib and listen for Becky's sweet breath. When my wife discovered my habit, she chided me for being so overprotective, and for a moment, I became suspicious of her. Surely, she could not be in league with any forces that would harm my daughter. In short order, I banished such thoughts from my head.

Well, at least I *tried* to . . .

Time continued its work, and Becky not only escaped the critical period of SIDS frequency, but she weathered bouts of commons colds, influenzas, chicken pox, measles, and mumps. It seemed like I blinked my eyes and she was four years old. She had been such a healthy baby and toddler, that I think I became lulled into a false sense of security during those years. We rarely allowed her to leave the house, other than to roam about our fenced-in yard. Whenever other children came over to play with her, I always watched them with a careful eye. I saw this movie once about a six-year-old serial killer. . . .

When it came to protecting your daughter, you couldn't be too careful.

It wasn't until Becky started pre-school that I began to realize how foolish, how *lax* I had actually been. There were so many ways she could be in danger, at first I had a hard time tracking everything—until I took a page from my accountant's training and logged everything in a wonderful ledger with cross-referencing columns and rows. Once I inflicted some *order* on the situation, I began to feel better about everything.

I didn't allow her to ride the school bus until I'd completed a dossier on the driver and had the vehicle inspected. The dossier thing worked so well that I used the same P.I. to work up files on everyone at the pre-school, my neighbors, and even Louise Smeak, the Sunday School teacher at St. Albans Episcopal. I wanted to have total control over everyone who would have any contact with my daughter.

You could never be too careful . . .

I heard this radio talk show where this guy who called in had postulated that many fatal diseases were actually transmitted by those plastic "sporks" they give out at fast-food eateries. I had never thought much about this, but it certainly made sense if you stopped to consider everything.

And then somebody told me that peanut butter is a major killer of small children. People feed it to them on the end of a spoon and it gets lodged at the intersection of the esophagus and the bronchial tubes or something like that. It's so dangerous that even the Heimlich maneuver doesn't work and of course there is always the truth that a spoon is pretty damned close to a spork. But can you imagine, that Death hides even in a peanut butter jar?

Well, you can bet that my Becky didn't eat any more of *that* stuff.

The years slipped away from me; I had risen through the ranks at P&G until I was the chief of the entire financial division. Sure, I had plenty of time on my hands, but still not enough to administer to Becky's needs as well as I would like. Retirement was still many years off and my wife did not seem to share my over-riding concern for my daughter's welfare.

In fact, I was beginning to realize that perhaps Rhonda was not the ally I'd always supposed.

Becky turned ten, and that meant a whole new ledger, a whole new set of variables that I would have to start tracking. She was a very pretty girl and despite my efforts to discourage contact with other people, lots of the kids in her class wanted to be her friends. More dossiers. More money. But what did I care? I was being a good parent.

It was also around this time that Rhonda actually turned against me. It started slowly and with much subtlety, but I recognized it early on because I'd sensed it coming. She told her sister I had too much pressure at my job, that I was not adjusting well to Becky's pre-teen years, and worst of all, that I needed a hobby. Can you imagine such foolishness? I could have gotten very angry, but I knew how outward displays of domestic unrest can be harmful to children. An article in the *International Enquirer* said depression and teen suicides tended to be caused by bad parenting, so by remaining tranquil, I was being a wise and caring father.

I knew that I would eventually discover a solution to the problem Rhonda was becoming. If I remained patient and vigilant, I would be given a sign, an answer. And it came to me the day I realized that Mr. Death had changed his tactics. I mean, it was no secret he'd been after Becky since we'd brought her home from Cook Memorial Hospital. It was only through my stalwart efforts she'd remained as safe as she had.

But Mr. Death is slick and he took to impersonating regular people that might come in contact with Becky. That's why I had to cancel all her dental visits and of course there would be no more examinations by Doc Wilson. The biggest problem were those unexpected situations that could not be planned. For example, when Becky answered the door one after-school day to admit the meter reader for the local gas and electric company, I almost lost my usual composure.

(Where was her mother? you might ask—as I certainly did. How could she allow the child to do something so dangerous as *answer the door*? The answer lay ahead, as you shall see.)

You can already imagine how horrible it could have been if the gas-man had actually been The Gas-Man—if you get my meaning . . .

Yes, I realized I must learn from this experience. And learn I did indeed. After pulling Becky from her school, I arranged to have her education continued at home under the care of a carefully checked-out tutor. The young boys who had already begun sniffing around the hems of my daughter's skirts received stern warnings from me to simply stay away. I reinforced my messages with letters to all the boys' parents.

That seemed to help matters very much until a man in a charcoal suit with a red tie knocked on the door. He said he was from the State Department of Health and Mental Hygiene, and that he wanted to ask me a few questions. He also said he had a warrant to inspect my premises. He showed me some ID that said his name was Silverstein and some papers with official seals and notary stamps on them. He didn't know I recognized his true identity, and therefore misinterpreted my smile as I led him into the kitchen. I directed him to a chair at the dinette where I offered him a cup of coffee. He said yes and I asked him what kind of questions he had for me. I was going to grab my aluminum baseball bat right away, but I was curious as to what Mr. Death would want to ask me. Didn't he already know everything? And so I poured two cups of Maxwell House and sat down to listen.

He said a few things right up front about Becky that made me very angry. I almost reached for the baseball bat twice, and both times I thought maybe I should listen a little longer, even though it was making me very angry.

"After reading copies of the letters you sent the Wizniewski and Harrison boys, I decided to contact you directly," said Mr. Death. "Initially, I spoke to your wife, and she told me about your . . . tendency to . . . ah, go on at length about your daughter."

I asked him what exactly Rhonda had said.

"Exactly? Well, sir, she said that she is very much afraid of you. Did you know that?"

I told him no. Anything else? I asked.

"She said that she had decided a long time ago she would tolerate your behavior—"

Tolerate?

"Yes, as long as it remained within the family, she figured it was safer, better for everyone involved."

Safer . . . yes, I see, I told him. But then, why are you here, Mr. Silverstein? (I needed to allay any suspicions he might have that I knew his true identity.)

"Well, it's hard to explain, but we've received a petition to have your case examined by a state psychiatrist," he said. "We have statements by neighbors and relatives and parents at Holbrook Elementary, plus an interesting letter from a private investigator, Lucius Mallory. It was forwarded to us from Lieutenant Karsay at the 3rd Precinct."

I moved away from the table, close to the pantry door where my aluminum buddy awaited my touch. And what do these statements and letters have to do with me?

Mr. Death almost chuckled. Can you imagine his audacity? "I think you know what this is all about. Your daughter, Rebecca, is dead, sir. She died when she was three months old from SIDS. More than nine years ago."

I think that's when I lost it—when he mouthed such a cruel lie, a heinous blasphemy in my house. I screamed something about what a liar he was and how I knew his true identity and how I would stop him from taking my daughter away from me.

He went down like a clumsy palooka from the first impact to the base of his skull. As his life fluids seeped across the tiles of the kitchen floor, I realized I'd made a mistake. This man, Silverstein, was a mere mortal. Another of Death's clever tricks, no doubt. I checked my watch, and knew I had little time. Rhonda would be due home from her part-time job at the neighborhood library at any moment.

There was no need to clean up the mess, however. None at all.

It has been a long week-end. The scent of death I mentioned earlier is getting heavy in here. The crowds of neighbors and police cars that have surrounded my little bungalow have been a terrible distraction, and I fear that Mr. Death will get in while I am forced to deal with the foolish meddling of those outside. The television says there is a dangerous hostage situation here. I think it is a good thing they don't know about Silverstein and Rhonda. They probably think I might do harm to Rebecca, which reveals them to be the fools they are.

Don't they know I'm her father?

And a father can't ever be too careful. . . .

The Powers Of Darkness

Richard Lee Byers

"Are you a devil worshipper?"

Startled, Harper lurched around. The woman had stolen up behind him so silently that it was almost as if she'd coalesced out of the twilight. "What?" he said. "I don't think I heard you right."

The woman swallowed. She was fat, and wore a Tampa Bay Giants T-shirt, cutoffs, and flipflops. Her feet were dirty, her teeth stained and crooked. All in all, a perfect example of the new neighbors that he was making a conscientious effort not to think of as rednecks. "Are you a devil worshipper?" she repeated.

"No," Harper said. He couldn't decide whether to be annoyed or amused. "Why would you ask that?"

The woman hesitated. "Somebody told me."

"Who?"

"I shouldn't say." She turned and lumbered away from the road.

Puzzled, Harper continued his walk through the subdivision. Each of the homes lining the street occupied at least a half acre of land; most were trailers, with only the occasional house. As darkness fell, mosquitoes began to whine around his ears. Occasionally, he caught a whiff of skunk, cow manure, or somebody's barbecue grill.

Despite the bugs and the muggy Florida heat, up to now he'd enjoyed his evening walks, and not only because they

244

got him away from his wife. Before inheriting Aunt Joanie's house, he'd spent most of his life in the brick-and-concrete heart of one Northern city or another, and so the burrowing owls, gopher turtles, and choruses of braying frogs in his new neighborhood interested him.

But now he found he couldn't focus on Nature. The more he thought about his exchange with the fat woman, the more it bothered him.

He guessed he understood where her accusation had come from. He wrote fantasy novels, epic potboilers full of black magic and evil spirits. The local paper had profiled him, so people knew it. And recently he'd thrown a costume party for the Tampa science fiction club, and had people in hooded cloaks and monster masks parading around his yard.

But Jesus Christ, so what? It was all *imaginary*. How could anybody get upset about it?

Surely, most people weren't. And as for the couple morons who were, well, what difference did it make? He tried to put the matter out of his mind.

A door slammed. Harper jerked in his chair, and the half-formed sentence in his head burst like a bubble. The cursor on the computer screen winked at him mockingly.

Grimacing, he looked at his watch, and was surprised to discover it was almost five. He could knock off for the day if he wanted, and the way his back had begun to ache, he did. He saved his text, stood, and stretched till his spine popped. Then he headed for the front of the house to see what all the racket was about.

In the living room, a cluttered space festooned with prints by fantasy artists like Whelan, Maitz, and Cherry, he found his son and wife. Kevin's face was twisted and red beneath his tousled, sandy-blond hair. Mary, slim and fair-skinned, with curls the color of honey, had dropped to one knee to look the ten-year-old in the eye. Harper had seen the tableau a hundred times. Something had upset Kevin, he was reluctant to talk about it, and his mother was coaxing the story out of him.

"What's up?" the writer asked.

Mary turned her head, a glint of annoyance in her gray

eyes. "That's what I'm trying to find out. He was playing with some of the neighbor kids."

"Did you get in a fight?" Harper asked. He looked the boy up and down for bruises.

"No," Kevin said. He quivered. "But Mrs. Porter says I can't play with Frank and Robbie anymore."

Mary's lips thinned, as if she was annoyed with Kevin for yielding the truth to his father instead of her. "Why, sweetheart?" She hesitated. "Did you do something?"

"No!" Kevin said. "She said they were only allowed to play with Christian kids."

"You are Christian," Mary said. Harper supposed she was right. They didn't go to church, but the boy had been baptized. "Did you tell her that?"

Kevin said, "No. She wouldn't listen to me." He glanced at an assortment of gaudy plastic figures scattered across the worn beige J. C. Penny sofa. "She said the X-Men are Satanic."

"Don't worry about it," Harper said. "I'll talk to her."

"Maybe you should let it go," Mary said. "I'm not sure these are the right friends for Kevin anyway, and you don't want to stir things up worse than they are already."

Harper said, "I won't. Give me a little credit." He smiled at his son. "Can you show me the right house?"

Kevin looked at his father, then his mother. Harper could tell he felt caught in the middle. Finally the boy shuffled to the window and pointed at a weather-stained double-wide trailer across the street. There were several kids hanging around in front of it. "There."

"I see it," Harper said. He opened the door, and the late-afternoon sun seared his face. Carthoris, the family's white-and-gray tomcat, ran up and rubbed against his feet. He stooped and scratched the animal behind the ear, causing him to flop over onto his back. "This should only take a minute."

As Harper passed his curbside mailbox, the children in the yard noticed him coming, and started whispering back and forth. When he got closer, he smiled at them, and they scattered. Slightly dismayed by their reaction, he climbed the rusty wrought-iron steps to the trailer's screen door. The voice of a television preacher twanged from the dimness beyond.

Harper knocked. A vague form heaved up, occluding the glow of the TV. As it trudged closer, it turned into a sun-bronzed woman in her early twenties, surprisingly young to be the mother of any of the kids outside. Sweat glistened on her forehead and neck. Her floral-print blouse was sodden with it.

"Hi," Harper said. "I'm Bruce Harper. Kevin's dad. Are you Mrs. Porter?"

The black-haired woman stared at him. "Uh huh."

"I understand there was some kind of a problem this afternoon. Could we talk about it?"

Mrs. Porter sighed. "If we have to. I think it would be better if our kids stayed away from each other."

"Why?" Harper asked. A drop of sweat oozed down his temple. He wished Mrs. Porter had invited him in. Not that it seemed to be any cooler inside the trailer, but he felt awkward talking through the screen. "Because he brought his superhero toys? They're not anything"—he floundered, groping for an appropriate word—"*bad*, just characters from a comic book."

"I know what *X-Men* is. Witchcraft, smut, and violence. My boys aren't allowed to look at trash like that."

Harper gave her what he hoped was a winning smile. "You know, our generation read comics too, and most of us turned out all right. Kids understand the stories aren't real, just fairy tales with spandex."

"Frank and Robbie never looked at fairy tales, either, or anything else that goes against the Bible."

Harper felt an almost irresistible impulse to launch into his patented spiel on the value of fantasy for kids and grownups alike. He quashed it. He could tell that he'd never convince this woman, and he'd come over here to help his son, not debate. "All right. I respect your feelings. Kevin will leave the figures at home from now on."

Mrs. Porter shook her head. "No. I'd rather he just stayed away."

"But why? He's a good kid!"

"I gave him a chance. For his great-aunt's sake. But everyone's heard about you, Mr. Harper."

"What do you mean?" Harper demanded. "What have you heard, and who said—"

Mrs. Porter closed the inner door.

Harper lay in the darkness, staring at the shadowy form of the ceiling fan. Even with the wooden blades swishing around and the AC rumbling, the bedroom seemed hot and close. Mary lay beside him, a couple feet away. He sensed that she wasn't asleep, either.

"God, I hate his place," she said at last. "The humidity. The toilets overflowing—"

"Come on, that only happened one time. Since the guy pumped out the septic tank, they're fine."

"Back in civilization, we didn't have to worry about things like that. We had sewers. As opposed to hillbilly neighbors out of *Deliverance*."

"There were fundamentalists who thought all fantasy was evil in Cincinnati, too. Remember when they picketed Halley's Comics?"

"Yes. But they didn't live near us, and they didn't dump on our kid."

Outside the window, Carthoris yowled, probably chasing off another cat. Harper rolled onto his side and put his hand on Mary's shoulder. "Look, I'm upset too, but let's not blow this out of proportion. So a couple of idiots have weird ideas about us. Kevin'll meet other kids."

She squirmed away from his touch. "I just wish we could move back where our friends are."

"Well, we can't," Harper snapped. "Not right now. We can't afford rent. You know that as well as I do."

"We could if you hadn't spent a year and a half writing that World War I thing. Your *breakout* book," she sneered.

Harper's muscles tightened, shooting a twinge through his lower back. He tried to rein in his temper. "Not every project sells. That's the nature of the business. All a writer can do—"

"Your agent warned you nobody would buy it."

"You know, if I haven't told you lately how much I appreciate your support, there's a reason." He flung off the sheet, sat up, and fumbled for the clothes he'd tossed on the chair. "I need some air."

By the time he reached the living room, his anger had cooled to a weary frustration. Mary was right, he'd screwed up, but was she going to hold it against him forever? Couldn't she see that no matter how little money they had or where they were forced to live, life would be more pleasant if they were kind to each other?

He sighed. Maybe she'd wake up in a better mood. Maybe they could make peace then.

He opened the door just in time to see the black bulk of a pickup truck rolling by. Metal clanged, then clattered, something rolling in the street. The vehicle roared away.

Curious, he trotted down the rutted strip of ground that served as his driveway. Carthoris, ghostly in the moonlight, bounded along beside him. Harper figured that a piece of the truck, a hubcap or muffler perhaps, had fallen off. But when he reached the street, he saw his own dented mailbox lying on the pavement. Someone in the back of the pickup had clubbed it off its wooden post.

Mary rose from the dining room table and started prowling around, her coffee mug shivering in her hand. "We can't live like this," she said.

Harper pushed his raisin bran away untasted. The discussion had spoiled what little appetite he'd sat down with. "How do you know it had anything to do with what Mrs. Porter said? Maybe it was just teenagers playing a prank."

"Were any of the other mailboxes on the street knocked down?"

He sighed. "Not that I noticed."

Her lip curled. "Well, then."

"Okay, maybe it was somebody who thinks we're Satanists. It's still no big deal. It took me about a minute to nail the damn thing back on its pole."

"It's *harassment*," Mary hissed. "I don't know how you think we're going to manage in a place where everyone's against us."

Harper closed his eyes. He hoped that if he couldn't see

her, he wouldn't feel quite as angry. " 'Everyone' is not against us."

"Oh, yeah? How do you know?"

"Because it's 1993, and we're in America, fifteen miles from a major city. The vast majority of our neighbors happen to be rational, educated people. You just want to assume otherwise to convince yourself this is a hellhole and there's no choice but to leave."

"I know you think I'm a selfish bitch, but this isn't about me. I can stick it out here if that's what it takes to make you happy. I mean, God forbid that you should have to get a job or anything. But can you imagine what it'll be like for Kevin, going to a school where all the other kids treat him like a freak?"

"That won't happen," Harper said. As a timid, bookish child, he'd been bullied himself, and the suggestion that he was setting his son up for the same treatment infuriated him. "Look, I admit, we're having a problem. But it's a stupid problem, easy to solve. We just have to let people get to know us. As soon as they see we don't have cloven hooves, the rumor will collapse under the weight of its own absurdity."

Mary grimaced. Her shoulders slumped, as if she was suddenly as sick of the quarrel as he was. "Fine. You fix it, then."

The nearest bar was a small, concrete-block box about a mile from Harper's house. Pit bulls prowled the yard of the trailer next door, and a Baptist church stood directly across the street.

Harper thought that in the darkness, the tavern looked forbidding, like a pillbox on a battlefield, or a blockhouse in a prison complex. Trying to rein in his imagination, he opened the door.

The interior of the building was nearly as drab as the facade. The floor was the cement foundation slab. The mismatched tables, chairs, and barstools looked as if they'd been purchased at some of the subdivision's ubiquitous yard sales. Even though it was Friday night, there were only a few customers. Perhaps most of the area residents preferred to drink farther afield, in more congenial surroundings.

Harper headed for two guys, one tall and barrel-chested, the other short and wiry, sitting shrouded in cigarette smoke at the bar. The smaller man glanced over his shoulder, twitched, and elbowed his companion in the ribs. The big man looked around too.

Trying not to choke on the acrid blue haze, Harper said, "Hi. Hot out there. Too hot not to stop for a beer." He looked at the bartender, a gawky, pimply kid who looked too young for the job. "I'll have a draft. And give these gentlemen a refill."

The wiry man raised his hand, revealing a faded eagle tattoo. "No. We're fine. I take it you're walking?"

"Yeah," Harper said. "I do it a lot. At night, when it's cooler. For the exercise."

The tattooed man grimaced. "Most people around here get all the exercise they need on the job. Must be nice to get paid for sitting on your ass making up stuff."

Harper said, "I guess I don't need to introduce myself."

The big guy shook his head. The glow of the fluorescent lights rippled across his close-cropped, graying hair. "No," he said. "People have heard about you."

Harper looked him in the eye. "What have they heard?"

The big man shifted uncomfortably on his stool. His friend answered for him. "That you're in some kind of cult. That a bunch of the other weirdos came to your place and you all danced naked around a bonfire."

"Well, it's all true," Harper said. "I worship Lucifer. I guess it had to come out sooner or later. Even if nobody had spotted the coven celebrating the Black Mass, eventually somebody would have noticed my wife flying around on her broom, or me setting the remains of our human sacrifices out on trash day." He realized the other men weren't grinning, just staring at him stonily. "Jesus, I'm kidding! You guys don't believe in that kind of creature-feature mumbo jumbo, do you?"

The big man shrugged his massive, rounded shoulders.

"Well, you shouldn't," Harper said, "I've researched the

occult, for my writing. Take it from me, demons, curses, and the rest of the powers of darkness are fun ideas to play around with in fiction, but they also violate the laws of science. They can't exist in the real world. So even if you did have a neighbor who worshipped Satan, you wouldn't have to be afraid of him. He'd just be a harmless crank.''

The tattooed man scowled. ''Are you saying Manson was harmless? Or those devil lovers who rape little children?''

''I don't think Manson claimed to be a Satanist. And there aren't really hordes of depraved cultists running around America molesting kids. That's just an urban legend.'' The two friends exchanged sceptical glances. Harper could tell he was losing them. ''Well, all right, there might be a few sick people trying to practice black magic and actually doing some damage. But I'm not one of them! I'm normal. I have a family and work and bills and stupid, ordinary problems just like everybody else. I wish I knew who was telling people otherwise.''

The wiry man said, ''It would be real dumb to try and get revenge.''

Startled, Harper blinked. ''I don't want revenge. I just want to talk to him and convince him he's wrong.''

''I don't know who started the stories,'' the big man said. ''They're just going around. But I'll give you some advice: You won't do yourself any good by sneaking around in the dark, or speaking out in defense of devil worship, either.''

''I wasn't,'' Harper said. ''I was just—''

''We have to go,'' said the tattooed man, tossing a taped and faded five-dollar bill on the bar. He and his friend strode for the door, leaving their half-finished beers behind.

When Harper got home, he found Kevin and Mary huddled together watching a Hammer horror movie. The chanting of the busty, black-robed witch on the TV screen made his head throb, and his wife's greeting jangled his nerves still further. ''Well? Does everybody love us now?'' Kevin seemed to cringe at the edge in her voice.

In reality, Harper hadn't been able to tell if he'd done any good. None of the people he'd accosted in the bar and on the street had refused to speak with him, but many had seemed uncomfortable, guarded, or cold. But he was damned if he'd admit it when Mary was out to break his balls, and Kevin needed reassurance. "I met some people. I think it did some good."

"How much?" Mary asked. "At best, you talked to a tiny fraction of the people in the area. Even if you charmed every one of them—"

"I didn't say the problem was solved," Harper said. "But I made a start. I'll keep introducing myself, the neighbors I meet will talk to others, and gradually word will get around that we're okay."

Mary grimaced. "Assuming that even happens, how long will it take? And what's going to happen in the meantime?"

"Nothing," Harper said, "except maybe I'll have to put the mailbox back up again. You're panicking over a trivial annoyance." He put his hand on Kevin's shoulder and smiled down into the boy's anxious blue eyes. "I promise, everything's going to be fine."

The following night, Harper awoke to screaming, or at least he thought he had. But by the time he bolted upright, the night was still, though it still seemed to vibrate with the echo of a cry.

He was pretty sure he'd been having a nightmare. Had someone been shrieking in that? Befuddled, he ran his fingers through his sweaty hair.

"What is it?" Mary mumbled.

Harper didn't particularly want to answer. If he kept quiet, she might go back to sleep, and these days, he liked her better that way. But his heart was still pounding, his skin, crawling; it might help to be told that the scream had only sounded in his dreams. "I thought I heard something. Did you?"

"Maybe," she said, the grogginess draining out of her voice. "Carthoris screeching. Another cat fight. Except maybe he sounded different."

Out in the front yard, Kevin wailed, the sound of his voice unmistakable. Harper and Mary leaped up and scrambled for the front of the house, jamming together in the bedroom doorway. For an instant, he wanted to knock her aside.

They found their son sobbing on his knees. Carthoris, burned almost beyond recognition, squirmed feebly on the grass before him. Evidently someone had poured gasoline on the cat, then set him on fire. A sickening stench of charred meat hung in the air.

Mary knelt and put her arms around Kevin. The boy twisted and buried his face in her nightgown. Harper noticed that his fingers were blistered, no doubt from touching the cat's still-smoldering flesh.

Mary sneered up at her husband. "Another 'trivial annoyance,' " she said.

Harper's fists clenched. "I'll call the vet."

The coppery stubble on the deputy's deeply cleft chin glinted in the sunlight streaming through the window. Harper, pacing restlessly, surmised that the green-uniformed officer was finishing up the graveyard shift. "How's the cat now?" he asked.

Mary said, "They had to put him to sleep." In her lap, Kevin sniffled.

"And nobody saw or heard anything," the deputy said.

"No," Harper said wearily. He wondered how many times the cop was going to take them over the same ground. "Just Carthoris crying."

The deputy clicked the nib back into his ball-point and closed his black fake-leather notebook. "Then I hope you realize, we may not be able to do much."

"What does that mean?" Harper demanded. "I told you what this is all about. If you find the people who think we're Satanists—"

"I thought Mrs. Harper said the whole neighborhood thinks so."

"Of course they don't." Harper shot Mary a venomous glance. "I'm sure it's only a couple idiots, five or six at the absolute outside. Start with Mrs. Porter across the street."

The deputy frowned. "Are you accusing her?"

"No. But I imagine she can point you at the people who did do it."

"Well, of course, we'll check around," the deputy said vaguely. "I didn't mean to suggest any different. But you

know, however it works out, in the long run it might pay
you to be a little less"—he hesitated—"provocative." He
waved his hands at the pictures of dragons, wizards, and
barbarian warriors on the opposite wall. "I mean, look at
this place."

Harper stared at him incredulously. "Are you saying that
what happened is our own fault?"

The deputy shrugged. "I grew up around here, Mr. Harper.
And I can tell you, it's a conservative, family-values kind of
community. If you want to live a wild life, I guess that's
your privilege, but maybe you'd be better off doing it in
California or someplace like that. But of course, that's for
you to decide. I am sorry about your pet." He got up, put
on his cowboy hat, and went out the door.

"So much for that," Mary said. "He's on *their* side.
Which means people are free to do anything they want to us.
Now can we leave?"

"No," Harper said. "What happened to Carthoris is horrible, but basically, nothing's changed. We still need to ride
this out."

"I knew I couldn't persuade you," Mary said. "You'd
oppose anything I suggested, just for spite. But maybe you'll
listen to your son." She squeezed Kevin's forearm. "Go on,
sweetheart, tell Daddy what you told me."

Kevin slowly raised his head. His eyes were red, his face,
blotched and puffy. He smelled of tears and mucus. "I hate
it here," he said haltingly. "I'm scared."

Though Harper knew he was being unfair, he couldn't help
resenting the boy for siding with his mother. Struggling to
keep his anger out of his voice, he said, "Kev, please, listen.
We have a right to be who we want and live where we want.
If we let ourselves be driven out of our home, we'll *always*
be scared, because we'll know that bad people can intimidate
us whenever it suits them. Do you understand?"

Kevin shook his head. "No." He started crying again, and
Mary wrapped her arms around him.

"Nice parenting," she said. "That really comforted him.
But you forgot to make another promise to solve the problem."

Harper's forearm twitched. He might actually have slapped

her if an idea hadn't burst into his head. "As a matter of fact, I'm going to solve it right now. If only to get you off my back." He took his keys out of his pocket.

"Wait!" Mary said. He turned, surprised by a softer note in her voice. She shifted Kevin onto the sofa cushion, rose, and hurried to him. "What are you going to do?"

"What do you care?" Harper said. "It's not like you think I can do anything *right*."

She put her hand on his chest. "Please. You're upset. You should calm down before you go anywhere."

For the first time in a long while, she actually sounded like she cared about him. But it was too little too late. She'd dumped on him one too many times, and now he had to *show* her. "Don't tell me what to do." He pivoted, shaking off her hand.

Two minutes later, Harper pulled into the parking lot of the Baptist church, among the fifty or so vehicles that had arrived before him. The building's spire gleamed like freshly fallen snow. Organ music and slightly off-key singing moaned from inside.

Harper had rushed here because he'd realized Mary had been right about one thing: It would take too long to win the neighbors over one and two at a time. He needed to talk to them en masse. He climbed out of the car and strode to the church's entrance.

The interior of the building looked as cheery and modern as the Cincinnati church where he'd gotten married. Potted palms flanked the altar. The walls and carpet were bright, pastel colors. The stained-glass windows beneath the vaulted ceiling shone. But evidently the air conditioning was broken, because the hall was hot and stuffy. Many of the people in the gleaming oak pews sat fanning themselves with the congregation newsletter.

As Harper marched down the aisle, they turned and stared. Murmurs arose, growing louder and louder, until the minister, a bald, middle-aged man in glasses, stopped the sermon in mid-sentence. "Can I help you?" he asked hesitantly.

"Yes," Harper said. "I need to talk to these people."

"We're in the middle of a service—"

"I apologize for interrupting. But it's important." He continued toward the pulpit. The bald man tensed, as if he intended to keep him out by force. Harper stared him in the eye.

"All right," the pastor said. "Since I can see you're in distress." He stepped back, and Harper took his place. Surveying the crowd, he spotted the fat woman, Mrs. Porter, and her children, and several other people he'd met.

"For those who don't know me, my name is Bruce Harper," he began. The microphone on the podium squealed and he pushed it farther away. "My family and I moved here a couple months ago. Recently, people have been harassing us; this morning, Kevin, my ten-year-old, is crying because someone burned our cat to death. Many of you know why these things are happening: There's a rumor going around that I'm a devil worshipper.

"If I knew who started it, I'd sue him for slander, because it's a lie. A *ridiculous* lie, without a shred of evidence to support it. I'll tell you the whole case against me. I take walks at night. I was involved in a costume party. My kid reads comics. If those are the infallible signs of devil worship, I suspect that nearly everyone here is guilty. Of course, I also do something that the rest of you don't: I write stories about spirits and magic. But they're just entertainment. Make-believe. They're not intended to convert people to a belief in witchcraft or anything else."

He wiped perspiration from his forehead: "You see? The whole thing's asinine. And even if it weren't, it would still be cruel and cowardly to kill a defenseless animal just because I owned it, or make a sweet little boy miserable simply because I'm his dad, or persecute my family any other way. We're Americans, right? We're supposed to respect each other's freedoms, including freedom of religion. And Christians are supposed to love their neighbors."

Sweat stung in his eyes. He blinked it away. "So I'm begging you: Don't spread vicious gossip about me, and don't give my wife and kid a hard time. If you don't want to be friends, just leave us alone, and we'll do the same for you." He realized he'd run out of things to say. He peered out at the crowd, to see if he'd moved or shamed them.

And was shocked at the sneer on every lip, the loathing in every eye. A malice like the contempt in Mary's voice, or the rage that churned his stomach when they fought.

He realized it didn't matter who'd started the rumor, how absurd it was, or how eloquently he defended himself. These people simply wanted someone to hate. He was a little different, and so he'd do.

Suddenly he was afraid.

"I guess that's it," he quavered. "Thanks for hearing me out. I'll let you get back to your service." He stepped down and started back up the aisle. Voices babbled on either side:

"He admitted to Doug that they drink human blood."

"Did you see the way he glared at Reverend Thomas? That was what they call the Evil Eye!"

"—sex with animals—"

"—piss and shit on the Bible—"

"And the bastard has the nerve to come into *our church*!"

Don't run, Harper told himself. Don't show fear. If you just keep walking, you'll be all right.

From the corner of his eye, he glimpsed a figure rising from its seat. His head jerked around. He tripped over someone's outstretched leg.

He fell to one knee, and the congregation roared. By the time he tried to get up, they were on top of him.

Snakes

Jack Ketchum

What she came to think of as *her* snake appeared just after the first storm.

She was talking on the phone with her lawyer in New York. Outside the flood-waters had receded. She could see through the screen which enclosed the lanai on one side, that her yard, which an hour before had been under a foot of water, had drained off down the slope past the picket fence and into the canal beyond.

She could let out the dog, she thought. Though she'd have to watch her. At one year old the golden retriever was still just a puppy and liked to dig. Ann had learned the hard way. Weather in south Florida being what it was she'd already gone through three slipcovers for the couch due to black tarry mud carried in on Katie's feet and belly.

The lawyer was saying he needed money.

"I hate to ask," he said.

"How much?"

"Two thousand for starters."

"Christ, Ray."

"I know it's tough. But you've got to look at it this way— he's already into you for over thirty grand and every month the figure's growing. If we get him he'll owe you my fee as well. I'll make sure of it."

"*If* we get him."

"You can't think that way, Annie. Look. *I* know you're

starving out there. I know what you make for a living and I know why you moved down there in the first place—because it was the cheapest place you could think of where you could still manage to bring up your kid in any kind of decent fashion. That's *his fault*. You've *got* to go after him. Just think about it for a minute. Thirty grand in back child support! Believe me, it will change your whole life. You can't *afford* to be defeatist about this.''

"Ray, I *feel* defeated. I feel like he's beaten the shit out of me."

"You're not. Not yet."

She sighed. She felt seventy—not forty. She could feel it in her legs. She sat down on the couch next to Katie. Pushed gently away at the cold wet nose that nuzzled her face.

"Find the retainer, Ann."

"Where?"

I'm trapped, she thought. He's got me. I barely made taxes this year.

"Trust me. Find the money."

She hung up and opened the sliding glass door to the lanai and then stood in the open screen doorway to the yard and watched while Katie sniffed through the scruffy grass and behind the hibiscus looking for a suitable place to pee. The sun was bright. The earth was steaming.

She couldn't even afford her dog, she thought. She loved the dog and so did Danny but the dog was a luxury. Its food was a luxury, its collar, its chain. Its shots were an extravagance.

I'm trapped.

Outside Katie stiffened.

Her feet splayed wide and her nose darted down low to the ground, darted up and then down again. The smooth golden hair along her backbone suddenly seemed to coarsen.

"Katie?"

The dog barely glanced at her, but the glance told her that whatever she saw in the grass, Katie was going to play with it come hell or high water. The eyes were bright. Her haunches trembled with excitement.

Katie's play, she knew, could sometimes be lethal. Ann would find the chewed bodies of ginkos on the lanai deposited there in front of the door like a some sort of present. Once, a small rabbit. She watched amazed and shocked one sunny afternoon as the dog leapt four feet straight up into the air to pluck a sparrow from its flight. She was thinking this.

And then she saw the snake.

It was nose to nose with Kate, the two of them fencing back and forth not a foot apart, the snake banded black and brown, half-hidden behind the hibiscus bushes, but from where she stood, six feet away, it looked frighteningly big. *Definitely* big enough, she thought, whether it was poisonous or not, to do the dog serious damage if it was the snake and not Katie who did the biting.

She heard its hiss. Saw its mouth drop open on the hinged jaw.

It darted, struck, and fell into the black mud at Katie's feet. The dog had shifted stance and backed away and was still backpedaling but the snake was not letting it go at that. The snake was advancing.

"Kate!"

She ran out. Her eyes never left the snake for an instant. She registered its fast smooth glide, registered for the first time actual *size* of the thing.

Seven feet? Eight feet? Jesus!

She crossed the distance to the dog faster than she thought she'd ever moved in her life, grabbed her collar and flung all seventy-five pounds of golden retriever headfirst past her toward the door so that it was behind *her* now, *shit*, head raised, gliding through the mud and tufts of grass coming toward her as she stumbled over the dog who'd turned in the doorway for one last look at the thing and then got past her and slammed the screen in the goddamn face of the thing just as it hit the screen once and then twice—a sound like a foot or hammer striking—hit it hard enough to dent it inward. And finally, seeing that, she screamed.

The dog was barking now, going for the screen on their side, enraged by the attempted intrusion. Ann hauled her away by the collar back through the lanai and slid the glass doors shut and even though she knew it was crazy, even though she knew the snake could not get through the screen, she damn well locked them.

She sat down on the rug, her legs giving out completely, her heart pounding, and tried to calm Katie. Or calm herself by calming Katie.

The dog continued to bark. Then to growl. And finally just sat there looking out toward the lanai and panting.

She wondered if that meant it was gone.

Somehow she doubted it.

She was glad it was President's Day weekend and that Danny was with his grandmother and grandfather at Universal over in Orlando. The trip was a present to him for good grades. She was glad he wouldn't be coming home from school in an hour as usual. Wouldn't come home to *that*.

The dog was still trembling.

So was she.

It was two o'clock. She needed a drink.

She could pinpoint the moment her fear of snakes began exactly.

She had been eight years old.

Her grandparents had lived in Daytona Beach, and Ann and her parents had come to visit. It was Ann's first visit to Florida. Daytona was pretty boring so they did a little sightseeing while they were there and one of the places they went to was a place called Ross Allen's Alligator Farm. A guide gave them a tour.

She remembered being fascinated by the baby alligators, dozens and dozens of them all huddled in one swampy pen, but seemingly very peaceful together, and she was wondering if maybe the reason they weren't biting at one another was that they all came from one mama, if that were possible. She stood there watching pondering that question until she became aware that the tour had moved on a bit and she knew she'd better catch up with them but she still wanted an answer to her question about the alligators so when she approached the group she did what she'd been told to do when she had a question, never mind how urgent.

She raised her hand.

As it happened the tour guide had just asked a question of his own. *Who wants to put this snake around his neck?* And Ann, with her hand in the air and thinking hard about the peaceful drowse of baby alligators found herself draped by and staring into the face of a five-pound boa constrictor named Marvin, everyone smiling at her, until her father said *I think you'd better take it off her, I don't know, she looks kinda pale to me*, and she fainted dead away.

There had been green snakes in the garden by her house and they had not bothered her in the slightest and there were garter snakes down by the brook. But nothing like a five-pound boa named Marvin. So that afterwards she avoided even the greens and garters. And shortly after had the first of what became a recurrent dream.

She is swimming in a mountain pool.

She is alone and she is naked.

The water is warm, just cool enough to be refreshing, and the banks are rocky and green.

She's midway across the pool, swimming easily, strongly, when she has the feeling that something is . . . not right. She turns and looks behind her and there it is, a sleek black watersnake, lithe and whiplike, so close that she can see its fangs, she can see directly into the white open mouth of it, it is undulating through the water toward her at stunning speed, it's right behind her and she swims for dear life but the snake is gaining by steady effortless degrees and she knows she'll never make it, not in time, the banks loom ahead like a giant stone wall bleeding gleaming condensation and she's terrified, crying—the crying itself slowing her down even more so that even as she swims and the water thickens she's losing her will and losing hope, it's useless, there's only her startled frightened flesh driving her on and the snake is at her heel and she can almost feel it and

she wakes.

Sometimes she's only sweating. Twisted into the bedsheets as though they were knots of water.

Sometimes she screams herself awake.

Screams as she's just done now.

Goddamn snake.

Seven feet long and big around as a man's fist. Bigger. The snake in her dream was nothing compared to that.

She got up and went to the kitchen and poured herself a

glass of vodka, added ice and tonic. She drank it down like a glass of water and poured another. The shaking stopped a bit.

Enough for her to wonder if the snake were still outside.

The dog was lying on the rug, biting at a flea on its right hind leg.

The dog didn't look worried at all.

Take a look, she thought.

What can it hurt?

She unlocked the door, opened it, and stepped out onto the lanai, then slid the door closed behind her. She didn't want Katie involved in this. She picked up a broom she used to sweep up out there. Behind her Katie got to her feet and watched, ears perked. She scrabbled at the door.

"No," she said. The scrabbling stopped.

"Good dog."

She peered through the screens.

Nothing by the door.

Nothing in the yard either that she could see, either to the left, where the snake had first appeared and the hibiscus grew up against the picket fence, nor to the right, where a second, taller plant grew near the door. The only place she *couldn't* see was along the base of the screened-in wall itself on either side. To do that she'd have to open the door.

Which she wasn't about to do.

Or was she?

Hell, it was ridiculous to hang around wondering. There was every chance the snake had gone back through the fence the way it had come and was rooting around for mice down at the banks of the canal even as she stood here.

Okay, she thought. Do it. But do it carefully. Do it *smart*.

She opened the dented screen door to just the width of the broom and wedged its thick bristles into the bottom of the opening. She peered out along the base of the longer wall to the left.

No snake.

She looked right and heard it hiss and slide along the metal base near the hibiscus and felt it hit the door all at once, jarring its metal frame.

She slammed it shut.

The broom fell out of her hands, clattered to the concrete floor.

And then she was just staring at the thing, backing away to the concrete wall behind her.

Watching as it raised its head. And then its body. Two feet, three feet. Rising. Slowly gaining height.

Seeming to swell.

And swaying.

Staring back at her.

It was nearly dusk before she got up the courage to look again.

This time she used a shovel from the garage instead of the broom. If it came after her again with a little luck she could chop the damn thing's head off.

It was gone.

She looked everywhere. The snake was gone.

She took another drink by way of celebration. The idea of spending the night with the snake lying out there in her yard had unnerved her completely. She thought she deserved the drink.

If she dreamed she did not remember.

In the morning she checked the yard again and finding it empty, let Katie out to do her business, let her back in again and then went out the front door for the paper.

She took one step onto the walkway and hadn't even shut the door behind her when she saw it on the lawn, stretched to its full enormous length diagonally from her mailbox nearly all the way to the walk, three feet away. Head raised and moving toward her.

She stepped back inside and shut the door.

The snake stopped and waited.

She watched it through the screen.

The snake didn't move. It just lay there in the bright morning sun.

She closed the inner door and locked it.

Jesus!

She was trapped in her own home here!

Who the hell did you call? The police? The Humane Society?

She tried 911.

An officer identified himself. He sounded young and friendly.

"I've got a snake out here in my yard. A big snake. And he . . . he keeps coming right at me. I honestly can't get out of my house!"

It was true. The only other exit to the condo was through the kitchen door that led to the garage and the garage was right beside the front door. She wasn't going out that way. No way. No thanks.

"Sorry, ma'am but it's not police business. What you want to do is call the Animal Rescue League. They'll send somebody over there and pick it up for you. Get rid of it. But I gotta tell you, you're my third snake-call today and I've already had four alligators. Yesterday was even worse. These rains bring 'em *all* out. So Animal Rescue may make you wait a while."

"God!"

He laughed. "My brother-in-law's a gardener. You know what he says about Florida? '*Everything* bites down here. Even the *trees*'ll bite at you.' "

He gave her the number and she dialed. The woman at Animal Rescue took Ann's name, address and phone number and then asked her to describe the animal, its appearance and behavior.

"Sounds like what you've got is a Florida banded," she said. "Though I never heard of one that big before."

"A what?"

"A Florida banded watersnake. You say it's seven, eight feet? That's big. That means you've got maybe thirty pounds of snake there."

"Is it poisonous?"

"Nah. Give you a darn good nasty bite though. The banded's aggressive. He'll hit you two three four times if he hits you once. But again, I never heard of one *goin' after* you the way you're saying. Normally they'll just defend their own territory. You sure you didn't go after *him* some way?"

"Absolutely not. My dog, maybe, at first. But I pulled her

away as soon as I saw the thing. Since then he's come at me twice. With absolutely no provocation whatsoever.''

"Well, don't start provokin' him now. Snake gets agitated, he'll strike at anything. We'll be out just as soon as we can. You have yourself a good day now.''

She waited. Watched talk shows and ate lunch. Stayed purposely away from both the front door and the lanai.

They arrived about three.

Two burly men in slacks and short-sleeve shirts stepping out of the van carrying two long wooden poles. One pole had a kind of wire shepherd's crook at the end and the other pole a V-shaped wedge. She stood in the doorway with Katie and watched them. The men just nodded to her and went to work.

Infuriatingly enough, the snake now lay passive on the grass while the crook slipped over its head just beneath the jawbone and the V-shaped wedge pinned it halfway down the length of its body. The man with the crook then lifted the head and grabbed it under the jaw first with one hand and then the other, dropping his pole to the grass. Its mouth opened wide and the snaked writhed, hissing—but did not really seem to resist. They counted to three and hefted him.

"Big guy, ain't he.''

"Biggest banded I've seen.''

They walked him across the street to the vacant lot opposite into a wide thick patch of scrub.

Then they just dropped him, crossed the street, got the pole off the lawn and walked back to the van.

She stood there. She couldn't believe it.

"Excuse me? Could you hold on a moment, please?''

She walked outside. The bald one was climbing into the driver's seat.

"I don't understand. Aren't you . . . moving him? Aren't you *taking* him somewhere?''

The man smiled. "He's took.''

"*That's* supposed to keep that thing away from here? That *street*?''

"Not the street, ma'am. See, a snake's territorial. That means that wherever he sets down, if there's enough food 'round to feed on, that's where he's gonna stay. Now, he's gonna find lizards, mice, rabbits and whatever over there in that lot. And see, it leads back to a stream. When he's finished with this patch he'll just go on downstream. You'll never see that guy again. Believe me."

"What if you're wrong?"

"S'cuse me?"

She was angry and frustrated and she guessed it showed.

"I said what if you're wrong! What if the damn thing is *back here* in half an hour?"

The men exchanged glances.

Women. Don't know shit, do they.

"Then I guess you'll want to to call us up again, ma'am. Won't happen, though."

She wanted to smash furniture.

She talked to Danny in Orlando that night and told him about the snake. She must have made it sound like quite an adventure because Danny expressed more than a little pique at missing it. By the time she finished talking to him she almost thought it *was* an adventure.

Then she remembered it hissing, racing through the grass. Rising up to stare at her.

As though it knew her.

She fell asleep early and missed the evening news and weather report. It turned out that was the worst thing that happened to her all day.

The following morning she cleaned house from top to bottom, easier to do with Danny gone, and by noon had worked herself up into a pretty good mood despite thinking occasionally of her lawyer and the money. She had considered how she might raise the cash for his retainer but had come to no conclusion. Her ex-husband had seen to it that her credit was shot so that a loan was out of the question. Her car was basically already a junker. And her parents had barely enough to get by on. *Sell the condo?* No. *Everything in it?* Dear God.

Once in a while she'd go out and check the yard. And maybe those guys were right, she thought. Maybe they knew their business after all. Because the big banded watersnake had not appeared again.

She showered and dressed. She had a lunch date with Suzie over at the Outback set for one-thirty.

Suzie, too, had missed the weather the night before and when they came out of the restaurant around three—aware that it was raining but not for how long nor nearly how hard—the parking lot was ankle-deep in floodwater. Hurricane Andrew be damned. Here they were, standing in the midst of the worst damn rainstorm of the year.

"You want to wait it out?"

"I was cleaning. I left the second-floor *windows* open. I can't believe it."

"Okay, but be careful driving, huh?"

Ann nodded. Suzie lived nearby, while her house was over a mile away. Visibility was not good. Not even there within the parking lot. Sheets of rain driven by steady winds gave the grey sky a kind of thickness and a warm humid weight.

They hugged and took off their shoes and ran for their respective cars. By the time Ann unlocked hers and slid inside her skirt and blouse were see-through and her hair was streaming water. She could taste her hair. She could see almost nothing.

The windshield wipers helped. She started the car slowly forward, following Suzie out through the exit to the street where they parted in different directions.

Happily there was almost no one on the usually congested four-lane street and cars were moving carefully and nobody was passing. The lane-lines had disappeared under water. She was moving through at least a foot and a half of it.

Then midway home she had to pull over. The windshield wipers couldn't begin to cope. The rain was pounding now—big drops sounding like hailstones. The wind gusted and rocked her car.

She sat staring into the fogged-over rearview mirror hoping that some damn fool wouldn't come up behind her and rear-end her. It was dangerous to pull over but she hadn't had a choice.

She looked down at herself and wished she'd worn a bra.

It was not just the nipples, not just the shape and outline of her breasts—you could see every mole and freckle. The same was true of the pale yellow skirt gone transparent across her thighs. She might as well be naked.

So what? she thought. Who's going to see you, anyway? In *this*.

The rain slowed down enough so that the wipers could at least begin to do their job. She moved on.

The water in the street was moving fast, pouring toward some downhill destination.

Curbs were gone, flooded over.

Lawns were gone. Parking lots. Sidewalks.

The openings to sewers formed miniature whirlpools in which garbage floated, in which paper shopping bags swirled and branches and bits of wood.

In one of them she saw something which chilled her completely.

A broken cardboard box was turning slowly over the grate. The box was striped with black and brown and the stripes were moving.

Snakes. Seeking higher ground and respite from swimming.

She had heard about this happening during storms in Florida but she'd never actually seen it. *Everything bites*, said the man.

This goddam state.

She turned the corner onto her street.

And she might have guessed if she'd thought about it, might have expected it. She knew the street she'd turned off was elevated slightly over her own. She'd noted it dozens of times.

But not now. Not this time. She was too intent on simply getting there, on getting through the storm. So that her car plunged into three and a half feet of water at the turnoff.

She damn near panicked then. It took her totally by surprise and scared her so badly that she almost stopped. Which would no doubt have been a disaster. She knew she'd never have gotten it started again. Not in this much water. She kept going, hands clutching the wheel, wishing she'd never dreamt of having lunch with Suzie.

The water was halfway up the grille ahead of her, halfway up the door. The car actually felt *lighter*, as though the tires had much less purchase than before.

Almost crawling, expecting the car to sputter and die any moment, she urged it on. Talking to the car. Begging to the car. *Come on, honey.* Her condo with the open second-floor windows only four blocks away.

You can do it, honey. Sure you can.

One block.

Going slowly, the car actually rocking side to side in the current like a boat, her foot pressing gently on the accelerator.

Two blocks.

And home just ahead of her now, she could see its white stucco facade turned dull grey in the rain, see the wide-open window to Danny's bedroom like a dark accusing eye staring out at her, the front lawn drowned and flooded with water.

And as she passed the third block, going by the overpass to the canal, she could see the roiling.

At first it wasn't clear just what it was. Something large and black moving in the water ahead like some sort of matter in another whirlpool over another sewer grate only bigger.

Then she came closer and she almost stopped again because now she saw what it was clearly dead ahead but she didn't stop, my God, she *couldn't* stop, she inched along with her foot barely touching the accelerator, letting the idle do the work of moving the car forward like a faintly beating heart somewhere inside while she desperately tried to think how to avoid the writhing mass of bodies and what the hell to do.

There must have been dozens of them. All sizes.

All lengths.

The water was thick with them.

They moved over and through one another in some arcane inborn pattern, formed a mass that was roughly circular in shape and maybe six or seven feet in diameter, thickest at the center, lightest at the edges, but all in constant motion, some of them shooting like sparks off a sparkler or a catherine wheel and then swimming back into the circle again that formed their roiling gleaming nucleus.

Driving through them was unimaginable. She had to go around them but it was impossible to see where the street

ended and lawn began and like every street in the development
the curbs were shallow—she would feel very little going over
them.

But she had to try.

*And in fact she felt nothing as she passed to the right onto
her neighbor's lawn and into her neighbor's mud and she
tried not to see them out the driver's side window as the car
lurched once and shuddered and stopped while her wheels
spun uselessly on.*

Her first response was to gun the thing but that was no
good, all it did was dig her deeper into the mud on the
passenger side.

Well. *Not exactly all.*

It also stirred them, seemed to annoy them all to hell. She
heard them hit the front and back doors on her side. *Bump.
Bump. Bumpbumpbumpbumpbump.* She dared to glance out
her window and saw that the circle had become an oblong
figure stretching the entire length of the car—as though something protoplasmic were trying to engulf her.

She put the car in park and let it idle. Fighting a growing
panic. Trying to consider her options.

She could sit there. She could wait for help. She could
wait for them to disperse.

But there wouldn't be any help. There was practically
nobody on the main road let alone this one, no one but her
dumb enough to be out on side streets in a storm like this.

And they wouldn't be dispersing either.

That much was obvious. Now that the car was quiet the
circle had formed again. Almost exactly as before.

Except for these two. Crawling up over the hood.

A black snake. And something banded yellow and brown.
Crawling toward the windshield. Looking for higher ground.

*And she could feel them with her inside the car. She could
hear them on the seat in back. Crawling up to her seat.
Crawling up to her neck and over her neck and down across
her breasts and thighs.*

She had to get out of here. That or go crazy. There was
one option she simply could not tolerate and that was just to
sit there listening to them slither across the roof and over
the hood. She could imagine them, see them, thick as flies,

blocking her view through the windshield, crawling, staring in at her. *Wanting* in.

She had to get out.

She could run. She could run through the water. It wasn't that deep. Go out the passenger side. Maybe it was free of them.

She shifted seats.

It wasn't. Not completely. But there weren't many. Just sparks on the catherine wheel. Darting back and forth beneath the car.

The black snake was at the windshield. Another yellow and brown appeared just over the left headlight, moving up across the hood.

How long before the car was buried in them?

Her heart was pounding. There was a taste in her mouth like old dry leaves.

You can do this, she thought. You haven't any choice. The only other choice is giving up and giving in and that will make you crazy. When you have no choice you do what you've got to do.

Don't wait. Waiting will make it worse. Go. Go now.

She took a deep breath and wrenched at the door handle and pushed hard with her shoulder. Warm floodwater poured in over her feet and ankles. The door opened a few inches and jammed into the mud. The spinning tires had angled the passenger side down.

She pushed again. The door gave another inch. She tried desperately to get through.

It wasn't enough.

She threw herself across the seat onto her back, grabbed the steering wheel above with both hands for leverage and kicked at the door with all her might, kicked it twice and then got up and rammed her body into the gap. Buttons popped on her blouse. She screamed and kicked as a brown snake glided over her leg above the ankle and into the car and she pushed again and then suddenly she was through.

Mud sucked at her feet. The water was up to mid-thigh. Her skirt was floating. She slogged a few steps and almost fell. A green snake twisted by a few feet to the left—and what may have been a coral snake, small and banded black, yellow and red swam back toward the car beside her. She lurched away. Corals carried poison. She turned to make sure it had gone back to the swirling hell it came from and that was when she saw him.

Her snake.

Perched atop the roof of the car. Coiled there.

Looking at her.

And now, beginning to move.

The dream, she thought, *it's the dream all over again* as she saw the snake glide off the roof and into the water and she hauled herself through the water, making for what she knew was the concrete drive in front of her house, its firmer footing, but now she was still on the lawn next door, her feet slapping down deep into the soft slimy mud, legs splashing through the water so that she was mud from head to toe in no time and not turning back, not needing to—the snake gaining on her as real in her mind's eye as it had been in her dream.

When she fell she fell flat out straight ahead and her left hand came down on concrete, the right sunk deep into mud. She gulped water, spit it out. Scrambled up. The torn silk blouse had come open completely and hung off one shoulder like a filthy sodden rag.

She risked a glance and there it was, taking its time, gliding, sinuous and graceful and awful with hurt for her just a few feet away.

A black snake skittered out ahead but she didn't care, her feet hit the concrete and suddenly she was splashing toward the garage because its door was kept unlocked for Danny after school; there were keys to the house hidden by the washing machine, there were rakes and tools inside.

She hit the door at a run and turned and saw the snake raise its head out of the water ready to strike and she bent down and reached into the warm deep muddy water, her head going under for a terrible moment blind as she clawed at the center of the door searching for the handle and found it and pulled up as the massive head of the thing struck at her, barely missing her naked breast as she lurched back and fell and it tangled itself, writhing furiously, in her torn nylon blouse.

Floodwater poured rushing into the garage, the thick muscular body of the snake turning over and across her in its tide, caressing the flesh of her stomach and sliding all along her back as she struggled to free herself of the blouse and twist it around its darting head. She stumbled to her feet and ran for the washing machine, found the keys and gripped them tight and ran for the door.

The snake was free. The blouse drifted.

Ann was standing in two feet of water and she couldn't see the snake.

She fumbled the key into the lock and twisted it and flung open the door.

The snake rose up out of the water and hit the lip of the single stair just as she crossed the threshold and then it began to move inside.

"No." she was screaming. "I don't let you in I didn't *invite* you in. Goddammit! You bastard!" Screaming in fear but fury too, slamming the wooden door over and over again against the body of the snake while the head of the thing searched her out behind the door and she was aware of Kate barking beside her, the snake aware too, its head turning in that direction now and its black tongue tasting dogscent, womanscent, turning, until she saw the vacuum cleaner standing by the refrigerator still plugged in from this morning and flipped the switch and opened the door wide and hurled it toward the body of the black thing in the water.

The machine burst into a shower of sparks that raced blue and yellow though the garage like a blast of St. Elmo's Fire. The snake thrashed and suddenly seemed to swell. Smoke curled puffing off its body. Its mouth snapped open and shut and opened wide again, impossibly wide. She smelled burning flesh and sour electric fire. The cord crackled and burst in its wall-socket. Katie howled, ran ears back and tail low into the living room and cowered by the sofa.

She grabbed a hot pad off the stove and pulled the plug.

She looked down at the smoking body.

"I got you," she said. "You didn't get me. You didn't expect that, did you."

When she had hauled the carcass outside and closed the garage door and then fed Katie and finally indulged in a wonderful, long, hot bath, she put on a favorite soft cotton robe and then she went to the phone.

The lawyer was surprised to hear from her again so soon. "I'm having a little garage sale," she said.

And she almost laughed. Her little garage sale would no doubt relieve her of everything she was looking at, of practically everything she owned. It didn't matter a damn bit. It was worth it.

"I want you to go after him," she said. "You hear me? I want you to get the sonovabitch."

And then she did laugh.

Riki Tiki Tavi, she thought.

Snakes.

Joyce Carol Oates

It was the most beautiful house I had ever seen up close. Or was ever to enter. Three storys high, broad and gleaming pale-pink, made of sandstone, Uncle Rebhorn said, custom-designed and *his* design of course. They came to get me—Uncle Rebhorn, Aunt Elinor, my cousin Audrey who was my age and my cousin Darren who was three years older—one Sunday in July 1969. How excited I was, how special I felt, singled out for a visit to Uncle Rebhorn's house in Grosse Pointe Shores. I see the house shimmering before me and then I see emptiness, a strange rectangular blackness, and nothing.

For at the center of what happened on that Sunday many years ago is blackness.

I can remember what led to the blackness and what followed after it—not clearly, but to a degree, as, waking vague and stunned from a powerful dream, we retain shreds of the dream though we remain incapable of making them coalesce into a whole; nor can we "see" them as we'd seen them during the dream. So I can summon back a memory of the black rectangle and I can superimpose depth upon it—for it could not be flat, like a canvas—but I have to admit defeat, I can't "see" anything inside it. And this black rectangle is at the center of that Sunday in July 1969, and at the center of my girlhood.

Unless it was the end of my girlhood.
But how do I know, if I can't remember?

I was eleven years old. It was to be my first time ever—
and it was to be the last time, too, though I didn't know it
then—that I was brought by my father's older step-brother,
Uncle Rebhorn, to visit his new house and to go sailing on
Lake St. Clair. Because of my cousin Audrey, who was like
a sister of mine though I saw her rarely—I guessed this was
why. Mommy told me, in a careful, neutral voice, that of
course Audrey didn't have any friends, or Darren either. I
asked why and Mommy said they just didn't, that's all. That's
the price you pay for *moving up* too quickly in the world.

All our family lived in the Detroit suburb of Hamtramck
and had lived there for a long time. Uncle Rebhorn too, until
the age of eighteen when he left and now, how many years
later, he was a rich man—president of Rebhorn Auto Supply,
Inc., and he'd married a well-to-do Grosse Pointe woman—
and built his big, beautiful new house on Lake St. Clair
everybody in the family talked about but nobody had actually
seen. (Unless they'd seen the house from the outside? Not
my parents, who were too proud to stoop to such a maneuver,
but other relatives were said to have driven all the way to
Grosse Pointe Shores to gape at Uncle Rebhorn's pink mansion, as much as they could see of it from Buena Vista Drive.
Uninvited, they dared not ring the buzzer at the wrought iron
gate, shut and presumably locked at the foot of the drive.)
Uncle Rebhorn, whom I did not know at all, had left Hamtramck far behind and was said to "scorn" his upbringing
and his own family. There was a good deal of jealousy of
course, and envy, but since everybody hoped secretly to be
remembered by him sometime, and invited to share in his
amazing good fortune—imagine, a millionaire in the family!—they were always sending cards, wedding invitations,
announcements of births and christenings and confirmations;
sometimes even telegrams, since Uncle Rebhorn's telephone
number was unlisted and even his brothers didn't know what
it was. Daddy said, with that heavy, sullen droop to his voice
we tried never to hear, "If he wants to keep to himself that's
fine, I can respect that. We'll keep to ourselves, too."

Then, out of nowhere, the invitation came to *me*. Just a telephone call from Aunt Elinor.

Mommy, who'd taken the call, of course, and made the arrangements, didn't want me to stay overnight. Aunt Elinor had suggested this for it was a long drive, between forty-five minutes and an hour, and she'd said that Audrey would be disappointed, but Mommy said no and that was that.

So, that Sunday, how vividly I can remember!—Uncle Rebhorn, Aunt Elinor, Audrey, and Darren came to get me in Uncle Rebhorn's shiny black Lincoln Continental, which rolled like a hearse up our street of woodframe asphalt-sided bungalows and drew stares from our neighbors. Daddy was gone—Daddy was not going to hang around, he said, on the chance of saying hello and maybe getting to shake hands with his step-brother—but Mommy was with me, waiting at the front door when Uncle Rebhorn pulled up; but there were no words exchanged between Mommy and the Rebhorns, for Uncle Rebhorn merely tapped the car horn to signal their arrival, and Aunt Elinor, though she waved and smiled at Mommy, did not get out of the car, and made not the slightest gesture inviting Mommy to come out to speak with *her*. I ran breathless to the curb—I had a panicky vision of Uncle Rebhorn starting the big black car up and leaving me behind in Hamtramck—and climbed into the back seat, to sit beside Audrey. "Get in, hurry, we don't have all day," Uncle Rebhorn said in that gruff jovial cartoon voice some adults use with children, meant to be playful—or maybe not. Aunt Elinor cast me a frowning sort of smile over her shoulder and put her finger to her lips as if to indicate that I take Uncle Rebhorn's remark in silence, as naturally I would. My heart was hammering with excitement just to be in such a magnificent automobile!

How fascinating the drive from our familiar neighborhood into the city of Detroit where there were so many black people on the streets and many of them, glimpsing Uncle Rebhorn's Lincoln Continental, stared openly. We moved swiftly along Outer Drive and so to Eight Mile Road and east to Lake St. Clair where I had never been before, and I could not believe how beautiful everything was once we turned onto Lakeshore Drive. Now it was my turn to stare and stare. Such mansions on grassy hills facing the lake! So many tall trees, so much leafy space! So much sky! (The sky in Hamtramck was usually low and overcast and wrinkled like soiled laundry.) And Lake St. Clair, which was a deep rich aqua, like a painted lake! During most of the drive, Uncle Rebhorn was talking, pointing out the mansions of wealthy, famous people—I only remember "Ford"—"Dodge"—"Fisher"—"Wilson"—and Aunt Elinor was nodding and murmuring inaudibly, and in the back seat, silent and subdued, Audrey and Darren and I sat looking out the tinted windows. I was a little hurt and disappointed that Audrey seemed to be ignoring me, and sitting very stiffly beside me; though I guessed that, with Uncle Rebhorn talking continuously, and addressing his remarks to the entire car, Audrey did not want to seem to interrupt him. Nor did Darren say a word to anyone.

At last, in Grosse Pointe Shores, we turned off Lakeshore Drive onto a narrow, curving road called Buena Vista, where the mansions were smaller, though still mansions; Buena Vista led into a cul-de-sac bordered by tall, massive oaks and elms. At the very end, over-looking the lake, was Uncle Rebhorn's house—as I've said, the most beautiful house I had ever seen up close, or would ever enter. Made of that pale pink glimmering sandstone, with a graceful portico covered in English ivy, and four slender columns, and dozens of latticed windows reflecting the sun like smiles, the house looked like a storybook illustration. And beyond was the sky, a pure cobalt blue except for thin wisps of cloud. Uncle Rebhorn pressed a button in the dashboard of his car, and the wrought iron gate swung open—like nothing I'd ever seen before in real life. The driveway too was like no driveway I knew, curving and dipping, and comprised of rosy-pink gravel, exquisite as miniature seashells. Tiny pebbles flew up beneath the car as Uncle Rebhorn drove in and the gate swung miraculously shut behind us.

How lucky Audrey was to live here, I thought, gnawing at my thumbnail as Mommy had told me a thousand times not to do. Oh I would die to live in such a house, I thought.

Uncle Rebhorn seemed to have heard me. "*We* think so, yes indeed," he said. To my embarrassment, he was watching me through the rear view mirror and seemed to be winking at me. His eyes glittered bright and teasing. Had I spoken out loud without meaning to?—I could feel my face burn.

Darren, squeezed against the farther arm rest, made a sniggering, derisive noise. He had not so much as glanced at me when I climbed into the car and had been sulky during the drive so I felt that he did not like me. He was a fattish, flaccid-skinned boy who looked more like twelve than fourteen; he had Uncle Rebhorn's lard-colored complexion and full, drooping lips, but not Uncle Rebhorn's shrewd-glittering eyes; his were damp and close-set and mean. Whatever Darren meant by his snigger, Uncle Rebhorn heard it above the hum of the air-conditioner—was there anything Uncle Rebhorn could not hear?—and said in a low, pleasant, warning voice, "Son, mind your manners! Or somebody else will mind them for you."

Darren protested, "I didn't say anything, sir. I—"

Quickly, Aunt Elinor intervened, "Darren."

"—I'm sorry, sir. I won't do it again."

Uncle Rebhorn chuckled as if he found this very funny and in some way preposterous. But by this time he had pulled the magnificent black car up in front of the portico of the house and switched off the ignition. "Here we are!"

But to enter Uncle Rebhorn's sandstone mansion, it was strange, and a little scary, how we had to crouch. And push and squeeze our shoulders through the doorway. Even Audrey and me, who were the smallest. As we approached the big front door which was made of carved wood, with a beautiful gleaming brass American eagle, its dimensions seemed to shrink; the closer we got, the smaller the door got, reversing the usual circumstances where of course as you approach an object it increases in size, or gives that illusion. "Girls, watch your heads," Uncle Rebhorn cautioned, wagging his forefinger. He had a brusque laughing way of speaking as if most subjects were jokes or could be made to seem so by laughing. But his eyes, bright as chips of glass, were watchful and without humor.

How could this be?—Uncle Rebhorn's house that was so spacious-seeming on the outside was so cramped, and dark, and scary on the inside?

"Come on, come on! It's Sunday, it's the Sabbath, we haven't got all day!" Uncle Rebhorn cried, clapping his hands.

We were in a kind of tunnel, crowded together. There was a strong smell of something sharp and hurtful like ammonia; at first I couldn't breathe, and started to choke. Nobody paid any attention to me except Audrey who tugged at my wrist, whispering, "This way, June—don't make Daddy mad." Uncle Rebhorn led the way, followed by Darren, then Aunt Elinor, Audrey and me, walking on our haunches in a squatting position; the tunnel was too low for standing upright and you couldn't crawl on your hands and knees because the floor was littered with shards of glass. Why was it so dark? Where were the windows I'd seen from the outside? "Isn't this fun! We're so glad you could join us today, June!" Aunt Elinor murmured. How awkward it must have been for a woman like Aunt Elinor, so prettily dressed in a tulip-yellow summer knit suit, white high-heeled pumps and stockings, to make her way on her haunches in such a cramped space!—yet she did it uncomplaining, and with a smile.

Strands of cobweb brushed against my face. I was breathing so hard and in such a choppy way it sounded like sobbing which scared me because I knew Uncle Rebhorn would be offended. Several times Audrey squeezed my wrist so hard it hurt, cautioning me to be quiet; Aunt Elinor poked at me, too. Uncle Rebhorn was saying, cheerfully, "Who's hungry?—I'm starving," and again, in a louder voice, "Who's hungry?" and Darren echoed, "I'm starving!" and Uncle Rebhorn repeated bright and brassy as a TV commercial, "WHO'S HUNGRY?" and this time Aunt Elinor, Darren, Audrey, and I echoed in a chorus, "I'M STARVING!" Which was the correct reply, Uncle Rebhorn accepted it with a happy chuckle.

Now we were in a larger space, the tunnel had opened out onto a room crowded with cartons and barrels, stacks of lumber and tar pots, workmen's things scattered about. There were two windows in this room but they were small and square and crudely criss-crossed by strips of plywood; there were no windowpanes, only fluttering strips of cheap transparent plastic that blocked out most of the light. I could not stop shivering though Audrey pinched me hard, and cast me an anxious, angry look. Why, when it was a warm summer day outside, was it so cold inside Uncle Rebhorn's house? Needles of freezing air rose from the floorboards. The sharp ammonia odor was mixed with a smell of food cooking which made my stomach queasy. Uncle Rebhorn was criticizing Aunt Elinor in his joky angry way, saying she'd let things go a bit, hadn't she?—and Aunt Elinor was frightened, stammering and pressing her hand against her bosom, saying the interior decorator had promised everything would be in place by now. "Plenty of time for Christmas, eh?" Uncle Rebhorn said sarcastically. For some reason, both Darren and Audrey giggled.

Uncle Rebhorn had a thick, strong neck and his head swiveled alertly and his eyes swung onto you before you were prepared—those gleaming, glassy-glittering eyes. There was a glisten to the whites of Uncle Rebhorn's eyes I had never seen in anyone before and his pupils were dilated and very black. He was a stocky man; he panted and made a snuffling noise, his wide nostrils flattened with deep, impatient inhalations. His pale skin was flushed, especially in the cheeks; there was a livid, feverish look to his face. He was dressed for Sunday in a red-plaid sport coat that fitted him tightly in the shoulders, and a white shirt with a necktie, and navy blue linen trousers that had picked up some cobwebs on our way in. Uncle Rebhorn had a glowing bald spot at the crown of his head over which he had carefully combed wetted strands of hair; his cheeks were bunched like muscles as he smiled. And smiled. How hard it was to look at Uncle Rebhorn, his eyes so glittering, and his *smile*—! When I try to remember him now miniature slices of blindness skid toward me ▄▄▄▄▄▄▄▄▄▄▄▄▄▄▄▄ in my vision, I have to blink carefully to regain my full sight. And why am I shivering, I must put an end to such neurotic behavior, what other purpose to this memoir?—what other purpose to any effort of the retrieval of memory that gives such pain?

Uncle Rebhorn chuckled deep in his throat and wagged a forefinger at me, "Naughty girl, I know what *you're* thinking," he said, and at once my face burned, I could feel my freckles standing out like hot inflamed pimples, though I did

not know what he meant. Audrey, beside me, giggled again
nervously, and Uncle Rebhorn shook his forefinger at her,
too, "And you, honeybunch,—for sure, Daddy knows *you*."
He made a sudden motion at us the way one might gesture
at a cowering dog to further frighten it, or to mock its fear;
when, clutching at each other, Audrey and I flinched away,
Uncle Rebhorn roared with laughter, raising his bushy eye-
brows as if he was puzzled, and hurt. "Mmmmm girls, you
don't think I'm going to hit you, do you?"

Quickly Audrey stammered, "Oh no, Daddy—*no*."

I was so frightened I could not speak at all. I tried to hide
behind Audrey who was shivering as badly as I was.

"You *don't* think I'm going to hit you, eh?" Uncle Rebhorn said, more menacingly; he swung his fist playfully in
my direction and a strand of hair caught in his signet ring
and I squealed with pain which made him laugh, and relent
a little. Watching me, Darren and Audrey and even Aunt
Elinor laughed. Aunt Elinor tidied my hair and again pressed
a finger to her lips as if in warning.

I am not a naughty girl I wanted to protest and now too *I
am not to blame*.

For Sunday dinner we sat on packing cases and ate from
planks balanced across two sawhorses. A dwarfish olive-skinned
woman with a single fierce eyebrow waited on us, wearing a
white rayon uniform and a hairnet. She set plates down before
us sulkily, though, with Uncle Rebhorn, who kept up a steady
teasing banter with her, calling her "honey" and "sweetheart,"
she did exchange a smile. Aunt Elinor pretended to notice
nothing, encouraging Audrey and me to eat. The dwarf-woman
glanced at me with a look of contempt, guessing I was a poor
relation I suppose, her dark eyes raked me like a razor.

Uncle Rebhorn and Darren ate hungrily. Father and son
hunched over the improvised table in the same posture, bringing their faces close to their plates and, chewing, turning
their heads slightly to the sides, eyes moist with pleasure.
"Mmmmm!—good," Uncle Rebhorn declared. And Darren
echoed, "—*good*." Aunt Elinor and Audrey were picking
at their food, managing to eat some of it, but I was nauseated

and terrified of being sick to my stomach. The food was lukewarm, served in plastic containers. There were coarse slabs of tough, bright pink meat curling at the edges and leaking blood, and puddles of corn pudding, corn kernels and slices of onion and green pepper in a runny pale sauce like pus. Uncle Rebhorn gazed up from his plate, his eyes soft at first, then regaining some of their glassy glitter when he saw how little his wife and daughter and niece had eaten. "Say, what's up? 'Waste not, want not.' Remember"—here he reached over and jabbed my shoulder with his fork—"this is the Sabbath, and keep it holy. Eh?"

Aunt Elinor smiled encouragingly at me. Her lipstick was crimson-pink and glossy, a permanent smile; her hair was a shining pale blond like a helmet. She wore pretty pale-pink pearls in her ears and a matching necklace around her neck. In the car, she had seemed younger than my mother, but now, close up, I could see hairline creases in her skin, or actual cracks, as in glazed pottery; there was something out of focus in her eyes though she was looking directly at me. "June, dear, there is a hunger beyond hunger," she said softly, "and this is the hunger that must be reached."

Uncle Rebhorn added, emphatically, "And we're Americans. Remember *that*."

Somehow, I managed to eat what was on my plate. *I am not a naughty girl but a good girl: see!*

For dessert, the dwarf-woman dropped bowls in front of us containing a quivering amber jelly. I thought it might be apple jelly, apple jelly with cinnamon, and my mouth watered in anticipation. We were to eat with spoons but my spoon wasn't sharp enough to cut into the jelly; and the jelly quivered harder, and wriggled in my bowl. Seeing the look on my face, Uncle Rebhorn asked pleasantly, "What's wrong now, Junie?" and I mumbled, "I don't know, sir," and Uncle Rebhorn chuckled, and said, "Hmmmm! You don't think your dessert is a *jellyfish*, do you?"—roaring with delight, as the others laughed, less forcefully, with him.

For that was exactly what it was: a jellyfish. Each of us had one, in our bowls. Warm and pulsing with life and fear radiating from it like raw nerves.

* * *

▬▬▬▬▬▬ ▬▬▬▬▬▬▬ flicking toward me, slivers of
blindness. Unless fissures in the air itself?—fibrillations like
those at the onset of sleep the way dreams begin to skid
toward you—at you—into you—and there is no escape for
the dream *is* you.

Yes I would like to cease my memoir here. I am not
accustomed to writing, to selecting words with such care.
When I speak, I often stammer but there is a comfort in that—
nobody knows, what comfort!—for you hold back what you
must say, hold it back until it is fully your own and cannot
surprise you. *I am not to blame, I am not deserving of hurt
neither then nor now* but do I believe this, even if I cannot
succeed in making you believe it.

How can an experience belong to you if you cannot remember it? That is the extent of what I wish to know. If I cannot
remember it, how then can I summon it back to comprehend
it, still less to change it. *And why am I shivering, when the
sun today is poison-hot burning through the foliage dry and
crackling as papier-mâché yet I keep shivering shivering shivering if there is a God in heaven please forgive me.*

After Sunday dinner we were to go sailing. Uncle Rebhorn
had a beautiful white sailboat bobbing at the end of a dock,
out there in the lake, which was a rich deep aqua-blue scintil-
lating with light. On Lake St. Clair on this breezy summer
afternoon there were many sailboats, speedboats, yachts. I
had stared at them in wondering admiration as we'd driven
along the Lakeshore Drive. What a dazzling sight like nothing
in Hamtramck!

First, though, we had to change our clothes. All of us,
said Uncle Rebhorn, have to change into bathing suits.

Audrey and I changed in a dark cubbyhole beneath a stairway. This was Audrey's room and nobody was supposed to
come inside to disturb us but the door was pushing inward
and Audrey whimpered, "No, no Daddy," laughing nervously and trying to hold the door shut with her arm. I was
a shy child; when I had to change for gym class at school I
turned my back to the other girls and changed as quickly
as I could. Even showing my panties to another girl was

embarrassing to me, my face burned with a strange wild heat. Uncle Rebhorn was on the other side of the door, we could hear his harsh labored breathing. His voice was light, though, when he asked, "Hmmmm—d'you naughty little girls need any help getting your panties down? Or your bathing suits on?" "No, Daddy, please," Audrey said. Her eyes were wide and stark in her face and she seemed not aware of me any longer but in a space of her own, trembling, hunched over. I was scared, too, but thinking why don't we joke with Uncle Rebhorn, he wants us to joke with him, that's the kind of man he is, what harm could he do us?—the most any adult had ever done to me by the age of eleven was Grandpa tickling me a little too hard so I'd screamed with laughter and kicked but that was years ago when I'd been a baby practically, and while I had not liked being tickled it was nothing truly painful or scary—was it? I tried to joke with my uncle through the door, I was giggling saying, "No no no, you stay out of here, Uncle Rebhorn! We don't need your help no we don't!" There was a moment's silence, then Uncle Rebhorn chuckled appreciatively, but there came then suddenly the sound of Aunt Elinor's raised voice, and we heard a sharp slap, and a cry, a female cry immediately cut off. And the door ceased its inward movement, and Audrey shoved me whispering, "Hurry up! You dumb dope, hurry up!" So quickly— safely—we changed into our bathing suits.

It was a surprise, how by chance Audrey's and my bathing suits looked alike, and us like twin sisters in them: both were pretty shades of pink, with elasticized tops that fitted tight over our tiny, flat breasts. Mine had emerald green seahorses sewn onto the bodice and Audrey's had little ruffles, the suggestion of a skirt.

Seeing my face, which must have shown hurt, Audrey hugged me with her thin, cold arms. I thought she would say how much she liked me, I was her favorite cousin, she was happy to see me—but she didn't say anything at all.

Beyond the door Uncle Rebhorn was shouting and clapping his hands.

"C'mon move your sweet little asses! Chop-chop! Time's a-wastin'! There'll be hell to pay if we've lost the sun!"

Audrey and I crept out in our bathing suits and Aunt Elinor

grabbed us by the hands making an annoyed "tsking" sound
and pulling us hurriedly along. We had to push our way out
of a small doorway—no more than an opening, a hole, in
the wall—and then we were outside, on the back lawn of
Uncle Rebhorn's property. What had seemed like lush green
grass from a distance was synthetic grass, the kind you see
laid out in flat strips on pavement. The hill was steep down
to the dock, as if a giant hand was lifting it behind us, making
us scramble. Uncle Rebhorn and Darren were trotting ahead,
in matching swim trunks—gold trimmed in blue. Aunt Elinor
had changed into a single-piece white satin bathing suit that
exposed her bony shoulders and sunken chest; it was shocking
to see her. She called out to Uncle Rebhorn that she wasn't
feeling well—the sun had given her a migraine headache—
sailing would make the headache worse—could she be excused?—but Uncle Rebhorn shouted over his shoulder,
"You're coming with us, God damn you! Why did we buy
this frigging sailboat except to enjoy it?" Aunt Elinor winced,
and murmured, "Yes, dear," and Uncle Rebhorn said, snort-
ing, with a wink at Audrey and me, "Hmmm! It better be
'yes, dear,' you stupid cow-cunt."

By the time we crawled out onto the deck of the sailboat
a chill wind had come up, and in fact the sun was disappearing
like something being sucked down a drain. It was more like
November than July, the sky heavy with clouds like stained
concrete. Uncle Rebhorn said sullenly, "—bought this frigging sailboat to enjoy it for God's sake—for the family and
that means *all the family*." The sailboat was lurching in the
choppy water like a living, frantic thing as Uncle Rebhorn
loosed us from the dock and set sail. "First mate! Look
sharp! Where the hell are you, boy? Move your ass!"—
Uncle Rebhorn kept up a constant barrage of commands at
poor Darren who scampered to obey them, yanking at ropes
that slipped from his fingers, trying to swing the heavy, sodden main sail around. The wind seemed to come from several
directions at once and the sails flapped and whipped helplessly. Darren did his best but he was clumsy and ill-coordi-
nated and terrified of his father. His pudgy face had turned
ashen, and his eyes darted wildly about; his gold swim trunks,
which were made of a shiny material like rayon, fitted him

so tightly a loose belt of fat protruded over the waistband and jiggled comically as, desperate to follow Uncle Rebhorn's instructions, Darren fell to one knee, pushed himself up, slipped and fell again, this time onto his belly on the slippery deck. Uncle Rebhorn, naked but for his swimming trunks and a visored sailor's cap jammed onto his head, shouted mercilessly, "Son, get *up*. Get that frigging sail to the wind or it's *mutiny*!"

The sailboat was now about thirty feet from the safety of the dock, careening and lurching in the water, which was nothing like the painted-aqua water I had seen from shore; it was dark, metallic-gray and greasy, and very cold. Winds howled about us. There was no cabin in the sailboat, all was exposed, and Uncle Rebhorn had taken the only seat. I was terrified the sailboat would sink, or I would be swept off to drown in the water by wild, frothy waves washing across the deck. I had never been in any boat except rowboats with my parents in the Hamtramck Park lagoon. "Isn't this fun? Isn't it! Sailing is the most exciting—" Aunt Elinor shouted at me, with her wide fixed smile, but Uncle Rebhorn, seeing my white, pinched face, interrupted, "Nobody's going to drown today, least of all *you*. Ungrateful little brat!"

Aunt Elinor poked me, and smiled, pressing a finger to her lips. Of course, Uncle Rebhorn was just teasing.

For a few minutes it seemed as if the winds were filling our sails in the right way for the boat moved in a single unswerving direction. Darren was holding for dear life to a rope, to keep the main sail steady. Then suddenly a dazzling white yacht sped by us, three times the size of Uncle Rebhorn's boat, dreamlike out of the flying spray, and in its wake Uncle Rebhorn's boat shuddered and lurched; there was a piercing, derisive sound of a horn—too late; the prow of the sailboat went under, freezing waves washed across the deck, the boat rocked crazily. I'd lost sight of Audrey and Aunt Elinor and was clutching a length of frayed rope with both hands, to keep myself from being swept overboard. How I whimpered with fear and pain! *This is your punishment, now you know you must be bad*. Uncle Rebhorn crouched at the prow of the boat, his eyes glittering in his flushed face, screaming commands at Darren who couldn't move fast enough to prevent the main sail from suddenly swinging around, skimming over my head and knocking Darren into the water.

Uncle Rebhorn yelled, "Son! Son!" With a hook at the end of a long wooden pole he fished about in the sudsy waves for my cousin, who sank like a bundle of sodden laundry; then surfaced again as a wave struck him from beneath and buoyed him upward; then sank again, this time beneath the lurching boat, his arms and legs flailing. I stared aghast, clutching at my rope. Audrey and Aunt Elinor were somewhere behind me, crying, "Help! help!" Uncle Rebhorn ignored them, cursing as he scrambled to the other side of the boat, and swiping with the hook in the water until he snagged something and, blood vessels prominent as angry worms in his face, hauled Darren out of the water and onto the swaying deck. The hook had caught my cousin in the armpit, and streams of blood ran down his side. Was Darren alive?—I stared, I could not tell. Aunt Elinor was screaming hysterically. With deft, rough hands Uncle Rebhorn laid his son on his back, like a fat, pale fish, and stretched the boy's arms and legs out, and straddled Darren's hips and began to rock in a quickened rhythmic movement and to squeeze his rib cage, *squeeze and release*! *squeeze and release*! until driblets of foamy water and vomit began to be expelled from Darren's mouth, and, gasping and choking, the boy was breathing again. Tears of rage and sorrow streaked Uncle Rebhorn's flushed face. "You disappoint me, son! Son, you disappoint me! I, your dad who gave you life—you disappoint me!"

A sudden prankish gust of wind lifted Uncle Rebhorn's sailor cap off his head and sent it flying and spinning out into the misty depths of Lake St. Clair.

I have been counseled not to retrieve the past where it is ▮▮▮▮▮ blocked by ▮▮▮▮▮ like those frequent attacks of "visual impairment" (*not* blindness, the neurologist insists) but have I not a right to my own memories? to my own past? Why should that right be taken from me?

What are you frightened of, Mother, my children ask me, sometimes in merriment, what are *you* frightened of?—as if anything truly significant, truly frightening, could have happened, or could have been imagined to have happened, to me.

So I joke with them, I tease them saying, "Maybe—*you!*"

For in giving birth to them I suffered ▓▓▓▓▓▓ slivers of ▓▓▓▓▓▓ too, which for the most part I have forgotten ▓▓▓▓▓ as all wounds heal and pain is lost in time—isn't it?

What happened on that lost Sunday in July 1969 in Uncle Rebhorn's house in Grosse Pointe Shores is a true mystery never comprehended by the very person (myself) who experienced it. For at the center of it is an emptiness ▓▓▓▓▓▓▓▓▓▓ black rectangular emptiness ▓▓▓▓▓ skidding toward me like a fracturing of the air *and it is ticklish too, my shivering turns convulsive on the brink of wild leaping laughter.* I recall the relief that my cousin Darren did not drown and I recall the relief that we returned to the dock which was swaying and rotted but did not collapse, held firm as Uncle Rebhorn cast a rope noose to secure the boat. I know that we returned breathless and excited from our outing on Lake St. Clair and that Aunt Elinor said it was too bad no snapshots had been taken to commemorate my visit, and Uncle Rebhorn asked where the Polaroid camera was, why did Aunt Elinor never remember it for God's sake, their lives and happy times flying by and nobody recording them. I know that we entered the house and once again in the dark cubbyhole that was my cousin Audrey's room beneath the stairs we were changing frantically from our bathing suits which were soaking wet into our dry clothes and this time Aunt Elinor, still less Audrey, could not prevent the door from pushing open ▓▓▓▓▓▓▓▓▓▓ ▓▓▓▓▓▓▓▓▓▓▓▓ crying "Daddy, no!" and "No, please, Daddy!" until I was crying too and laughing screaming as a man's rough fingers ▓▓▓▓▓▓ ran over my bare ribs bruising ▓▓▓▓▓▓ the frizzy-wiry hairs of his chest and belly tickling my face ▓▓▓▓▓▓ until what was beneath us which I had believed to be a floor fell away suddenly ▓▓▓▓▓▓ dissolving like ▓▓▓▓▓▓ water *I was not crying, I was not fighting I was a good girl: see?* ▓▓▓▓▓▓

████ waking then like floating to the surface of a dream as
again the tiny pink pebbles exquisite as seashells were being
thrown up beneath the chassis of the shiny black car, and
Uncle Rebhorn rosy-faced and fresh from his shower in crisp
sport shirt, Bermuda shorts and sandals drove me the long
long distance back to Hamtramck away from Lake St. Clair
and the mansions like castles on their grassy hills, on this
return ride nobody else was with us, not Audrey, not Aunt
Elinor, not Darren, only Uncle Rebhorn and me, his favorite
niece he said, beside him in the passenger's seat in the air-
conditioned cool inside the tinted windows through which,
at the foot of the graveled drive, as the wrought iron gate
swung open by magic, I squinted back with my inflamed eyes
at the luminous sandstone mansion with the latticed windows,
the portico covered in English ivy, the slender columns like
something in a children's storybook, it was the most beautiful
house I had ever seen up close, or was ever to enter in my
life. And nothing would change that.

Story Backgrounds

GARY BRANDNER

This is as close to autobiographical as anything I have written. Allowing for some juggling of time sequences and dramatic structuring, Billy Bobbick's story is my story. The scene on the merry-go-round is as accurate as I can remember it. My ticket phobia continues to this day. The ending, let us hope, is completely fictional.

RICHARD LEE BYERS

What scares me the most is simply the human propensity to treat other people cruelly for the silliest reasons imaginable, or for no reason at all. To put it another way, as my protagonist discovers too late, spite, ignorance, prejudice, and shortsightedness are the true powers of darkness, and they can destroy any one of us. The story was inspired by events in real life. I live in a suburural (an odd term that means more rural than suburbia, but more residential than honest-to-God farmland) subdivision, and, because of my involvement in fantasy, I have fundamentalist neighbors who think I'm a Satanist. I do take evening walks through the neighborhood, and twice I've had people stop me and ask in all seriousness if I'm a devil worshipper.

MAX ALLAN COLLINS

My biggest fear doesn't have a name. It is tied to a character trait of mine—or possibly flaw—perhaps best demonstrated by the fact that I still live in the small town I was born and raised in, forty-some years ago, and that at age twenty, I married my childhood sweetheart to whom I am still blissfully wed.

Possibly the best term for this form of dread is fear of change. It's a fear that my world will be taken out from under me—that my lifeline will be cut, my security will be lost. It is this fear that makes us cower before sadistic, unreasonable bosses—the parental figures of our careers.

And, so, it all goes back to that truly primal fear: fear of your parents. Fear of the punishment, the wrath of those who gave you life, those who sheltered you, shaped and controlled you. Or even worse, the fear of losing them. . . .

You don't have to have been abused (and I certainly wasn't—I was if anything pampered) to understand this basic fear. If there wasn't some truth to what I'm saying, then who among the grown-ups reading this anthology has never shared with a mate or a confidant the startling news that one or both of your parents is driving you crazy.

NANCY A. COLLINS

I moved to Manhattan—to be more precise, the Lower East Side, the "Mean Streets" of Scorsese fame—in the summer of '92. The most unrelentingly urban of American inner cities. Everyone has commented on how well I've adapted to my environment. Maybe that's because by the time I got to New York, I already had a career and a name for myself. I didn't have to wrestle this anaconda of an urban center on a day-to-day basis to just get by, like so many others are forced to. The fact that hundreds—perhaps thousands—of people move to this city every year without any job or housing prospects never ceases to amaze me. All the situations related in "Avenue X" are true, although fictitious. Ol' Blue Eyes was right—if you can make it here, you can make it anywhere. But if you *can't* make it, the city will grind you up like a chicken bone in a spiralling corkscrew disposal unit.

MICHAEL GARRETT

I have, unfortunately, been on both sides of the desk in the "Unfinished Business" scenario and am all too familiar with the volatile emotions and stress that accompany both firing and being fired. I fear that violence in the workplace will worsen before it ever improves.

JEFF GELB

My mother's death in 1991 was a life-altering event in ways I am still exploring and will continue to do so until my own death—and hopefully, beyond. It seems to have lessened my own fear of death, which was The Big One for me prior to Mom's "dropping her body." But it also pointed out that family is truly what counts in life. To lose my family would be akin to losing my reason to live, and so it has become my greatest fear.

"Home Again" is dedicated to my mother.

STEPHEN GRESHAM

After I published my second horror novel, I suffered through several agonizing months struggling with a question: could a horror novel impact a reader in such a way as to "trigger" psychotic behavior? The question haunted me in a most intimate and soul-wrenching manner. Most frightening of all, the question generated other questions, other issues, leaving bloody tracks on my psyche. I've followed those bloody tracks, and what continues to haunt me is that . . . I haven't answered the question.

RICK HAUTALA

Remember that old gem of college bathroom graffiti wisdom: *"Death is the biggest trip of all—that's why they save it for last!"* Well, I think it's probably safe to say that most horror writers write what they do because—bottom line—they're afraid of death. But I want to clarify a small point about my contribution to *Fear Itself*. At first I was going to say that I'm not so much afraid of death as I am afraid of *dying*, but it's even more subtle than that. I think my biggest fear—the one that leaves me bathed in a cold sweat in the middle of the night—is the terrifying *subjectivity* of the death experience. Imagine when you finally "check out"—as we all must—what you will *experience*, and the worst thing is, you won't be able to *describe* it to anyone! I have no doubt that all of my writing, perhaps even the source of my inspiration to write, is this fear of the subjective experience of death. Certainly all of my novels and most of my short stories have been driven by this fear, but "Perfect Witness" was written with it clearly in mind . . . staring me right in the face.

JACK KETCHUM

The events in "Snakes" are an amplification and rearrangement of real ones which occurred to a very real woman and her dog during a Southwest Florida storm. The recurring dream about the water-snake is, of course, my own—it's me and not her who's scared of them. The childhood incident at the 'gator farm (yes, that kid with his hand in the air was me) is probably the reason. I think that ever since then snakes represent to me the unseen, unnoticed, and unexpected threat that exists in nature and in everyday life—literally the "snake in the grass" you step on right before he bites you—the sudden conscienceless enemy, thoroughly unforseen. You meet him now and then. And he chases you through your dreams.

PAUL KUPPERBERG

When I was in my early 20s, on my own for the first time, I went through my starving-artist-in-a-garret phase. I was usually flat broke, hung out with a largely bizarre and often motley crew of people, was not on unfamiliar terms with various altered states of reality, and firmly believed that living somewhere out there on the neurotic, self-destructive edge was the only way to go for a young, creative type.

Now, years later, my wife and I live in our own house in the suburbs, I hold down a 9-to-5 job, and no longer have the patience for the largely bizarre or for altered states of reality. I'm convinced that there's as much creativity in happiness as there is out on the edge, but sometimes, when I'm struggling to make a story work, I feel the smallest bit of panic. The fear that maybe I've become too much the "normal" citizen to be able to still hack it. Intellectually I know there's no connection between self-destructive behavior and creativity . . . but I haven't completely abandoned neurosis (we all need to keep a *little* something of the beast inside us). Just to be on the safe side.

GRAHAM MASTERTON

When I was very small, the statues of London had a profound effect on me. They stood in the ruins of the Blitz, dark and menacing but somehow sad, too, as if they contained all the heroism and all the terrible suffering of war.

There was Winged Victory on top of the arch at Hyde Park Corner, with her chariot and her horses. There was a naked David with a sword, in the brownest and glossiest of bronzes. There was the body of an infantryman from the Great War, covered with his helmet and his cape. To me, they were real. I was sure that they could feel; I was sure that they could speak.

One night when I was five I had a vivid nightmare that I was being pursued by a mounted statue, and I can remember that feeling of absolute terror even today.

Statues can be erotic; statues can be heroic. Statues can be disturbing. But there is always the feeling that they are more than metal, more than stone. They have a kind of frozen soul, too.

I find religious effigies particularly disturbing. The melancholy statues of Christ; the pale madonnas. There is a bronze in the Groeninge Museum in Bruges of three heavily cowled nuns, and to my mind it is one of the most frightening pieces of sculpture ever created.

There are plenty of other hair-raising sculptures in Bruges, however, and "The Gray Madonna" is one of them.

TH. METZGER

We all wear emotional armor—a fragile membrane that protects us from what's outside and protects the world beyond us from what breeds in our inner darkness. "Pyre" is about the collapse of this armor, the dissolution of boundaries. Emotions are explosive, dangerous; they take us to places we fear to go. "Pyre" is the story of a man who gives in to the emotional chaos inside himself.

REX MILLER

"Sewercide" is a twist on the stalker theme, but inside the story are fearsome things I refuse to amplify in print. Folks say putting your mouth on some things can make them happen. I won't take the chance. Suffice it to say there are elements of the story I won't articulate.

THOMAS F. MONTELEONE

While the fear that underlies this story may be fairly obvious and require little clarification, I think I can comply with your Good Editor's wishes to come up with *something* to fill this white space. As the father of three children, I think I'm qualified to speak for most parents when I say there is nothing to strike more terror within me than to enter my child's room in the middle of the night and find Old Cowl'n'Bones in the shadows. Gilda Radner and Christopher Lee redux—only it's not for laughs. The death of a child is one of those incomprehensible things to me. Just the thought of it *staggers* me as I write these words. How anyone survives it is one of life's greatest mysteries. I honestly don't know that I could; and I'm the kind of asshole who thinks he can still play ice hockey with twenty-year-olds as I skate along on the wrong side of forty-five. Several of my friends suffered through this scenario, and every time it disturbed me so totally, I was unable to say anything to any of them—other than to say I lacked the vocabulary of grief necessary to deal with such a limitless tragedy. During those moments, I've never felt so helpless in my life.

JOYCE CAROL OATES

It's night. It has been night for a long time. Hours pass—yet it's the same hour. I can't sleep. My mind is fractured like broken glass. Or a broken mirror, shards reflecting shards. I am incapable of thinking but only of receiving, like a fine-meshed net strung tight, mere glimmerings of thought. Teasing fragments of "memory"—or is it "invented memory"?—rise and turn and fall and sift and scatter and rearrange themselves into arabesques of patterns on the verge of becoming coherent, yet do not become coherent. As in a childhood riddle never explained. As in one of those ingeniously intricate childhood puzzle-drawings in which shapes—faces, figures of animals—are superimposed upon one another, obscured by clouds, trees, natural objects. Something wants to speak—but what? This insomniac state is perhaps but the nighttime, and therefore the most obvious expression of a general fascinated bafflement of consciousness, for I have to acknowledge that occasionally—not frequently (which would be madness) but occasionally—such fugue states grip me by day, in public places; I am especially vulnerable while being introduced to give a lecture or a reading, for instance, or, on rarer occasions, while being cited for some honor or award. At such times one must sit gravely listening, one must not be seen to demur, still less to be assailed by gusts of wild hilarity, disbelief. Yes, I think ironically, as an enthusiastic stranger's voice extols the public achievements of the largely fictitious "Joyce Carol Oates," yes but no: you don't know *me*. If you knew me, you would not say such outlandish things.

What should be said in place of these "outlandish things," I have no idea.

Yesterday in Manhattan, on the twenty-third, penthouse floor of a Fifth Avenue office building facing Trump Tower, at a lavish luncheon in my honor, in the grip of a powerful fugue state I felt as if I were about to remember something—but could not, cannot. Wanting desperately to reread a certain passage from Pascal's *Pensées*, which I have virtually memorized yet can't trust my memory to replicate with the full dignity and gravity these famous words demand.

> This is our true state; this is what makes us incapable of certain knowledge and of absolute ignorance. We sail within a vast sphere, ever drifting in uncertainty, driven from end to end. When we try to attach ourselves to any point and to fasten to it, it wavers and leaves us; and if we follow it, it eludes our grasp, slips past us, and vanishes forever. Nothing stays for us. This is our natural condition, and yet most contrary to our inclination; we burn with desire to find solid ground and an ultimate sure foundation whereupon to build a tower reaching to the Infinite. But our whole groundwork cracks, and the earth opens to abysses.

Unless you are more protectively self-deluded than Pascal, this is true for you, too.

Certainly for me.

"Joyce Carol Oates"—more helpfully comprehended as an imagination and a writing process, and not an individual—very possibly feels little of this existential anxiety, except in and through her fictitious personae; but I, who encompass, yet am hardly identical with "JCO," am in the grip of this anxiety whenever the momentum of my life slows, and its surface distractions fade. At such times, like the narrator of my story ▮▮ (its title refers precisely to the "abyss" of which Pascal speaks: a kind of black hole of the spirit) I seem about to remember and to know something—but what?

The story in this anthology is but one of any number of fictions I've created to attempt to comprehend, even in the face of ceaseless failure, this abyss, and the mystery surrounding it. The story is *not* autobiographical, except emotionally; I stand in awe of the possibility that being hypnotized by ▮▮ is a key to my putative industry.

At the same time, I think I am probably representative of the legion of people, women perhaps more than men, yet surely there are many men in our ranks as well, who are both fascinated by the contents of the unconscious and in terror of their uncontrolled eruption. The sudden incursion of an unwanted memory in our lives: how can we assimilate it into what we want to believe of ourselves? We build personalities, like "fictions," to withstand the roiling waters. Or we build fictions, like "personalities."

ELSA RUTHERFORD

This story comes from a fear that manifests itself in a recurring nightmare in which I must dig up dead relatives who, on being exhumed, come back to life. *But in varying states of decomposition.* I've come to understand that the basis of this horrifying dream and the fear it symbolizes is attributable to present-day medical technology. Today life can be prolonged by extraordinary means. It is fast becoming the norm for the elderly, no matter how severely impaired, to live to advanced ages with the aid of medical science. Even the so-called "brain dead" can be kept alive indefinitely. For the first time in history, families are making soul-wrenching decisions concerning the care and quality of life for their elderly and infirm. In some cases, truly life or death decisions. This is a new and profound dilemma raising new and profound fears. Fears that most of us must eventually face: How far will we go to keep family members alive? How much emotional and financial burden can we bear? How will we handle the moral ethics involved? And whatever decisions we make, how can we be certain those decisions won't come back to haunt us?

JOHN SHIRLEY

Whom can you trust? What if even those you've known for years, those intimates whom you think you know, you really don't know? What if you can't trust them at all? What if your wife is nurturing a secret psychosis that's going to bear fruit in your murder some three am as you sleep beside her? What if your best friend is really your profoundest enemy? What if your beloved child hates you and is just waiting for the right moment to show it? *Whom can you trust?*

TIA TRAVIS

I'm twenty-six and don't have a driver's license because I'm afraid of killing myself in a car. I'm afraid of physics and pain, afraid of J.G. Ballard's "brutal, erotic and overlit realm." I'm afraid that death really is the extinction of the personality and that, ultimately, we have no control over how our lives will end. I'm afraid that death isn't *eternal rest*, it's *cerebral silence*. No electrical activity in the brain. Not now, not ever. *Cerebral silence:* The End. Think about *that* for five minutes and then tell me what you're afraid of.

"Shatter" is dedicated to Johnnie.

SCOTT H. URBAN

My own death isn't something I worry about. No matter how prolonged, it's eventually over. But having to watch a member of my own family terrorized, raped, or even killed— and not being able to do anything about it? I don't think I could live with that.

Writing "Victims" was definitely a disturbing experience. I've even been pricing burglar alarm systems.

EDO VAN BELKOM

I used to work for a newspaper in a city an hour's drive from where I lived. The route I took was Highway 401—one of the largest and busiest highways in Canada. Needless to say, the weather wasn't always conducive to driving. One drizzly winter night, I had to stop on the side of the highway to refill my car's reservoir with windshield washer fluid. While I poured anti-freeze into the reservoir I was forced into a position that placed my back to the highway and my head under the hood—a vulnerable position to say the least. With each semi-trailer that screamed by—at what sounded like breakneck speed—the car shook violently, as if the trucks were passing within inches of it. Well, being forced to remain in that position while the reservoir took *forever* to fill up, my mind kindly began thinking about all the terrible things that could happen to me.

GRAHAM WATKINS

This is, in reality, the only true phobia I can ever remember being troubled by; but, while it existed, it was a true phobia, a source of almost everyday terror. As I look back on it now, it seems to me that it existed from the time of my earliest memories; it was, at times, so bad that it was difficult for me to look at pictures of spiders in a book. Nothing else affected me that way, nothing. I was downright fond of snakes and insects, keeping so many of them as pets that my parents often felt we were living in a zoo.

If pinpointing the origin point of the phobia is difficult, even attempting to assign some cause is impossible. My family often told horror stories about children bitten by black widows who died in agony, but to many members of my family, all sorts of creatures were deadly; truly dangerous creatures like rattlesnakes and copperheads provoked no fear at all.

Later, as I became a teenager, I suppose I sort of made an active decision that for me, for my life-style, an arachnophobia was impossibly crippling. In an effort to get over it, I actively courted the spiders, studying them, handling them— and to a great extent, my efforts were successful. Still, though, some residue remains; I still jump, I still have an adrenaline rush, when one drops down on me unexpectedly— and, somehow, I always seem to know instantly when it's a spider as opposed to some insect. It still strikes me as peculiar that some harmless spider like a jumping spider (always, for whatever obscure reason, one of the worst for me) provokes such a reaction when an insect capable of really hurting you— like a hornet, a wheelbug, or a horsefly—engenders no other response than to brush it away.

One other note: the areas described in the story actually exist in the Red River Gorge area of Kentucky; I've actually mapped some of those caves, and the "natural traps" described are real enough too. None that I know of has a small enough chimney to actually trap someone (although the side comments about Floyd Collins are quite true), but the rooms beneath them are, in some cases, just as they are in the story—a gathering place for ambush predators like snakes and spiders. Contrary to the belief of the story's protagonist, the black widow, uncommon generally in the Gorge, is abundant in those pits. During my collecting days as a Zoology major at the University of Kentucky, I captured exceptionally large specimens of several species of spiders, widows included, from those pits.

But I never stayed in any of those rooms very long—and the notion, the utterly terrifying notion, of somehow losing my carbide was always in my mind. This memory, perhaps more than any other, was the inspiration for the story.

Author Biographies

GARY BRANDNER

The prolific Brandner is the author of 24 novels, including the famous *Howling* series, *Cameron's Closet*, and *Walkers*, plus nearly 100 short stories, five screenplays, and six adaptations of his books by others for movies and TV miniseries. Brandner lives in California.

RICHARD LEE BYERS

Byers is the author of such horror novels as *Dead Time*, *Dark Fortune*, *Vampire's Apprentice*, *Fright Line* and *Deathward*. His short fiction has appeared in *Freak Show*, *Grails*, *Confederacy of the Dead*, and others. The Floridan also writes young adult titles like *Joy Ride* and *Party Till You Drop*.

MAX ALLAN COLLINS

Iowa's Collins is a two-time winner of the "Shamus" Best Novel award for his Nate Heller historical thrillers *True Detective* and *Stolen Away*. He is the author of four other mystery series and his novel of the Clint Eastwood film *In The Line of Fire* was an international best-seller. He scripted the *Dick Tracy* comic strip from 1977–1993, and his comic book credits include *Ms. Tree*, *Batman*, and *Wild Dog*. His story for *Fear Itself*, "Mommy," is soon to be a major motion picture.

NANCY A. COLLINS

Collins's first novel, *Sunglasses After Dark*, won Horror Writers and British Fantasy Society awards. She has also been nominated for the Campbell Award and the comic industry's Eisner award for her work on *Swamp Thing*. In comics, she is also the writer of *Wick*, while in books, her latest are *Wild Blood* and *Walking Wolf*. The New Yorker is presently working on the third Sonja Blue novel, *Paint it Black*, and her first collection of short stories, *Nameless Sins*.

MICHAEL GARRETT

Garrett's first novel, *Keeper*, has been optioned for a movie. His short stories have been published in numerous periodicals and anthologies. He is an Editorial Associate with *Writer's Digest* magazine and is co-editor of the *Hot Blood* series. He lives in Alabama.

JEFF GELB

Gelb, a California resident, is the editor of the *Shock Rock* anthologies and co-editor of the *Hot Blood* series. His novel, *Specters*, was published in 1988. He is an avid comic book collector and a frequent contributor to *Comics Buyer's Guide* and other comics magazines.

STEPHEN GRESHAM

Gresham, an Alabama resident, has had 12 novels published since 1982. Number 13, scheduled for publication in

1994, is titled *Primal Instinct*. He has also written 18 published short stories and recently completed a young adult horror novel.

RICK HAUTALA

Maine resident Hautala is the author of 10 horror novels including *Ghost Light*, *The Mountain King*, *Dark Silence*, and the upcoming *The Pack* and *Twilight Time*. His short fiction has appeared in *Predators*, *After the Darkness*, *Narrow Houses*, *Ultimate Zombie*, and *Shock Rock 2*.

JACK KETCHUM

Ketchum's novels include *Off Season*, often credited as the first splatterpunk novel, as well as *Hide and Seek*, *Cover*, *She Wakes*, *The Girl Next Door*, *Offspring*, and *Road Kill*. Short fiction credits include *Vampire Detectives*, *Stalkers III*, and *Book of the Dead III*. Ketchum lives in New York.

PAUL KUPPERBERG

Connecticut's Kupperberg is an eighteen-year veteran writer in the comic book field, with over 600 stories to his credit, including work on Superman and Batman. He is the author of the novels *Crime Campaign* and *Murdermoon*, and has had short stories published in the anthologies *Further Adventures of Batman Vol. 3*, and *Larger Than Life*. He is an editor at DC Comics.

GRAHAM MASTERTON

England's Masterton is hard at work on several new horror novels, including *Burial*, *The Sleepless*, and *Flesh & Blood*. He has had over 50 short horror stories published, including the award-wining "Absence of Beast."

TH. METZGER

New York's Metzger is the author of *Big Gurl*, *Shock Totem*, *This Is Your Final Warning*, and *Drowning In Fire*. His work has also appeared in anthologies including *Shock Rock 2* and *Bizarre Obsession*.

REX MILLER

Missouri's Miller is the creator of the enormously popular Chaingang character from *Slob*, *Savant*, and other books in the series, and the writer of *Profane Men* and others. His short fiction career began in *Hot Blood* with prolific work following in *Thrillers*, *Freak Show*, and others. He has just completed co-scripting a comics mini-series with novelist Andrew Vachss.

THOMAS F. MONTELEONE

Monteleone won the 1993 Bram Stoker Award for Novel for *The Blood of the Lamb*. His next novel will be either *The Final Quartet* or *Nights of Broken Glass* in late '94. To date, he has edited four annual *Borderlands* anthologies, and has numerous short fiction credits including *Peter Straub's Ghost Stories*, *Love in Vein* and *Thrillers*. The Maryland resident has a regular column in *Cemetery Dance* magazine.

JOYCE CAROL OATES

The incredibly prolific Oates is the author of 27 novels, 17 collections of short stories, seven books of poetry, five volumes of essays, 15 plays and more than two dozen works published by small, independent presses. She is also the author of four suspense novels under the pseudonym of Rosamond Smith. The multi-award-winning writer lives in New Jersey.

ELSA RUTHERFORD

Rutherford is a native Alabamian. A former newspaper columnist, she sold her first novel, *The Water and the Blood*, in 1987. Her short fiction has been published in numerous European countries as well as the U.S. She teaches fiction writing at a university.

JOHN SHIRLEY

California's Shirley is the author of more than 17 books under his own name and a dozen under pseudonyms. His best-known books include *City Come A-Walkin'*, *Heatseeker*, *Cellars*, *Wetbones* and *The Brigade*. He is also a successful songwriter who fronts his own band, *The Panther Moderns*.

TIA TRAVIS

Travis's latest work appears in *Chills*, *Shock Rock 2*, and *Young Blood*. She lives on the Canadian prairies, "where the highways are straight and visibility is excellent in all directions."

SCOTT H. URBAN

A frequent contributor to the dark fantasy small press, Urban's work has appeared in *Doppelganger*, *Thin Ice* and others. The North Carolina writer's short fiction credits include *Shock Rock 2* and *The Beast Within*. He is developing comic book scripts and screenplays.

EDO VAN BELKOM

Ontario's van Belkom has sold over 40 short stories to such books as *Year's Best Horror Stories*, *Hot Blood 4*,

Shock Rock 2, *Deathport*, and *Northern Frights*, along with numerous magazines.

GRAHAM WATKINS

North Carolina's Watkins is the author of *Dark Winds*, *The Fire Within*, and *Kaleidoscope Eyes*, as well as numerous pieces of short fiction in *Hottest Blood*, *Shock Rock 2* and other leading anthologies.